For those who have not read Howard Headworth's *The Al-Andalus Chronicle*, why not learn how Pedro Togeiro came to be befriended by Don Gonzalo Fernández of Córdoba, how he came to meet Raquel and later King Fernando and Queen Isabel, and how later he came to be a crew member on Christopher Columbus's very first voyage of discovery to the New World…

Spain's Pursuit of Destiny
The Columbus Years

Spain's Pursuit of Destiny
The Columbus Years

Howard Headworth

 **New Generation Publishing**

Acknowledgements

My sincere thanks to Frank and Karen Villafana and my wife, Sarah, for so diligently proofreading the manuscript of this book, and for finding the spelling errors, repetitions and inconsistencies which inevitably arose during the three years it was being researched and written. To many friends in the village who showed a keen interest in the book's preparation and thereby helped sustain my enthusiasm to complete the task. To my good friend and Spanish tutor, José Golderos in Almería, who, through his understanding of the broader canvas of Spanish history through the ages, allowed the short timeframe of this book to be placed in context. To Malcolm Ecclestone in Norwich, an expert on Early Music and a collector and exponent of medieval instruments, for helping bring Chapter VI alive. And lastly, to many people in the Dominican Republic, museum curators, archaeological site guides etc., for so helpfully showing me around.

Howard Headworth
San José, Almería
March 2008

Cover: The castle of Vélez Blanco, Almería, with the 5,100 ft limestone peak La Muela (the Molar) behind. The castle was built by the Marquéz de Los Vélez, Pedro Fajardo, in 1506–15. The bridge to the right leads to a lower enclosure comprising what remains of the original Moorish alcázar.

Author's Note – Use of Names

In this book set largely in Spain, I have adopted the approach used by other English authors and have used the Spanish names of the kings and queens, their children and other personages who were born in Spain. Thus, I have used Fernando and Isabel rather than Ferdinand and Isabella, as they are known in England, and their children Isabel, Juan, Juana, María and Catalina, not Isabella, John, Joan, Mary or Catherine.

However, I have kept the names of personages from other countries in their anglicised form, since in most cases that is how they were known at that time or are known historically. So, Philip the Fair of Austria and his son Charles V have been used, not Felipe and Carlos. King John of Portugal has been used instead of the Portuguese Joáo.

The explorer Christopher Columbus is universally known by this name, which I have adopted in this book. In fact, it is no less correct than the Spanish Cristóbal Colón, as the explorer came from Genoa in Italy and not from Spain. But I have retained the Spanish Christian names of his brothers, Bartolomé and Diego.

At this time, the Iberian Peninsula comprised the separate kingdoms of Portugal, Castile, Aragón and Navarra, with Cataluña a semi-independent dukedom within the kingdom of Aragón. Although the Muslim kingdom of the Nazarí had only just been conquered (with the surrender of Granada in 1492), it retained its separate identity for some time afterwards. But to avoid unnecessary repetition, Spain is mostly used as a generic term to cover all these lands excepting Portugal.

Castile and Seville have been used instead of Castilla and Sevilla, but otherwise the Spanish cities or regions of Almería, Andalucia, Córdoba, Jaén, Málaga and Vélez have been used, since this is also their anglicised form.

Historical Setting

It is early 1494. The Catholic Monarchs, Isabel of Castile and Fernando of Aragón, are into the twenty-fourth year of their dual monarchy; the impetuous Charles VIII is on the throne of ever-powerful France; Maximilian in Germany is bringing sense and stability to the Holy Roman Empire; and Henry VII is on the throne of England, having vanquished Richard of York at Bosworth nine years before. King John of Portugal has realised his error in rejecting Christopher Columbus's overtures to fund his voyage of discovery across the Ocean Sea, and the young king is determined not to lose out on the riches to be had in the newly discovered lands. Lastly, the brilliant but lecherous Rodrigo Borgia of Spain has assumed the papacy in Rome as Alexander VI.

It is only two years since the 700-year kingdom of Muslim Granada in al-Andalus was overthrown by the Christians after a ten-year war, and the sad Sultan Boabdil has left Spanish shores for Morocco with his followers. Christopher Columbus has set off on his second voyage to the New World with a thirst for gold, and hundreds of thousands of resourceful Jews have been forced to leave their homeland in Spain for ever.

Spain's place on the world stage is in Isabel's and Fernando's sights. Moreover, they have five children coming of age to use in the political power game. Spain's destiny beckons. But will it be fulfilled?

Contents

I	The End of a Brave Man	19
II	Letter from the King	24
III	The Mob	33
IV	Tordesillas	51
V	The Treaties	60
VI	The Banquet	70
VII	Yazíd	80
VIII	Columbus's Ambitions	92
IX	Storm Clouds over Italy	99
X	Don Gonzalo Fernández of Córdoba	104
XI	The First Italian Campaign	110
XII	A Royal Invitation	120
XIII	Wedding Bells	130
XIV	Flanders	135
XV	The Partisans	141
XVI	Tuscany	151
XVII	The Cottage in the Clearing	162
XVIII	The Crypt	170
XIX	Annus Horribilis	179
XX	The Sorceress	186
XXI	Scandal and Intrigue in Rome	192
XXII	Columbus's Third Voyage	196
XXIII	The Baron of Montecorvino	203

XXIV   The Granada Revolt   213

XXV   Affairs of State   224

XXVI   Home at Last   233

XXVII   Nobility and Peasantry   241

XXVIII Caribbean Catastrophe   244

XXIX   The Orphan Girl   250

XXX   Action on All Fronts   260

XXXI   Shock Waves across Spain   268

XXXII   Forces Unleashed   274

XXXIII A Kingdom Pulled Three Ways   283

XXXIV   Spain in Turmoil   293

XXXV   Triumphant Return   302

XXXVI   A New Land and a New Life   309

Historical Postscript   318

Appendices
    A   La Española   321
    B   Chapter Components   325
    C   Calendar of Historic Events   332
    D   Bibliography – Alphabetical   346
    E   Bibliography – by Subject   349

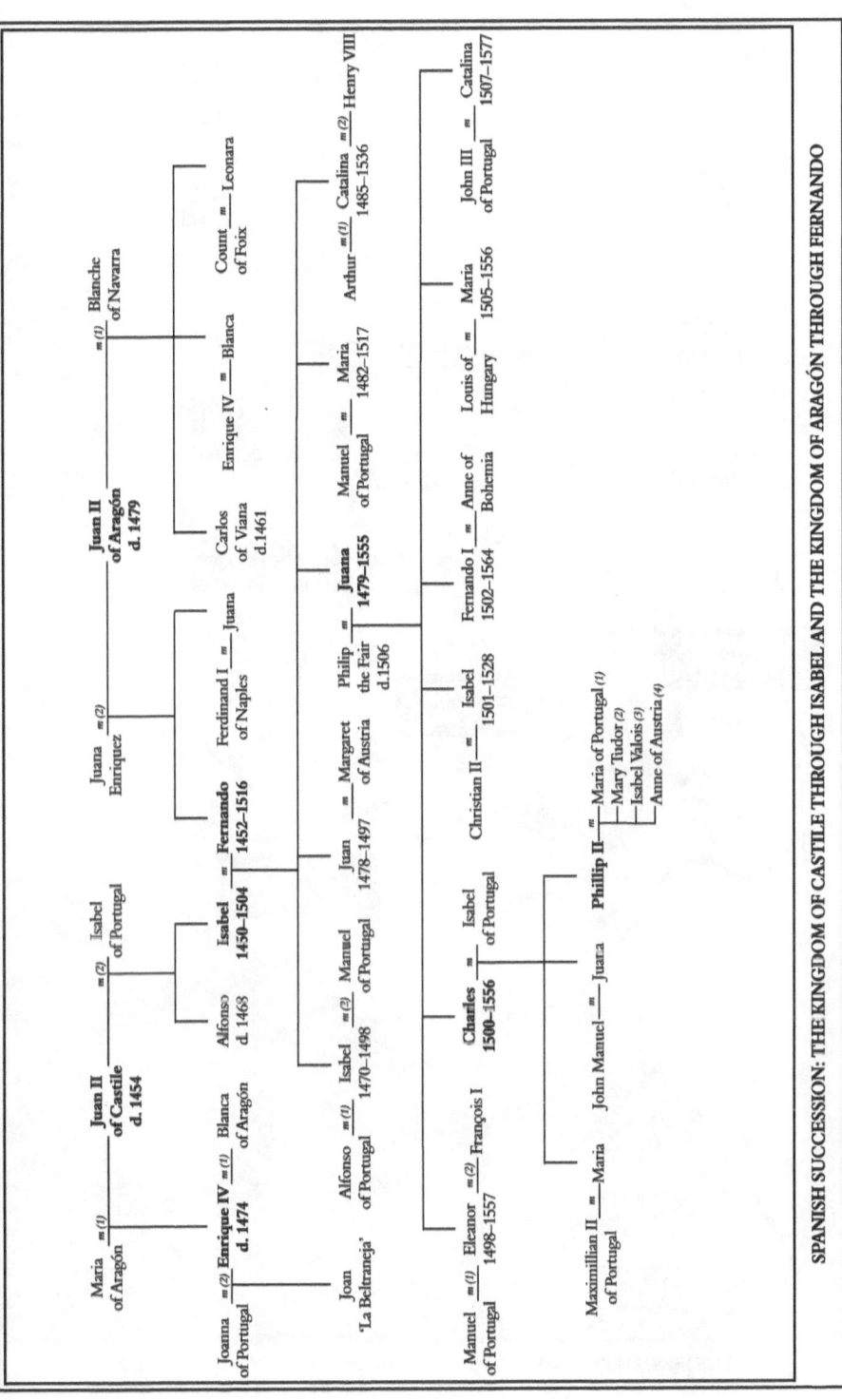

SPANISH SUCCESSION: THE KINGDOM OF CASTILE THROUGH ISABEL AND THE KINGDOM OF ARAGÓN THROUGH FERNANDO

THE IBERIAN PENINSULAR AT THE TIME OF THE RECONQUEST (1492)

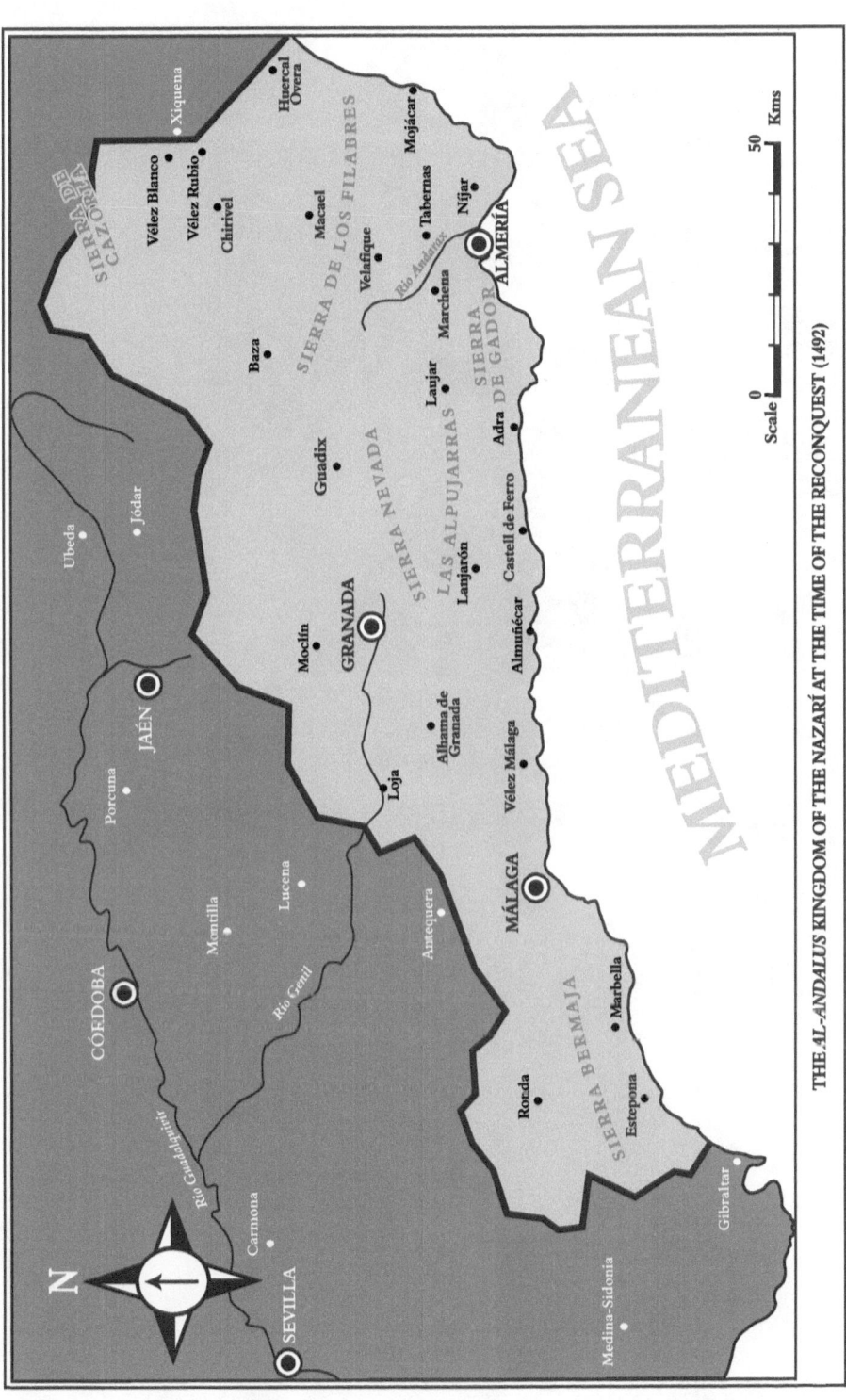

THE *AL-ANDALUS* KINGDOM OF THE NAZARÍ AT THE TIME OF THE RECONQUEST (1492)

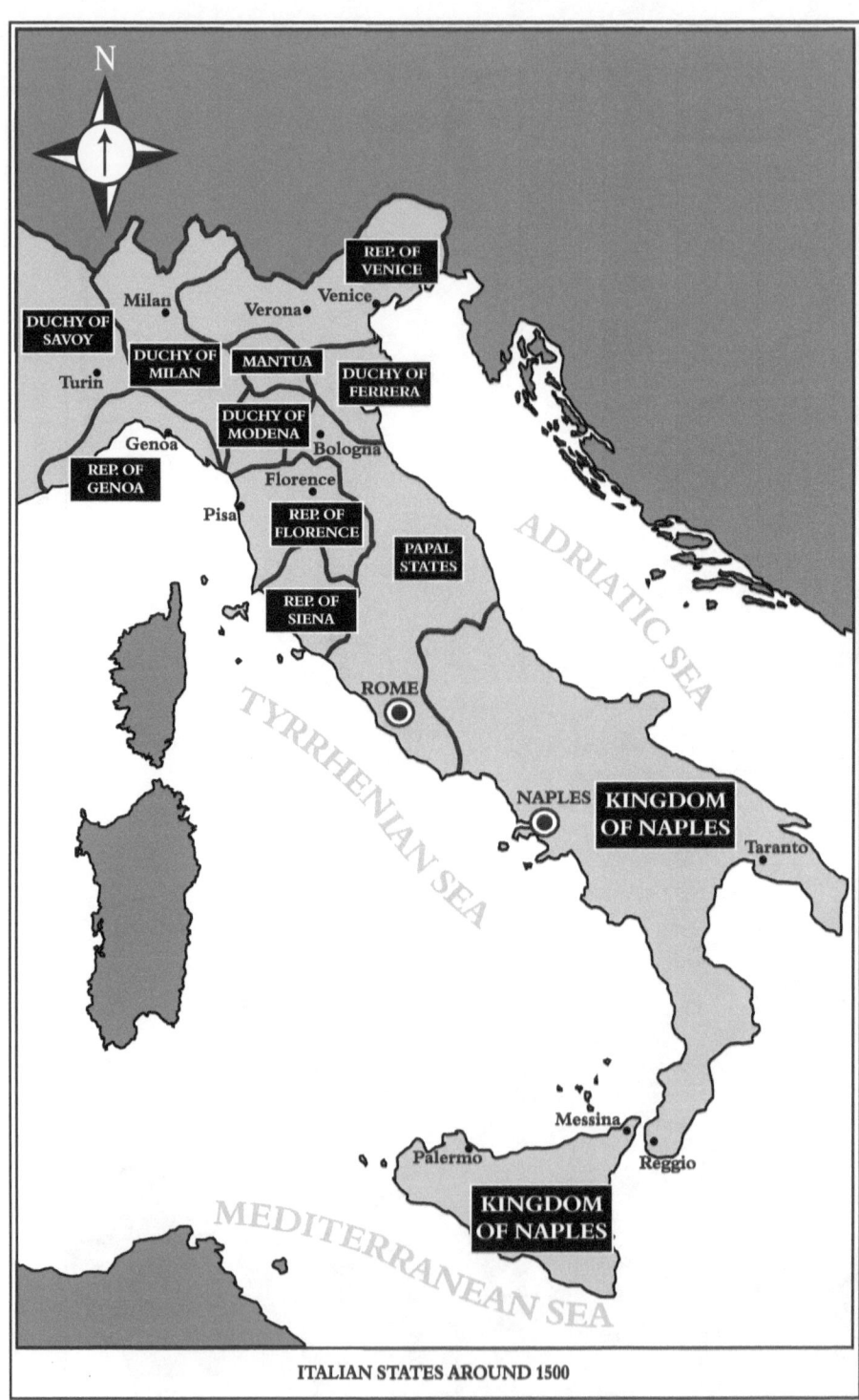

ITALIAN STATES AROUND 1500

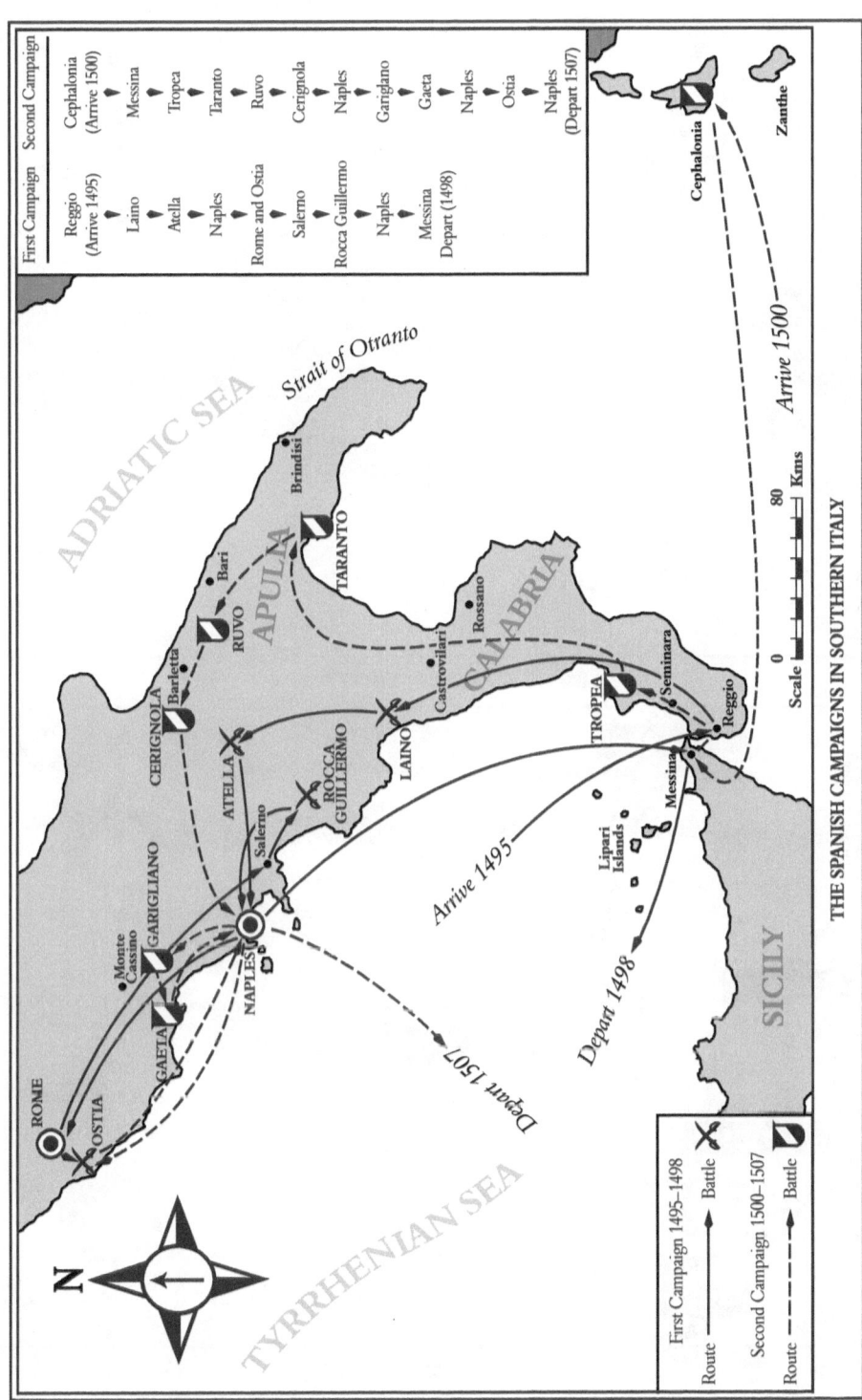

THE SPANISH CAMPAIGNS IN SOUTHERN ITALY

First Campaign	Second Campaign
Reggio (Arrive 1495)	Cephalonia (Arrive 1500)
Laino	Messina
Atella	Tropea
Naples	Taranto
Rome and Ostia	Ruvo
Salerno	Cerignola
Rocca Guillermo	Naples
Naples	Garigliano
Messina Depart (1498)	Gaeta
	Naples
	Ostia
	Naples (Depart 1507)

First Campaign 1495–1498	
Route	——
Battle	✗
Second Campaign 1500–1507	
Route	- - -
Battle	◣

Scale 0 · · · · 80 Kms

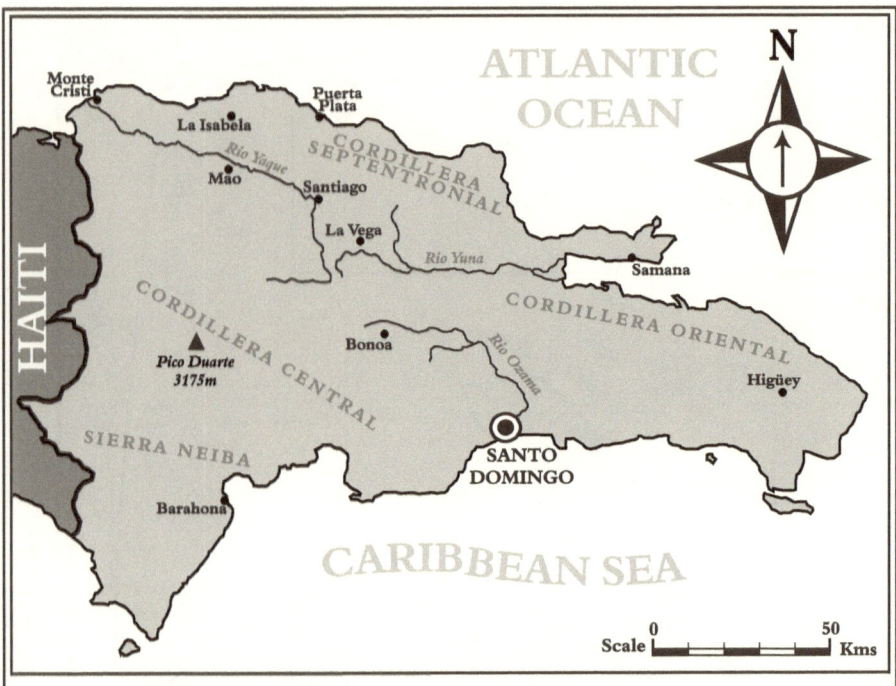

LA ESPAÑOLA (DOMINICAN REPUBLIC)

THE CARIBBEAN ISLANDS

I: *The End of a Brave Man*

March 1494. Tlemcen, Morocco

They stood silently side by side alongside a recently filled grave. A cold drizzle swept in from the Mediterranean to the north, stinging their eyes. Rivulets of water ran down the mound of soft earth to gather in puddles around their feet. A woman hidden by a deep red *salhama* or thick woollen tunic with a black *milhafa* or silk scarf over her head stood alone a few yards away. Well shod for the inclement weather, she wore *hirkasa* or high sheepskin boots. She stood at the head of the grave, which was marked by a rough headstone placed against the mound of earth, but was yet to be fixed in place. The man was above average height, slender and lithe with brown hair and blue eyes. He was well dressed and stood bareheaded in homage to the deceased man lying at his feet. The woman by his side, eighteen years of age and two years his junior, was strikingly beautiful, with golden skin and raven hair cascading down her back like a waterfall in moonlight. A full figure was concealed beneath her robes. Like her young husband, she had pulled back her hood in homage to the dead lord. They stood motionless, indifferent to the rain.

'When did he die, Pedro?' she asked in a hushed voice, as if others might hear in this empty, unkempt city graveyard.

'A month or so ago, Raquel. I'm not sure exactly,' replied Don Pedro Togeiro de Gozco. He was King Fernando's recently appointed ambassador to the Sultan of Morocco, and had been knighted befitting his new station.

'I received a note from Prince Ahmad in Fez five days ago that his great-uncle had died here in Tlemcen. It must have been Ahmad's father, Boabdil, who had the headstone inscribed.'

'But rather badly, by the looks of it, Pedro,' Raquel remarked. Her Castilian was poor but improving by the day. She had been born in the small al-Andalus village of Mecina Fondales in the western Alpujarras, which even now remained a Muslim stronghold. She had followed her mother, Raghad, and had been baptised into the Christian faith soon after her marriage to Pedro towards the end of the previous year. 'There's no future in being a Muslim here now,' was her mother's resigned comment after the fall of the Nazarí kingdom of Granada to the Catholic Monarchs. Most Muslims chose to retain their religion and customs as Mudejares living within the Christian community, but many had been baptised and adopted Christian names. Many more had abandoned their country of birth and emigrated to other Arab countries, chiefly to Morocco.

'Yes, Raquel, the stone's been badly inscribed,' replied Pedro. 'I'll get a new one made and replace it. It's the least I can do for the memory of such a great man, and I'm sure the King would approve.'

'What did he die of? Do you know?'

'No, I don't. He seemed well enough when we saw him last. It might have been the plague, which is still raging here. Moving among the villagers as he did meant that he was always prone to catch it.'

'How terrible,' replied Raquel. 'But it might explain why he was buried in this hastily dug grave… What an end to a great man!' she sighed.

They remained there silently, each deep in thought.

Doña Raquel had met the former King of Almería just the once, soon after she and Pedro had moved from Spain to Morocco to take up Pedro's appointment as ambassador. Mohammed Abú Abdalá – dubbed *El Zagal* by Fernando and Isabel, meaning the Valiant One – had been shabbily treated by Mohammed al-Burtuqali al-Wattasi, the Moroccan sultan, who unjustly blamed him for the loss of Granada. Abú Abdalá had been roughly taken by Moroccan soldiers soon after his arrival in Morocco from al-Andalus in 1490. A crucible of boiling copper with green flames dancing over its surface had been passed back and forth across his face and blinded him. Then he had been cast into the streets with a placard around his neck saying, 'This is the man who lost Granada.' Yet the fall of Granada did not happen until nearly two years later!

Mohammed Abú Abdalá, tall and angular, a cruel and devious man but a born leader, had wandered from village to village as a beggar. By chance, Pedro had encountered him some time later, after Pedro had accompanied Boabdil to Morocco following the latter's departure from al-Andalus in October 1493. Then, the nineteen-year-old, half-Christian and half-Jewish by birth, had found and paid for lodgings for El Zagal and for a kindly widow to care for him. The change in the old warrior was immediate, and with new raiment, a trimmed beard and a clean bandage around his slanting eyes, he looked like the El Zagal of old – upright, proud, dignified and lordly.

Pedro remained standing by the grave, his eyes welling up. His mind wandered back to the time when he had met Abú Abdalá for the first time. It was five years before. Then, Don Gonzalo Fernández of Córdoba – Abú Abdalá's implacable but respected foe – had sent messengers from the Christian castle of Moclín, thirty miles north of Granada, to enquire if the Muslim lord, uncle of the then sultan Boabdil, would conduct Pedro to Almuñecar, still in Muslim hands. There, Pedro could board a boat to return to his home town of Vélez Blanco on the Almería–Murcia border. Pedro grinned as he recalled how

El Zagal had put the fear of death in the two Christian soldiers guarding the high U-shaped pass of Ventas de Zafarraya leading to the coast. Oh, how he had terrorised them!

Raquel had different memories. She had met Abú Abdalá just once when she had accompanied Pedro to check how the blind man was being cared for in his lodgings. While grateful to the young ambassador for the attention he had paid him, El Zagal retained the haughty air of a lord to one of his subjects. But not so with Raquel. Using their native language, he soon melted to her female charm and soft voice, gently passing his rough hands across the smooth features of her face. Pedro and she had promised to visit him soon afterwards, but it was not to be.

Mohammed Abú Abdalá I'b Saïd, to give him his full name, was the younger brother of Abú Hasan Alí, known as Muley Hassan, who, as the then Sultan of Granada, had died in 1485. His son, twenty-three-year-old Mohammed XII, known as Boabdil, had bound himself to King Fernando as a vassal king, believing that this would secure the peace with the Christians, who were hell-bent on putting an end to the Nazarí kingdom once and for all. Furious, Abú Abdalá dissociated himself from his weak nephew and continued the fight, until eventually and inevitably the Muslims were overwhelmed by the superior forces of Christendom. After bequeathing the keys of the city of Almería to the Catholic Monarchs on 26 December 1489, El Zagal retired to his estates near Laujár in the Alpujarras, but within months he had emigrated to Morocco. That was in 1490. Now, four years later, at an age of around forty, he lay buried in the city graveyard. A sad end to a noble man.

A woman in black approached Pedro and Raquel.

'You must be Pedro Togeiro?' she whispered in Arabic. 'My father told me about you.'

'Ah!' replied Pedro, 'then you must be Jadicha. He said he had a daughter who lived in Almería.'

'Yes. When my father fell out with Boabdil, he moved there from Granada to continue his fight against King Fernando. I and my mother…'

'Equivilia, Yusuf IV's daughter?'

'Yes, that's right. We moved there to join Yahya al-Nagar, the Prince of Almería.'

'Who's now the Bailiff of Granada?'

'Yes, but with the name of Pedro de Granada Benegas. Reluctantly, I too have converted to Christianity. Three weeks ago, I received a message from Abraham Ibn Zayal, my father's former secretary, who decided to move back to al-Andalus. He wrote to say that my father had died here, so I've come over to pay my last respects.'

'He was a great man, Jadicha. I revered him. In many ways, it's a pity he didn't become sultan instead of Boabdil.'

'Maybe. But you know, Pedro, if he had become sultan the struggle would have continued between our people and the Christians. There would have been more cities put to the sword like Málaga six years ago, more suffering, more deaths. And it wouldn't have made the slightest difference to the eventual outcome. Fernando and Isabel would have still triumphed. I tried to explain this to my father many, many times, but he was too stubborn; too much a fighter.'

'And that's how I'll remember him, Jadicha; a warrior to the end, brave and fearless.'

The three of them stayed silent for a while.

'Jadicha,' said Pedro, breaking the silence, 'I'll arrange for a proper grave to be constructed here for your father with a nice headstone. But we need to inscribe it.' He pulled out a piece of paper from his pocket. 'I've drafted some words. How do these sound to you? Raquel has corrected the Arabic for me.'

He read it out:

FY DIKRA MOHAM-MED ABU ABDU AL-LAH, YBN SAYD MAXHUR KASZ-SZGAL BEN SAYD ABU NARS, BEN ALY, BEN YUSUF AZ-ZANY, BEN MOHAMED ALJAMIS. MALIK ALMARYA FY SZMAN ALKADYM. NADIL ALMUHAFIDZA ALA MAMLAKA AN-NASRYA DUNA JAUF. HUA MAT, RAHIMATU-LLAH, FY HAMZEM, FY SANAUAT AN-NEBY, UA KANA AMRAHU ARBAYN. TARAKA SZAUYATUHHU AKBYLYA UA YBNATUHU HADYXA.

Translated, it said:

IN MEMORY OF MOHAMMED ABÚ ABDALÁ I'B SAÏD, KNOWN AS EL ZAGAL, SON OF SAÏD ABU NARS, SON OF ALÍ, SON OF YUSUF II, SON OF MOHAMMED V. AT ONE TIME KING OF ALMERÍA. HE FOUGHT FEARLESSLY TO PRESERVE THE KINGDOM OF THE NAZARÍ. HE DIED IN TLEMCEN IN THE YEAR OF THE PROPHET 899, AGED FORTY. HE LEFT A WIFE, EQUIVILIA, AND A DAUGHTER, JADICHA. MAY HIS SOUL FIND PEACE.

'That's lovely, Pedro. You've obviously given it a lot of thought. Thank you so much, and you too, Raquel.'

Jadicha stretched up to kiss Pedro on both cheeks; both their faces were chilled and flushed by the rain. She did likewise with Raquel. Slowly they drew aside and parted. In silence, the young ambassador and his wife retraced their steps to the entrance gates of the graveyard, where their horses were tied beneath some trees. A rider drew up, hurriedly dismounted and ran towards them. The end of a soiled white turban streamed out behind him.

'Yazíd!' cried Pedro. 'What brings you here in such a hurry? We'll be back home in a day or so!'

'I thought you'd like to see this dispatch from the King. A messenger delivered it yesterday. It must be very important.'

II: *Letter from the King*

Pedro, Raquel and Yazíd found an inn in Tlemcen. It was getting late, and the weather was too inclement to consider returning home that day. After seeing their horses properly housed and fed, they donned dry clothes and descended to the smoky, dimly lit parlour, pulling some chairs up around the fire. On such a miserable night, it was nice and cosy and, best of all, they had the place to themselves.

'Come on then, Pedro, what does it say?' Yazíd was as impatient as ever.

'All in good time,' replied his boyhood friend, putting on a nonchalant air, as if letters from the King arrived every day.

The royal communiqué was folded in half and sealed with the King's big wax seal. Pedro prised it open with a knife and held it behind the candle on the table. He read it slowly to himself. A smile flicked across his face, followed by a chuckle. The other two could barely contain themselves.

'So what does the King say?' they asked together in exasperation.

Pedro read the letter aloud.

'Palacio de Cordón, Burgos, 25 February 1494.

'Despatch from Hernando de Zafra, Secretary to Their Royal Majesties, to Don Pedro Togeiro, Ambassador to the Sultan of Morocco…

'Their Royal Majesties send their greetings and trust that you are in good health. You have had little time in your new post in Fez, but already they have received reports indicating that relations between Morocco and our kingdoms have improved and they commend you for this. They send their greetings to Doña Raquel and also to your mother, Miriam, who they hope has now settled in comfortably in the castle of Xiquena with their former most loyal servant, Captain Agustín López. The Queen retains fond memories of her meeting with your mother in Santa Fe following the cessation of hostilities with the Moors two years ago.

'This letter conveys a request from Their Majesties for your attendance forthwith at Tordesillas, and that of Doña Raquel if you so desire. I have already written to Sultan al-Wattasi on their behalf, indicating that you will be absent from your duties for several months. As you know, some sensitivity exists between Portugal and Spain over the future division of lands to be discovered across the Ocean Sea.[1] King John strongly contests the proposition of Pope Alexander VI in his bull *Inter Caetera* made in May last year, proposing a north–south line dividing future Spanish and Portuguese areas of influence. It is clear that a new division needs to be negotiated and a treaty agreed between our counties if serious conflict is to be avoided. More will be explained to you when you attend Their Majesties.'

Pedro paused and looked up at Raquel and Yazíd to see if they were listening. He need not have worried; they were in rapt attention. He continued.

'King John recalls that a young man, who quite clearly is you, accompanied Christopher Columbus when he, the King, granted the Admiral an audience following the latter's landfall in Lisbon on his return from the Indies in March last year. Being impressed by the warmth with which Christopher Columbus described your sterling conduct during the terrible storm when so many of the crew were confined below deck, sick, King John was not altogether surprised to learn that you are now in Their Majesties' service. You made sufficient impression on him then to prompt his request to meet you again during the negotiations shortly to commence in Tordesillas. However, there is a more obvious reason for Their Majesties requesting your attendance there, and that is that the discussions will no doubt include the territorial and fishing rights of our countries along the coast of Africa, currently subject to the Treaty of Alcáçovas of 1479. They consider that it is as well that you are aware personally of these matters in your future dealings with Sultan al-Wattasi. It is for this reason that they wish you to be there.

'King Fernando and Queen Isabel are presently in Burgos, but intend to move their court in May to Medina del Campo. This lies half a day's ride from Valladolid. It is expected that the negotiations with King John will take place in the Convent of Santa Clara in Tordesillas, a walled town on the banks of the River Duero, and more or less midway between the two forementioned cities. I suggest that when you arrive you find your way to the Convent of Santa Clara. You will have no difficulty finding suitable accommodation in the city. You will be reimbursed for the costs of the journey and your stay here.

'Kindly confirm as soon as possible your attendance on Their Majesties.

'Obediently yours,

'Hernando de Zafra.'

---

[1] The term 'Atlantic Ocean' did not emerge until long after Columbus's time, maybe not until the 17th century. Columbus conferred on himself the title 'Admiral of the Ocean Sea'. This led to, or derived from, a map of the western hemisphere, with the New World on one side and Europe on the other, produced by Juan de la Cosa around 1500. He was a cartographer and friend of Christopher Columbus and what we now know as the Atlantic Ocean he showed as *Mare Oceanum*. A map from 1586 showed it as *Mare Oceano Occidentale* and one from 1621 as *Oceanus Occidus*, 'the western ocean'.

'Where's Valladolid?' asked Yazíd.

'As my appointed envoy, Yazíd, I thought you might know!' scoffed Pedro. 'It's many days ride from here.'

'Will you go?'

'Of course! This is a royal summons. I must go.'

'Will Raquel go with you?'

'We'll see. Now leave me, please, both of you. I must reply to Hernando de Zafra. Then, Yazíd, you can take it to Melilla to catch the afternoon boat tomorrow. Raquel and I will return to Fez to pack our things for the journey and to collect young Sara. We'll meet you in Melilla within the next thirty-six hours. Then we'll all take the ferry across to Adra.'

'Not Cartagena?'

'No, the Adra boats are more frequent and, in any case, we'll return first to Vélez Blanco to leave Sara with my mother. We can spend a short time there, but we'll need to set off for Tordesillas soon.'

'So you'd like me to come with you?' asked a rather peeved Raquel, putting on a diffident air, as if meeting the King and Queen had little appeal to her. She would like to have been consulted.

'Of course, my dear… that's if you wish,' added her suitably admonished husband. 'You'll enjoy meeting the Queen. Austere she may be, but she is very considerate and never forgets a face.'

They arrived in Vélez Blanco five days later. The town of some 6,000 souls, still mostly Muslim, was situated on a curved spur in a limestone crag at a height of almost 4,000 feet. Opposite it, across the valley, loomed the dominant, flat-topped mountain, Cerro de La Muela, some 2,000 feet higher, aptly named 'The Molar.' The town was enclosed by two walls, a higher wall bounding the *alcázar*, or fortified palace[2], together with an underground *aljibe*, or water cistern, cut into the solid rock. Alongside it lay a small mosque, already renamed the Church of Santa Magdalena. It was in this church, on a cold, snowy day, just six months before, that Pedro and Raquel had been married. The lower wall of the town was bounded at each end by deep ravines, which defined the spur and from which perennial springs discharged. Vélez Blanco was the birthplace of Pedro Togeiro and his Muslim friend, Yazíd, who was one year younger. Yazíd was a short, stocky lad who could run like the wind for hours without stopping, as if in a trance, but then not know where he was. Four miles below this town lay Vélez Rubio, its sister town of fewer than 1,000 souls. Vélez Rubio took its name from older and pale purplish marls underlying the towering limestone crags which formed the Sierra María. The

---

[2] Between 1506 and 1515, the beautiful and imposing castle of Vélez Blanco was built alongside.

Río Vélez drained the area and flowed eastwards to Lorca, some twenty-five miles away. The city of Murcia lay a further forty miles beyond. Just six miles from Vélez Blanco was the small but imposing red sandstone castle of Xiquena. This was set on an isolated rocky hill above a sloping plain planted with almonds, and it guarded the valley and the route to Lorca.

It was to this castle that Pedro, Raquel and their two-year-old daughter, Sara, headed. Yazíd had taken his leave of them to return to his parents – Yakub Ibn Hayyan and his wife Fátima – in the higher town. Yakub was a leather trader and sold hides to local craftsmen for shoes, saddles and a multitude of domestic and farming items. Raquel was more than keen to accompany Yazíd to Vélez Blanco to be reunited with her mother, Raghad, who now lived there, but that would have to wait until the morrow.

The studded wooden gates into the castle grounds were opened by a huge bearded man wearing a coat of mail and a steel helmet. He must have stood nearly six and a half feet and had the shoulders of an ox. In his hand he held an eight-foot Swiss halberd with an ash staff as thick as a tree, topped by two feet of tempered steel. Behind him, a gravel path wound its way steeply up the enclosure between flanking battlements which ran up and around the hill. A high, square tower topped the fortification, but Xiquena's main accommodation comprised an isolated square keep located in the centre of the castle grounds. It was neither large nor especially commodious.

Pedro and the huge man recognised one another. They both stood there, startled. The gatekeeper may not have worn a helmet of brass, but he was a veritable Goliath. However, it was the youngster who was first to put a name to the face.

'Matute... *Mat*!' Pedro exclaimed. He knew him best by his shortened name. 'Do you remember me?'

The giant stood there looking down at Pedro and Raquel with his mouth open. The words would not come.

'You remember... seven years ago... I was thirteen then... after the November earthquake in Almería... when you were with a party of soldiers from the Inquisition... you took me to Jaén as prisoner!'

The man mouthed some words, but they did not come.

'You remember, surely! You pinned that loathsome Zak down to the ground after he and his evil partner had... had... had their way with me, in that barn. It was the last night before we reached Jaén... when Captain Ortiz sliced open Zak's scrotum with his knife and cut out his balls...' Pedro paused. 'You remember, surely?'

'Y-y-yes, I do remember now. It seems a long t-t-t-time ago,' he stuttered.

Matute's stutter was so bad that he preferred to remain silent. Then he laughed with a great roar and slammed his halberd hard on the ground.

'By G-G-God, didn't he squeal! And all that blood. What became of him? Him and the other evil f-f-f-fellow?'

'Gaz?'

'Yes, Gázquez.'

'They both met their end at the Santa Fe camp outside Granada.'

'By your hand?'

'Yes. I had a score to settle. They'd murdered my father and sister.'

'Ah, n-n-now I understand,' he said slowly. 'I heard the c-c-captain talking to Abel about that. But I didn't really understand what they were saying.'

'Abel?' asked Pedro.

'Yes, Abel. Abel Jiménez. Him and me both j-j-joined the captain here after the war with the Moors ended. We s-s-started here two months ago while you were in M-Morocco.'

Pedro was lost for words.

'I can't believe it. Abel Jiménez!' he exclaimed after a few moments. 'It was Abel who tipped off Gonzalo Fernández that I'd been taken to the Inquisition cells in Jaén. If it hadn't been for him, I would now be dead or, at the very best, a cripple for life.'

'You know D-D-Don Gonzalo, then?' Mat asked in amazement.

'Yes, Mat, very well. Indeed, he came to our wedding up there in Vélez Blanco.'

Pedro pointed over his right shoulder to the town high on the hillside 'But it's a long story, Mat. I'll have to tell you another time.' He then asked, 'Is Captain López at home?'

'No, but he'll be b-b-back shortly with Abel. But your mother's here. I'll t-t-take you both up to the keep.'

He did not need to. Pedro's mother Miriam had heard the voices and was already hurrying down the path to the gatehouse. When she saw who it was, she ran to meet Pedro, Raquel and her granddaughter, Sara. She hugged and kissed them all. Holding little Sara's hand, she led them swiftly up to the house. Matute closed the gate and followed them up the path. He was not going to miss the excitement. There was little enough of that at Xiquena.

'I don't know why you've come home, Pedro and Raquel. But it's lovely to see you both and, of course, little Sara. My word, hasn't she grown!'

'She has, Mama, but she's been very poorly. She's had this chesty cough for months and we're very worried.'

'Never mind, my dear,' replied Miriam heartily, not really taking in what Raquel had said. 'We'll soon have her right. You'll have a surprise when you see who's here, Raquel. What a coincidence! Ooooh!' she cooed.

Miriam bounded up the path like a two-year-old. She could not contain her glee.

Reaching the doorway of the hall was Raquel's short, stocky mother, Raghad. Her new husband, Pedro's loveable uncle, Joshua, was a step behind. In a triple ceremony the previous November, Pedro and Raquel, Raghad and Joshua, and Miriam and Agustín López, lately a captain in the service of Queen Isabel, had all been married. All four, Raghad and Joshua, and Miriam and Agustín, were widows or widowers, and each had found fulfilment and happiness with their new partners in marriage.

It took a while for the handshakes, backslapping and kissing to subside. Apologising for the modesty of the accommodation afforded in the keep, Miriam led them up a flight of stone steps to an arched door leading into the manorial hall. Steps beside the door led to several bedchambers in the floor above. The hall was pleasantly warm. The square hall had a high, cross-vaulted ceiling. Barred windows looked out on two sides. A study and small library occupied a narrow arched niche on the third side. A cavernous hearth, accommodating a chain-driven iron spit, topped by a tapering chimney, occupied the remaining side. A fire glowed in the grate, from which smoke spiralled quietly up the chimney. Níjar rugs covered the cold flagstones of the floor. On the bare stone walls on each side of the fireplace were faded, moth-eaten battle flags won from the Moors long ago. Xiquena had been on the frontier between the two kingdoms and had changed hands many times. On two walls, taking pride of place, hung Miriam's colourful tapestries. These had been created by her embroidery school during her eight long years of captivity in the Alhambra after her abduction by slavers in the port of Aguilas. Pedro was then just eight years old. His Jewish father, Abraham, a renowned apothecary, wrote her out of his life, resigned to the conviction that she had been sold in the slave markets in Damascus or Baghdad, where fair-haired white women commanded a high price.

Joshua, Abraham's younger brother whom Pedro adored, poured some red wine from an earthenware jug sitting in the hearth. As he did so, a clatter of feet up the steps brought forth Miriam's husband, Agustín. Shock and surprise were written all over his face. Captain Agustín Jaime López Marín had served twenty-five years in the service of the Queen before retiring. When Miriam had been discovered in the Alhambra after the fall of Granada on 2 January 1492, the Queen had commanded him to return Miriam safely to her home in Vélez Blanco. During that long ride home with Miriam's tapestries secured on a packhorse, she and the captain, then three years her senior at forty years of age, had been captivated by each other; he by her grace and beauty, she by his manliness and calm authority, and not least by his smart officer's uniform. During the reception in Miriam's family home after the triple wedding in Vélez Blanco the previous November, Don Gonzalo Fernández of Córdoba, the victor of so many of the battles with the Muslims in the years leading up to the fall of Granada, had, on behalf of King Fernando, announced the King's appointment of Agustín as Bailiff of Vélez Blanco, granting him the castle of Xiquena as his future residence.

'So what's brought you home, Pedro?' asked Miriam during a lull after the greetings had subsided. She had been dying to ask.

Pedro retrieved the King's letter from his jacket pocket and read it out slowly to the gathering.

It was later in the evening, while Miriam was showing the womenfolk the new tapestry on which she was working, that Pedro and Agustín had a chance to talk. Pedro had been thrilled beyond words that his mother, so long interned in the harem of the Sultan in the Alhambra, had found true contentment with this former officer of the Queen's guard. Theirs had proved a perfect match. However, so speedily had Pedro and Raquel taken up their duties in Fez after the wedding that he had found little time to discover what Agustín's future duties entailed.

'I'm sorry to appear so ignorant, Captain...'

'Agustín, please, Pedro! I'm not in the army now, you know! Besides, you're a knight of the realm and much superior to me in rank! So – Agustín, please.'

'Thanks. But please tell me, Agustín, what does the post of Bailiff of Vélez Blanco entail? I should know, but to be honest I've little idea.'

'Well, basically, Pedro,' he replied slowly, 'I administer the whole estate for the Fajardo family. This covers all the area around – Vélez Blanco, Vélez Rubio, María, Chirivel and many other villages besides. I see that taxes are collected and dues paid, and that civic buildings are kept in good repair. The Moorish people here are now classed as Mudejares, so they're allowed to keep their religion, customs and dress. I work closely with Mohammed Adbuladin, their mayor, to help promote peace and harmony between his people and the growing Christian community here. But in truth things have continued to be unstable after the reconquest, and at times they're very volatile. So both Mohammed and I spend a lot of time encouraging the tradesmen in the town. Take your friend Yazíd's father, for instance, Yakub Ibn Hayyan, the leather trader. He's now sending his leather products to Murcia and even as far away as Valencia, and he's become very prosperous. He's been made an elder of the Mudejar community, and he's very useful to us in calming the troubled waters that arise all too frequently.'

'So if you manage the estate, Agustín,' asked Pedro, 'who are you answerable to?'

'Essentially, Juan Chacón, the owner, but in due course to his son, Pedro Fajardo, who will succeed to the title. He's only sixteen as yet.'

Pedro looked puzzled.

'But if the ruling family's name is Fajardo and young Pedro is also a Fajardo, how come his father's name is Chacón? It doesn't seem to make sense.'

Agustín laughed.

'That's a paradox which I need to explain to you. You see, Vélez Blanco and the surrounding district originally lay within the domain of one Don Pedro Fajardo, who was the Count of Cartagena and grandfather of young Pedro. Old Don Pedro died twelve years ago without a male heir, but he left four daughters. The eldest of these, Luisa, succeeded him as Governor of Cartagena and the surrounding region; but such is the strategic importance of Murcia, and the harbour of Cartagena, that the choice of her future husband was determined, can you believe, by none other than the Catholic Monarchs. Not much seems to avoid their scrutiny! They conceded that Luisa's future husband need not be of high nobility, providing he was loyal to the Crown and would act with vigour in the defence of this strategic region. Luisa's husband turned out to be Juan Chacón, whose mother was a confidante of Queen Isabel, so you can see where the connection lay. Juan Chacón was heavily involved in the Granada war. Indeed, he's reputed to have saved the life of Fernando in an incident when he was surrounded by a Moorish contingent lead by that rascal El Zagal, whom you held so dear.

'Now, what's intriguing, Pedro,' he continued, 'is that the marriage contract between Luisa and Juan Chacón stipulated that only their firstborn would carry the family name, Fajardo, and that all other offspring would carry their father's name, Chacón – an unusual arrangement, to say the least!'

'So that's why Juan Chacón's son, Pedro, retains the family name Fajardo?'

'Exactly! Odd, isn't it? Although Vélez Blanco and the surrounding towns still lie within the jurisdiction of the Fajardo family, Juan spends most of his time administering the family estates in Murcia and Cartagena. He only comes here a couple of times a year.'

'So you're left to your own devices for most of the time?'

'Yes, and that suits us fine. Your mother's abiding passion continues to be making tapestries, and she's now assembled a group of local women to help, as she did during her confinement in the Alhambra for all those years. These so impressed Isabel when she learnt of them. Since your mother speaks Arabic well she's become an influential figure in the community here, helping the poorer Mudejar families.' Agustín paused.

'Tell me, Pedro,' he continued, 'do you plan to take Raquel with you to Tordesillas?'

'Yes, I do. Although she pretends to be disinterested, I think she'd hate to miss meeting the King and Queen.'

'And can you blame her? What an opportunity for her!' he commented. 'I'd like to accompany you there, Pedro,' he continued, 'but at the moment I need to stay here. There's some unrest brewing in the town over the changes we're going to make to the Caños de la Novia fountain on the way into the town, and I need to be here. Mohammed Adbuladin is wholly behind the changes, but nevertheless, I feel I should be here. Luckily, Mat will ensure that no serious trouble arises! The villagers are terrified of him. With his mass of fair hair, they think he's a Viking!'

'I'd be terrified too, Agustín. He's awesome!'

'But very gentle… Miriam is devoted to him. However, all things considered, Pedro – particularly for the sake of Raquel – I think it's wise if someone goes with you both.'

'How about Abel?'

'I was going to suggest Abel. He's married now and has taken a Mudejar wife, Eva, from Vélez Rubio. They live in a cottage along the road to Lorca, but I'm sure Eva won't mind. She helps Miriam in the kitchen here and they get on like a house on fire. Abel would be ideal, and he'd love to go with you. He's a hardened soldier, absolutely reliable and good in a crisis. What's more, he comes from Galicia in the north of the country and has travelled the road between Granada and Valladolid many times. He knows the route well. I can't think of anyone better to accompany you. When do you plan to leave, Pedro?'

'In a week or so, Agustín. How far is it to Valladolid, in fact?'

'It's a long way. Almost 400 miles from Granada, and we're over 120 miles from there ourselves. It'll take you over ten days to get there.'

III: *The Mob*

May 1494

The three of them set off from Xiquena on the first day of May. It was a warm, sunny day. The almond trees in the nearby orchards shone with a haze of pink blossom. The alcázar of Vélez Blanco on the distant hill to their right glowed in the golden morning light, while Cerro de la Muela, rising precipitously opposite them, still had a dash of glistening snow left on its summit. It was a glorious morning. Pedro had been itching to set off for days, as had Abel, but Raquel had been apprehensive. She had never travelled far and was unusually quiet and subdued.

'Don't worry,' Miriam had said to her. 'It'll be a wonderful adventure for you, and you've got Abel and Pedro to look after you. You have nothing to fear. And you'll enjoy meeting Queen Isabel. I found her charming.'

But Raquel remained silent. She said nothing about her dream the week before. Maybe it was preying on her mind…

Abel led the way on his black stallion. He was a smallish, robust man with a round, cheery face. Underneath his outer cotton shirt he wore a coat of mail which protected his neck, covered his arms to his wrists and reached over his thighs. Beneath the linked mail, he wore a soft woollen shirt. He rode bareheaded, his dark hair billowing in the light breeze, but a steel helmet hung from the pommel of his high saddle. Abel was armed with his broad, heavy sword. A long, razor-sharp hunting knife was sheathed at his side. A four-foot ash staff, less brittle than one of oak, swung from his right side. Its end was sheathed in iron to give it more clout. In a ruckus, the staff was more manageable than a lance. So Abel rode well protected. He had insisted that if he were to make the journey to Tordesillas he must act the part. 'Forearmed is forewarned,' he had said. 'Who knows what we'll encounter?'

Pedro rode Indy, his faithful chestnut mare, which had been abandoned by the villagers of Mecina Fondales in the Alpujarras when they left their village two years before. Miraculously, Pedro had intercepted them as they trudged out of the village in the pouring rain with what few belongings they could carry. Raquel and her mother, Raghad, and baby Sara were among the bedraggled party. But for this chance encounter, Raquel would have been lost to him for ever.

Pedro rode beside her. He was clad in a leather jerkin and thick woollen trousers. His favourite red floppy hat was on his head. Like Abel, he wore riding boots to protect his legs against bushes and thorns. Pedro was armed as ever with his beautiful Toledo sword, so wonderfully crafted for his thirteenth birthday by David Levy in Lorca. His matching dagger was on his belt. Like Abel, an ash staff swung from his saddle, although his was shorter and not tipped with iron. Pedro had considered taking a mail shirt with him, but had decided that the thick leather jerkin, almost as good as a breastplate, would provide adequate protection.

Raquel had become a confident rider and had chosen to wear loose-fitting Arab clothes which were far more commodious on a warm day. So she had on a red *yubba*, a woollen tunic with broad sleeves, and a white *sarawil* or baggy cotton trousers. Her long black hair was tied in a bun and concealed in a *mandil* or silk scarf. The saddlebags of all three horses were well laden with spare clothing; Pedro with clothes of a courtier, albeit very modest, and Raquel with some finery as befitted a lady. Abel's more powerful mount carried some blankets and waterproof clothing, lanterns, several water skins and emergency provisions, as well as some more beautiful clothes for Raquel made by Miriam. Well, she was to meet the Queen.

By dusk they had reached Baza, some forty miles on, and by the following afternoon had passed through Guadix, where in December 1488 El Zagal, its then king, had handed over the keys to the city to no lesser a person than King Fernando himself. The third day saw them on the road heading north towards the fine walled town of Úbeda. Facing south to the mountain wall of the high sierras, Úbeda had already been earmarked for magnificent palaces by princes and bishops alike.

It was late in the afternoon when the party of three approached Jódar, a morning's ride from Úbeda. Jódar, an old Arab town, bleached almost white by the sun, lay on a limestone ridge overlooking an undulating plain. This was planted with olive groves which ran as far as the eye could see to the hazy massif of the Sierra de Cazorla many miles to the east. The plain's patchwork quilt of pale marly soils – yellows, mauves and creams – was seemingly hand-stitched by lines of olive trees, resplendent in their green livery of spring.

They had ridden in silence for nearly an hour, deep in their own thoughts. It became evident what Abel was thinking about.

'You told me last week, Pedro, about your voyage to the Indies with Christopher Columbus. What became of him afterwards?'

'As you must have heard, Abel, he had a triumphant arrival in Barcelona last April in front of the Palau Reial Major, where he presented the King and Queen with his log of the journey.'

'Were you there?'

'No. By then I had returned home to my mother in Vélez Blanco.'

'But it must have been quite an occasion?'

'Yes, so I was told. Six of the Indians he brought back from Cuba and La Española[1] were paraded through the streets and caused a real sensation with the people in the city, what with their plumes of coloured feathers, the parrots and the giant lizards[2].'

'So where's Christopher Columbus now?'

'At the end of September last he sailed to the Indies with another fleet.'

'You didn't go?'

'No!' interjected Raquel. 'Pedro was planning our wedding... although really,' she added with a touch of venom, 'he was awaiting a message from that good-for-nothing sultan of his, Boabdil, to join him when he fled to Morocco.'

'He didn't flee, Raquel,' protested Pedro. 'It was part of his agreement with Fernando and Isabel.'

Abel grinned but ignored the family squabble. He shared Raquel's opinion about the former sultan.

'How many ships did Columbus take this time?' he continued.

'It was a big fleet, by all accounts, and assembled very hastily. I think the King and Queen were worried about the intentions of King John of Portugal.'

'Who you've met?'

'Yes, when I accompanied the Admiral to the Portuguese court after our return in March last year. I'd come back in the *Niña* with the Admiral, although I'd set off in the *Pinta*. We lost sight of Martín Pinzón in the *Pinta* in the terrible storm off the Azores, and we had no idea that he'd survived it until after we'd returned to Palos. Quite amazingly, the *Pinta* sailed into Palos that very day, just a few hours after us in the *Niña*.'

'Did Pinzón sail with Columbus on this second voyage?'

'No, he died soon after he returned from the Indies. It was very sad. He treated me harshly, but I liked the man. He was a great sailor.'

'What did he die of?'

'I'm told he died of something he picked up in Cuba. His skin was all blotchy and he had terrible headaches. He died before the end of the month.'

'So Columbus's second voyage must have been organised very rapidly?'

'Yes, maybe too rapidly. Time will tell. Shortly after the Barcelona procession, the Admiral received instructions from the monarchs to prepare for a second voyage. By August they had become insistent that he should sail forthwith.'

'Because of the Portuguese threat?'

---

[1] Now comprising the Dominican Republic and Haiti.
[2] Iguanas

'Yes, I suppose so. King John is a charismatic character. But he is also tough and very determined to uphold Portuguese rights in the Ocean Sea – or what he considers Portuguese rights.'

'How many people set off on this second voyage?'

'Around a thousand, I believe.'

As they rode wearily up towards the town, a dozen or so people were tearing down the hill towards them, looking back in terror as a hundred or so men chased them, brandishing sticks and clubs.

'Please help us,' the leader said, panting, as they reached Abel and Pedro. The elderly man was on the point of collapse. He had a full grey beard and was clearly more a man of learning than of the soil.

'They're going to kill us!' he gasped, barely able to catch his breath.

The group cowered in a tight knot between the horses, clinging in desperation onto their bridles and harnesses and the riders' legs. There were three men and three women of middle age, several youngsters, and a very elderly couple, evidently grandparents. Abel pushed them away and rode forward to meet the angry mob. Pedro jumped off his horse, telling Raquel to stay where she was. She was safer in the saddle. Pedro was immediately submerged by arms and bodies.

'Why are they chasing you?' he asked the bearded leader, trying to push the throng away from him.

'We are Jews... *conversos*,' replied the breathless leader. 'You see...'

He got no further. Fifty yards up the road, Abel had placed his horse across the road to block the baying crowd, all dressed in white cotton *qamis* and white baggy *sarawils*. The crowd swarmed around him. He had barely drawn his long staff from its holder when a bare-chested young man, wearing only a *sarawil*, jumped up behind him and dragged him to the ground. Abel was submerged in a sea of flailing arms and clubs. His helmet clattered across the road. But the mob barely stopped. Like a frothing white tide, it poured down the road, leaving Abel sprawled and unconscious in a pool of blood which left a dark stain as it soaked into the dust. Within seconds, the mob was upon Pedro and the party of Jews. Mercifully, Raquel was left on her horse. She had had the sense to pull off her *mandil* and shake out her dark hair. Spiritedly, she shouted at the mob in Arabic. Maybe that was what kept them away from her. Pedro was ejected from the melee like a pip from a squashed orange as the mob set upon the Jews. Clubs reigned down to the screams of the vanquished and the baying of the mob: *'Judios, Judios, Judios!'*

Momentarily, the mob drew back from the families lying in the dust. The attackers wiped the blood and sweat from their faces with the backs of their hands. Their first taste for blood was satiated. Most of those lying on the ground pulled themselves to their knees slowly, blood pouring from open wounds on their heads and faces. It was safer to face the mob kneeling than to lie prostrate on the ground. Many held their sides in agony, finding it difficult to breathe. Several of the youngsters got to their feet valiantly, ready to defend themselves as best they could from further assault. The two grandparents, if that is what they were, remained motionless on the ground, their bodies broken and twisted. Up the road towards the village, Abel was getting to his knees.

Raquel had seen all this from the vantage point of her horse. She had witnessed such incidents before back home. It was the lull before the storm, and she knew it was crucial to take action now.

'You there!' she shouted angrily in Arabic, adopting the rough dialect of her home village. 'Why do you attack these people? Can't you see that they're unarmed!'

She knew she was playing for time. But if she could hold them off for just a minute it might stop a second onslaught. The next time the beating would be more focussed, more severe. Most would surely die.

'Can't you see there are women and children here? The two old people are already dead. Is this the way Muslim people behave?' she hollered, her voice gaining in force as she became more confident. 'Haven't we Muslims suffered enough at the hands of the Christians without you behaving like the filthy creatures they are? Stand aside, I say. Leave these poor people alone. Leave them alone, I say,' she repeated, with even more force.

Taken by surprise, the mob took a step back. But the leader, a powerful man in his thirties, stood his ground.

'Who do you think you are,' he spat, 'riding into our village, interfering in our affairs? You know nothing of what's going on here,' he said with utter contempt. 'Ahmed!' he shouted to another man, who could have been his brother. 'Pull that woman off her horse. We'll take them all up to the village.'

'Wait!' shouted Raquel, again in her rough Arabic. 'I'm Doña Raquel, and my husband is His Majesty's ambassador to Morocco. But I'm one of you. I was brought up—'

She could get no further. She pushed away the man who was trying to manhandle her from her horse and dismounted slowly and proudly, smoothing her cascade of raven hair back behind her head. With her dark complexion, in the evening light she looked both stunning and formidable.

'What do I care whether if you're the ambassador's woman or the Queen herself?' mocked the leader. 'Ahmed, take these two up to the village, and that fellow lying on the ground up the road. And round up all these accursed Jews. Leave the two who are dead. The crows can have them.'

But Abel was now on his feet, his big stallion having trotted back to him. The animal knew where safety lay. Abel saw the commotion down the road and had heard Raquel's strident voice over the uproar, quelling the violence. What a woman, he thought. What a spirit! Although he did not understand what she was saying, his opinion of her soared. He saw Pedro and Raquel's belongings in their horses' saddlebags being ransacked, Pedro's sword and dagger being taken from him. His precious jade ring, given to him by Queen Isabel for saving her and King Fernando's lives in the encampment fire at Gozco nearly four years ago, was snatched from his finger. Raquel's gorgeous dresses to wear before the Queen were being paraded around by one of the ruffians. Pedro and Raquel's hands were being bound behind their backs with rough esparto cord. He could see Pedro gesticulating to him with his head as much to say 'get away while you can'. Pedro was right. Abel knew he must get away and do so quickly. He ran across the road and retrieved his helmet and his iron-headed staff which lay nearby. In a couple of strides, he was on his horse and riding full tilt up the hill. There was no way other than through the village. But he would not be threatened now.

The mob pushed the Jews towards the village, half a mile away. Those who lagged behind were cuffed and beaten. The youngsters, who showed a bit of spirit, were clubbed viciously. Pedro and Raquel followed some distance behind. There was little they could do now for the poor people and instinctively they wanted to separate themselves from them. Their horses were led off elsewhere. Indy looked back anxiously at Pedro, the whites of her dark eyes showing her fear.

The sun had set over the hills to their left, leaving behind a golden glow in the sky. As the Jews were paraded through the village, the wives and children of the mob came out of their houses, screaming, *'Judios, Judios!'*, waving their fists and throwing stones at them. The Jews trooped on silently, muted by the fear of what might lie in store for them. Pedro and Raquel were held back as they approached some stone cottages on the edge of the village. Now empty and largely in ruins, their roofs of pale brown pantiles had long fallen in.

'Where are you taking us?' demanded Raquel, repeating her rough village dialect.

'You'll soon see,' was the curt reply.

'You have no right to treat us this way,' complained Pedro in Arabic, finding his voice at last. 'We're on our way north at the King's behest. What goes on in this village is of no concern to us. Release us, and return our horses and belongings, and we'll be on our way.'

The mob leader sneered at him with disdain. The couple were led up the road towards the centre of the village and then down a side street. Without any words being spoken, they were directed into a two-storey stone house and pushed down some steps to a cellar. A door was opened, their hands were freed and they were pushed inside. The door was bolted behind them. It was pitch-black, or appeared so at first. It had a dry, musty smell which they could not place. Some of the fading light of day entered through a small grill high in the wall, which must have been more or less at street level. It allowed some welcome fresh air into the dark room. Their plight could have been much worse, and the cellar was commodious compared with the freezing cell in which the thirteen-year-old Pedro had been incarcerated in Jaén seven years before by the Spanish Inquisition. In comparison, this cellar was dry and contained sacks of straw and empty boxes stacked on one side. Quietly, the cellar door opened and a large pitcher of water and two mugs were placed inside. Pedro only caught a glimpse of their gaoler, but he was young and clean-shaven and not one of the street mob. Pedro pulled some boxes down from the stack and poured some water into the earthenware mugs. The couple were both parched.

'What do we do now, Pedro?' asked Raquel. Her earlier fortitude was wavering.

Pedro put his arms around her. He could feel her shaking.

'You were wonderful out there, my darling,' he said tenderly. 'If you hadn't made the stand you did, that group of poor people would undoubtedly have been beaten to death, there and then.'

'What will happen to them now?'

'I don't know.'

'Why were they attacked?'

'One of them said they were *conversos*, Jews who have adopted the Christian faith.'

'But why would the villagers attack them for this?'

'After the fall of Granada,' he explained, 'the Jews were given four months to leave Spain and thousands did, as the Muslim villagers did in your village at Mecina. I don't know what's happened here in Jódar. I expect we'll find out eventually, but the prospects for these Jewish people look pretty grim to me.'

'What will happen to us?' asked Raquel, tears forming in her eyes.

'When things calm down, the people here will soon realise that they've made a great mistake and they'll set us free. Remember, Abel is free and will fetch help. He's not called "able" for nothing. He's a very resourceful man.'

'I do hope you're right, my dear,' she said.

'We'll make ourselves as comfortable as we can on these straw mattresses and see what the morrow brings.'

'I'm glad I wasn't separated from you, my love,' she added as they spread the mattresses on the stone floor. 'I don't know what I'd have done.'

'Nor me,' Pedro said. 'I'd have been worried out of my mind.'

They cuddled up together on the floor, happy to be together even under these uncertain circumstances.

'What will happen tomorrow?' asked Raquel after a while.

'Let's wait and see, dear. There's no point worrying now. But I'm sure we'll be released soon.'

They lay together contentedly. Raquel had clearly been looking for a good moment to tell Pedro something important. After a while, excitedly yet a little tentatively, she whispered, 'Pedro, I've been waiting for a suitable moment to tell you. I think I'm expecting a baby.'

'Well, in prison seems as good a time as any to give me the news!' he mocked. 'But that's wonderful news, Raquel. When will you know for certain?'

'I spoke to Mama before we left. It seems pretty certain. I'll know for sure in a couple of weeks' time.'

'That will be wonderful. But it does mean that we can't linger too long in Tordesillas.'

'Oh, don't be silly! Think of all the doctors the Queen has in court. I'm sure I couldn't be in a better place.'

But Pedro could not sleep and, absently, his mind returned to Abel's questions about the second voyage of the Admiral of the Ocean Sea, Christopher Columbus. Pedro pondered how he was progressing.

In fact, in talking earlier to Abel, Pedro had greatly underestimated the number of crew and passengers who sailed in the seventeen ships. In total, they carried nearly 1,500 crew and passengers, including a few women. Christopher Columbus had chosen the ships carefully for their manoeuvrability, and they included the *Niña*, his favourite ship from the first voyage. All but two of them were square-rigged; the remainder were lateen-rigged with triangular sails. As with the first voyage, most of the crew came from Palos, near Seville, but there were many Basques and some were Genoese. One such Genoese was Diego, Columbus's brother, who always dressed as a priest. Among the contingent were 200 volunteers who paid for their own passage. These included many who would later become governors of several of the countries of Latin America, plus Pedro de Las Casas, father of Bartolomé de Las Casas. Later, Bartolomé reconstructed Columbus's ship's log of the first voyage after it was lost, and he did more than any other to promote the interests of the Indians against the inhumane treatment of the conquistadors. Problematically for Columbus, many of these volunteers were appointees of the monarchs and were more loyal to the Crown than to him. Also present were twenty armoured horsemen and their chargers. Columbus was deeply worried by the presence of so many high-ranking and influential people who owed him no allegiance. There were two doctors, plus priests and Benedictine monks who, again, were effectively agents of the Crown.

Columbus had on board three Indians as interpreters. He had brought back ten natives from his first voyage, but the remainder had died. His fleet could well have included Noah's ark, since he also took twenty-four horses, ten mares and two mules, as well as pigs, goats and sheep. The majority of the crew were farm workers, there to eventually work the fields and mine the gold.

In early October, at about the time that the deposed Sultan of Granada, Boabdil, had abandoned al-Andalus for Morocco with his family and followers, the fleet arrived in Gomera in the Canaries. There, Columbus bought pigs, more mules and some chickens. A festival was organised in honour of Beatriz Bobadilla, Gomera's beautiful governess, whom the Admiral idolised and to whom he had paid court on his first voyage. The fleet left there on 13 October, taking an initial route to the south-east which, after twenty days, brought them to several small islands, starting with Martinique[3], which were inhabited by the cannibal tribe, the Caribes. Columbus had encountered these hostile people the previous year. These beautiful and leafy islands are in the centre of the Lesser Antilles archipelago, which forms the eastern edge of the Caribbean Sea. There they captured twelve fat but beautiful girls and two boys, all of whom were later returned to Spain.

The expedition proceeded to Dominica and then on to Guadalupe, where they found thatch huts containing human skeletons, the first signs of human burial. They learnt that some youngsters had been castrated, and the women there told of being treated with terrible cruelty by the Caribes, who maintained that human flesh – when roasted on a grill with parrot and duck and other delights – was the finest in the world. These cannibals used human tibias and arms to make the points of their spears. The travellers spent just six days in Guadalupe, since Christopher Columbus's aim from the outset was to return quickly to the Villa de la Navidad, the fort on the island of La Española. There, the previous Christmas, he had left a party of thirty-nine crewmen from the *Santa María* to establish a small colony, after this ship had run aground and foundered on a sandbank. The fleet sailed on to Montserrat, where the Caribes had slaughtered all the inhabitants. They pressed on to Antigua, which was well populated. But in a short skirmish two of the Spanish were injured and one died, the first casualty of the expedition.

Moving ever westwards, with brief stops on Santa Cruz, the Virgin Islands, and Puerto Rico, where the natives were terrified of the Caribes, they arrived at La Española on 28 November, just eleven months after leaving the colonists there with arms, a year's supply of wine and food and ship's timbers to build a fort. Columbus was mortified to find the fort silent and reduced to ashes. Hoping to attract the settlers, if by chance they were still alive and still in the

---

[3] The modern names for the Caribbean islands have been used, not those given by Columbus.

vicinity, they fired their small cannons or bombards all at the same time. The concussion of the guns reverberated around the mountains like thunder, but it was in vain. In a deserted native village nearby, Columbus's men found many articles belonging to their missing crew, including caps, shoes, pieces of cloth and the large anchor from the *Santa María*. The Spaniards never found out what happened to their compatriots, but the brother of Guacanagarí, the local chief, who had befriended Columbus a year before, said that the Spanish colonists had left the fort to capture natives and search for gold. A battle had taken place some two months before. Guacanagarí's brother said that, judging by the condition of the bodies, they might well have been killed by the Caribes. Mercifully, Columbus refused to avenge their deaths.

At the beginning of January, after a difficult sea passage along the northern coast of La Española, they stopped at Monte Cristo. Some twenty miles inland from there, they constructed the fort of La Isabela. This would be the strategic base for the Spanish for many years to come. The whole expedition landed there, including the animals. Everyone was very fatigued after the stop-start journey. La Española possessed a large population of friendly Tainos Indians. As before, they demonstrated a pleasant disposition and were receptive to Christianity. They knelt before the altar set up by the priests onboard and joined boisterously in the Ave Maria. All declared their wish to become Christians, yet their huts contained all sorts of gods and idols!

So Columbus established La Isabela in a valley where the previous year Martin Pinzón had claimed to have found gold. In a short time, they had constructed 200 cabins around a central square. The water in the river was clear and drinkable. Exaggerating, as was his habit, Columbus compared the small river there to the Guadalquivir running through Seville, the fields surrounding their community with the best to be found in Castile, and claimed that the two nearby lakes and their flocks of turkeys could not be bettered anywhere in the world. Soon, however, discord broke out in the settlement, with the Admiral unable to control the rapacity of his men, who treated the Tainos with utter brutality. His men had little idea of how to farm or hunt, and Columbus failed to find gold enough to pay them for their labours as planned. Many of the settlers wanted to return immediately to Spain. As matters deteriorated, the settlers took the Tainos as slaves and Columbus contemplated starting a trade in slavery with Seville. A week after disembarking at La Isabela, he sent a party of fifteen men inland in search of gold. Columbus wanted the expedition's horses for this enterprise, but their lordly owners refused to release them.

The party went sixty miles inland and, on their return, reported optimistically that they had seen gold in many places – so much, they claimed, that their ships would be too small to return it all to Spain. This was a great relief to

Columbus, since before departing he had promised the Catholic Monarchs that he would find as much gold as there was iron in northern Spain.

At the beginning of February, Antonio de Torres returned to Spain from La Española with twelve ships, leaving Columbus with just five caravels. On 12 March, the Admiral set off with 500 men to explore the 'island of gold'. They travelled by horse and on foot. The journey was tough, and they used the natives as beasts of burden and to help cross the rivers. Columbus found some rocky ground showing signs of gold, and he commanded the construction of a fort there, which he named 'St Thomas'. Following growing insubordination, several of his party were flogged and had their ears or noses cut off. One was hanged.

After two weeks, Columbus returned to La Isabela in time to receive an urgent message that the natives were planning to attack the fort at St Thomas, and he immediately sent 400 men to reinforce it. But they had no scruples and acted with awful cruelty, flogging the natives and cutting off their ears. The consequence was predictable. The natives at La Isabela refused to give them food, and – with all their flour consumed – the colonists had to ration their supplies. Already it was clear that the climate did not suit the growth of the seeds and plants which they had brought with them. Illnesses proliferated and, worryingly, they had only found a small amount of gold. Ignoring the growing unrest, Columbus sailed westwards towards Cuba, leaving his brother Diego in charge. From that time on, Columbus never recovered his authority.

Antonio de Torres and his twelve ships landed in Cádiz on 7 March after thirty-five days' passage, and a month later reached the royal castle of La Mota in Medina del Campo, built sixty years before. They brought back to Spain with them gold, cinnamon and peppers, plus a group of Indians as slaves, as well as several hundred of the crew and passengers who had left Spain just four months before. More ominously, they also carried back to the Old World the contagious disease which had smitten Martín Pinzón and which would soon spread across Europe.[4] Torres told the monarchs of the discontent among the colonists and the paucity of gold, food and supplies. He also reported on the maltreatment of the natives. Yet, in contrast, he carried a letter from the Admiral which lauded the thick veins of gold they had found. Columbus wrote that they were to return cannibal slaves to learn Castilian, and predicted again that they could plant wheat, sugar cane and vines on the island, as well as rear cattle and pigs. He complained about the insubordination of the horsemen, who saw themselves as outside his authority and, while they were useful to defend the encampment of Isabela, were not under his direct command.

---

[4] Syphilis

Fernando felt deceived by the rosy tone of Columbus's letter and the lack of gold returned by Antonio de Torres, since he desperately needed money to finance the threatened conflict in Italy. A week later, the monarchs wrote to Christopher Columbus, saying that they had ordered Bartolomé Columbus, his brother, to sail to the Indies with three caravels filled with provisions. Bartolomé was well thought of by the monarchs, so in May – while Pedro and Raquel were still incarcerated in the house in Jódar – Bartolomé departed for Gomera in the Canaries, to take on board a hundred sheep to take to the Indies.

The light was streaming through the grill in the wall when Pedro and Raquel were roused the next morning by their gaoler, a pleasant enough young man called Yusuf.

'I've brought you some food and some more water,' he said in Arabic. 'You'll be leaving here in a short while.'

'Where to?' asked Raquel. 'Are you releasing us?'

'I can't say,' Yusuf replied. 'But Mohammed ibn Zárkara, who's the mayor of Jódar, has heard about your being taken prisoner. He'll know what to do with you.'

The young man said no more and left, bolting the door behind him.

An hour later, two women dressed in colourful *durra'as* over white *qamis* beckoned Pedro and Raquel to follow them. The two women were young and very pretty and immaculately groomed. They led the couple up the road to the village square. An imposing house stood to one side, and they were taken to this and led upstairs to a bedroom overlooking the square. The shutters on the inside of the barred window were half-open, and they could see that the room was comfortably furnished with a soft mattress and cushions, and a low dressing table. A pitcher of fresh water stood on the marble top washbasin, and clean linen towels had been provided.

'Whose is this house? Why have we been brought here?' Pedro and Raquel asked the two young women. But they received no reply, just a kindly smile and a graceful tilt of the head.

It was half an hour later when Mohammed ibn Zárkara unlocked the door and entered. He was a tall, imposing man in his fifties with a well-manicured black beard and a black *'imam* wound about his head.

'I'm Mohammed ibn Zárkara,' he said in a lordly manner in Arabic. 'I'm the alcalde of Jódar. I regret that you were treated so roughly yesterday. Please accept my apologies. I hope that you'll find this accommodation more acceptable.'

'Ibn Zárkara,' started Pedro. 'As you might have heard, my name is Don Pedro Togeiro de Gozco and I'm the King's ambassador to Morocco. And this is my wife, Doña Raquel.'

'Who is a very spirited young woman, I gather!' he chuckled. 'Yes, I know who you are.'

'So why are we being kept here? We're on our way at the King's behest to Tordesillas. King Fernando will not take kindly to our detention here. Why are we being locked in this room? Why were those people attacked yesterday?'

'They were Jews,' he replied. 'They profess to be *conversos*, but in reality we know that they still practise their religion in secret. You know that the Jews were required to leave al-Andalus two years ago this month, and they were given four months to do so. Those who chose to remain could only stay if they were baptised into the Christian faith. Many did so. However, the Jews here shut themselves in their enclave on the edge of the village. They claim that they were converted to Christianity, but we know that this is not so.'

'But—' interrupted Pedro.

'Please let me finish,' said Ibn Zárkara firmly. 'As you know, life for we Muslims in the kingdom of Castile – all-powerful now after the fall of Granada – has become difficult and dangerous. If we were found to be harbouring families of Jews, we would be the ones to be punished and probably forced to leave our village and sail to distant lands. This is why the villagers here rose up against the Jews yesterday. We simply cannot afford to be seen sheltering them in our midst. We used to be left in peace, but no longer. Squadrons of the King's horses pass through here regularly, taking what they choose and molesting our young woman. I dread to think what they'd do if they had strayed into the Jewish commune.'

'What will become of these people?' asked Raquel.

'That's no concern of yours, Doña Raquel,' Mohammed ibn Zárkara replied firmly.

'So will you release us now?' asked Pedro. 'You know that we've nothing to do with the affair yesterday, and that we were simply passing through your village.'

'That I understand. But I'm obliged to consult with the *alguacil* here. Only then can I release you. But you need have no fear. Your life is not threatened and you'll be treated well. My two wives, Jaduya and Aisha, who you've met, will care for all your needs. So please be patient. We wish you no harm.'

Pedro paused a few moments, looked the tall Muslim in the eyes and stood up slowly. He enunciated his Arabic very clearly.

'Ibn Zárkara, we have listened to you patiently without interruption. Now you can listen to me. By holding us here against our will, you are threatening yourself and possibly the whole of your village. You clearly have no comprehension of the gravity of what you are doing. Your villagers have stolen our horses and saddlebags and all our belongings, including my precious Toledo sword. The saddlebags contain the summons from the King and Queen for us to attend them in Tordesillas for an important state occasion involving the kingdoms of Castile, Aragón and Portugal. To say that the monarchs will be displeased to hear of our confinement here in your house is a gross understatement.'

'And what is more,' added an angry Raquel, recovering her fury from the day before, 'your villagers have stolen all our personal belongings and,' she was almost incandescent now, 'they have defiled my beautiful clothes, which were especially made for me for the palace ceremonies – parading them around among themselves as if they belonged to the village harlot! What value are they now, even if they're returned to me?'

She glowered at the Muslim mayor, ready to pounce on him, but Pedro restrained her and continued.

'One of your mob ripped from my finger the Queen's jade ring, which she presented me with three years ago for saving her and the King's lives from a fire at the encampment at Gozco outside Granada. Only a handful of her closest courtiers and nobles are privileged to wear such a ring, which guarantees safe conduct across this country. To hold such a ring unlawfully incurs the severest punishment.'

'But you must understand, Ambassador,' stammered the Muslim, now starting to realise the implications of his actions and those of his villagers, 'I have to wait to hear from the *alguacil*. I cannot release you until I have his authority.'

'You needed no authority to place us in custody,' spat Raquel, who was ready to fly at the man.

'Exactly,' added Pedro, 'and you need no authority to release us. Listen, ibn Zárkara, and listen carefully,' Pedro continued, lowering his voice and speaking with absolute gravity. 'Abel Jiménez, who is accompanying us to Tordesillas, is an ex-soldier. By now he might already be returning from Úbeda or Baeza with a squadron of lancers – *jinetes*, as you would understand them – fast and lightly armoured and ruthless. I truly dread to think what they'll do if they find us captive in your house, or for that matter, what will befall your village and your villagers. I strongly urge you to release us now – not in half an hour, not this afternoon, but *now* – and return all our belongings intact, our horses and saddlebags, as well as the Queen's jade ring and my wife's clothes, although they are worthless now. Even then, I have no idea what retribution will follow. But be very clear about what I am telling you. Abel knows where we are, so if any harm befalls us in any way, then... well, you will have to guess as to the consequences.'

Mohammed ibn Zárkara sat down on the low divan, shaking so badly that he had to feel for it behind him. His eyes stared blankly at his hands, which were clasped in front of him, but he could not stop them shaking. He sat thus for a few minutes, then wobbled to his feet, took an unsteady course to the door, fumbled with the key and departed without locking the door behind him.

'I'll see that your things are assembled downstairs,' he mumbled as he left, steadying himself down the stairs against the handrail. Raquel started to follow him down the stairs, maybe even to assist him on his way, but Pedro counselled caution. It was safer to stay where they were for the moment.

The previous evening, Abel Jiménez had galloped through the village on his big stallion without anything going amiss. With his ire now roused and with sword unsheathed, he was not going to be molested. Úbeda lay fifteen miles to the north, and he arrived there before nightfall. It was a modest town, protected by city walls which were started by the Moors in the year 850. Now a Christian town, it was growing rapidly and would, in the next hundred years, contain some of the most ornate churches and wealthiest palaces in the whole of Spain. Abel followed the road into the centre from the west gate. This led to the main square by the thirteenth-century church of San Pablo. Úbeda still possessed a garrison, a leftover from it being a frontier town some years before, and the barracks were easily found, since a handful of soldiers lounged around outside chatting and looking bored. They directed Abel inside to the refectory, where two officers were eating. Abel introduced himself.

'Sit down, my man, have some food and drink with us,' a captain said. 'It's always good to meet an old comrade-in-arms. If you've been riding all day, you must be tired and thirsty.'

Abel quaffed several quarts of water and half as much wine, and over some bread and soup told the officers what had occurred at Jódar. The response was immediate and enthusiastic: 'We'll ride in the morning!'

Captain Ruiz led a troop of two dozen lancers out of Úbeda early the next day. Abel rode alongside him, he and his horse glad of the night's rest. With lances and sabres they were well armed, but they travelled light with thick padded jerkins as their sole body protection, plus steel kneecaps and close-fitting steel helmets.

'Who was involved in the riot, Abel?' asked the captain as they trotted on.

'The leader of the mob was a burly fellow in his mid-thirties. He was clearly the ringleader. And I heard him address another fellow as "Ahmed", a bit younger I'd say.'

'Ah! They would be the two brothers, Abul and Ahmed Kaisan. They're always causing trouble, and effectively rule the village. They're bad news, and I fear for your two friends. We'd better make haste.'

He thrust out his jaw, leant forward on his horse and spurred it into a gallop.

Pedro and Raquel had been wise to stay where they were. For the next hour there was a continuous hubbub in the square below as, bit by bit, their belongings were returned and dumped unceremoniously in the dust at the door of the alcalde's house. First were their saddles, then the horses' harnesses and reins, then the saddlebags. Finally Pedro's sword and dagger, both sheathed, were placed carefully by the door. Three women then arrived in the square, pursued by a laughing gaggle of children. The women disported themselves in Raquel's gorgeous dresses, with the remainder slung over their arms. Wearing nothing underneath, and to the ribald jesting of the crowd now gathering, they unashamedly pulled the dresses over their heads, prancing around naked to the delight of the crowd, who clapped their hands in time as the prancing became a high-stepping, rhythmic dance.

Pedro recognised the two brothers, Abul and Ahmed Kaisan, as they strutted into the square to loud cheers. They pushed their way into the circle now formed around the three women, who had been joined by others, younger and more nubile. They lifted two of the women high off the ground, their copious breasts swinging around like bags of pork fat, to the delight of the crowd. It was becoming a great village fiesta. The crowd quietened for just a moment as a clatter of horses entered the square. A big cheer went up as two youths, riding bareback, rode Pedro's and Raquel's mounts to the door of the alcalde's and dismounted. Then, as a final curtain raiser, Ahmed Kaisan, his woman still appended to him, approached Mohammed ibn Zárkara in mock homage, pulled Pedro's jade ring from his finger and placed it on the mayor's outstretched but still shaking hand.

But if the clatter of Pedro's and Raquel's horses drew the attention of the villagers, it was nothing to the thunder of horses' hooves a few minutes later when Captain Ruiz's lancers rode into the square. He had divided his force in two. Abel took a dozen lancers around the back of the village so that the two squadrons of horsemen, shouting blood-curdling cries, their sabres to the fore on outstretched arms, rode into the square from different directions. They were an awesome and terrifying sight. Even then the riders split up, completely encircling the crowd, which ran screaming in all directions to escape the riders; but there was nowhere to go. The square was effectively sealed.

Pedro and Raquel had watched all the celebrations of the villagers through the shutters of their upstairs room. Now they ran down the stairs and burst out past the alcalde into the arms of Abel, who had dismounted in front of the house.

'Thank God you're both safe, Pedro!' he exclaimed. 'These two men here are brothers and the ringleaders of the mob. They're notorious troublemakers. I feared for your safety. Come, let's gather up your things and saddle your horses. We'll leave Captain Ruiz to sort out these people.'

The good captain had wasted little time. With half his men still mounted and standing guard, the remaining lancers herded the villagers into a group using the flats of their sabres and made them sit cross-legged on the ground. The villagers were more than happy to obey, since a wild orgy of retribution was less likely to follow if they acquiesced. Too often, sabres and bloodletting go hand in hand. With rape and hot-blooded cavalry equally associated, the three hussies became shy and bashful, borrowing shawls and scarves from the other women to cover themselves up. But the riders were well disciplined, and wasted little time in arresting ibn Zárkara, while the two brothers were clapped in irons.

'What will you do now?' Pedro asked Captain Ruiz.

'The villagers can go home. They seem to have returned all your belongings. These two,' he said, pointing to the two brothers, 'will be hanged this evening in this village square. They have a long history of causing mischief, and this gives me a chance to settle many scores. Even the villagers here will know that I've little option.'

'Come, Pedro and Raquel,' said Abel Jiménez, 'we've recovered all your belongings. Let's be on our way and leave Captain Ruiz to wrap up this sorry affair.'

'What will become of ibn Zárkara?' asked Raquel, who was now a lot calmer and more rational.

'I don't know,' replied Abel, 'he's a broken man, as you can see. The Captain may reckon it's best to leave it to the villagers to decide what to do with him. Come, let's be on our way.

'Thank you for your help, Captain,' said Abel, shaking his hand, as he mounted his stallion.

'My pleasure, Abel,' replied Ruiz. 'I was glad of the chance to sort out this den of cut-throats. And in any case my men needed a ride out. God speed you on your journey north.'

'Heavens, what an experience, Pedro!' was Raquel's comment as they trotted out of the village. 'I had a premonition in a dream some weeks ago that something nasty was going to happen to us on our journey.'

'You never said!' replied Pedro.

'I didn't want to worry you, dear. Anyway, it wouldn't have made any difference, would it? We'd still have come.'

They had gone about a mile out of the village, descending a long slope. A cluster of pine trees lay a hundred yards to the left on a clayey knoll.

'What's that among the trees, Pedro?' queried Abel. 'I can't make it out, can you? Let's go and see.'

They reached the trees together. Two long timbers had been placed between branches, ten feet or more above the ground. Twisting in the breeze were the bodies of the dozen or so Jews who had sought their protection the previous day – men, women and children. With ligatures tightened around their necks, their heads lay at acute angles. Their blackened faces were a hideous sight, having already been etched by the crows. The trousers of the men hung around their ankles, soaked in blood. The symbol of their faith, their circumcision, had been sliced away.

IV: *Tordesillas*

May–June 1494

The rest of their journey to Tordesillas was largely uneventful, but neverthe-less it was a great adventure for Pedro and Raquel. The roads of Spain were atrocious, having deteriorated progressively after the departure of the Romans in the fifth century. They were stony, rutted and dusty in summer and lakes of glutinous mud in winter. For horse and coach alike they made travelling slow, uncomfortable and hazardous. The sheep fared much better. The three seventy-yard wide, age-old drove roads which ran for hundreds of miles from Extremadura on the Portuguese border eastwards into the heartland of Castile provided far more commodious routes. Unfortunately for those sheep des-tined for market, it was in one direction only.

Pedro, Raquel and Abel joined the old Roman route which led from Córdoba to Toledo. Within days, they descended into the winding Pass of Despeñaperros, a gorge cut deep into the granite mountains of Sierra de Morena. Narrow, with precipitous walls on each side, it was a perfect place for ambush. Yet in the year 1212 the Muslims, being forced ever southwards by the Christians in their centuries-long quest to drive the Arab invaders from Iberia, had failed to take the strategic advantage of the gorge, and on the rolling plain which opened up to the south, they suffered a massive defeat. There, at the famous battle of Navas de Tolosa, they lost 30,000 men to Alfonso VII's army. It was a rout of immense proportions and heralded the end of the Muslim occupation of the peninsula.

This occupation had started in 711 with the invasion led by Tariq ibn Ziryab, when 7,000 Yemenis, Syrians and mainly Berbers crossed the Straits at Gibraltar.[1] In just over ten years, the Arabs had occupied nearly the whole of the Iberian peninsula. But a little remained outside their grasp in Asturias in northern Spain, and it was in this mountainous region that the flame of Christianity was kept alive. Visigoth Christians, who were unwilling to live under Muslim rule, moved northwards to Asturias to swell the small band of resistance fighters there. In 722, they won a crucial battle at Covadonga in the Picos de Europa, which checked the Muslim advance northwards. It was a

---

[1] The name 'Gibraltar' is derived from *jabal-tariq*, 'Tariq's rock'.

crucial turning point in Spanish history.[2] Given impetus by the miraculous yet timely discovery in 813 of the bones of St James in a field[3], the Christians started to drive the Muslims southwards across Castile. This thrust, lasting some 700 years, is known in Spain as the Reconquest.

In 1085, Alfonso VI took the ancient stronghold of Toledo for the Christians, who were in the fervent grip of the crusades to the Holy Lands. They continued their drive southwards, consolidating their hold on the country and building lines of castles from east to west along the shifting frontier, often little more than a day's ride apart. Never put to the test, these magnificent structures became, in truth, follies for the aggrandisement of the nobility. By the beginning of the thirteenth century, the Reconquest had carried the Christians to the very gateway of Muslim al-Andalus at the Pass of Despeñaperros. Driving south after the battle of Navas de Tolosa, they took the capital of the ruling Almohads dynasty at Córdoba. Nine years later they captured Jaén, and three years later Seville in 1248. From that time on, until the fall of Granada in 1492, the Nazarí, the last of the Muslim family dynasties, were confined to the mountainous region of Granada, Málaga and Almería, known collectively as al-Andalus.

Pedro, Raquel and Abel were glad to reach Toledo and give themselves and their horses a few days' rest and to enjoy the hospitality and splendours of one of Spain's greatest cities. Their journey there across La Mancha had been an incredible experience. La Mancha was the very heartland of Spain, with endless plains, unremitting winds which swept the land clean, and gigantic skies across which sailed towering white clouds. The plains were now largely deserted, as the Roman and Moorish plough had given way to sheep pasture. Yet while La Mancha seemed boundless, faint purplish lines of hills were always visible on far horizons, maybe thirty or more miles away. In the incessant heat of summer, clouds would tower heavenward, point a dark finger windward, and illuminate with lightning flashes distant storms with pinkish light. Yet La Mancha was not all featureless plain. Fingering out eastwards from Portugal and eventually petering out across the country were several mountain chains made of granite. One of these the three travellers had already traversed at the Pass of Despeñaperros. Another – higher, wider and wilder – was the Sierra de Guadarrama, over which they would need to ride to reach Tordesillas. La Mancha's true *meseta* comprised a dissected plateau of layered pink and white sands. which rose sharply 200 feet from the plain and on which was located the

---

[2] In recognition of the important role Asturias played in the Reconquest, the monarch's firstborn is accorded the title of Prince or Princess of Asturias.

[3] Which became the site of the cathedral of Santiago de Compostella, and the focus of pilgrimages.

modest town of Madrid, later to become Philip II's capital. The river Tajo[4] skirted the southern scarp face of the plateau to curl around Toledo on its way to the sea at Lisbon. Tributaries of the Tajo meandered sluggishly across the plain, forming marshy wetlands and shallow lakes, with rushes and feathery tamarisk trees masking the water's edge and offering shelter to wading birds and wildlife. Drinking water was not that difficult to come by. Although at an elevation of well over 2,000 feet, dug wells could find water at little more than thirty feet of depth, and the numerous *pozos* and *norias* gave testament to this ease of water abstraction, if not its abundance.

Enshrined in the Treaty of Alcáçovas of 1479, Portugal jealously guarded its trading and fishing rights around the coast of Morocco and down the bulge of Africa. Nevertheless, the Spanish fishermen at Palos and Moguer along the estuary of the Rio Tinto, fifty miles west of Seville, remained aggrieved and did not feel constrained by the treaty. With warlike noises coming from Portugal over the incursions into their preserve by the fishing boats from these towns, King Fernando imposed a sanction on Palos and Moguer by requiring them to provide ships and three months' supplies for Columbus's first voyage of discovery, thereby reducing his obligation to part-fund the voyage. It was a typical ploy of the wily king.

At this time, Castile and Portugal were like squabbling sisters, bonded by centuries-old ancestries yet separated by jealousies. Portugal had won its independence from Spain in 1297 in the Treaty of Alcañices which, despite later takeovers by Spain, fixed the borders between the two realms for perpetuity. War could have broken out again at any time between them over petty issues. Yet, in fact, a royal marriage might have merged the kingdoms into one for ever. But it was never to be. It is against this background of bitchiness and rivalry that the prospective meeting of the two kingdoms at Tordesillas must be viewed.

Christopher Columbus had spent two years in Portugal in the middle 1480s, seeking support from King John II for his planned voyage across the Atlantic to find a new route to the Spice Islands. Frustrated, Columbus's brother, Bartolomé, went to England and France to lobby support, but to no avail. Finally, Christopher Columbus received the blessing of the Spanish monarchs, but they insisted that the war with Granada had first to be won. Columbus waited with growing impatience, as the chance of fulfilling his epic journey seemed to be slipping away, but the monarchs were true to their word and, after haggling over the financing of the voyage and over Columbus's entitlements, the navigator set sail in August 1492 on his historic voyage.

---

[4] Tagus in Portugal

The Admiral returned from the Indies in March 1493, when the *Niña* made its landfall at Lisbon. King John was thus able to learn at first hand of the explorer's discoveries. John realised that he had made a serious error of judgement in not supporting Columbus's voyage. Not only had a new and probably easier route to the Spice Islands of Asia gone begging, but his trade routes down the Atlantic coast were threatened. He sought the Pope's inter-vention. Within a month, Pope Rodrigo Borgia, Alexander VI, received a copy of Columbus's eight-page letter to his faithful supporter in Palos, Luis de Santangel, printed in Barcelona in Castilian in April of that year. This historic letter described the voyage and the discoveries made, and it became a mo-mentous document. A Latin translation, *Epistola de insulis repertis de nouo*, was printed in Rome soon afterwards. In response to Portugal's bidding, Alexander VI issued the bull *Inter Caeteras*, proposing a line dividing Portuguese and Spanish interests in the Atlantic. This dividing line ran north to south from pole to pole, and lay one hundred leagues to the west of the Azores and the Islas de Cabo Verde, which were both Portuguese domains. This papal bull proposed that Spain would control interests to the west of the line and Portugal interests to the east. But King John rejected this proposal – his sea captains wanting more sea room in the Atlantic when sailing south and demanding that the line to be drawn further to the west.[5] With war again threatening between Spain and Portugal, the two sides agreed to meet to resolve the conflict of interests, and it was this which drew the Catholic Monarchs to Tordesillas and led them to request Pedro's attendance there.

The three travellers, refreshed from their stay in Toledo, took the road northwards to Ávila. Although much used by monarch and peasant alike, the route was wearisome, winding through mountainous country, all the time ascending. It was the heartland of Castile; what later became known as *Castilla la Vieja*.[6] Castles, big and small, square and round, towers and lookouts, stretched into the distance on each side of the road. Riders carrying the royal mail waved to them as they raced past to every corner of Spain. They overtook carriages bearing powdered ladies adorned in their finery and with their accompanying outriders. Even with four horses, these lumbering coaches struggled up the slopes and had to be constrained going down. Other carriages, richly painted, heavy and slow, transported the great and the good on their way

---

[5] Recent computer simulations of ocean currents have shown that the Portuguese sailors, in their voyages down and later around the west coast of Africa, are likely to have taken advantage of currents circulating southwards and sweeping close to the South American coast.

[6] In the Spanish constitution of 1983, Old Castile (*Castilla la Vieja*) became the self-governing region of Castilla y Leon, and New Castile (*Castilla Nueva* – the region of La Mancha) became Castilla y La Mancha.

to bless, baptise or burn their suffering congregation. Pedro recognised the crooked tree insignia of the Spanish Inquisition on one such carriage, and wondered if the curtained windows concealed the much feared Inquisitor General of Castile himself, Tomás de Torquemada.

'Where's that ahead of us?' shouted Raquel, as the three riders reached the top of another rise. She could not believe how far they were from home. Until her and Pedro's move to Morocco, she had never gone more than forty miles from the Alpujarran village where she grew up.

'That's Ávila,' replied Abel, slowing down to ride beside her.

'But it's incredible!' cried Raquel, standing up in her stirrups to get a better view. In the distance, six or seven miles away, a walled city straddling the brow of a hill had come into view.

'Yes, it's an amazing place,' replied Abel. 'The walls are all of two miles around and it's got eighty-eight round towers and ten gates.'

'Incredible!' repeated an overwhelmed Raquel. 'Can you see it, Pedro?'

'Yes, what a sight! I've walked the city walls of Almería, Granada and even Fez, but that's a spectacular sight.'

'When was it built?' asked Raquel, now bubbling with curiosity.

'The castle? Oh, a long time ago, over 200 years ago,' he added.

'Has the city ever been besieged?' asked Pedro.

'Not that I know of. Like all the castles and city walls we've passed, which the Christians built to secure their newly won lands as the Moors were being driven further and further south, they've proved quite superfluous.'

The city drew closer as they climbed the near 4,000-foot plateau on which Ávila sat. It was the highest city in Castile. A biting wind blew across the plateau, and they were glad to reach the shelter of the south gate. The gothic cathedral lay alongside, housing dozens of tombs of the kings and queens of Castile and Leon, and even some much older seventh-century ones, containing the very first kings of Asturias.

It being a market day, the city was crowded and the three, having found an inn for the night and stables for their horses, wandered around relaxed and happy, stopping at stalls to sample the fresh bread, cured meats and sweet buns. Like all markets days, it was a day out for the womenfolk, and consequently was noisy, bustling but good-humoured.

They stayed a couple of nights in Ávila before setting off on the last phase of their journey to Tordesillas and Valladolid. Medina del Campo lay in their path fifty miles away and was the nearest of these three royal cities, which lay within only half a day's ride from one another. They reached Medina that evening. Medina del Campo was an old town, but what made it particularly distinctive was the imposing castle of La Mota, a favourite residence of the Catholic Monarchs, completed just sixty years before. Set within a broad, circular earth motte, the castle was faced with brick and possessed a deep, dry moat between the square skirting wall and the castle itself. What few windows it possessed lay high up in the walls. With its immense square tower, it was impregnable. Not knowing what to expect, the three riders tinkled the bell at the gatehouse and after a wait were allowed over the causeway into the inner sanctum of the castle. Two young girls were playing with skipping ropes in the courtyard, but were much more interested in the horses being led into the enclosure than in the three visitors. Steps led up to the main entrance where, in due course, a stately man came and greeted them.

'I'm Hernando de Zafra, the monarchs' private secretary. Welcome to La Mota. You must be Don Pedro Togeiro... and this must be Doña Raquel?'

'Yes sir,' replied Pedro. 'And this is Abel Jiménez, a former soldier who's accompanied us here. We hope we're not intruding by coming to La Mota?'

'Not at all, young man. I'm pleased to make your acquaintance and, of course, that of your beautiful young wife. I'm delighted that she was able to come with you. I recall you now from the day the King and Queen entered Granada two and a half years ago, don't I? If my memory's correct, you were a member of the Queen's personal guard, dressed in a fine uniform!'

'Yes,' Pedro replied, laughing. 'Are Their Majesties here, Don Hernando?'

'No, they and their court left for Tordesillas two weeks ago. They'll both be there now. They'll be expecting you.'

'Where will we find them?'

'They're staying in the palace overlooking the river, but you're best to go straight to the Convent of Santa Clara alongside it. That's where the Spanish delegates are meeting with the representative of King John.'

'Is he there?'

'No, he decided in the end that it would be prudent to avoid a direct meeting with Their Majesties, and I think he was probably right. Matters are too delicate between our countries to risk them crossing swords – I'm speaking figuratively, of course!' chuckled Hernando.

'Their Majesties arrived here at La Mota last month to meet the Portuguese delegates. There are three of them. You'll meet them. One is Ruy de Sousa, a confident of King John, an expert mariner who has been ambassador to the English court; his son, Pedro, the Portuguese customs and excise chief, again an experienced mariner; and Aires de Almeda, who has also served at the English court. They seem a formidable trio to me. I understand also that four other experts are travelling directly to Tordesillas. Look, Pedro, I'm riding to Tordesillas myself tomorrow with important documents for Their Majesties, and if you wish we can travel together. We'll have a posse of riders accompanying us, so Abel will be in good company.'

'Who are the young children playing outside, Don Hernando?' asked Raquel.

'They're the Princesses María and Catalina. Maria is twelve years old and Catalina, the baby of the family, is just nine. Juan and Juana are both at Tordesillas with their parents. You'll meet them, too.'

'Can I go and say hello to the princesses?' pleaded Raquel. 'I'd love to meet them. We don't see too many princesses in our part of the world!'

'Of course. They'd love to have someone to play with. But before you go outside, I'm arranging for some rooms to be made ready for you and, if you're agreeable, we'll dine at eight. But Pedro, why don't you and Abel take some refreshments in the refectory? I've some state papers to finish off, otherwise I'd join you. Oh, and by the way,' he added, 'the town has its annual fair here this week, and it's recognised as being one of the very best in all Castile. So if you want some real fun after dinner you can go into the town. It's just a short walk from here.'

'Can we take María and Catalina with us, Don Hernando?' pleaded Raquel.

'Why not? But they'll need to have Doña María of Aragón with them as their chaperone. She's a lady-in-waiting to the Queen. Her Majesty would insist on that.'

The fair was indeed memorable. People flocked to it to sample the luxuries of medieval life normally beyond their reach: woollens and silks, perfumes and cosmetics, spices and honey. Raquel took the opportunity of trying on and buying some new silk dresses at a fraction of the price of those in Toledo and Ávila, as well as some small ones for two-year-old Sara back home. Pedro secretly bought a gold pendant with a big pearl for Raquel to celebrate her pregnancy, if this were later confirmed, as well as some unusual wool dyes for his mother's tapestries which she could not obtain locally.

Leaving the two youngest royal princesses at La Mota in the capable hands of Doña María de Aragón, the party set off for Tordesillas the next morning, arriving there three hours later. The walled city was built on a steep bluff bordering the fast-flowing Duero River, and was reached over a Roman bridge. A road slanted up the bluff and led into the small central square comprising shops, inns and hostelries situated beneath colonnaded balconies.

'If you've nowhere to stay as yet, Pedro,' said Hernando de Zafra as they crossed the bridge, 'I can recommend the Bodega de Muelas fifty yards up the road from the plaza mayor. It has comfortable rooms upstairs, and although it doesn't serve food, there are plenty of places in the square where you can eat. Tell Señora Angela Villanove that I sent you. The representatives from Portugal and Spain only meet in the mornings to allow them to confer among themselves in the afternoons. I suggest you come to the palace this evening. I'll try and arrange an audience for you with Fernando and Isabel. Both have state papers to sign, but since these are in my care I'm sure I can arrange a break in their duties. As you know they are a very dutiful and conscientious couple.'

In the early evening, the bodega owner Doña Ana of Beamonte arrived. A sprightly and aristocratic woman in her mid-forties, she greeted Pedro and Raquel rather formally, but her stern countenance started to melt as they walked to the palace. She led them down through the city square and quickly reached the parade overlooking the Duero River. Flowing clear and wide, it was bordered on both sides by tall poplars. The royal palace, as much a castle as palace, lay immediately to their left. It had been a residence of the Kings of Castile for generations. Beyond the royal palace, at the end of the riverside parade was the convent of Santa Clara. Started as an Arab palace in 1340, it was built around a courtyard, whose arcade of keyhole-shaped arches and their rich plaster ornamentation was the work of Alhambra craftsmen, fashioned soon after the latter's completion.

Pedro and Raquel were led into the royal palace and to a small, poorly lit room where Hernando de Zafra was in conference with Fernando and Isabel. The palace had been an enduring residence of Castilian monarchs for centuries and was starting to show its age.[7]

'Ah!' said the King, rising from his high-backed chair, 'the young man who saved us from the encampment fire at Gozco, and who is doing such sterling work for us in Fez! Welcome to Tordesillas.' He turned to Pedro's wife. 'And you must be…'

'Raquel, Your Majesty; this is my wife, Raquel.'

'Yes, of course. I'm delighted to meet you, young woman.'

'I trust you both had an uneventful journey here?' asked the Queen.

'Yes, thank you, ma'am.' Pedro saw little point in mentioning the events at Jódar.

'And how is Juan Chacón?' asked the Queen. 'His father, Gonzalo, was a close confidant of mine in my younger days.'

'I haven't met Señor Chacón as yet, ma'am. As you know he spends most of his time in Murcia and Cartagena. He only visits Vélez Blanco occasionally. But my stepfather…'

'Agustín López?'

'Yes, ma'am.'

'How is he enjoying his retirement? And how is your mother…?'

'Miriam, ma'am.'

'Oh, yes, Miriam. What a charming women she is! Is she still doing her tapestries, Don Pedro?' she asked.

---

[7] Because of its poor state, it was pulled down in 1771. The site is now occupied by an apartment block.

'Yes, ma'am. She's even got some of the Mudejar women in the town helping her. It's become quite a little industry.'

'As she did in the Alhambra with her tapestry school? Hmm... that's interesting!'

The Queen paused for a moment in thought, but refrained from commenting further.

V: The Treaties

Queen Isabel was a phenomenon, and unquestionably the woman of her time. Forty-three years of age, her early years had been forged on the anvil of a Castile which was on the verge of civil war and which bordered a self-confident and bullish Portugal. Portugal had already liberated itself from the Muslims, and by then had established its own Cortes to govern the country. It was in an aggressive mood.

Isabel was born on April 1451 in Madrigal de las Altas Torres, a town of 700 souls lying fifteen miles south of Medina del Campo. Also there, three years before, her mother, Isabel of Portugal, had married King Juan of Castile. Isabel and her younger brother, Alfonso, had grown up in Arévalo, a walled city close by, lying midway between Ávila and Medina del Campo. A triangle – with sides of only fifty miles, with Valladolid in the north, Ávila in the south and Salamanca in the west – an easy day's ride to the Portuguese border, was the vibrant heart and power base of Castile, and embraced all the forementioned towns and cities.

Isabel was very devout and was later accorded the title 'Isabel la Católica' by the Pope. She was of medium height, comely rather than pretty, plump rather than slim, and she had blue-green eyes and auburn hair. Her mouth was rather pouting and her chin weak; but not so her character. The premature death of Alfonso in 1468 at the age of fourteen brought Isabel forward as heir to the throne – or so it seemed. But Enrique, her stepbrother by King Juan's first wife, María of Aragón, had assumed the crown and sought to make Juana 'La Beltraneja' heir to Castile. But Enrique IV was impotent and openly homosexual. He was the laughing stock of his court, where the gossip was that La Beltraneja was not his daughter but the issue of María of Aragón and Pedro de Castile, a tall and handsome courtier. So in order to secure his wife's illegitimate daughter as heir to the throne of Castile, Enrique tried to marry off Isabel to his brother, King Alonso V of Portugal, a widower in his forties. Other royal suitors came forward for the hand of the twenty-year-old princess; from France, England and Aragón.

The three from overseas had no appeal to the strongly willed Isabel, and after written overtures to Fernando of Aragón, the couple met and were married in October 1469 in Valladolid by Archbishop Carillo of Toledo. Isabel was then eighteen and Fernando, who was her second cousin, was sixteen.

While Isabel was sometimes described as fair and fair-skinned, Fernando had dark hair and a ruddy complexion. Heir to the throne of Aragón, and holding the title King of Sicily, Fernando was said to be experienced in the art of war as well as in love, since he had already sired two children. After an aborted child, his and Isabel's firstborn, another Isabel, soon followed. Of similar age, which was somewhat unusual in royal circles at this time, the couple were physically attracted to one another; but more significantly they foresaw the political wisdom of a union between their two kingdoms. Nevertheless, storm clouds were gathering. On Enrique's death in 1474, his brother, Alfonso V of Portugal, continued to promote his niece, Juana La Beltraneja, as rightful Queen of Castile, having in mind to marry her himself and thereby add the crowns of Castile and Leon to that of Portugal. He raised an army of 15,000 foot soldiers and 5,000 cavalry and entered Spain through Extremadura. The turncoat Archbishop Carillo joined his cause, as city after city declared for Alfonso and the illegitimate Juana. The French king, Louis XI, always looking to cause mischief, threatened to invade Navarra in northern Spain on the side of Alfonso.

The situation started to look precarious for Isabel. But four crucial grandees declared for her, plus the new Cardinal of Spain, Pedro González de Mendoza. Others started to follow suit. With their help, Isabel gathered together a scratch force of 25,000 peons, and on 2 March 1475, in the pouring rain on the banks of the Duero River, her young husband, the twenty-three-year-old soldier-king Fernando, led and won a crucial battle in the civil war at Toro, near Zamora, forty miles from the Portuguese border. Tordesillas, as ever close to the centre of action, lay only twenty miles up the road, and there Isabel stayed anxiously awaiting news of the action which would determine her kingdom. But Castile was secured for her, and Isabel and Fernando were acclaimed in all cities from Burgos to Córdoba as the dual monarchs of their united kingdoms.

However, Isabel and Fernando's problems did not cease after overcoming this Portuguese threat. Far from it. Both inherited jealous and feuding nobles, who were self-serving and semi-independent lords of their domains. So they set about bringing order to their kingdoms; placing their own appointees in charge of provinces; selecting compliant bishops and competent and loyal captain-generals to the regions; putting the kingdoms' finances on a proper footing; raising taxes and levies. It was a monumental task, and they did not spare themselves one jot. While Valladolid was the administrative centre of Castile, and Zaragoza that for Aragón, the royal couple were rarely there, choosing to move together continually around their kingdoms from one city to another, staying a few weeks or months in each. For instance, the year before, in 1493, having received Columbus in Barcelona, they spent a week in Córdoba, fifteen days in Extremadura, two weeks in Valladolid and three weeks in Zaragoza. In each city they held court, heard petitions, approved budgets, resolved difficulties and put down local insurrections and discord. It was a punishing routine which eventually took its toll on Isabel.

Nothing better illustrated her devotion to duty than her weekly routine. On every Thursday and Saturday, one hour was dedicated to signing briefs and documents; letters and petitions were handled promptly every evening. Monday afternoons were allocated to her secretaries; Tuesdays to cabinet meetings; Wednesdays to the royal auditor; Thursdays to memorials and Fridays to fiscal matters. Aside from signing documents for an hour, Saturdays were left free.

Devout in their faith and dedicated to each other and their royal duty, they laid the foundations for Spain's bid for greatness. Indeed, their joint thirty-year reign would provide the primary impetus in Spain's pursuit of destiny.

'Well now, Don Pedro,' concluded the King, after the pleasantries had been observed. 'You've come here to be party to our negotiations with Portugal over the division of the lands in and beyond the Ocean Sea, as well as down the coast of Africa. As my ambassador in Fez, this will be of more interest to you. The negotiations are nearing conclusion. So tomorrow morning at eleven come to the royal monastery of Santa Clara, next door, where you will meet my three representatives. The deliberations are taking place in the great hall, which has a big table where maps can be spread out. You are there to listen to the proceedings, and I would counsel you against speaking – that is, unless you are consulted. After all, you'll be the only one there who has actually been to the Indies! Sadly, I can't be there myself, since I've work to do here, but I do try and drop by and listen when I can.'

'May I ask, sire, how the Admiral is progressing on his second voyage to the Indies?'

'Yes indeed. Antonio de Torres returned to Cádiz in March with twelve ships and reported to me soon afterwards. Things don't appear to be going too well in La Española, although what Antonio tells me is in conflict with the buoyant letter he brought me from the Admiral. They appear to have found little gold, and they are desperately short of supplies. There's also discord among the colonists. So I've despatched Bartolomé Columbus with five caravels loaded with provisions, and he set sail two weeks ago. He'll visit Gomera on the way there to collect more supplies. I like Bartolomé. He seems a sound man.

'Tell me, Doña Raquel,' asked the King. 'What will you do while Pedro is in Santa Clara? You won't be very much interested in the proceedings there.'

'Why doesn't she join my ladies in the court?' interjected the Queen. 'Would you like that, Doña Raquel?' she asked.

'Oh yes, ma'am, I would,' she replied, her eyes lighting up.

'Good, I'll ask Ana to meet you and bring you here tomorrow. You seem a lovely young woman, Raquel, and Pedro is a lucky fellow to have you as his wife. Your youth and radiance will not go amiss in the palace here, will it, Fernando?'

'No, it certainly won't.' The point had not been lost on Fernando. He had an eye for the ladies and had had several mistresses.

'But now you must leave us,' the King concluded. 'We still have matters to resolve with Hernando.'

'Candidates for your little book?' asked the King after they had departed. The Queen's close confidantes believed that she kept a book in a locked casket in which she noted the names of people who had served her well and deserved advancement or might be of future use to her.

'Who? Pedro and Raquel?'

'Yes, but I was thinking more of Pedro's mother, Miriam…'

'Hmm!' replied Isabel thoughtfully. 'Maybe. Thank you for mentioning it.'

While the Portuguese delegates, and particularly their team of experts, were experienced in state matters and knowledgeable in maritime affairs, those from Spain were decidedly not. One was Enrique Enríquez, an uncle of the King who, despite his title of Admiral of Castile, had scarcely been to sea and was there because his daughter, María, was the fiancée one of Pope Alexander Borgia's sons. Another was Gutierre de Cárdenas, the royal chief accountant, who had made his fortune by importing lichen from the Canaries; a voyage there from Cádiz was the full extent of his maritime experience. The third was Rodrigo Maldonaldo de Talavera, a lawyer and member of the King's council. Three supposed experts on geography, all knight-commanders, were also present, but none had any knowledge of the Indies. Inexplicably, Antonio de Torres was not included in the negotiating team, although he had just returned from La Española. And he was present for much of the proceedings.

Doña Ana of Beamonte accompanied Raquel to the palace that morning, her rather frosty and haughty air of the previous evening dissolving before Raquel's sparkling dark eyes and laughing smile.

'You look the picture of good health, Raquel. Morocco must suit you,' remarked Ana as they walked through the city square. A market was in full swing and the place was alive with traders and townsfolk, bartering noisily and looking for bargains.

'I am,' replied Raquel, 'but I'm starting to feel queasy in the mornings. I think I might be pregnant, but I'm still not sure of this yet, and I don't want to worry Pedro.'

'You're not sure you're pregnant?' checked Ana. 'In that case, you must see Salomón Byton, the Queen's physician. He's the best in the land and has seen her Majesty safely through all her pregnancies. He's at court now and I'll speak to him. You couldn't be in a better place!'

Pedro arrived nervously at Santa Clara mid-morning, not knowing what to expect and not knowing what was expected of him. He need not have worried. He was conducted into the inner sanctum of the former royal palace to the long, panelled room where the negotiations were being held. Six men, immaculately but soberly dressed, faced each other across the long table, three on each side. Several others sat behind them along the walls. They were very mixed, some grey, weather-beaten and grizzled, others young and fresh-faced. Pedro took a seat alongside a man in his forties. Evidently, the three in front of him were the Spanish delegates, and those facing him on the far side of the table were from Portugal. He was introduced to the assembly, and he was rather relieved that apart from a few heads turning no one showed any interest. He and the man seated next to him whispered their introductions. Fortunately for Pedro, the man was Antonio de Torres, recently arrived from the Indies. He could have added much to the debate. Later, Pedro and he were able to compare notes on their experiences on their respective voyages.

It was clear that the negotiations were reaching a conclusion, and the atmosphere in the room was electric as each side sought to push their own ideas or dismiss those of their opponents. The negotiations were conducted in mixed Castilian and Portuguese, which were then dialects of the same language. It soon became clear to Pedro that the Portuguese delegates were much surer of themselves, with the three from Spain needing constantly to turn to their experts seated behind them to check details and fortify their arguments. At issue was the large chart on the table in front of them. Bejewelled fingers from each side stabbed at it, moving to the left or right a ruler which lay across it. Pedro was able to catch sight of the map during a mid-morning break, when the assembly dispersed to the riverside balcony. A fresh breeze from the river and a glass of chilled white wine helped cool tempers as the delegates from each side mingled and chatted among one another. It was Pedro's first experience of such high-powered diplomacy, and he relaxed appreciably when he saw how delegates could be at each others' throats one minute and socialise amicably the next. Antonio de Torres took Pedro's elbow and led him to a quiet corner.

'What's the map on the table, Señor Torres?'

'Antonio will do, Pedro. We're both in this together, aren't we?' he chuckled. 'I'm surprised you don't recognise the map!' He grinned. A wicked smile broke across his face.

'Why, Antonio?' Pedro was not sure if he was being made fun of.

'Why? Because it's Columbus's map which he drew in La Española last year, during his first voyage. Didn't you see him making this map?'

'No,' replied Pedro. 'He kept all his charts very much to himself. Only once did he show them to Martín Pinzón when they were arguing about which route to take, some weeks before we actually discovered land. What does the Admiral's map show?' Pedro asked.

'It's a map of the Ocean Sea, with Europe and Africa on the right side and Asia on the left, which Columbus claims to be Japan and China. The only thing discernible to me on the map is Cuba sticking out like a thumb from a rather imprecise mainland, plus an island next to it which, I assume, is La Española.'

'So why is the ruler placed down the middle of the map?'

'Ah! That's what all the debate's about, Pedro!' Antonio laughed again. He obviously found the whole proceeding highly amusing.

'Last year, Pope Alexander in Rome proposed a north-to-south line to divide Portuguese and Spanish interests. His proposed line lies one hundred leagues to the west of the Azores and the Islas de Cabo Verde which lie due south of them. The Portuguese rejected this. These deliberations here in Santa Clara have been about fixing a new line which will satisfy both sides. A lot rests on this, and both countries are aware of it. Spain wants unhindered trade westwards to China and Japan, and Portugal wants to have a monopoly of its trade south and eastwards to the Spice Islands.'

'Surely the Pope's dividing line would do that?'

'It should do, but Portugal is reluctant to concede all the exploration to the west to Spain.'

'There were stories about "lands across the sea" before the Admiral's first voyage,' commented Pedro. 'Do you think Portugal knew something of these?'

'I'm beginning to think they might well have done. That's why they've been pushing to fix the line much further towards the Indies.'

'So are the two sides reaching agreement yet, Antonio?'

'I think so. Over the last two weeks, the Portuguese have pushed the line westwards to a point virtually midway between Cabo Verde and La Española. That's, of course, as they're shown on Columbus's chart.'

'But how accurate is his chart, Antonio?'

'You tell me – you were there!'

'Well, all I know is that while I was on the *Pinta* I helped the pilot, Cristóbal Sarmiento, to measure how far we sailed each day. But for all the care he took, it was pretty crude. I'd throw a piece of wood into the sea at the bows, and Cristóbal would count the number of chants he made until the piece of wood passed the stern. Then he worked out our speed.'

'And how did he time his chants?'

'He said that he checked them repeatedly against his wife's kitchen sand timer, and then timed that against the half-hour-long hourglasses on board. From these, he prepared a table of figures which then gave him the ship's speed. We did three such float runs each time, and often several times a day if the wind was changeable. The pilots on the *Santa María* and *Niña* did the same. With this information and his compass bearings, the Admiral marked the ship's position on his chart each day, but nobody was allowed to see this.'

'So what was Columbus's conclusion? How far are the Indies from Spain?'

'Well, he told me when we were on the way to see King John in Lisbon after our return that our landfall on San Salvador[1] was 960 leagues west of the Canaries[2], although I imagine it would have been shorter if the route had been direct and had not looped south. He also said that using his night sightings of the Pole Star he put Cuba at a latitude of 21° north of the equator.[3] Those are the only figures I can recall him mentioning.'

'That figures, then, since the two sides seem to have settled on a distance of 370 leagues between the Islas de Cabo Verde and La Española in the Indies. I think I'm right in saying that Cabo Verde lies about 150 leagues west of the Canaries, although a bit further south. So what's proposed is virtually midway between the Canaries and La Española.

'Midway? That seems a reasonable compromise.'

'Yes, it does, Pedro. But time will tell. Time will tell,' Antonio replied.

Pedro stood there looking over the river, a frown forming on his face.

'What's troubling you, Pedro?'

'Something's not right, Antonio. What the two sides are agreeing is a fixed line dividing their interests in the Ocean Sea, yes?'

'That's right. Roughly midway between the Canaries and the Indies.'

'But it's all based on the Admiral's calculation of how far the Indies are from the Canaries.'

'Of course.'

'But that could be in serious error. If it turns out when more measurements are taken that the Indies are nearer to the Canaries than Columbus's figure, then Portugal will have gained more territory than Spain. While if the distance turns out to be much larger, Spain will have gained more territory.'

'Well, I suppose...'

---

[1] It's now considered that Columbus's first landfall was at Samana Cay in the Bahamas, and not San Salvador (Watling Island).

[2] At 3.3 nautical miles to a league, this placed San Salvador 3,200 nautical miles from the Canaries, compared with 3,100 actually along the same assumed route. So Columbus's dead reckoning was remarkably correct.

[3] Bearing in mind that the Pole Star then lay 3.5° from the celestial pole (now less than 1°), his observations were very accurate. The correct latitude for Cuba is 21°18'.

Pedro was now in full swing.

'Look, Antonio, we've just been discussing the crudeness of the way we determine the speed of a ship through the water. That is, how quickly the float passes along the boat from bow to stern.'

'Yes. Go on.'

'Well, if a ship is being carried along on a current then its total speed is greater than if it were simply being blown along by the wind.'

'That follows.'

'But if a ship is carried along on a current, the current is impeding the float from passing down the side of the boat. Then the float takes longer in its journey, and consequently the boat would appear to be sailing more slowly than it actually is. Therefore, with a following current a ship would travel a greater distance than as measured by the floats. So the actual distance from the Canaries to the Indies would be consequently greater.'

'And the reverse if the boat is heading into a current?'

'Yes, then the Indies would appear to be closer than they really are.'

'Hmm! It seems to me, Pedro, that you should be involved in the negotiations! But I suggest you keep your views to yourself. It would raise a hornet's nest if you propound your theories now. Come,' he said, guiding Pedro to the door, 'the meeting's reconvening. We'd better go back inside.'

TRATADOS DE TORDESILLAS

Don Fernando e doña Isabel por la çraçia de Dios rrey e rreyna de Castile, de León, de Araçon, de Sequília, de Granada, de Toledo, de Valençia, de Çalilza, de Mallorcas, de Seuilla, de Cerdeña, de Córdoba, de Córceça, de Murçia, de Jahén, del Alçarbe, de Alçezira, de Çibraltar, de las yslas de Canaria, conde e condesa de Barçelona e señores de Vizcaya e de Molina, duques de Atenas e de Neopatria condes de Rosellon e de Cerdania marqueses de Oristán e de Çoçeano, en vno con el prínçipe don Juan, nuestro muy caro e muy amado hijo primoçénito heredero de los dichos nuestros rreyes e señoríos. Por çuanto por don Enrrique Enrriques, nuestro mayordomo mayor, e don Çutierre de Cárdenas, comendador mayor de León, nuestro contador mayor, e el doctor Rodríço Maldonadó, todos de nuestro Consejo, fue tratado, asen tado e capitulado por Nos y en nuestro nonbre e por virtud de nuestro poder, con el se renísimo don Juan, por la çrasia de Dios, rrey de Portuçal...

...and so it continued, folio after folio.

The lawyers had had a field day drafting this preamble to the two treaties. The first treaty related to the disputed fishing grounds off the Moroccan and African coasts, and the second to the division of seas, lands and islands in and around the Ocean Sea. The wordy preamble defined the parties to the treaties, with all their many titles and possessions, and credited those who negotiated the treaty. It tied the agreement for posterity through later heirs to the thrones, and it defined the geographical points to which the treaty limits applied. This laborious, repetitive, multi-folio document was the vehicle to which the two treaties were appended, specifying the agreed geographical limits, and to which royal seals would be affixed.

Pedro sat through three more days of negotiations, which eventually concluded after both sides had repeated their demands ad nauseam. Eventually, irritable and exhausted, the six delegates agreed upon the two treaties, the geographical demarcations of which, in truth, had barely shifted in weeks. But both sides were satisfied with the outcome; the Portuguese more than the Spanish, who later professed to having been short-changed in the negotiations. With the tension removed, there was much hilarity and backslapping.

The following day, 7 June 1494, the royal couple, their two children, Juan and Juana, the delegates, their experts, and members of the court, assembled in a house a short way along the river terrace to sign the treaty.[4] Pedro joined Antonio de Torres to witness the historic event. A long table had been erected on a stage at the end of the central hall. Dressed soberly in black doublet and hose, gorgeously adorned with gold tracery, the delegates initialled the two treaties. These were signed and ratified by the Catholic Monarchs in Arévalo on 2 July and by King John of Portugal on 4 September. With much ceremony, the royal court dispersed two days later when the monarchs left for La Mota in Medina de Campo.

So what did the treaties specify? The first treaty divided the sea as much as the land, placing a line 370 leagues to the west of the Islas de Cabo Verde. This line ran north–south from pole to pole, granting Spain the lands, islands and oceans to the west of the line and those on the east side to Portugal.[5] With only minor violations, the treaty was upheld by both countries throughout the centuries. It has remained a rare example of a treaty agreed mutually between two parties in peacetime and not imposed unilaterally on the vanquished after conflict.

The second treaty signed that same day resolved the disputes relating to the African coast. Essentially, it ratified the Treaty of Alcáçovas of 1479, which regulated the fishing and trading rights, assigning to Spain the African Atlantic

---

[4] This former building is now called La Casa de los Tratados, and it houses a tourist office and a small museum related to the historic treaty.

[5] At the time of the treaty, no land was known to exist south of La Española, but subsequent exploration discovered South America. The north-eastern part of this new continent lay within Portugal's domain and became Portuguese-speaking Brazil.

seaboard as far south as Cape Borjador. This lay on the African coast just south of the Canaries. But in addition – and significantly – the treaty divided the Muslim Kingdom of Fez between Spain and Portugal for their future conquests, and allocated to Spain Moroccan territories along the Mediterranean coast. This pact was of particular value to Spain, since it cleared the way for the future ascendancy by Spanish Christendom over Islam in northern Africa. Being on the crest of a religious wave, after expelling the Muslims from al-Andalus two years earlier, this was one of the primary objectives of the Catholic Monarchs in the negotiations with Portugal, and it was why Fernando invited Pedro to be present during the deliberations. The Treaties of Tordesillas were endorsed by Pope Alexander VI the following year.

Two days before, Doña Ana of Beamonte, the Queen's matron of honour, who had taken Raquel under her wing, had accompanied Raquel to Salomón Byton, the Queen's physician. He confirmed that Raquel was expecting a second child and that she was already in the second month of her pregnancy. She and Pedro were delighted with the news, and they and Ana celebrated the news that evening in the royal palace with their own special banquet, at which Pedro presented Raquel with the pearl droplet on the gold chain.

With the treaties concluded, it was time to go home; but not before a celebration.

VI: The Banquet

June 1494

With the negotiations concluded and the treaties ready for the royal seals, it was time to celebrate. On 8 June, the day before the court dispersed, a royal banquet was held. While Pedro had attended a royal banquet in the new city of Santa Fe soon after the fall of Granada – and indeed was the guest of honour for saving Their Majesties' lives from the encampment fire at Gozco – that banquet was nothing when compared with the one now to be held in the royal palace of Tordesillas. With 200 guests invited, among them Spanish and Portuguese, princes and princesses, lords and ladies, gentlemen and their ladies, cardinals, archbishops and their retinue, it was to be a truly sumptuous affair. Held at four in the afternoon, much later than the late-morning start which was usual in the other royal houses of Europe, it gave time for the invitees to complete their toilet and dress at their leisure.

In the upstairs room in the Bodega de Muelas, Pedro and Raquel laid out and pressed afresh their costumes for the banquet. Although much had been stolen at Jódar, the market stalls at Medina del Campo had furnished Raquel with replacements for much of what had been pilfered. Thus far at court, she had worn conventional court attire of a square-necked, long satin robe with full sleeves, loosely belted. But she found this unbearably heavy and cumbersome.

'What do you think, Pedro?' she asked. 'Can I wear my own people's dress? It'll be much more comfortable during the banquet.'

'Why not?' replied Pedro. 'You'll be a sensation.'

'But will Muslim dress be acceptable?'

'I don't see why not. After all, you're baptised now. If you wear your gold cross and chain around your neck, I'm sure that there'll be no problem. People will know that you're a convert and will respect you for it.'

And a sensation she proved to be. To go with her tawny skin and dark eyes, she wore a pale green silk, knee-length *gilala* or blouse over baggy silk *sarawil* or trousers of the same colour held up by a *tikki*, or cord, and an open, ankle-length, pink silk *yubba* around her shoulders. Over her hair, she wore a fine white silk *lifafa* or scarf which reached to her waist and which was speckled in gold. With gold earrings and the gold cross and chain around her neck, she was stunning.

In contrast, Pedro was dressed in the fashion of a young nobleman and, accordingly, had had his hair trimmed tidily to the nape of the neck. He wore a white silk shirt with a square neck. The sleeves were full and tapered and gathered at the wrist. Miriam had made the shirt especially for him and embroidered the neck and wrist with black silk thread. 'Well,' she teased Pedro, 'if Queen Isabel can make Fernando's shirts and finish them with black silk, as I'm told she does, then I can do the same for my lord!' Pedro's high-waisted jacket, made in one piece with seams under the arms, was made of blue velvet. In the fashion of the time, the ample sleeves were open at the shoulder and elbows, and the undershirt puffed out into these openings. His jacket was laced down the front. Over his jacket he wore a thigh-length, dark red cloak with a wide collar which reached over the shoulders. Pale blue woollen hose covered his legs and he wore leather slippers which were open at the back. To complete his outfit, he wore a black floppy bonnet topped by a couple of white swan's feathers. And lastly, he wore the Queen's jade ring on his finger. He might not match the elderly nobles there for brocaded splendour, but few if any there were privileged to wear the Queen's ring.

Pedro knew how punctilious the royal couple were about time, and he and Raquel, staying just a few minutes' walk away from the palace, arrived to join the other guests waiting their turn in the antechamber to meet the royals. Each couple was announced loudly by the haughty, black-clad royal chamberlain flourishing a silver-headed ebony wand. Everyone was dressed in his or her finery. Silk, velvet and ornate brocade, interwoven with gold and silver, were much to the fore, often covering very portly figures. While the fashion for both sexes demanded that arms were fully covered, the female fashion was for bare backs and shoulders, high waists, flattened chests and protruding stomachs. Headgear was mandatory for everyone, with upturned rimmed or floppy bonnets for men and high, ornate creations for the ladies. Wearing the costume of a young courtier, Pedro was not out of place in the gathering, but Raquel was a sensation and, to the great consternation of the ladies present, she was a magnet for lordly, if not priestly, eyes.

Eventually the couple reached the monarchs, who were accompanied by Prince Juan, then sixteen, Juana, a year less, and the babies of the family, María, twelve, and Catalina, nine. The eldest child, Isabel, twenty-four, was already a widow after the death of Prince Alfonso of Portugal from a riding accident just a few months into their marriage, six years before. Shortly afterwards she shut herself away in a convent. Raquel had already introduced herself to the two youngest princesses at La Mota a few weeks before, and they quickly recognised her among the invitees and waved.

King Fernando, ruddy-faced and blue-chinned, was notorious for his dull Spanish clothes, but for once was dressed in his finery. Taking his cue from his rival, Henry VII of England, he was wearing a gown of large-patterned gold brocade with deep sleeves. Its collar was ermine, as were the edges of the sleeves. Over this he wore an open, calf-length robe of crimson velvet, with openings for his arms, with an embroidered silk shirt evident at the neck and wrists. A heavy double gold chain hung around his neck. On his head he wore a black velvet bonnet with a castellated upturned rim and a gold dress crown secured on it, although he would remove this later when the banquet got underway.

Queen Isabel, now in the twentieth year of her reign, looked worn and tired. The ten-year war in Granada, recently concluded, had taken its toll on her. Even more than her husband, who interfered incessantly with his generals on the battlefield (and once near Málaga was encircled and had almost been taken prisoner), Isabel had personally directed every aspect of the long campaign through her devoted lieutenant, Don Gonzalo Fernández of Córdoba: ensuring her forces were fed, armed and clothed; finding the money, often by selling her jewellery, to pay her soldiers and to buy cannons and machines of war from Italy. The list of her responsibilities was endless. Now her auburn hair was fading, her eyes were dull and her face was becoming lined and drawn. But for this occasion, with loyal nobles and friends around her, some of the sparkle returned. Normally shunning expensive clothes, she was wearing a low, square-necked, emerald green and gold brocade gown with a floral pattern which trailed behind her on the stone floor. The sleeves were long, turned back and lined with miniver. On her head she wore a black squarish cap, the back of which reached over her shoulders. Like Fernando, she also wore a lightweight dress crown but later removed it. As ever, a jewelled cross hung on a double gold chain around her neck.

It was a festive gathering, and the noise of the chatting and laughter echoed around the bare stone walls. The banquet promised to be a lavish affair. The royal courts of Europe competed with one another on a grand scale to flaunt their status, power and influence. Today would be no exception. In the vaulted chamber that led to the great hall sat two welcoming musicians. One played a large lute, his fingers caressing the five courses of strings to produce music of such beauty and quality that Pedro and Raquel, and all the other guests who passed by, paused to marvel at his dexterity. A second musician sitting alongside played a bass viol, his bow lightly stroking the strings to provide a solemn accompaniment to the lute. Filing slowly forward with the other guests towards the monarchs and wholly entranced by the musical rhapsody, Pedro was startled to find himself in front of the King, who was still in business mode.

'Ah, my young ambassador for Morocco!' greeted Fernando. 'And your young wife. My word, my dear, you look delightful,' he said turning to Raquel.

'So cool on a warm day... I hope that you found the negotiations with the Portuguese instructive, Pedro?'

'Y-y-yes, sire,' stammered a startled Pedro, quickly regaining his wits. 'And thank you for inviting me here. However, I must admit that much of the deliberations went over my head.'

'But do you think we got a fair deal?' asked the King. 'Bearing in mind that you've been to the Indies?' There was already growing unease among the Spanish that they had been hoodwinked by the Portuguese. This feeling would persist until silver started to flow back to Spain from Mexico thirty years later.

'That's not for me to say, sire. But I'm sure that your lords Enrique Enríquez and Gutierre de Cárdenas did the very best they could on your behalf,' Pedro replied diplomatically.

'Well said, young man!' chipped in the Queen, who was quietly chatting to Raquel, for whom she had developed quite a liking. 'I can see that your diplomatic skills accord with the reports we've received.'

'And you will need them,' added the King, becoming very serious. 'You will remember in the agreement, Pedro, that we and King John have pretensions on Morocco. Sultan al-Wattasi will not be too pleased when the terms of the Treaty become known to him, as they surely will. You'll need to be on your guard against a strong reaction from him.'

'The King is right to caution you, Pedro,' added the Queen, now addressing both him and Raquel. 'If there's any sign of trouble, or if you are threatened in any way, you must return to Spain immediately. Are you clear about that?' She gazed at them for a moment. 'But have no fear,' she added, breaking into a smile. 'There are many other ways in which you can serve us. We don't intend to lose you from our service that easily.'

'And that applies to both of you!' added the King.

'Now, we must move on. Do enjoy the festivities.'

'Thank you, ma'am,' they added in unison, one bowing and the other curtseying.

They passed through into the banqueting hall. Set in an old palace of the Castilian kings, the hall was long but relatively narrow. Curved cruck beams descended from the central master beam of the roof and were supported on horizontal square spars projected from the wall, each ending in a carved figure. In this way the hall was able to have been widened by a yard or so on each side. The bare stone walls were part-covered with wall hangings, many of them now rather drab. Campaign flags, mainly won from the Portuguese but, more recently, from the former Nazarí kingdom of Granada, hung from angled poles set in the walls. The banqueting hall was illuminated by the flickering light of burning lanterns fixed high on the bare stone walls. A few rather worn carpets on the stone floor dampened the sound of feet, but they did not muffle the exquisite music of the ensemble playing on the minstrels' gallery high on the wall.

A long narrow table, supported on trestles, stood on a raised platform along one long wall of the banqueting hall, and five similar tables stood at right angles to it, but at floor level. The guests were already taking their places when Pedro and Raquel entered through the arched doorway, and they were conducted by a page to their places on wooden seats on a side table, a few places from the royal table. Pedro recognised only a few of those gathered there, but he was pleased to find himself opposite Antonio de Torres. Antonio was a widower, his wife having died in childbirth five years before, and he was partnered by his sister, Juana, who was governess to Prince Juan. Their meeting with Juana de Torres at Tordesillas would one day prove to have been a fruitful occurrence.

After introductions had been made, Pedro asked Antonio about his plans.

'Will you be returning to La Española, Antonio?'

'Yes, very shortly, Pedro. Indeed, you'll remember that I'm designated as its governor. So I must return. Have you ambitions to return to the Indies, Pedro? Your knowledge of the islands could be a real asset to us, and you know Columbus well.'

Pedro laughed.

'Who knows, Antonio? One day, maybe! For the moment I have a job to do in Fez, and that's where we'll be returning shortly.'

'Well, take care, Pedro. It's clear to me that the King and Queen desire to follow their Granada triumph and gain papal favour by winning over Morocco to Christendom. Al-Wattasi there will not be amused.'

'Yes, the King has already warned me.'

'Good. I wish you luck, and hope we can keep in touch from our respective outposts of the kingdom. I'm sure we're destined to meet again.'

High above and behind the King's table was a wooden balcony jutting out from the wall where the royal musicians stood. They were dressed similarly in crimson woollen robes and black bonnets. Their robes looked decidedly thick and heavy, but for most castles and palaces – draughty, with patchy heating – they were clearly a necessity. The eight musicians in their lofty perch were playing a mixture of wind, stringed and brass instruments. Each musician played several instruments and switched from one to another as demanded by the music they were playing. The wind instruments were led by the raucous shawms. These were reed instruments, later evolving into an oboe, which were first introduced to Spain by the returning Crusaders, who had heard them being played by the infidels. They were joined by the noble cornets and sackbuts, the latter the forerunner of the trombone, and much admired by the King for its regal sound. Quieter interludes with flutes and recorders gave some respite from their noisier brethren. The music was scored and had been composed especially for the occasion. Raquel as much as Pedro was enchanted by the mellifluous blend of sounds, the harmonies, counterpoint and rhythms, constantly changing. They could not believe how so many instruments could be played at the same time without producing discord, shrillness and stridency.

The music stopped and people rose to their feet as a fanfare by trumpeters of the Queen's personal guard announced the entrance of the monarchs and their four children into the banqueting hall, preceded by the haughty royal chamberlain in his black garb. The jewels on the dresses of the Queen and Juana twinkled in the bright flickering light of the flaming wall lanterns. A deep drum thudded a rolling beat as the monarchs, with Juan and Juana, María and Catalina, slowly made their way to the top table. There they stood for a moment as a herald cried, *'Viva el Rey Don Fernando y la Reina Doña Isabel!'*

A cheer went up from the guests, and the monarchs received their acclaim with raised hands and a slow nod of their heads. A warm smile flickered across the lips of the sombre Queen. Prince Juan took his seat next to his mother, while Princess Juana sat next to the King and close to where Pedro was seated. They made eye contact and the princess smiled broadly at him. What had her mother told her? Seated each side of the prince and princess were the three Portuguese delegates who attended the negotiations, Ruy de Sousa and his son, Pedro, and Aires de Almeda. Alongside them, near the end of the table, sat the younger princesses, María and Catalina.

Raquel and Pedro were spellbound by such a wonderful occasion, and it would remain long in their memory – but no less so than the dishes about to be served. Antonio was passed the *carta del día*, and the four of them studied it.

'But it's in French!' exclaimed Raquel, who was totally perplexed. She was only now becoming accustomed to Castilian.

'Yes,' laughed Antonio de Torres. 'It's now the vogue to adopt the style of the Flemish court in Brussels. Not just for menus, but also clothes, architecture, furniture, paintings – everything. Soon we'll all be speaking French!'

'I don't know what it says,' complained Raquel. 'But there seem lots of dishes. You'll have to tell me what they are.'

'Don't worry, Raquel,' said Antonio. 'You won't be expected to eat all of them. You eat what takes your fancy and leave the rest.'

With a chuckle in his voice, clearly revelling in the occasion, he read out in good French what the menu said and translated the dishes listed into Castilian.

Goblets marked each place setting and servants were placing on the tables jugs of red wine from the local vineyards in the Duero valley. Fresh water from the deep palace well filled large earthenware jugs.

Pedro glanced along the top table at Juana, just a few places from him. Chatting and laughing a few minutes ago, the fifteen-year-old was sitting there silently, as in a trance, her eyes glued to her hands placed in her lap. She seemed oblivious to the noise and revelry around her and to the lovely music being played on the gallery behind her.

Antonio banged his spoon on the table to gain attention from the other three.

'Right,' he said. 'Let's see. A few light dishes to start with. *Petits vol-au-vents à la Reine... Croquettes à la royale... Fromage de brebis de Manchega dans l'huile d'olives*. Hmm. Best to avoid these, otherwise you'll become filled even before you start! Now four fish and shellfish dishes. *Turbot, sauce aux truffes, de Pontevedra... Truite saumonée régionale... Escalopes de chevreuil portugais... Huîtres de l'estuaire de La Coruña*. Oysters. Oh, lovely! One of my favourites. Now the soups. *Potage de pigeons á la marinière... Potage de céleri... Consommé de volaille... Potage d'agneau gallois*. Welsh lamb! Do you know, Pedro, that ever since Henry Tudor gained the crown of England seven or eight years ago, Welsh lamb has become very popular. Not surprising, though,' he added, 'always very tasty. Now for the fowl. *Aiguillettes de canard à la bigarrade... Cygne de palais royal... Faisans fourrés avec cailles bardées*. Pheasant stuffed with quail! Oh, you'll love that, Raquel.'

'But you might like the duck more than the swan,' chipped in Antonio's lively sister, Juana. 'Swan's flesh is a bit too chewy for me.'

'Now the meats,' Antonio continued. '*Filet de boeuf à la Vizcaya... Chevreuil á la broche... Sangliers rôtis de Picos de Europa*. Wild boar? A bit heavy. I'll stick to the venison. And lastly, if you have any room left, the desserts. *Gaufres aux raisins d'Almería... Gelée de groseilles*. Hmm. Perfect! Gooseberry jelly after honeycomb with raisins. That will freshen our palates. And finally, Pedro... *Thé de cannelle infusé avec des oranges de Sevilla*.'

'I think that's been put on the menu just for you, Raquel!' laughed Antonio's sister. Whether the King heard what she said or not, he glanced across at Raquel, raised his glass and nodded approvingly. The movement caught Pedro's eye, and he saw the King lean across and shake Princess Juana roughly. She looked up, startled as if from a trance, and smiled sheepishly at her father. Conscious that someone was looking at her, she turned and smiled at Pedro, this time giving him a mischievous wink. But why? he thought.

'Well, there you are, Pedro. Eighteen gorgeous dishes for you to sample. Choose wisely and be selective. Just take a little of those which take your fancy, and with luck you'll be able to walk home unaided.'

'But *eighteen* dishes!' commented Raquel. 'It's really quite excessive. My mother will be appalled when I tell her about this.'

'And you are right, Raquel. But this is a modest affair compared with those in the other royal courts of Paris, Windsor and Brussels. The English king thinks nothing of a banquet with 600 or 700 guests and an array of dishes which makes this affair seem like a picnic by the river. So treat this as a once-in-a-lifetime experience, and enjoy the food and music to the full.'

Already, the menservants, all similarly clad in smart grey doublet and hose, were wheeling trolleys holding the fish dishes and placing three plates of each on every table. At the top table, pages in the service of the court were doing the same. Others were filling silver goblets with wine.

With plates and bowls being replaced as needed and the minstrels playing with gusto, the banquet got underway. After the soups and consommés had been served and consumed, Raquel and Juana preferring the lighter celery soup while the two men chose the thicker lamb broth.

An interlude was called and the guests rose to stretch their legs and wander out into the garden overlooking the Duero. It was early evening and a cool breeze was blowing from the river. The musicians descended from the gallery, and at a side table tucked voraciously into a thoroughly deserved meal. The King and Queen retired to their quarters to rest and change into more casual attire. Other guests, with lodgings nearby, did the same.

Princess Juana, who was now the soul of the party, located Pedro and Raquel looking out across the tree-lined river to the low hills beyond and the wheat fields already turning golden.

'Don Pedro?' she said.

'Yes, Your Highness.' Pedro stretched out his left leg in front of him and bowed low, sweeping his arm across his body.

'And Doña Raquel?'

'Yes, Your Highness.' She curtseyed gracefully, something Doña Ana of Beamonte had taught her while she was at court.

'Oh, please – Juana will do,' said the princess, placing her hand affectionately on Raquel's arm. 'Ana tells me that you're expecting a baby?'

'Yes, Juana, in about six months' time – so Salomón Byton, the physician, thinks.'

'Oh, that's wonderful. I hope it all works out well for you.'

At fifteen, Juana was pretty, with a narrow waist and already a full bust. She had auburn hair, like her mother's, but fairer, with a central parting. She had slightly bulging brown eyes and a high forehead. She had a weakish chin and a small, pouting mouth. The princess was good at sewing and embroidery, and was already an accomplished musician, playing several instruments. She spent hours in her room playing her clavicord. As she would demonstrate after the banquet had finished and the tables had been cleared away, she was a lively court dancer, and enjoyed entertaining the guests with her quick steps. The princess was well versed in Latin and was fluent in French. Not surprisingly, her parents were justly proud of her. Yet she could be moody and withdrawn.

'My mother thinks that you might like to see the tapestries in our quarters here,' she remarked. 'They're quite famous. She tells me, Pedro, that your mother runs a school of tapestry in your home town, so I'm sure she'd love to hear about them. Do please follow me.'

Juana led them back into the palace and through a side door in the ante-room into the royal quarters. Several more doors led them into a well-furnished lounge, with divans and upholstered armchairs placed around the fireplace, although no fire was burning. The carved oak table, chairs and cupboards, all now nearly black with age, had been commissioned by Sancho IV 200 years before.

'There,' she said, pointing to four tapestry panels on the left-hand wall. 'These depict the story of the Holy Virgin and were made by Jan van Eyck in Flanders.[1] You can see they're woven in wool and silk, and with silver and gold thread. Aren't they beautiful?'

'Yes, they are,' enthused Raquel, a bit lost for words. 'Miriam, Pedro's mother, would love to see them. The stitching is so fine and regular.'

'Yes, they're very beautiful. And we have another set of tapestries in Zamora cathedral, forty miles from here, depicting the Trojan War.'

'Were they also made by Jan van Eyck, Juana?' Pedro enquired.

'No, by another famous weaver in Flanders, Peter van Oppenom. The Flanders weavers are still the finest in Europe. But who knows, one day your mother's work might be just as famous,' said the princess, adding with sincerity, 'I do hope so.'

Skipping along nimbly, she led them back into the banqueting hall, where the guests were reassembling for the second part of the banquet. Already Fernando and Isabel were in their places, having changed into lighter clothing. Many guests had done the same.

When the meal was concluded, the tables were cleared and moved to the side of the hall to make space for the dancing which was to follow. The minstrels descended from the gallery and four of them took their places by the side of the high table. If Flemish art and fashion were dominant in the courts of Europe, Italian dances were the vogue. The dancing started with a *bassadanza*, a slow elegant dance which drew the couples to the floor. As the tempo of the wind instruments grew apace, this gave rise to the *quaternaria*, a four-beat walking step with a stamp on the last beat. Antonio and his sister persuaded Pedro and Raquel to join them on the floor and, quick to learn, they soon picked up the rhythm of the dance. After years at court, Prince Juan and his sister were in their element, but not more so than when the music picked

---

[1] After Juana's years of solitude in later life in this palace, these tapestries were affectionately cherished by her descendants.

up apace to a lively *tarantella*. The dancers moved to the side and joined Fernando and Isabel in clapping their hands gleefully to the music, as brother and sister showed their virtuosity in this lively dance, kicking and hopping with true dexterity, each trying to outdo the other in their nimbleness of foot and height of their prances. None of the guests could be persuaded to join the couple, such was their stylish exhibition of the *tarantella*.

Soon the dancing returned to the quieter and more serene *bassadanza* and, in due course, the guests started to depart the banquet. Taking their turn, Pedro and Raquel approached the royal table, bowed and curtseyed to the royal couple, and, with the moon's reflection zigzagging across the river below them, they wandered back in the cool of the night, arm in arm, to their lodgings in the bodega. It had been a memorable day.

VII: Yazíd

The following day, Pedro, Raquel and Abel Jiménez joined the royal court as it left Tordesillas. They tagged onto the end of the dozens of carriages and wagons and scores of riders who crossed the Roman bridge heading south. It was only a few hours to Medina del Campo. There, waving to the royal couple, who were riding out in front of the throng with Juan and Juana, the trio spurred their horses to a gallop and headed south to Ávila and onwards to Andalucía.

By this time, Christopher Columbus – on his second voyage – was off the coast of Cuba with his seventy-ton *San Juan* and two smaller caravels. Firstly they discovered a beautiful island close to the north-east coast, which he named Tortuga[1] on account of the great size and abundance of the turtles there. They then crossed the narrow strait and followed the southern coast of Cuba for a thousand miles to a point close to its western end where, inexplicably, Columbus turned back. By then he was convinced that no island could be so long, and it fortified his belief from his first voyage that Cuba was attached to the mainland of Asia.[2] This conviction was reinforced when they came across footprints of a griffin, a fabulous creature with an eagle's head, as well as signs of other giant creatures. This was all the proof he needed that they had landed on a continental coast. The three ships turned back at Guantánamo Bay, and on 5 May they landed in a beautiful bay which he named Santa Gloria[3] on the north coast of Jamaica, one hundred miles south of Cuba. The Tainos Indians there were friendly, and after making a landfall further east he named the island Santiago. The Spaniards remained there ten days and saw many giant iguana lizards. While there, Columbus made the ship's lawyer, Fernán Pérez de Luna, prepare a declaration for all the seamen to sign agreeing that they had reached *tierra firme* of Asia, which Columbus believed was probably China or Malaya. Only one crew member refused to sign the declaration: Miguel Cuneo was convinced that they had no idea where they

---

[1] Now the island of Great Inagua
[2] As shown on his map of the Indies, used in the deliberations at Tordesillas. It is known as the *Carta Nautica de Colón, 1494*, a copy of which is on display, among others, in the Tordesillas museum devoted to the Columbus explorations.
[3] Now Saint Anna Bay

were! Yet Columbus maintained the belief for years that the island he called Cuba was part of the Asian mainland, despite the fact that the Tainos, both on this and the previous voyage, had told him repeatedly that Cuba could be sailed around and was therefore an island. Stubbornly, Columbus held his view and tried to placate the Catholic Monarchs. They themselves believed that *tierra firme* would have to possess greater riches and wonders than those which Columbus described.

'Did you see Yazíd on your way back?' asked a very anxious Miriam when, after nearly two weeks wearisome riding, the trio arrived home at Xiquena.

'No, why?'

The welcoming kiss to the trio had almost been forgotten. Miriam, Agustín, Yazíd's father, Yakub ibn Hayyan, and his mother, Fátima, were standing together on the forecourt of the castle looking down on the gatehouse below and across the valley to the towering, flat-topped presence of Cerro de la Muela opposite them.

'He left here five days ago, Pedro,' sobbed a distraught Fátima. 'He... he...' What she wanted to say was all too much for her.

'I'd better explain,' said Yakub, cutting in. 'A week ago, a despatch rider from Valladolid delivered a letter from Hernando de Zafra asking Yazíd to rendezvous with a horseman in Chirivel—'

'Why Chirivel?' interrupted a puzzled Pedro.

'We don't really know why. The letter bore the royal seal, so we knew it was authentic. Yazíd was required to meet a rider there, who had a sealed packet of money for him to deliver to the Sultan in Morocco. I guess quite a large sum.'

'But why Chirivel?' asked Pedro. 'It doesn't make sense.'

'Nor to us. We could only assume that the rider would have ridden through Baza and had to return forthwith to Granada. Maybe those in court thought that Chirivel, in the domain of Juan Chacón's estate as we are here, was sufficiently close for a suitable rendezvous.'

'Well, so it is,' remarked Abel. 'It's barely a morning's ride from here.'

'Yes, we know,' said Fátima, wiping her tears from her eyes on her sleeve. 'But Yazíd didn't ride there, he set off on foot.'

'What! *Why*?' asked Abel, flabbergasted.

'You know Yazíd. He's always been more comfortable on foot than on a horse. He said he'd take a short cut over the mountains and avoid going down through Vélez Rubio.'

'Hmm,' interjected Pedro, 'that sounds like Yazíd. But really that's madness. It might save a few miles, but the path to Chirivel through the sierras is very rough and not easy to follow. It would be quicker to walk the long way around.'

'We told him that, too,' said Yakub, 'but he wouldn't listen. He's never happier than when he's in the mountains. He'd made his mind up, and nothing we said would change it.'

Pedro knew Yazíd better than anybody; even better than his parents. The two boys had grown up together in Vélez Blanco, and while different in every respect they were inseparable. Pedro was half-Christian and half-Jew, while Yazíd was Muslim. One was tall and slim with his mother's blue eyes, while the other was tawny skinned, muscular and stocky. From a young age, Yazíd had the wanderlust in his soul. He could always outrun Pedro and could keep on running seemingly for hours without stopping. Many times, he would disappear from home and find himself miles and miles away without knowing where he was or how he got there. Villagers and shepherds alike were dumbfounded when the young boy would ask them where he was and what road he should take to return home. Even more inexplicably, Yazíd would turn up by the side of Pedro during his travels across al-Andalus and just as suddenly disappear. Was Yazíd a sprite or a sylph? Even now, Pedro was not sure. Once Yazíd had saved Pedro's life in the Alpujarras, when Pedro fell into an old mine shaft with absolutely no prospect of extricating himself.

'How did you know I was trapped down there?' Pedro asked afterwards.

'I just knew,' was Yazíd perplexing reply.

The mineshaft, hidden among bushes in the floor of the valley, was 200 miles from Los Vélez. Even now, three years later, Pedro continued to ask himself, *How did he know I was trapped? How did he find me?* Sometime afterwards, when Pedro had reached Palos de la Frontera, 400 miles from their home, in order to witness the departure of Columbus's ships on his first voyage of discovery, Yazíd had appeared by Pedro's side as he attended a young cabin boy who was on his way to board the *Pinta*, then still at anchor in the estuary. The lad had been knifed in the chest and was bleeding to death in Pedro arms.

'Look, Pedro!' Yazíd had exclaimed. 'Look at the boy's kitbag. It's got your name written on it, hasn't it? *Pedro Tegero*. It must be a sign! You must take the boy's place and join the ship. The last of the sailors are already being rowed across to it.'

Pedro did so, but the consequence for Yazíd had been terrible.

'So when did he set off?' asked Abel.

'Six days ago.'

'Well, he should be back by now. It's only some fifteen miles over the mountains, and even if he stopped overnight in one of the shepherds' stone shelters, he still should be back by now.'

'Yes, we know. That's why we're so worried,' bemoaned Fátima as tears continued to stream down her face.

'Look,' said Pedro positively. 'I know the tracks over the sierras like the back of my hand. Yazíd and I spent half our childhood among them. I know every pass, every path, every cave. If anybody can find him, I can. If Mat would accompany me, just in case of trouble, we're sure to find him or what became of him.'

It was agreed. Abel ran down the path to the gatehouse to tell the giant Matute to collect his things and be ready to leave shortly. Pedro ran upstairs, freshened himself up and donned some fresh clothes. The womenfolk packed some cured ham, cheese and dried fruit and plenty of water for the two men to take. There was not a drop of water to be found in the limestone mountains in the summer. For their part, Agustín and Yakub retrieved Pedro's knapsack, which the leather trader Yakub had had made for Pedro several years before. It had plenty of space and cleverly it allowed Pedro to carry his Toledo sword in a slot placed in the back. His sword was out of the way, but it could be drawn quickly from behind his head. Within half an hour, Pedro and Matute were ready to set off.

'It's late afternoon, but we've got several hours of daylight left,' said Pedro, tired from his journey home, but now reinvigorated for action. 'We'll take the defile through the mountain wall, between Vélez Blanco and the caves.'

Yakub knew exactly where he meant and winked at Pedro. As boys, Pedro and Yazíd had frequented their secret hideaway for years, but later felt quite deflated when Yakub let slip that the cave overhang had been his secret hideaway too when he was a boy.[4]

'If you ride to the foot of the defile,' offered Abel, 'I'll bring your horses back here. Then tomorrow I'll ride with them to Chirivel and meet you in the square there. In that way, we can all ride back here together.'

'Brilliant idea, Abel.'

None suspected that the horses would be needed for another purpose.

Matute deigned not to carry a sword. His heavy ash staff was all he needed. His immense size and fierce countenance – surrounded by a mass of blonde hair – were enough to put his foes to flight.

The single defile through the limestone wall was a hundred yards wide. Leaving their horses in Abel's care, Pedro and Matute quickly ascended the gentle grass slope, coming out onto a rocky plateau. A path led through thorn bushes to the left, while the one to the right veered close to the 6,000-foot summit of the Sierra de María, then down through a pine forest and eventually entered the village bearing the same name. But they took the left path. Several

---

[4] The Cueva de los Letreros is a *Monumento de Patrimonio de la Humanidad en España* and contains pictograms from the Neolithic age. Indalo Man, the symbol of Almería province, is said to be derived from there.

miles on, the path forked, with each track heading through the mountains and down to Chirivel, less than ten miles away. Either could have been used by Yazíd, and Pedro opted for the right fork. There was no way of knowing which was more likely. After several hours hard trekking, it started to get dark, and with the path treacherous and difficult they found a shepherd's shelter and settled down for the night, glad that they carried sufficient water and food with them. Not much more than six feet across and five feet high, such round stone enclosures were common, and afforded the shepherds some protection from the elements.

They reached Chirivel mid-morning on the next day. They had seen no sign of Yazíd. Abel was in the village square waiting for them. Alongside, a footpath ran down to a double-plank footbridge across the *rambla*, which, it being summer, was bone dry. What few trees the village possessed were along the banks of the stream. Abel had asked around, and nobody had seen any sign of Yazíd. But across the square a grizzled old man wearing a faded *qamis* had taken a seat in the shade of a tree.

Pedro approached him.

'Excuse me, sir,' asked Pedro courteously in Arabic. 'We're looking for a young Muslim man who we believe came here a few days ago. He's a stocky fellow and probably a bit scruffily dressed.'

The old man looked up and squinted at Pedro standing with his back to the sun. His gnarled hands were propped on a stick in front of him. He did not reply immediately.

'Yes, there was such a fellow. Three or four days ago. Young, strong-looking, lively. He entered the square from the direction of Vélez. He waited around all morning, pacing back and forth. Eventually a rider came from the other direction...'

'Baza?'

'Yes, I suppose so. The rider dismounted and they were in conversation for quite a while. The rider was a Christian and well dressed. An ex-soldier, I'd say. He had a beautiful horse.'

'What happened then?'

'I'm not sure, but I think the rider handed your Muslim friend a package... but I can't be sure since they were in the shade on the far side of the square. Then they shook hands, and the rider mounted his horse and galloped away – at quite a speed, I can tell you!'

The man was silent for a while. Pedro and the two ex-soldiers waited patiently. To press the old man might be counterproductive. But he continued after a while.

'Eventually, your friend gathered up his things – he was carrying a shoulder bag – and headed off the way he had come.'

'Did he speak to anyone else?' asked Abel, with his smattering of Arabic.

'No… Oh, but now I remember! Standing in the far corner of the square, half-concealed by the corner of the old mosque, was a rough-looking fellow. Soon after your Muslim friend had departed, the man himself disappeared. Perhaps he followed your friend?'

'Can you describe this fellow for us, sir?' asked Abel.

'If my memory serves me, he was small and somewhat hunched. He might have had a hunchback. He had an unkempt black beard and wore very old clothes, the clothes of a beggar. I couldn't tell whether he was Christian or Muslim, but he was quite dark-skinned. Oh yes, he had a limp, and I think he had a stick, too. I recall the sound of it clumping on the stones of the square.'

'Anything else you can tell us about this man?' asked Pedro. 'You've been very helpful.'

'No, I'm sorry. That's all I remember.'

Pedro thanked the old man for his help and shook his hand, transferring a golden *dobla* into his palm in the process.

The three conferred, reverting to Castilian.

'It sounds quite ominous to me,' said Abel. 'I saw no sign of Yazíd or this bearded man while I rode here along the main road, so I can only think that Yazíd returned the way he had come, over the mountains.'

'In that case, he must have returned via the other path from the one we came down. Mat, I think the sooner we're on our way back the better. Abel, perhaps you'll hang around here to see if you can learn anything more, or in case we return here.'

Pedro and Matute had gone a few hundred yards when Pedro had an idea. They turned back to the square and spoke to the old man again.

'Sir,' asked Pedro. 'Do you recall seeing the bearded man later? Did he return to this village?'

'No,' he replied. 'I sit in the shade here during much of the heat of the day, and I'm sure that the ruffian with the crooked back didn't return here.'

'Thank you again kindly, sir,' Pedro replied. 'Hmm,' he said, turning to Mat. 'That's bad news. It means that the beggar might well have followed Yazíd.'

Pedro and Matute wasted no time in following the trail back over the mountains, taking the right-hand path, which Yazíd was sure to have followed. Most of the path was rocky and stony, but they stopped to examine a twenty-yard dusty section. Sure enough, they could see Yazíd's tracks with his distinctive pointed shoes, but they were often overwritten by other footprints. Matute, silent but astute, studied them carefully on his hands and knees.

'It's clear, P-P-Pedro,' he said with his stutter, 'that the person following Yazíd had a limp. Can you see? His left f-f-footprint is deeper than the right. And you can see the marks of his stick!'

They pressed on with even more urgency. They must have travelled several miles and were reaching the crest of the route when Matute, always in the lead, stopped, holding his right arm out to caution Pedro. The path had narrowed between thorn bushes and was now dry and dusty.

'What is it, Mat?'

'There was a scuffle here, and there's blood. Can you see? The footprints are all blurred.'

Matute followed the trail slowly, Pedro trying in vain to interpret what he could see. For the next thirty yards, the dusty trail was scuffed and there was a line of dark blotches. Matute looked around at Pedro and shook his head, as if warning him. Something had been dragged through the dust. There were no footprints. He cautioned Pedro to stay where he was. For all his immense size, Matute had a second sense and he feared the worse.

He followed the trail. The scuff marks stopped. Some thorn bushes to his right had been disturbed.

'Stay where you are!' he called back to Pedro.

Matute pulled the bushes aside to his right. A pair of legs appeared beneath the undergrowth, which had clearly been disturbed. He forced his way through the thorns, getting terribly scratched, and pulled back the flattened undergrowth. A body lay there, and a massive stone, nearly a cubic yard in size, lay on the body where its head and chest had been. The remains of what must have been Yazíd were unrecognisable.

By this time, Pedro was by Mat's side and saw for himself the ghastly remains of his dear friend. He recognised his worn clothes and the pointed sandals he wore. But there was nothing else by which to identify him.

Pedro retreated to a boulder ten yards away and sat down. With his elbows on his knees and his face in his hands, he was overcome by grief. Tears rolled down his face, and he cried and cried and cried.

Poor Yazíd! His only true boyhood friend. True and faithful to the last. The friend with whom he had shared so many good times in their cave hideaway in the mountain wall below their home in Vélez Blanco; the friend who had saved his life from the mineshaft and later had appeared by his side at Palos; the friend who had appeared out of nowhere when Fernando and Isabel had been handed the keys of Almería by El Zagal on a drizzly December day five years before. Poor Yazíd... Soon after he had appeared out of nowhere at Palos, Pedro had entrusted him with his precious sword, an ornamental dagger given to him by Boabdil, the deposed Sultan of Granada, and the Queen's jade ring. But in handing in the cabin boy's wages for the voyage to the local alcalde, Yazíd had been arrested for his murder. Without even a summary trial, he had been sent to the galleys from which there was no return. Only the intervention of Don Gonzalo returned him safely to his home, to appear miraculously under the arm of the great man himself at Pedro and Raquel's wedding on that snowy day in Vélez three years before. Poor Yazíd! Pedro sobbed and sobbed and sobbed, reliving all the wonderful times they had had together as boys and the experiences they had shared.

Matute, a silent man but with deep feelings, placed his arm around Pedro's shoulders. He had only met Yazíd once, but he shared Pedro's grief. Squeezing Pedro's shoulder compassionately, he arose and walked silently to Yazíd's crushed body. He placed his arms around the enormous boulder. His hands could just reach the far corners, and with every sinew and muscle in his body taking the immense strain, he slowly heaved it off Yazíd's head and chest and hurled it aside. Looking up, he could see where the stone must have been dislodged. A flattened knife still embedded in Yazíd's chest showed that he had been stabbed and was probably dead before the boulder had been dislodged.

Matute untied the bedroll which he had been carrying and wrapped it around what remained of Yazíd's body. He tied it tightly and lifted it on his shoulders.

'I'll take Yazíd back down to Chirivel, Pedro,' he said. 'You stay here as long as you like.'

Pedro stayed mourning Yazíd's death until the sun started to set over the sierras to his right. But the two hours of daylight remaining were enough for him to return to Chirivel.

'Where's Mat?' Pedro asked Abel, who was waiting patiently with the horses in the square.

'He rode off soon after he brought poor Yazíd's body down from the mountains. I'm so sorry, Pedro. I know how close you two were.'

'Thank you, Abel. He was like a brother to me. So where did Mat go?'

'He went off to hunt down Yazíd's killer. He said he thinks he knows where he can find him. If he does find him, Pedro, he'll kill him. You can be sure of that. Mat and I joined the King's forces at the same time twenty years ago, and if anybody can find Yazíd's killer, Mat can – even if it takes him a year and he has to follow him across the breadth of Spain. Pedro, I've tied Yazíd's body across Indy. We can ride back to Xiquena together on my horse. He's a lot bigger and stronger than Indy.'

Two hours after leaving Abel, Matute arrived in the burgeoning settlement which would grow to become Vélez Rubio. He asked around, his stammer miraculously ceasing as his self-consciousness disappeared.

'Yes,' he was told by an elderly couple in the main street. 'We've seen such a person with a hunchback and a stick here from time to time. A rough-looking fellow, always skulking around. Never up to any good.'

'Do you know where I can find him?'

'I don't think he lives in this village. We'd soon know if he did. He's probably to be found on the hill opposite among the old Arab ruins. There are a lot of bad people up there.'

'Thank you, kind people,' replied Mat. 'It's what I suspected.'

'I wouldn't go up there alone, if I were you,' they cautioned. 'You'd need a squad of soldiers to sort out that den of thieves.'

Mat laughed. 'Don't you worry about me,' he roared, looking down on the two villagers from his six-and-a-half feet, 'I'm my own squad of soldiers!' There was nothing Mat liked more than facing a challenge on his own, where his strength and wits could be put to the test.

It was already early evening, and Matute had worked out his plan. The old hill fort of Vélez al-Almar stood on the summit of an isolated mountain a mile away from the hamlet. An alcázar with a broken-down tower and several other ruined buildings lay on the domed summit, and a wall encircled the whole enclosure. There were enough buildings there to conceal Ali Baba and his forty thieves! A single path to the top ran from the dry river bed on the far side of the mountain. Matute studied the fort carefully from the highest vantage point he could find. Then, moving cautiously, he crossed the Baza road and started to ascend the mountain, taking a difficult route through thickets of bushes where its steepness precluded him from being seen from the top. He reached the perimeter wall, now largely collapsed, and followed it around to its highest point where, out of sight, he could look down on the buildings near the old alcázar and tower, fifty or so yards away.

In due course, half a dozen ruffians congregated near the tower and began arguing about the division of spoils from their various sorties that day. These lay spread out on a blanket in front of them, much of it vital food and drink. And Mat's man was there! Dark-skinned and with a distinct hump and a limp, Yazíd's killer stayed on the edge of the group. But why? Where was his contribution to the spoils? Where was Yazíd's money packet?

It was getting dark as the thieves dispersed to their various abodes among the derelict buildings, each bearing something in his hands. Matute watched the hunchback move off to his left, and the giant ran quickly around the outside of the wall to keep him in sight. The killer entered one of the stone ruins and Mat raced across the open space to another ruin fifteen yards away. The killer came out of the tumbledown house holding a packet in his hand, looked around furtively in case any of his colleagues were watching, then disappeared into another adjacent ruin which was little more than a pile of stones and a collapsed roof. Mat got closer, and through what remained of the doorway he saw the hunchback remove a stone from the inside wall and conceal the packet inside, then replace the stone. Mat noted exactly where the stone was located.

The hunchback returned to his lair and, clearly content that he had hood-winked the other thieves by concealing his gains from them, sat down outside and cut himself a thick slice of cured ham to be followed by a flagon of rough wine – undoubtedly all stolen. Perfect. This was just what Mat had hoped for.

Never losing sight of the killer, Mat bided his time until it was dark and the moon was well past its zenith in the southern sky. Now, with his eyes perfectly accustomed to the darkness, he moved slowly and stealthily to the hunchback's lair. The man was inside asleep and snoring loudly. Mat leant over him and placed his powerful hands around the man's neck and, ensuring that he did not cry out, slowly, but ever so slowly, throttled him. When he was done, he raised the man's shoulders, put one hand behind his head and jerked it forward forcefully. The snap was audible. He had to be sure.

Matute ran across to the adjacent ruin and quickly found the telltale stone concealing the money. With Yazíd's money safe in his possession, Matute circled the enclosure to his left until he found the path which descended to the *rambla*. Nobody would stop him now.

Yazíd was buried in the Muslim cemetery a quarter of a mile outside Vélez Blanco later that same day. Pedro and Abel had returned to Xiquena with Yazíd's body the previous evening. There was more a mood of sadness than one of tears. Yakub and Fátima had already braced themselves for tragic news, and Fátima had no more tears to shed. With them at the cemetery that evening were the mullah and the mayor, Mohammed Adbuladin. Yusuf and Fátima were accompanied by their other two grown-up children and their families. Agustín and Miriam were there, plus Pedro, Raquel and young Sara with her wheezing cough. Matute and Abel were present to show their last respects. All the women folk wore black shawls over their heads. In addition, Pedro's uncle, the loveable Joshua, and his wife, Raghad, Raquel's sparky mother, had come down from the upper part of the town, where they lived contentedly in Pedro's former family house. After the mullah spoke some final prayers, Pedro gave a short peroration in Arabic, lauding their close friendship for so many years and reflecting in a lighter vein on some of their adventures together.

Later, Yakub and Pedro agreed upon a short inscription on Yazíd's tombstone. It would read in Arabic:

IN MEMORY OF YAZÍD IBN HAYYAN, SON OF YAKUB, WHO DIED TRAGICALLY AGED 19 ON 22 JUNE 1494 (IN THE YEAR OF THE PROPHET 901). HE WAS A YOUNGSTER WITH UNFLAGGING ENERGY AND AN UNQUENCHABLE SPIRIT WHO SHOWED UNSTINTING LOYALTY TO ALL THOSE HE LOVED. HE SHALL BE GREATLY MISSED. MAY HIS SOUL FIND THE TRANQUILLITY WHICH EVADED HIM IN LIFE.

They all returned to Xiquena from the cemetery. Their mood was very sombre. The full shock of Yazíd's death was only now sinking in.

'Oh, Mama, I'm so sorry, in all the worry over Yazíd I forgot to give you Queen Isabel's letter,' said Pedro.

'For me?' questioned Miriam.

'Yes, a rider overtook us after we left the royal party at Medina and handed it to me.'

'For me!' exclaimed Miriam again. 'I can't believe it. What could it be about?'

'Well, open it and see!' chided Agustín. 'She probably wants you to return to the harem in the Alhambra!'

Miriam scowled at him, then read it aloud.

'To Señora Miriam López, Xiquena, Vélez Blanco, Andalucía.

'From her Majesty, Queen Isabel…' Miriam looked up and gave an excited giggle. 'From the Queen herself, and in her own hand!' she exclaimed breathlessly.

'My dear Señora,' she read:

'Firstly, please treat what I am about to tell you in the strictest confidence. I anticipate that you will inform your husband, my loyal Captain Lopez, of this letter's contents, as well as your son and daughter-in-law, Don Pedro and Doña Raquel. But not a word of this must be divulged to anyone else until a formal announcement is made from the royal court. We pray that this will be later this year.

'We are in negotiation with Emperor Maximilian of the Holy Roman Empire for the dual betrothal of Prince Juan to his daughter, Princess Margaret of Austria, and Princess Juana to his eldest son, Archduke Philip. We are very excited about the prospects of these royal matches, and foresee much good coming from such links with the noble house of Austria. Already our minds are turning to wedding gifts and all the planning which royal weddings entail.

'Juana is unusually devoted to the panels of Jan van Eyck's tapestries in the palace at Tordesillas depicting the story of the Virgin Mary, which she showed your son and daughter-in-law during the banquet there to celebrate the signing of the Treaties. With this in mind, I would like to present her with a set of tapestries of historical significance, and I can think of no better theme than the conquest of Granada, which was recently concluded and fully merits recording for posterity. For this, I envisage three panels. The first depicting the handing over of the keys of the city of Almería in December 1489 to the King and me by Mohammed Abú Abdalá who, I gather, died recently; a second depicting our entrance to the city of Granada in January three years later, when we received the keys of the city from his nephew, the Sultan Boabdil; plus a third panel showing the wonderful view of the Alhambra palace as seen from the Albaicín hill, with the snow-covered sierras behind. I believe that these three tapestries would embody perfectly the triumph of our ten-year Conquest.

'The reason for my writing will now become obvious to you. Nothing could be more appropriate after your years in captivity in the Alhambra, or give Juana and I more pleasure, than for you to take on such a task. Thus I am writing to ask if you would be prepared to take on this commission. Of course, this is a gigantic task for you and your team of needlewomen to tackle, and I am sure that you will need to add to their numbers considerably and train them appropriately. I will be writing to Juan Chacón to ask him to facilitate all that you might require.

'But an early start is essential, and that is why I am writing to you well ahead of a formal announcement of the betrothals, since you will need all the time at your disposal. You and your team will be paid generously for the work. Already artists at court are depicting for me the three panels and will transfer these images onto tapestry canvas for you to work on.

'In anticipation of your positive response to my request, I have placed an order for wool thread from England, where the finest wool is now to be obtained, and these will by dyed into an array of colours for you. Others you can add by yourself. If you wish, crowns and suchlike can be picked out with gold thread, and swords and other arms with silver thread. These and many other details can be worked out later.

'In the meantime, will you be so kind as to indicate you willingness to take on this commission? Royal messengers ride weekly between Medina del Campo and both Granada and Murcia. Please ask Captain López to arrange delivery of your reply to one or other city.

'I look forward to receiving your positive response. It will be truly fitting for you to do this work. Please convey our royal greetings to your husband and your family. You are indeed blessed by a fine son and a beautiful daughter-in-law. Both I know will be returning to Fez shortly.

'Isabel of Castile,
'6 May 1494.'

VIII: Columbus's Ambitions

January 1495

Pedro had returned to Fez in Morocco just a week after Miriam had so excitedly received the letter from Queen Isabel. But relations between Spain and Morocco had started to deteriorate after Sultan al-Wattasi learnt of the contents of the second of the Tordesillas treaties, which spelt out Spain's aspirations to colonise and Christianise his country. Under the watchful care of her mother and mother-in-law, Raghad and Miriam, Raquel had remained in Xiquena on her return from Tordesillas to enjoy an easy and trouble-free pregnancy. The menfolk in the castle, even the giant Matute, had been as anxious as the two women as Raquel's time approached, knowing how hazardous and life-threatening labour was to expectant women. So Pedro had returned from Fez at the end of December, and was in time for Raquel's delivery of a fine healthy boy on 2 January, three years to the day from Boabdil's surrender of Granada to the Catholic Monarchs. Pedro would not return to Morocco again.

Raquel was sitting up in bed nursing the baby when Pedro and young Sara were allowed into her bedchamber by Raghad, who had helped the midwife from Vélez Blanco to deliver the baby. In her eyes it was as much her baby as Raquel's, and she fussed around her daughter as Pedro embraced his wife and took the youngster in his arms. Sara, approaching three years old, was not going to be left out, and jumped up and down on the bed with glee at the prospect of having a baby brother to play with. The boy was rosy-cheeked and had blue eyes and fair hair, just like his grandmother, Miriam.

'You can see who he takes after!' laughed Raquel. 'There's no doubt that he's a real Christian boy!'

Her mother, Raghad, scowled in the corner. Although now baptised, she was still a Muslim deep down.

'What shall we call him, Pedro?'

'I've avoided thinking about names, Raquel. I didn't want to tempt fate by doing so. But what would you like to call your son? After all, you're the one who brought him safe and sound into this world.'

'Why not Antonio – after that charming man we met in Tordesillas? It's such a nice name. Antonio has a certain ring about it… Antonio and Sara Togeiro. Don't they sound nice together?'

'They do indeed. Very well, my dear; Antonio it shall be.'

Raquel must have had a premonition. Two days later, Abel Jiménez brought a letter back from Murcia, where he had been conducting business on behalf of Agustín. It was from Antonio de Torres.

To Don Pedro Togeiro, Xiquena, Vélez Blanco, near Murcia

From Antonio de Torres, La Isabela, Isla de La Española

20 October 1494

Greetings to you and Raquel from the Indies. I expect by the time you receive this that you, Raquel, will be close to the birth of your child. I pray sincerely that you will be safely delivered of a fine child. I think of you daily.

I arrived back here at La Isabela two weeks ago with four caravels loaded with food and other provisions, as well as letters to Christopher Columbus from Fernando and Isabel. Three ships are returning to Spain in a few days' time and so it's opportune to write you a hasty report on how things have been here since I left here last February. In fact, things seem to have deteriorated badly. Since he returned a month ago from his exploration of the south coast of Cuba and Trinidad, CC has been confined to his bed with gout and dysentery and is in a lot of pain. In August, his brother Bartolomé arrived with three shipments of supplies which were desperately needed, since it's clear the colonists here were starving after the failure of so many of last year's crops. While CC was away, our settlers took liberties with the Indians, who consequently hate us and refuse to obey us. Worse, almost half of our people in La Isabela have died of the contagious disease which they caught from native women. Painful and disfiguring, it's more often than not fatal. CC left his younger brother Diego in charge while he was away, and he's greatly disliked by all. He speaks little Castilian and there's clearly a strong feeling among the Spaniards against being ordered around by the Genoese – and, of course, that includes CC. The anger of the Tainos Indians boiled over some months ago, and they attacked and destroyed one of our coastal forts and burnt it to the ground, killing the dozen Spaniards there. Naturally, our people retaliated and captured scores of the Indians, and they are to be sent to Spain (with this letter) as slaves on the ships which brought Bartolomé two months ago. One positive thing to report is that the water mill which Diego had been building is operating and already grinding corn. So that's good news.

On his arrival, Bartolomé assumed immediate command of the island and he's proving to be very able and more popular than his brother. Moreover, he's an excellent navigator as well as a first-class mapmaker.[1] But not all the natives are against us. Friar Ramón Pané has had much success in converting them to Christianity, with the chief, Guacanagarí, adopting the name Juan. Other chiefs have followed suit. At the very least, the good friar has shown that baptism is an alternative to bloody conquest, and I support him in this.

I saw CC this morning. He's still in a lot of pain with his gout, but he's been cheered up considerably by the letters from F and I, who express their overall approval with developments here (but maybe they're relying too much on what I reported to them in April,

---

[1] For which he later became famous.

when things seemed a lot better). The monarchs informed him in their letters about the Tordesillas treaties and the agreements with the Portuguese and, of course, I was able to tell him how the discussions progressed which led to the agreements. He was intrigued to hear that you were present during the negotiations and he sends his best wishes to you. He recalls your sterling work on the Niña during the terrible storm on your return to Spain from the first voyage, when so many of the crew were sick and incapacitated below decks.

Two surveyors are on their way and will arrive shortly to determine the best land and most suitable crops for cultivation. F and I were in Madrid[2] when I left, attending Cardinal Pedro González de Mendoza, who is close to death. He's a great man who supported Isabel from the very first in her contest for the crown of Castile twenty or so years ago. He will be succeeded by Francisco Jiménez de Cisneros, the Primate of Spain and Archbishop of Toledo. Cisneros, as he is known, has a formidable reputation, but is very austere and chooses to go around barefoot. His appointment will not go down too well with the soft underbelly of the Church, I can tell you. But we shall see.

Well, Pedro, that's as much as I've got time for, since the ships sail on the morrow if the wind is fair; but I'll continue to keep in touch with you, and look forward with fingers crossed for good news concerning your second child. I will pray for Raquel. My sister Juana wishes to be remembered to you both.

Antonio

Columbus, despairing of finding gold and silver in quantity, decided to turn his attention to 'human gold' instead, in the form of slaves. Raiding parties were sent out to all parts of the island to capture natives, but they were not disposed to be clapped in chains and marched back to La Isabela. Thousands fled to the hills. It did not help that the settlers were unable to distinguish between the friendly Tainos, who were peaceful and easily converted to Christianity, and the Caribes, who were warlike cannibals and terrorised all the other tribes in the islands. Such was the rapacity of the Spanish settlers that Bartolomé de las Casas reported a few years later that two-thirds of the Indian population had been annihilated through conquest, disease and slavery.

Whether this was true or not, Antonio de Torres himself left La Isabela on 24 February with over 500 Indians destined for slavery. Diego returned with him, with the fleet reaching Madeira in a record twenty-three days. But half the Indians died on the voyage because of the cold weather, and the remainder were sick when they reached Cádiz. Nine were selected to be taught Castilian and to act as translators, while the rest were despatched to Seville for selling in

---

[2] Madrid was then a modest town. Fernando and Isabel earmarked it as the potential capital of Spain, but it was Philip II, their great-grandson, who in 1561 took the decision to move the Spanish court from Valladolid to Madrid, with all the consequential upheaval of ambassadors etc.

the slave market.[3] Fernando and Isabel themselves raised no objection to slaves, who were considered common currency, whether they were originally native islanders of the Canaries, Berbers from north Africa, Negroes from west Africa, or Slavs[4] from the Balkans. All were in great demand. Nevertheless, Archbishop Cisneros stood out against the slave trade from the Caribbean, and he supported Bartolomé de Las Casas in upholding the rights of the Indians.

By the time Antonio returned to Cádiz with his boatloads of slaves, Columbus was in the centre of La Española intending to subdue the whole island in the name of the Crown. He was accompanied by his brother, Bartolomé, and his old friend and ally, the Taino chief Guacanagarí, plus various of his men. Several forts were established and many Spaniards started to move to them from La Isabela with their Indian wives to set up home. Columbus reached agreement with many of the local chiefs that all their people between the ages of seventeen and sixty would pay regular tribute to the Crown, whether in the form of gold, cotton, flax, cereals or even fish. These were not idle promises. One Taino community at Cibao, for instance, agreed to hand over 60,000 pesos of gold in three instalments; a huge commitment. In exchange, Columbus agreed to prevent his men taking land without the consent of the tribal chiefs.

The large-scale clearing of land and the planting of crops which was now underway after the arrival of the two land surveyors, plus the steady export of slaves, were changing attitudes in Spain, where the Caribbean islands were starting to be considered as outposts of Andalucía or, as they would be known, colonies. Nevertheless, despite the complimentary sentiments expressed by the monarchs in their letters to Columbus, his imperial pretensions were starting to cause them concern and they were looking at ways to clip his wings. Having unified Spain after a lifetime of toil, they were not disposed to permit the Genoese explorer to establish his own sovereignty over the Caribbean. Their decree published in April 1495 changed things for good.

Some two months before the birth of baby Antonio, a muleteer arrived at Xiquena with two pack animals carrying the timbers to assemble three sturdy tapestry frames for Queen Isabel's commission. Excited though she was, Miriam did not interfere as the man rather laboriously assembled the frames and mounted the canvas on the rollers at top and bottom. A ratchet and pawl mechanism held them tight and allowed the canvas to be rolled up the frame as work progressed. The images which were to be woven onto the tapestries were

---

[3] It is worth observing that large-scale commercial slavery commenced eastwards to Europe from the Caribbean, and not westwards to the Caribbean from Africa.

[4] From which the word 'slave' derives!

already marked in colour onto the canvases, and the overall images were also shown on three scaled and coloured drawings. The muleteer also brought sacks of coloured wools, and within no time Miriam's team of needlewomen were busy on their task. Three could work on a canvas at any one time, and Miriam had fifteen keen villagers at her disposal who could do the work as and when they were able. Abel's wife, Eva, Raghad and Raquel were among them. Each canvas measured five feet by eight feet, and Miriam calculated that each of her three teams would need to sew some eight square inches per day over two years to complete the task. By the time Pedro had returned from Morocco, they had already made a good start; his mother was delighted with the progress and she had already written her first three-monthly progress report to the Queen.

Two weeks after the letter from Antonio de Torres, a rider arrived at Xiquena in the late afternoon. A biting cold wind was blowing from the north and flecks of snow were swirling in the darkening sky. Matute, guarding the gate as usual, immediately recognised the visitor as an old soldier and, bidding him welcome, led his horse to the shelter of the stables along from the gate, while directing the visitor up the path to the keep. After unsaddling the horse in the stable and ensuring that it had food and water, Matute followed the man quickly up the path.

'Do you remember me?' the visitor asked Pedro, when the latter came to the door.

'Yes, of course,' Pedro answered, the image of their first meeting coming quickly to mind. Its vividness had not diminished one jot over the intervening five years.

'Manuel Manzano? Don Gonzalo's right-hand man? What a wonderful surprise! Welcome to Xiquena. Do please come in out of the biting wind. It looks like we're in for some snow. And you, Mat!' he shouted. The giant was already halfway up the path.

'You'll love to meet Manuel,' Pedro said to Matute as he arrived at the door. 'Another old comrade-in-arms!'

Pedro could not get over his surprise at meeting Manuel Manzano again. All the family gathered in the main hall, where a fire was blazing in the cavernous grate. Abel joined them with an armful of logs. Despite the wind whistling in the throat of the chimney high above, the room was warm and commodious.

'I'm glad to arrive, Pedro, I can tell you,' said Manuel Manzano, rubbing his hands together. 'The weather's certainly turning worse and snow's already settling on the mountains around.'

'Have you come far, Manuel?' asked Agustin.

'From Murcia today. But I set off from Valencia several days ago. It's been a long ride, I can tell you.'

'Well, Manuel, we're glad you've arrived safe and sound,' said Miriam, introducing herself. 'Come and sit by the fire. You must be exhausted. I'll go and make a room ready for you.'

Abel threw some logs on the fire while Agustín handed the visitor a welcoming goblet of warm spiced wine from a jug standing in the fireplace.

'So how many years is it since we first met, Pedro?' asked Manuel after he had settled comfortably in a chair. 'It was in Jaén, wasn't it?'

'Yes, outside the *Casa de la Inquisición*. Don Gonzalo had just rescued me from the clutches of Tomás de Torquemada, the Inquisitor General of Castile. It was Abel here who had tipped off Don Gonzalo that I was imprisoned in their cells in Jaén. Without Abel and Don Gonzalo, I would have surely died there.'

'Yes, I remember now, Pedro. My word. You were in an awful state! Half-naked, with your arms half pulled out of your body after hanging from that hook! It seems a long time ago now.'

Pedro suppressed his curiosity as to why Don Gonzalo's man had ridden to see them until after they had eaten and the four former soldiers had exchanged their experiences while the wine flowed freely. After all, what else do old soldiers do?

'Now, Pedro, I expect you're wondering why I'm here,' said a replete Manuel Manzano.

Pedro nodded.

'You may not have heard, but the French have invaded Italy on the pretext of taking possession of the Kingdom of Naples. I'm told that this blatant invasion violates the terms of the Treaty of Barcelona between our two countries. Cutting a long story short, Pedro, King Fernando, whose uncle is the King of Naples, is raising an expeditionary force to expel the French from there.'

'But how does this affect me?' asked a bewildered Pedro. All this was news to him, although he had heard that the French king, Charles VIII, was young and headstrong.

'Don Gonzalo has been asked by Fernando to lead the expeditionary force and he has accepted it with alacrity. He's been at a bit of a loose end since the surrender of Granada three years ago.'

'But why have you come to tell me this, Manuel? I still don't understand.'

'Don Gonzalo wants you by his side, Pedro. Beyond that I can't tell you. He asked me to return home via Xiquena to give you this message – or, if you weren't here, to leave you this letter which I have with me. He asks that you come and visit him so he can tell you personally what he has in mind. He says that he has cleared with the King the termination of your ambassadorship in Morocco, which in any case, apparently, is becoming untenable after the Tordesillas treaties.'

Pedro was completely taken aback by Manuel's announcement, and looked around bewildered at his family. All seemed equally perplexed.

'How soon are you talking about?' asked Raquel, worried by the implications.

'Don Gonzalo is already raising contingents of soldiers in Córdoba and Granada, and others are doing likewise in Seville and other cities right across Spain. Putting it bluntly, Pedro, he'd like to see you very soon so he can finalise his plans.'

'That sounds like an order for Pedro to accompany you back home, Manuel,' commented Agustín.

'No, it's in no way an order, Agustín. But if Pedro were to ride back with me it would make the journey a lot pleasanter for both of us.'

'How long will it take?' asked Miriam.

'Don Gonzalo is presently at his home in Granada and he'll be there until the end of the month. It will take us around three days from here, depending on the weather and the conditions underfoot.'

'You'll have to go, Pedro,' said a tearful Raquel. 'After all, it's effectively a direct command from the King. I remember him saying at the banquet in May that he didn't intend to lose you from his service if you were to leave Morocco and that there were other ways in which you could serve him. Maybe this was in the back of his mind?'

'Actually, Raquel, it was the Queen who said this, and the King added afterward, "and that applies to the both of you!" So maybe he's got something up his sleeve for you, too!

'Very well, Manuel,' replied Pedro. 'We'll ride together to Granada when you've had a day's rest and when the weather improves. I must say, it will be lovely to meet Don Gonzalo again.'

IX: *Storm Clouds over Italy*

In July 1494 – at the time Pedro, Raquel and Abel had arrived back home – Charles VIII, the twenty-five-year-old King of France, had led a substantial invasion force across the Alps to invade Italy and claim the throne of Naples for his own. A semi-cripple, this impetuous and warlike young king was to precipitate conflicts across the breadth of Italy, cause divisions between the countries of Europe, and destabilise the region for years to come. For whereas by then the sovereign states of France, Spain, Portugal, England and the Holy Roman Empire of Maximilian existed with recognised governance and established borders, the peninsula of Italy enjoyed no such stability. Italy was then an amalgam of some ten republics and duchies, with the Kingdom of Naples occupying the whole southern half of the peninsula, including Sicily. The Papal States, essentially the Kingdom of the Vatican, dominated the middle of the country, centred on Rome. These were bordered on the west coast by two small independent republics of Siena and Florence. Under the right shoulder of the peninsula, the Duchy of Ferrara was wedged between the Papal States and the powerful Republic of Venice. The Duchy of Milan and the Republic of Genoa formed the left shoulder. These city states possessed their own administrations, armies, systems of taxation, traditions, enemies and alliances. Like a hand being thrust into a barrel of floating apples, any disturbance to the fragile peace in the peninsula jarred one state against another, upsetting the delicate balance which existed between them. This is exactly what the French invasion was to do. France was, as ever, the bully boy of Europe. With a population twice that of Spain and four times that of England, France – with its abundant riches and wealth – had meddled in the affairs of its neighbours for centuries. Charles VIII's action was wholly in keeping with his forebears.

But Charles was not the only protagonist. Fernando also had designs on Naples and Sicily, which had long been a fiefdom of his kingdom of Aragón. Nevertheless, the dominant power in Italy was the Pope, Rodrigo Borgia, whose influence across Catholic Europe was all-pervading, and he was to be drawn inexorably into the conflict which was soon to unfold.

It was Rodrigo Borgia who was instrumental in bringing together Spain and Portugal for the negotiations which led to the signing of the Treaty of Tordesillas. It was he who some years before had settled the thorny question of the 'unlawful' marriage between Fernando and Isabel, who were second cousins. Rodrigo could see clearly the merit of the union between Castile and Aragón to liberate al-Andalus and thus Western Europe from the Muslims, who were then threatening Venice and the Balkans. With this in mind, Rodrigo, then number two in the Vatican, forced through a papal bull legitimising the union of the two Spanish monarchs. Acting decisively again, Rodrigo drew the wrath of the Italian populace by accepting 300,000 Jewish refugees from Spain following their expulsion in May 1492. Lastly, in May the following year, he legitimised the Spanish conquest in America with a papal bull. Clearly, indecisiveness was not one of his failings.

Rodrigo Borgia became Pope Alexander VI in 1492. He was one of the most influential figures of his age, who increased the power of the Church and as much as anybody shaped the history of the time. He was an attractive man with a fine physique. He was elegant, prudent, decisive, perspicacious and a consummate diplomat. He was highly attracted by, and attractive to, beautiful women. This has led to his reputation as being corrupt, sexually promiscuous and guilty of nepotism; others say that he was no more than a man of his time. Like all popes of the late medieval and renaissance times, he was an absolute monarch who used his holy office to influence and interfere in all the affairs of Christendom.

He was born Rodrigo Borja in 1431 in the small hilltop town of Xàtiva, in Valencia, Spain. He was the son of low-ranking nobles Yofré de Borja and Isabel de Borja, who were, in fact, unrelated and had descended from different branches of a lineage which started in the twelfth century. On the death of his father, Rodrigo moved to Valencia in the care of his uncle, Alfonso Borja. Alfonso was then a cardinal and had a major influence on the development of his nephew. At the age of just seven, the youngster was inducted into the Catholic Church. At fifteen, he received papal dispensation to pursue an ecclesiastical career. He was, therefore, already marked for high office. Two years later, his uncle took him to Rome, where they lived in a convent-cum-fortress near the ruins of the Roman Coliseum and Forum. There, they italianised their name to Borgia, an appellation which would reverberate down through the ages.

At the age of twenty-two, Rodrigo went to the University of Bologna to study canon law and, just three years later, his uncle, now Pope Calixto III, made him a cardinal and then Vice-Chancellor. This was the second highest post in the Church, with practically unlimited powers. Also in the same year, Rodrigo was named general of the pontifical forces in Italy. Thus, at the age of twenty-six, he was a cardinal, Vice-Chancellor, a doctor of law and military supremo. To crown all these honours, a year later he was named Bishop of Valencia.

Rodrigo's palace in the Vatican became the centre of Roman life. Although in his private life he lived frugally, his banquets and cellar were legendary, as was the gluttony of the ecclesiastical hierarchy who coveted his hospitality. By then, Rodrigo had amassed an enormous income but also immense costs, spending large sums on improvements to the many churches within his jurisdiction.

When he was thirty, he took up with Vannozza Cattanei. At the time, she was nineteen, and with her Rodrigo formed a happy and stable relationship for over twenty years. The couple had four children, César, Juan, Lucrezia and Jofré. Each, as we shall see, was to play a part in the tangled affairs in the conflicts in Italy. By then, Rodrigo had had at least three children by other lovers. Born in 1474, Rodrigo's eldest son, César Borgia, was to become one of the most infamous personalities of the Renaissance. Aggrandised by legends of crime and cruelty, his sordid reputation has besmirched and overshadowed the whole of the Borgia dynasty.

When he was fifty-nine, Rodrigo started an illicit relationship with fifteen-year-old Julia Farnesio, who – despite an eye defect – was a noted beauty. Julia had arrived in Rome to marry Orso Orsini, the son of Rodrigo's cousin, Adriana Milà. This affair between uncle and second cousin, which was so openly conducted at the time of the marriage, totally scandalised Rome. Nevertheless, while history confers on Rodrigo an image of sexual and moral licentiousness and wantonness, including incest, it is only fair to record that his three papal predecessors, one so inaptly named Innocent VIII, had sixteen children between them.

In August 1492, the same month Christopher Columbus set off on his first voyage to the Indies, Rodrigo Borgia, at the age of sixty-one, at last assumed the papacy. He took the title Alexander VI. Throughout that year, ambassadors arrived in Rome from Florence, Venice, Sienna, Genoa, Naples, Spain and Germany. All expressed the hope that the Church would reassert its greatness under the dynamic new pope.

Few popes before or after were as adept as Rodrigo in political wheeler-dealing, or used alliances with other powers or arranged marriages for their offspring with such effect. These were the means then by which states secured their boundaries and faced threats from their adversaries. They were how the 'apples in the barrel' were kept in place.

Alfonso, the ageing King of Naples, had continued to cause unrest by seeking closer ties with the Medici of Florence. On his part, Rodrigo Borgia had sought to strengthen his alliance with the city state of Milan by marrying his thirteen-year-old daughter, Lucrezia, to twenty-six-year-old Juan Sforza, whose father was the influential Cardinal Ascanio Sforza. In April 1493, Alexander formed a defensive league with other city states of Milan, Venice,

Siena and Ferrara. This was to counter the conduct of Ferrante, Alfonso's son, who had commandeered several castles close to Rome. Nevertheless, aware of the growing threat from France, Rodrigo made a pact with Naples in August that year, whereby his youngest son, Jofré, aged twelve, was promised in marriage to Sancha, fifteen, who lay in direct line to the throne of Naples. To complete the trio of marriage alliances, Juan Borgia, his second son, married a young cousin of Fernando the Catholic in Barcelona. Thus Rodrigo, through the arranged marriages of his three adolescent children, strengthened his links with Milan, Naples and Spain. Following in his own footsteps, Rodrigo appointed César, his eldest son, as Cardinal and Bishop of Valencia; the title of cardinal being more political than religious.

The 'apples in the barrel' had continued to bobble around. In November 1494, the people of Florence had risen and expelled the ruling Medici family, promising to support the French king if he overthrew the Pope in Rome. Scenting the victor in the ensuing power struggle, several cardinals had rallied to the French side. By then, the French forces had already crossed the Alps. It was the largest force to do so since the time of the barbarians.

The army comprised over 50,000 men, including several thousand knights in armour, some of it beautifully adorned with gold. A large force of mercenaries from Switzerland and Germany formed the vanguard of the immense force with their phalanxes of heavy pikes. But it was the artillery which drew the gasps of the local population as it was drawn through towns and villages. Of the 140 bronze cannons, roughly a third were siege guns of the largest calibre ever cast. The remaining two-thirds were field guns, mobile and lethal against foot soldiers. The artillery was completed by 200 iron-hooped lombards capable of firing iron balls of eight inches in diameter. It was both a terrifying and yet awesome sight as the cannons rumbled through the towns and villages on their way to Rome. Every community through which the huge force passed prayed that it would continue without stopping. French forces, then and later, fed, watered and lodged themselves 'on the hoof', foraging far and wide to meet their every need.

Charles's army had entered Florence in early November. A week later, out of the blue, the fickle king announced that his main objective was to defeat the Turks and reconquer the Holy Lands. But first he would take Naples! Anxiously, Alexander VI had endeavoured to deflect Charles from his planned invasion of the peninsula by offering a payment on behalf of the Kingdom of Naples as an act of vassalage. But Charles had ignored the overture. On 28 November, his army had left Florence for Rome, which at that time was a city of 80,000 souls. Turning to an avowed foe who also sought stability in the region, the Pope had pleaded with Sultan Bayaceto in Constantinople for 45,000 ducats to oppose the French invasion. The German Emperor,

Maximilian, refused any assistance. From the heights of his squat, round fortress of Sant'Angelo on the right bank of the Tiber, Alexander could see the French horsemen advancing. He knew that Rome could not resist the invasion and ordered the gates of the city to be opened, thereby freeing the citizens of their obligation to defend the city and suffer the pillage which invariably occurred when a city was taken by storm. Unfortunately, it was the French who were besieging it. At the end of December, with the enemy encampment outside the city walls, the Pope received a delegation from the French king at the door of the Sistine Chapel, which had just been redecorated lavishly. Charles's passage through the Papal States could not be opposed by the papal forces. Effectively, they and the Kingdom of Naples were his to do as the French king chose.

Charles VIII entered Rome on 31 December 1494 to popular support and shouts of 'France, France!' He crossed the river into the old city and set up court in the Palace of St Mark's. Rodrigo stayed on the right bank of the river in the Vatican Palace alongside St Peter's Basilica. Eight cardinals went over to the French side. Already French soldiers were on the loose, with houses being broken into, sacked and pillaged, and with women being raped. Those inhabitants who resisted were killed. For two weeks, the soldiers continued their rampage through the old city, committing every sort of atrocity and violation. Finally, a pact was agreed which gave the French forces unmolested passage through the Papal States, with the Church paying for their costly provisioning. Stripped of his authority, Rodrigo Borgia was forced to concede César as hostage of the French king. In exchange, Charles would display an act of obedience to the Pope and would leave unmolested the latter's fortress of Sant'Angelo. As if forgotten in these machinations, no mention was made of Naples, the original target of the French invasion. On 19 January 1495, a special mass was held in the Vatican, which was connected to the Pope's Sant'Angelo fortress by a secret underground passage. Three times, Charles genuflected in front of the Pope, kissing his hands and feet. The authority of the Pope was intact. Then, with honours even, the French army departed for Naples. But the citizens of Rome have never forgotten the twenty-seven days in 1495 when their city was ransacked by the French.

Soon afterwards, Antonio de Fonseca, an envoy from Spain – whose brother, Archdeacon Rodríguez, was soon to play a dominant role in the Indies – met Charles to assert that the French had violated the Treaty of Barcelona, which had been signed specifically by the sovereigns of Spain and France two years before to protect the Kingdom of Naples from external interference. Consequently, Charles was informed very forcibly that Spain would be obliged to organise international resistance against the Kingdom of France. Fifteen years of turmoil were thus precipitated.

X: *Don Gonzalo Fernández of Córdoba*

February 1495

Don Gonzalo Fernández of Córdoba was Spain's greatest military commander. He was born in 1453 – the year which saw the fall of Constantinople to the Turks – and two years after the birth of Isabel of Castile, whom he served with devotion throughout his life. His father was lord of Montilla and of many estates around. The town of Montilla lay thirty miles south of Córdoba, and it was crowned by a beautiful hilltop castle, which was said to rival Ávila in its magnificence. Eighteen months after Gonzalo was born, his father died in a riding accident and his elder brother Alonso inherited the title and all the lands. Consequently, as the younger son, Gonzalo was obliged to make his own way in the world and seek his own fame and fortune.

At the age of thirteen, he became a page in the court of King Alfonso. Alfonso died two years later and his sister, sixteen-year-old Isabel, after fighting off the challenge of Juana 'La Beltraneja', assumed the throne. Gonzalo, then fifteen, was good-looking, eloquent, tall and of fine physique. He beat all the other youths at court in tournaments on horse and foot, as well as in competitions for throwing javelins and spears. He was generous beyond his means. He rode the best horses, wore the finest armour and kept a fine table.

Pages at court learnt from their squires how to ride and care for their mounts. They served food at mealtimes, prepared the sleeping draughts of spiced claret for their masters, and slept in their chambers. Pages learnt to wrestle, how to hone swords, burnish armour and oil leather cuirasses. Not least, they were initiated in the three mysteries of religion, war and love. Gonzalo's sponsor and friend was Martín of Alarcón, who was ten years his senior. They remained close friends throughout their lives.

After pages had demonstrated their prowess and valour in jousting, they reached knighthood, with its tradition of confession and night-long vigils in full armour. This medieval tradition was abolished by a peeved Isabel soon after Gonzalo's initiation; after all, why should she of all people be excluded from these time-honoured secret rites by virtue of her sex?

At the age of twenty, Gonzalo left the court following rumours that his relationship with Isabel was more than it seemed; their closeness was apparent to all. Whatever the truth in these rumours, he remained her loyal servant until her death. Three years later he married his cousin, Isabel de Sotomayor, and received a large estate plus 100,000 ducats from his brother Alonso. Widowed eleven years later without an heir, he married Doña María Manrique. She brought Gonzalo a considerable fortune and remained loyal to him throughout her life, despite their many years of separation. Elvira was his favourite of three daughters.

At the age of thirty, fluent in Arabic and with an estate near Córdoba, he was ideally placed to take a key role in the war to oust the Muslims from their kingdom of al-Andalus, then reduced to the regions of Granada, Málaga and Almería. Battles raged to east and west as the Christians, better equipped, better led and possessing the latest siege guns from Italy, drove the Moors back towards their fabulous city of Granada. In many of the ensuing battles, at Loja, Halava and Illora, Gonzalo led the assaults fearlessly with sword or lance or by being first to scale the fortifications. Yet he was more than a military leader. In the lulls between the battles which ebbed and flowed across the land, Gonzalo developed a close liaison with the sultan Boabdil. A mutual respect developed between them and this facilitated terms being mutually agreed for the surrender of Granada to Fernando and Isabel in January 1492.

The Spanish levies who fought the war were the stuff by which empires are forged. Coming from Castile, Aragón and Galicia in the north of Spain, the soldiers were tough, rough and proud. Washing was to be avoided, to the extent that Spanish men and women, even of noble birth, often took oaths of not washing or changing their clothes until a vow had been fulfilled. Isabel's personal vow was winning the Granada war. Her shift remained unwashed for over a year, and its musty shade of horn was adopted as a fashion in court.

Manuel and Pedro arrived in Granada to meet Don Gonzalo after a freezing journey of several days which skirted the rugged and snowbound, 5,000-foot mountains which hemmed in Granada to the east. Abel accompanied them, as much for old times' sake as to provide companionship to Pedro on the return journey. Don Gonzalo had moved from his castle home in Loja, thirty miles west of Granada, and was staying in his recently acquired house in Granada while enrolling officers and men for his expedition. It was to there that Manuel led the two men from Xiquena.

Pedro and Gonzalo shook hands warmly when Pedro entered his study, which had a fire burning brightly in the hearth. The two were of equal height. Now in his early forties, the elder man was still slim and agile, with his welcoming handshake giving testimony to his physical strength. Don Gonzalo had brown hair, cut shorter than was the custom, and finely etched features. He was wearing a thick scarlet doublet and a heavy woollen cloak with a fur collar and fur edges. It was fastened across his chest with a gold chain. The walls of the room were covered in maps, and a stand in one corner held Gonzalo's gold-rimmed steel helmet and his equally adorned half-suit of armour. His desk was well ordered, as befitted the man, but correspondence bearing the royal seal and several thick ledgers left little working space on it. His beautiful sword[1] lay across the front of his desk. The round boss at the end of the hilt was covered in gold and engraved with his family crest, while the forward-curving cross guard and strengthening loop were adorned with gold filigree. The blade itself was also engraved along the central furrow. It was indeed a superb piece of craftsmanship.

'It's lovely to see you again, Pedro. It can't be much more than a year since your wedding – on an equally snowy day, if I recall! And how is your beautiful Raquel, and your mother Miriam... and how has she settled down with Agustín?'

The questions were endless as the two caught up with the news. Don Gonzalo was at his charming best, and although Pedro was still in awe of him – as well he should be – he soon relaxed in his company.

'And this is Abel Jiménez, if I'm not right? How are you, my man?' They shook hands vigorously. 'You've taken up service with Captain López, I understand. Couldn't be with a better man. You know, Abel, if you hadn't tipped me off all those years ago that this young whippersnapper was in the dungeons of the Inquisition in Jaén, he'd probably still be there now – and certainly not here as a knight of the realm!' He paused, beaming, as Abel bowed.

'Well now, Pedro, I'm sure you're wondering why I asked you to come and see me,' Gonzalo continued.

'Yes sir, I am,' replied Pedro as he took a chair by the fire. A cut-glass decanter of fine wine and some glasses had been placed on a low table which held a plate of sweetmeats. Manuel and Abel had departed, leaving the two on their own.

'As I expect you know,' continued Gonzalo, now very serious and in military mode, 'Charles VIII of France has led an army into Italy with the purpose of taking the Kingdom of Naples. I understand that he's already reached Rome and caused wanton damage there. Charles claims hereditary right to Naples. Although it's strictly a fiefdom of the Vatican and under the Pope's protection, the historical rights to Naples lie with King Fernando, since Naples and Sicily, as well as Sardinia and Corsica at one time, have been part of the Kingdom of Aragón for centuries. It was Fernando's grandfather who foolishly ceded them to one of his sons, Alfonso. I've just heard that Alfonso died last month, and has been succeeded by his son, Ferrante, who's therefore Fernando's cousin.

---

[1] To be seen in the armoury of the Royal Palace in Madrid.

When twenty-five-year-old Charles set off last year, knowing that Alfonso's health was failing fast, he must have thought it was a perfect opportunity to take the kingdom for himself.'

'And you've been charged with stopping him?'

'Yes… King Fernando has ambitions to regain Naples for Aragón and he's asked me to lead a Spanish force to expel the French. My good friend Martín of Alarcón would have been Fernando's first choice, but Martín is a little old for the enterprise and, in any case, has not been too well recently. So I've been honoured by being asked to lead the force.'

'That's indeed an honour, sir,' commented Pedro.

In fact, there were many other great commanders in Spain beside Martín of Alarcón who could have been chosen to lead the campaign to Italy, including Gonzalo's elder brother, Alonso of Aguilar, as well as the Duke of Medina Sidonia, who did as much as anyone to win the war against the Nazarí. So why was Gonzalo chosen? The man appointed had to be more than a good commander. He had to be an able negotiator, a linguist and an intelligent man capable of quickly deciphering secret codes which were the means by which communications to foreign lands was conducted. But above all he had to be an elegant courtier who could mix comfortably with kings, princes and popes alike. The man wisely chosen by the Catholic Monarchs for this difficult and challenging role was Don Gonzalo Fernández.

'You're wondering why you're here, Pedro? I can tell from the perplexed look on your face. Or maybe it's the warm room and the wine!'

Pedro grinned sheepishly.

'Many of my former officers have volunteered to join me, and several hundred veterans of the Granada war have already signed up. And very eagerly, I might say. But I need someone to serve as my aide-de-camp during the campaign. Not to be involved in the fighting, but to act as my personal assistant.'

'But what would I do as your… "aide-de-camp"?' Pedro stammered over an expression he had never heard before.

'In effect, you'd be my secretary. You'd keep a detailed diary of the day's events; liaise with my comptroller, who looks after all the money matters, and with my quartermaster, who is responsible for food and forage, for arms and armaments and for uniforms bought and issued, as well as houses and farms commandeered for billeting – but for which, incidentally, we must pay a just rent.' Gonzalo sniffed.

'In wartime, I cannot keep tabs on all the things going on around me and I need someone reliable to act as my eyes and ears and help keep the machinery of my command running smoothly. Also, I'd need you to prepare letters – in strict confidence, you understand, and often in code – to King Fernando, Pope

Alexander, Ferrante and the French king and his commanders, and sometimes to deliver them under a white flag of truce.'

'All these things and many more, Pedro,' continued Gonzalo, 'require someone who I know well and have complete faith in to perform the tasks needed and, most importantly, to hold my confidence. In any army, you know, rumours spread like wildfire. Even calling an officer into my tent for a discussion can set off a spate of rumours which sweep through the ranks like a contagion and can travel across to enemy lines. I want someone close to me, someone who is always at hand and whom I can talk to in private and in confidence. I can think of nobody better to serve me than you.'

Pedro sat there with his mouth agape. The colour had drained from his face. He could not take it all in. Aide-de-camp... comptrollers... quartermasters... letters to Fernando and the French king... flags of truce... to be his eyes and ears... in strict confidence... *in strict confidence*. The words reverberated around his head.

Gonzalo rocked back on his chair and roared with laughter.

'I'm sorry, my boy, I do come over a bit strong at times! I'm sure it all sounds a monumental task I'm asking you to take on. But I wouldn't have asked you here if I didn't think you were the man for the job. In fact, I can think of nobody better.'

'But what about my work in Fez – and Raquel, and my two children?'

'I've spoken to the King. Your posting to Fez is coming to an end, as you yourself must suspect. The King is delighted with what you have done in Morocco and he's fully behind you joining me. As for Raquel and your young family, I understand your anxieties, but when service to one's country is concerned one has to make sacrifices, and being away from home for months or years on end is one of them. During the Granada war, I hardly saw my wife and daughters from one year to another. Think about the seafarers on long voyages and Christopher Columbus on his voyages to the Indies! Long family separations are unavoidable, and our womenfolk understand and accept this, as I am sure will Raquel. After all, she's in good hands at Xiquena, with a loving family around her. In any case, Pedro, you will not be in any *physical* danger. You will be no use to me dead or incapacitated through injury.'

Pedro simply did not know what to say. His mind was still in a whirl.

'You're staying in the city overnight, Pedro. Think on what I've said and talk it over with Abel and Manuel. They're military men and can explain more fully what I have been telling you. But think positively about the opportunities you'll have to see the world and the exciting times we'll have together. And remember, you're a knight of the realm and such service is expected of you. It was not for nothing that the King and Queen conferred this title on you.' He paused and looked the young man in the eye. 'Come back and see me tomorrow, Pedro. You're the man for the job and I'd love to have you with me.'

Pedro returned the next morning after a restless night and long hours spent talking with Manuel and Abel. They opened his eyes to the rigour and hardship of camp life but also the glory and exaltation of successful campaigns. Their eyes sparkled as they narrated their experiences, and it was this more than anything which made up Pedro's mind.

'Yes,' he said to Don Gonzalo, 'I will join you in Italy, and I'm flattered and honoured that you consider me worthy to be your aide-de-camp. I will serve you loyally and to the best of my ability.'

Don Gonzalo clapped him on the shoulder.

'I knew you wouldn't let me down, Pedro. And rest assured your wife will understand. My expeditionary force will be assembling in Málaga during April, and we will depart as soon as there's a fair wind. Meet me there.'

Pedro need not have worried about Raquel's reaction. Manuel Manzano had taken Agustín, Miriam and Raquel to one side when he had called at Xiquena the week before and acquainted them of the reason for Pedro's journey to Granada. They had little doubt that he would respond to the call of duty. After all, Gonzalo had become like a father to him.

XI: *The First Italian Campaign*

March 1495

With the rupture in relations with France and hostilities threatening in Italy, contracts were signed in Brussels by the Count of Nassau on behalf of Emperor Maximilian and by Francisco de Rojas on behalf of Spain, for the double marriage of Prince Juan, heir to the joint kingdoms of Castile and Aragón, with Princess Margaret of Austria, Maximilian's daughter. Also arranged was the marriage of Philip, Archduke of Austria, elder brother of Margaret, with Princess Juana. Neither bride was to be dowried. Juana was just sixteen and her brother a year more. The dual wedding fitted Fernando and Isabel's strategy of linking their kingdoms with other royal houses through marriage, and it followed the wedding in 1490 of Isabel – their eldest child, aged twenty – with Prince Alfonso of Portugal, five years her junior. Tragically, just seven months afterwards Alfonso died in a riding accident after being dragged along by his horse.

Spain's link with the House of Austria through the marriage of Juana and Philip would have ramifications for the whole of Europe for centuries to come.

Pedro reached Málaga towards the end of the month. He hardly recognised the city. He had been there eight years before, not long after the city had been sacked by Fernando's army. Then, Fernando had assembled an enormous force of 12,000 horseman and 50,000 soldiers outside the walls of the *alcazaba* and immediately had sealed off the busy port. Then his cannons set about destroying the walls, but the besieged Muslims had held out. By August, 20,000 citizens had died of disease and starvation. When finally the Christians had entered the city, Fernando wreaked a fearful retribution. The 15,000 inhabitants who were left alive were sold for 56 million *maravedís*, either into slavery or prostitution. The city was ransacked and left in ruins. If Fernando had meant this as a warning to the Nazarí kingdom that he would not be defied, he was successful. Never again did the Muslim towns or cities risk such a calamity. Guadix, Baza, Vélez Blanco and its surrounding communities, Almería and finally Granada, all sought a negotiated surrender, although they had precious little leverage in negotiating surrender terms.

But now, in March 1495, Málaga was alive with excited soldiers, all rising to the call for new military adventures in a distant land. They would get fed, armed and armoured. They would get paid – if they were lucky – and could look forward to rich pickings of booty, which was the norm in warfare. They knew this for certain, since they were responding to the call of their illustrious leader from the Granada war, Don Gonzalo Fernández of Córdoba, who was already a legend across the land. The soldiers were a mixed bunch, hailing from all parts of the peninsula, speaking Basque, Galician and Catalan as well as different dialects of Castilian. They roamed the streets of Málaga, sometimes armed, sometimes not, sometimes in armour and sometimes not. All were in high spirits and looking for merriment if not mischief.

The giant Matute was accompanying Pedro. Abel had declined Gonzalo's invitation to join him for the campaign, but Matute, unmarried and bored with being gatekeeper in a small, out of the way castle, had volunteered for action with alacrity. Raquel had resigned herself to losing Pedro for a lengthy period, so she was greatly relieved that the big man would be alongside her husband to keep him out of harm's way.

The two made their way through the boisterous streets from the port. They had arrived by boat from Aguilas and had left their war chests on board while they located Don Gonzalo's headquarters. Above them on their right were the partly rebuilt walls of the Moorish alcazaba rising sharply up each side of a steep ridge to the Castillo de Gibralfaro on the summit. Protected by this fortification, the port lay directly below. Started by the Phoenicians and later strengthened by the Romans, the anchorage was protected from fierce easterly winds by a breakwater which angled out for some distance from the waterside quay and by a smaller breakwater some hundreds of yards to the west. All sorts of craft were anchored within their protective arms, with boats being loaded or unloaded along the waterside quay or while at anchor. Single-masted, broad-beamed cargo boats and shallow-drafted Arab dhows with their lateen sails predominated, but among them, anchored some way out, were a couple of mighty Portuguese carracks, the latest and biggest naval ships then afloat, and closer inshore dozens or so of smaller caravels. Copied by the Spanish from the Portuguese, these sturdy and manoeuvrable ships were already transporting men and supplies back and forth to the Indies. They were Columbus's favourite vessel.

Soldiers milled around. They were bemused by Pedro's fresh, unscarred face and by the immense man with fair hair who accompanied him. The two had not gone far when shouts and cries of pain drew them to a crowd gathered in a circle around a ruckus. Two men, one of Pedro's height but more like a gorilla than a man, with great long arms and a huge barrel chest, and another, dwarfed and deformed, were setting about a youthful soldier with their boots and mailed fists, with the bigger man threatening to plunge his sword into the soldier's throat. The well-dressed youngster, wearing beautifully polished body armour and greaves protecting his shins, lay on the ground, his helmet being tossed around mockingly by the crowd.

'So you thinks you're a real soldier in all that tin plate, does you?' the bigger man scoffed. 'So let's see what you're made of!' he roared, as he and the dwarf kicked him fiercely in the lower back. The young soldier was already bleeding from his nose and had an open wound on his head. He was clearly in a bad way.

'Gonzalo wants real soldiers, not dandies all dressed up like peacocks!' the gorilla roared. The boots went in again.

Pedro was unarmed, but Matute, as ever, carried his long ash staff as thick as his wrist. Pedro had never lacked courage and the two burst through the baying crowd.

'What Don Gonzalo doesn't want in his army are ruffians like you!' Pedro shouted. 'Stand aside!' he ordered.

The bigger of the two ruffians turned from his vicious assault, looked at Pedro through a mass of matted black hair and roared with laughter.

'So you thinks you can stop me putting this pansy out of his misery, does you? Ho, ho!'

He stepped forward towards Pedro, his sword pointing at the knight's chest. 'So let's be having you,' he leered, beckoning Pedro forward with his other hand.

Pedro wavered.

'Huh! I can see you're no better than this little toad,' he mocked.

He turned and flicked his sword disdainfully at the young soldier, who was rising slowly to his feet.

Matute pulled Pedro aside. 'This is my b-b... b-business, Pedro. Leave this th-th-thug to me.'

'Can't talk proper, then?' mocked the ruffian. 'Can only talk like a little boy, can we! I'll soon make you wish you was still playing with your toy soldiers!'

The bully stepped forward towards Mat, the grin on his face being replaced by a leer. He threw aside his sword.

'I doesn't need that to deal with the likes of you.' He crouched forward. 'So make your play, big man.'

Mat was in a quandary as to whether to also lay down his weapon, and in that split second of uncertainty the man was upon him. He brushed aside Mat's staff as if it was a straw and grabbed him around his midriff in a fearsome bear hug, his long arms encircling the giant, forcing his chin back with the top of his head. The ruffian flexed his gorilla-like arms, squeezing the breath out of Pedro's friend. Mat's face reddened as he gasped for breath and as he tried to break the vicelike grip in which he was held. Mat felt his strength ebbing from him, but he had one overwhelming advantage – his height. Mat fell backwards, at the same time kicking the legs of the bully off the ground. As he fell, he used his momentum to toss the man over his head with his knees. The bully was forced to let go his grip and landed with a ground-shaking thud in the dust behind Mat, who was upon him in an instant. There could be only one winner now. Mat pinned him around the neck with his left hand, and with one jawbreaking blow of his right fist knocked him senseless. Cowering backwards, the dwarf turned and disappeared through the crowd.

Eventually, the big ruffian lifted himself stiffly onto his elbow and held his jaw. He scowled at Mat but could find no words. Pedro confiscated his sword and retrieved the young soldier's helmet from a bystander who, with a whimper, muttered, 'It wasn't me, honest.'

Mat stepped forward with fists still clenched and straddled the ruffian, who remained on the ground. He looked down at the man from his six-and-a-half feet, his stutter disappearing as always when he was aroused.

'If you think that you're going to join Don Gonzalo's expedition to Italy, you're very much mistaken. You're the last person he'd want in his army. We're on our way to see the great man now. But if I see you around here again or trying to board ship, I'll see to it that you're flogged to within an inch of your life!'

Mat continued to glare at the man for a few moments. Then he gathered up Pedro and the young soldier and left. The crowd parted like the Red Sea in the time of Moses and let them through.

'It's good to see you, Pedro,' said a welcoming Don Gonzalo when they reached his headquarters on the hilltop of Guadalfaro. 'You've arrived at an ideal time,' he continued in a businesslike way. 'I need your assistance in getting this embarkation underway. There's so much to do.' He paused. 'And who's this with you?'

'This is Matute. He's an ex-soldier and works with Abel at Xiquena. Agustín retained them both after the Granada war was over. Abel wasn't able to join you, but Mat's volunteered instead.'

'Well, welcome, Mat. By the look of it, you'll be worth two soldiers. But judging by the marks on your face, it looks as though you've already been in the wars!'

Pedro explained what had happened.

'Hmm,' pondered Don Gonzalo. 'That's interesting. You might be just the man I'm looking for, Mat, since I need someone to lead the camp guard; basically to keep the peace inside the camp – and that applies to Málaga, here and now, before we sail. Soldiers can be very undisciplined when waiting for action, and this leads to trouble. So how would you like to be Sergeant of the Camp Guard? You'll need three or four others to help you...'

'Y-y-yes sir,' Mat replied, his stammer returning. 'I'd l-l-like that—'

'That's good,' interrupted Don Gonzalo. 'You'll need a distinctive uniform and must be suitably armed. Pikes would be best. How about a scarlet jerkin over your mail shirt, plus a distinctive badge of authority? What did you say was the name of the young soldier you saved from that beating?'

'I think he said his name was Rodrigo... Rodrigo of Olvera.'

'Ah!' he exclaimed. 'That name sounds familiar! If I'm not mistaken, he's the grandson of the Marqués of Cádiz, who fought alongside me in the Granada war. He died soon after. He was a great man. Find the lad. Bring him to me. We'll see if he'd like to join your guard, or even be my standard-bearer. At least then we can keep an eye on him!'

Leaving Rome early in January 1495, Charles VIII of France's army of 40,000 had marched for Naples in two columns. One column marched along the coast and the other had taken a route through the mountains. On 22 February, after seven long months on the road, the French reached their goal, Naples. At the sight of the enemy making camp near his city, King Alfonso hastily heaped six galleys with treasure and sailed for Sicily to take refuge there. Alfonso had inherited the throne of Naples from his father, Ferrante, the previous year but his reign would be very short-lived. His son, also called Ferrante, had made some attempts to rouse the citizens and nobles to defend Naples, but he only encountered apathy, hostility and treachery. For the French army, their invasion of Italy had been roses all the way; no battles, no opposition, no problem.

With the French just days away from the city, the young Ferrante joined his ageing father in Sicily. They sent an urgent appeal to Fernando in Spain. 'The Kingdom of Naples would be irrevocably lost to the house of Aragón,' they pleaded, 'unless a Spanish army under an outstanding general were despatched without delay to lead an offensive to oust the French from Calabria and southern Italy.' Don Gonzalo Fernández of Córdoba's hour of greatness was nigh.

But Charles's day of reckoning had duly arrived. With Spain, Venice, the Papal States and Maximilian's Holy Roman Empire now united after signing the Treaty of Venice in March 1495, Charles was forced to withdraw from the peninsula. The promulgation of the Holy League was received with jubilation in Italy, with poets composing rhymes of eulogy to the Pope and with fiestas being held to celebrate the spirit of liberation. But it would prove to be a bit premature.

The Spanish armada of thirty ships set sail from Málaga at the end of April, having waited two weeks for a favourable westerly wind. Some 2,100 veterans of the Granada campaign were abroad. After some stormy weather, the sea calmed, and in bright warm weather the ships arrived at Messina in Sicily. This faced Italy six miles away across the straits. Pedro joined Gonzalo and his staff in going ashore to meet the King of Naples. Gonzalo's men grumbled at not being allowed ashore, but the next afternoon they sailed again across the narrow straits, landing at Reggio on the Italian mainland.

Charles abandoned Naples on 20 May. Leaving half his French soldiers to garrison towns and cities in the Kingdom of Naples, the remainder headed northwards. They made for a sorry sight as they headed back through Italy, ill and wretched after months of self-indulgence in one of Europe's most seductive cities. Charles swore to return, but like Princess Isabel's late husband, Prince Alfonso of Portugal, he later died after a riding accident.

The effects of his invasion of Italy were disastrous, both militarily and morally. From then on, Italy would become a battlefield for foreign kings with more money than sense.

Gonzalo's picked contingent landed at Reggio on the very toe of Italy just four days after Charles began his retreat. With the abdication of Alfonso through abject terror, his son Ferrante took command of the Neapolitan forces. But they and the contingents from Sicily and the surrounding province of Calabria, plus others belonging to the Papal States, lacked military training. They were disorderly, badly organised and had little experience of combat. Yet they had one advantage over Gonzalo's troops: they were much better paid. King Fernando, parsimonious by nature, expected his expeditionary force to live off the land. Alongside the inferior but better paid Neapolitan men, the Spaniards might well have felt aggrieved, with open mutiny threatening. However, always mindful of his soldiers' welfare, Gonzalo endeavoured to supply from his own pocket what Fernando withheld. This was a burden he would shoulder without complaint throughout his campaigns in Italy.

So, with the hasty departure of Charles and half his army, Gonzalo immediately set about clearing the surrounding villages of the garrisons they left behind. He then occupied from the sea three small ports around the toe of Italy which had been made over to the Spanish by Ferrante as a guarantee for their war expenses. The inhabitants of each of these towns celebrated the arrival of the Spaniards by dancing the vigorous *tarantella*, which Juana and her brother had displayed so expertly at Tordesillas the year before. Later, the Spanish soldiers would return to their homeland with sterling memories of the hot-blooded Italian girls, the *tarantella* dance and gold necklaces fashioned locally from the proceeds of their booty. Then, accompanied by 6,000 Neapolitan soldiers under the command of King Ferrante, Gonzalo marched inland through wooded hills to Seminara, some twenty miles north of Reggio.

By now, Pedro and Matute had settled into camp life, although Pedro did not see much of Mat, who revelled in his role of keeping order in the camp. He spent most of the day meeting and talking with the soldiers and eating with them in the evening around their campfires. 'Be seen' was his motto, and it paid dividends. His authority was never challenged.

Pedro took up the story of the campaign in his first proper letter to Raquel.

My dear Raquel,

Although I've sent you a few short letters to let you know how things are progressing, this is the first opportunity I've had to sit down and give you a proper account of our progress here and what my duties are as Don Gonzalo's aide-de-camp. Mat sends his love. I think he's enjoying every minute of his time here. Nobody's got a bad word to say for him and DGF (Don Gonzalo Fernández) loves him for the quiet way he goes around his business. In fact, Mat has found a lady friend in Reggio who I met the other week. She's a widow named Francesca and he tells me that she hails from Tuscany, from a small village in the mountains north of Florence. She's in her mid-twenties. She was told that her husband died earlier this year in Rome during the terrible happenings there when the French ransacked the city. They never found his body and one supposes his body was thrown into the Tiber, as were thousands. Terrible. Wherever the French go, there is unrest and blood-shed. But Francesca is delightful, and Mat is really taken with her. She's hot-blooded, dark and sultry like you, with a figure to match! Her home's now in Naples but she's here in Reggio looking after an aunt. Mat and his Camp Guard have taken to patrolling the streets of Reggio where he met her, so he gets to see her often. He can't wait to don his best clothes and 'head for town'. Camp followers aren't allowed in the camp, it's one of DGF's strict rules, so consequently many soldiers have found welcoming arms in the town. There are so many young women there who have lost their menfolk. But I suppose it's the same every-where where there's warfare.

You remember I mentioned in a note before we left Málaga a young soldier called Rodrigo of Olvera, who Mat rescued from some ruffians the day we arrived there? Well, DGF has taken him on his staff as his personal armourer. He's responsible for looking after his armour, but really I think DGF took a liking to the youngster and feels obliged to take care of him out of a sense of duty to his old friend, the Marqués of Cádiz. Rodrigo is a nice young fellow and we see a lot of each other in camp.

We eat very well, and I share Don Gonzalo's table for the evening meal in his pavilion, together with a selection of captains who he invites. It's obviously quite a perk for them, so I suppose I'm fortunate to be there each day. The soldiers' main meal is in the cool of the evening and it's largely the same every day. I'm told that it's the same the Roman soldiers ate, and it didn't seem to do them too much harm! It comprises onions, garlic, cucumbers and chillis chopped very finely, mixed with breadcrumbs, vinegar and water, and cooked all together in olive oil.[1] It's very tasty and also nutritious. When they can, they supplement this with what meat they can find – rabbits, hares and occasionally mutton from the market. We eat much the same in the pavilion, but it can be augmented by the odd partridge, chicken, duck or fresh fish, which DGF is particularly partial to. Most of the men carry a small leather wine bottle which they are allowed to top up each day, and camp

---

[1] Much like the popular dish *migas*, which is served in bars and restaurants in southern Spain today.

boys carry water skins around the camp throughout the day. There's a lot of joviality in the camp and the soldiers like nothing better than a sing-song and listening to ballads composed by one or other of them. Needless to say, swearing is prodigious, with the gesture of insolence used here being an arm raised with the thumb between the first and second fingers.

As I said last time, I am privileged to have a folding bed in the corner of DGF's large pavilion, which is in the centre of the encampment. It is very much the hub of the place. The men sleep in tents which are arranged in orderly lines, much as I observed at the Gozco encampment in the months before the fall of Granada. Then there were 50,000 soldiers, while here there are only some 2,000, although our numbers will rise when reinforcements arrive from Spain soon. DGF keeps me very busy, talking over ideas for the battles which lie ahead and the assaults he plans on the fortresses the French still hold. Of course, I do not dare proffer advice to the great man, but I think it helps clear his thoughts to talk to someone aloud before consulting more formally with his senior captains. I am responsible for keeping a daily log of progress of the campaign, and I liaise daily with the quartermaster, Rodriguez Ruiz, the comptroller, Perez Montoya, and Juan de Herrera, the land agent. He has the difficult task of smoothing over the problems which inevitably arise with the local town officials and villagers who we are freeing from the French invaders. DGF places much store in maintaining harmonious relations with the locals, but it's not easy; they are very emotional and, freed now of the French yoke, they are becoming very demanding.

DGF looks on me as his eyes and ears to forewarn him of matters which will need addressing, and for this Mat is very useful to me. DGF also dictates letters to King Fernando and Queen Isabel in Spain, which I prepare and he then signs, although he is writing fewer letters to them now since I think he is exasperated by the fickleness of the King.

I continue to have French lessons with Pierre d'Orléans, who is on DGF's staff here, and he says my French is now very good. But Don Gonzalo is amazing. He speaks fluent Arabic – although he says mine is more useful, being more colloquial – excellent French, and now can converse comfortably with King Ferrante and his officers in Italian! What a man he is! I can see why Isabel and Fernando selected him for this campaign.

Now to business. Our first battle proper at Seminara went badly. Seminara is only twenty miles north of our encampment here at Reggio. DGF is furious and wonders what the reaction in Spain will be to the news of the engagement. The French commander, Everard Stuart or Sire d'Aubigny, is a descendent of the Scottish House of Lennox, and mustered his garrison for an attack on our position. The young King Ferrante of Naples, who I like a lot, and his soldiers from the region around here are very impetuous and did not heed Gonzalo's warnings. DGF favoured a tactical retreat to the port of Tropea close by, but Ferrante marched out of Seminara with his men to confront the larger French force three miles outside the town. Our Spanish men feigned a withdrawal, a tactic they learnt from your Moorish soldiers in the Granada campaigns; but the Calabrians, misinterpreting our manoeuvre, sped from the battlefield, leaving some of their number encircled by the French. Fortunately, d'Aubigny, the French general, was a sick man and ordered camp to be pitched. Consequently, his forces failed to pursue King Ferrante's men. In a bid to salvage something from the debacle, DGF mounted his horse in full armour and charged the enemy at the head of our men and managed to extricate the surrounded Neapolitans. We had no other option than to march back here to Reggio. On the same day, can you *believe, King Ferrante sailed to Sicily and then onwards to Naples with a favourable breeze, where, we learnt subsequently, he arrived ahead of the news of his defeat at Seminara! Boosted by the return of their king, the inhabitants of Naples overwhelmed the small French garrison stationed there and threw open the city gates to welcome their kinsmen. So, incredibly, the impetuosity which lost Ferrante the battle of Seminara won him back Naples!*

Meanwhile, we have continued to subdue the weak French garrisons in the toe of Italy, although DGF learnt from a despatch rider the other day that during July in the north of Italy the mischievous French king, who has caused all this mayhem, fought his way past the forces of the confederation of city states at Fornovo and managed to escape to France. Good riddance, I say! Let's hope he doesn't come back!

Don Gonzalo dictated to me a letter to King Fernando and Queen Isabel describing how the battle at Seminara had been lost. He's not impressed by Ferrante. In his letter, he wrote that Ferrante wasn't the kind of leader he expected from the information he'd received before coming here. If Ferrante determines something, he insists that that course is best. Often he will make a decision and later change it, though it be good and sensible. The result is that he is almost always 'off target'.

DGF knew that the German and Swiss pike men were fighting alongside the French, but he did not know how our light infantry, the jinetes, *who are fast and mobile and use tactics adopted from your people during the Granada war, would fare against these heavily armed mercenaries. Many of our Spanish captains longed to show what they could do on the battlefield, but while they performed magnificently at Seminara, Ferrante's Neapolitan troops failed to understand our mode of charging, feinting and tactical manoeuvring, and took to their heels with the French cavalry in hot pursuit. As it was, Ferrante fell from his horse with his feet caught in his stirrups and was only saved from being captured by the French through some quick thinking of one of his officers! I'm sure half of the cavalry die from falling off their horses, and not from lances and sabres! But it has been a totally new experience for DGF to taste defeat. Added to his chagrin is the thought of how the defeat at Seminara will be received in Spain after this, our first foray in Italy.*

Well, my love, it's gone midnight, but my lord and master wants to confer with me so I must stop. There's a boat leaving Tropea tomorrow, so I can despatch this letter then. Please give lots of hugs and kisses to Sara and Antonio, who I miss terribly, and my love and best wishes to Mama and Agustín, as well as your mother and Uncle Joshua. I think about you all every day.

Your loving Pedro,

Reggio, September 1495

PS Don Gonzalo sends his greetings. Mat has just popped into the pavilion and sends his love. He's just been into town to meet Francesca and he's full of the joys of spring!

Ferrante's departure for Sicily left Gonzalo in sole charge. The Italians under his command desperately needed training and better discipline before anything could be expected of them. So, while overwintering in Reggio and waiting for more soldiers, clothing and supplies to arrive from Spain, Gonzalo drilled his Italian troops into better shape and trained them in guerrilla warfare, integrating them as best he could with his Spanish veterans. The spring offensive beckoned.

XII: A Royal Invitation

Things were starting to unravel for Christopher Columbus in the Caribbean. In April 1495, a decree was published in Madrid which invited Spaniards to equip expeditions to discover more islands in the Indies or *tierra firme* bordering the Ocean Sea. Clear rules were laid down. These were designed to protect the interests of the Crown as well as those of Columbus. For this reason, La Española was excluded from this decree. It stipulated that such explorers had to be known to the royal couple and receive from them a mandate for the expedition; all boats had to leave from Cádiz and be registered there; those who emigrated to the Indies at their own expense would receive free supplies from Spain for a year and be permitted to retain a third of the gold they discovered, with the other two-thirds going the Crown; the Crown would also receive one-tenth of the value of all other commodities produced; in addition, one-tenth of the cargo of boats going to La Española must be set aside for the use of the Crown, and one eighth for Columbus.

The royal declaration put an end to Columbus's monopoly. By then – month in, month out – flotillas of caravels were transporting men and goods back and forth to La Española and Cuba. As a matter of priority, Isabel and Fernando had to reassert their authority, since they were losing control of their new empire and losing much-needed revenue. To address this and to counteract the number of colonists who were returning home disillusioned, the King and Queen chartered a dozen caravels to supply the Indies with provisions and to transport new settlers, but with the proviso that, of the pearls, gold and silver found, one-fifth was to belong to the Crown. Each ship thereafter carried a notary to check on the cargo entering and leaving the Indies. Moreover, all boats were required first to return to La Española, and all ships had to be constructed in Spain. Slowly their controls took hold, establishing a heavy-handed bureaucracy which would continue for centuries.

Soon afterwards in June, as Don Gonzalo was landing on the toe of Italy, the monarchs sent their first reprimand to Columbus, instructing him, on the pain of death, to return to La Española, complaining that he had been absent for too long, sailing hither and thither around the Caribbean. On 5 August, Juan de Aguado, a royal magistrate, sailed from Seville with four ships full of provisions, but with the explicit mission of investigating Columbus's activities. It signified the end of Columbus's dream of his own personal empire. Aguado had with him a series of royal edicts which made clear to the Admiral that his monopolies were limited to La Española, and that the rest of the Indies, including the places that he had himself visited, were now outside his control and would be subject to a different administration. The Crown also demanded that the number of settlers receiving a salary be reduced drastically. Aguado had orders to return home after just a month in the Indies, but this demand was made void when his four ships foundered in a hurricane soon after they arrived at the island.

Convinced that he was surrounded by enemies, the Admiral wrote to the sovereigns in October with a litany of complaints: about Juan de Aguado and his officials, about the priests who were undermining his authority and about the monarchs' evident growing lack of confidence in him. Unknown to him, the court in Spain was abuzz with derision over the Admiral's obstinate conviction that he had reached the 'Indies'.[1] Finally, tired, exhausted and demoralised, after nearly three years in the Caribbean, Columbus decided to return to Spain to defend himself before the monarchs. But it would be six months later, in the following year of 1496, before he would leave La Isabela with two ships constructed in the Indies, carrying thirty slaves and some 200 disillusioned settlers. These included most of Aguado's men. After detouring through some of the smaller islands, he would finally arrive in Cádiz on 11 June, thus bringing to a close his second voyage to the Indies.

So what can be said about Columbus's second voyage to the Caribbean? On the positive side, journeys across the Atlantic had become a matter of routine. La Española and to a lesser extent Cuba were settled, and towns and villages established, as was an efficient bureaucracy to administer the islands. Gold was found in reasonable quantities, although it always would be insufficient for the Catholic Monarchs. On the downside, Columbus failed to discover the mainland of America, being convinced that Cuba was not an island, but an isthmus attached to Asia.[2] By then, others had realised that the natives on the Caribbean islands and their primitive Stone Age culture were hardly in keeping with the sophisticated oriental world of China and Japan, which were then well known from overland travellers and merchants. Consequently, Columbus was becoming a laughing stock in Spain. To compensate for the lack of gold found, Indians were starting to be transported as 'human gold' to Spain, where, as slaves, they were eagerly absorbed into Spanish society.

Amazingly, Raquel received Pedro's letter in October 1495, little more than three weeks after it was despatched on a boat which had been propelled by a fair wind. It arrived in Barcelona within a week. From there, it was carried by a

---

[1] Meaning, of course, his belief that he had reached the East Indies on the coast of Asia.
[2] As shown on his map, used during the Tordesillas negotiations, now on view in the Tordesillas Columbus Museum.

relay of riders the 500 miles to Vélez Rubio, which lay on the main highway to Granada. From there, it was a short distance then to Xiquena. With roads across Spain and Europe being atrocious, couriers carrying the royal mail and using relays of horses could ride some eighty miles in a day if they were lucky. For the ordinary traveller, it was much, much less than this. With communications between the capitals of Europe now an issue of great importance, most monarchies had in place efficient postal systems to service their needs. For Isabel and Fernando, who moved their court continually around their kingdoms, it was a pure necessity.

It was truly a red letter day for Raquel. Not only were her mother, Raghad, and Uncle Joshua down from Vélez Blanco for the day, but Abel and his Mudejar wife, Eva, were also there, helping in the castle with this and that. For all of them, Xiquena was as much their home now as Miriam's, Agustín's and Raquel's. Only Pedro and Mat were missing from the fold. All of them listened intently as Raquel read out Pedro's letter. She missed him terribly but she was very proud of him.

On this very same day, another horseman arrived, leading a mule laden with another consignment of coloured English wool for Miriam, and bearing moneys for her from the Queen as a further instalment for the work being done on the tapestries. Paco, the muleteer, also bore a letter for Raquel.

'Mama!' she exclaimed to Miriam, as Abel helped Paco unload the mule inside the castle gateway. 'I can't believe it! First a letter from Pedro and now Paco's brought a letter to me from Valladolid which bears the royal seal... A royal letter *to me!*' she added breathlessly.

But then Raquel paused. A letter to her from Valladolid, and not to Miriam. Why? She hesitated opening it. The letter must have been despatched after Pedro's letter had been sent from Italy, and must bring some terrible tidings. Miriam and Raghad saw the anxiety in her face, worrying about the contents of the letter from Valladolid. It had to be bad news about Pedro.

'Don't worry, my dear,' encouraged Miriam. 'Pedro's fine. He wrote his letter to you only three weeks ago. He explained quite clearly that for the moment hostilities with the French are over. Mat is there and he'll see that nothing happens to Pedro. In any case, Raquel, Paco the muleteer must have left Valladolid weeks and weeks ago, well before Pedro despatched his letter.'

'I suppose you're right, Mama,' responded Raquel, still reluctant to open the letter.

Miriam loved being called 'Mama'. She considered Raquel as much her daughter as was poor Cristina who, with her father, Abraham, was murdered outside their home by renegade soldiers of the Inquisition. They had been on the prowl 'hunting' for a Jewish apothecary who they believed must have had money and riches stashed away in his house.

'Come on, my dear, open the letter from Valladolid! I can't think why the Queen is writing to you, but it can't be bad news.'

Raquel looked around at the others, who nodded encouragement as she slipped a knife under the wax seal.

'It's not from the Queen, Mama! It's from Doña Ana of Beamonte, the Queen's maid of honour.'

Her relief was evident to all. She read it out aloud, now much calmer, with her voice a tone lower.

'From Doña Ana of Beamonte on behalf of Queen Isabel,

'Royal Palace, Valladolid, August 1495.

'Dear Raquel,

'I hope you remember me from your visit to Tordesillas last year for the signing of the treaties with the Portuguese. It seems such a long time ago. I know that your husband Don Pedro is now in Italy as Don Gonzalo's aide-de-camp, and I trust he is well and enjoying the experience. He cannot be with a finer and more caring general. Queen Isabel is delighted with the progress Señora López and her team of needlewomen are making on the tapestries, and she and the King send their best wishes to her, her husband Agustín and, of course, yourself.'

Raquel scanned the letter quickly, wondering why the Queen's most senior attendant was writing to her personally. Then she continued reading it out loud to her eager audience.

'As I expect you have heard by now, last May in Brussels the betrothals were signed for the marriages of Princess Juana with Archduke Philip of Austria, and her brother Prince Juan with Philip's younger sister, Princess Margaret. The King and Queen are thrilled to establish this link with the House of Austria, and see it as a means of containing French ambitions in central Europe.

'Princess Juana will travel by ship to Flanders, where she will marry Archduke Philip (an overland journey across France is obviously out of the question at the moment). The timing of this has not yet been fixed, since a fleet of ships will need to be chartered and made ready for this long and treacherous voyage across stormy waters. Much planning will be needed and the Queen is deeply engaged in this.

'It is intended that Princess Juana will be accompanied by several ladies from the court to oversee her every need and protect her from the reputed wantonness of the Habsburg court. The Princess and the Queen are drawing up a list of ladies-in-waiting who might make the journey, and they both would be thrilled if you would consider joining the Princess on what will be a wonderful adventure. Juana remembers you with affection from your short stay in Tordesillas last year. The Queen is keen to show the northern court of

Emperor Maximilian that the beauty and elegance of our Spanish ladies are second to none, and none will outshine you in these (indeed, the King still talks about you and how stunning you were in that pale green silk outfit and pink shawl you wore at the banquet at Tordesillas!).

'You would indeed grace the large party which will journey to Brussels, and we hope very much you will agree to accompany Princess Juana. Doing so might help lessen the burden of your separation from your husband, although I do appreciate it will mean a lengthy separation from your two children. I know that this will be a major determining factor in your decision.

'At this stage, all we seek is your response to this invitation (maybe via Paco, the muleteer, who is to set off shortly from Valladolid with more wool for Miriam). If you bless us with your agreement to come, we will inform you later about when you will need to travel north for the embarkation and what you must bring with you, but it is likely not to be before next autumn. At the very least, you will need lots of warm clothes! The winters in Flanders are truly horrible.

'We do hope you will accede to our request.

'With kind regards,

'Ana.'

There was a stunned silence in the great hall when Raquel finished reading out the letter. Typically, Raquel's mother, Raghad, was the first to speak.

'Oh, that's lovely, Raquel!' she cried. 'I'll be able to have Sara and Antonio to look after, all to myself!'

For Raghad, the eight-month-old baby was hers.

Miriam scowled at her. They were her grandchildren, too. 'Yes, Raghad. You must come and live here while Raquel is gone, then we can all look after the little dears,' she retorted with barely concealed venom.

Agustín looked across at Joshua, easy-going and good-natured as always, and winked. It took all their efforts to constrain the firebrand Raghad, loving and devoted though she was.

Raquel looked around at all of them.

'So, what do I do? What do I say to Doña Ana?' she asked. It was a terrible dilemma for the nineteen-year-old.

Agustín was the first to speak up, quietly and soberly.

'Raquel, Pedro is away in Italy with Gonzalo doing his duty for Spain. And he will be away for some considerable time yet. So you must also do your duty and serve Queen Isabel and Princess Juana. I was in the Queen's service for twenty-five years, and now it's your turn. Your duty is quite clear, my dear; you must go and you must reply to Doña Ana this evening. Paco will want to set off in the morning.'

'All of us,' he continued, 'and I mean all of us,' – he glanced at Raghad – 'will look after Sara and Antonio, just as Don Gonzalo's wife Doña María is looking after Elvira and their other two daughters.'

'But I do worry about Sara,' said Raquel. 'She's become so thin and pale with her coughing and wheezing. I don't want to leave her.'

'We'll take care of her,' intoned good-natured Joshua. 'Don't you worry, my dear. My mountain herbs will make her better.'

'Have no fear, Raquel,' concluded Miriam, 'Sara and little Antonio will be loved to death by all of us.'

All nodded in agreement, including Abel and Eva. After all, they were part of the family now. Raghad puffed out her cheeks and huffed, but nodded too. She knew Agustín was right. His common sense and straight talking always won the day at Xiquena.

That evening, with Agustín's help, Raquel wrote to Ana of Beamonte, accepting her invitation. Agustín promised to accompany her on the journey north.

Paco's delivery of wool for Miriam came just in time, since she and her team had nearly run out. The task they faced in the time available was enormous. Three hours of tapestry using the fine woollen thread was about as much as her ladies could individually do at any one sitting. With the longer days and better light of the summer months, Miriam doubled her team of needlewomen, with an afternoon team taking over from a morning team, with three women working on each tapestry at a time. More were not practicable. Even then, progress on the three tapestries – each forty square feet – was slow. The letter to Raquel from Doña Ana of Beamonte gave Miriam a time frame in which to work, with the summer and autumn of the following year as her target. Even then, it looked unlikely that she could complete the task, so she decided to give priority to the tapestry of the panoramic view of the Alhambra and set aside for later those of the monarchs' entrance to Granada and of El Zagal handing over the keys of the city of Almería. To this end, while the light of autumn lasted, the needlewomen from Vélez Blanco and several villages around worked in three shifts: morning, afternoon and early evening. The women loved it, but there were mutterings from their menfolk that their domestic and family chores were being neglected. By providing standbys for those needlewomen who were sick or otherwise unavailable, over forty women were engaged on the task. To this day, the women of Vélez Blanco still talk with pride of the Queen's commission. Miriam notified Queen Isabel by letter of her intention to concentrate on the Alhambra tapestry and received her blessing.

Gonzalo's supplies from Spain of money, clothing and armaments, including heavier and longer pikes and more arquebuses,[3] were long delayed, and it was only in February the following year, 1496, that he could continue his advance northwards through Italy. By the spring, locating his headquarters in Nicastro, some eighty miles north of Reggio, he had occupied the whole of upper Calabria, with the exception of one corner, where the French general Sire d'Aubigny maintained some of his forces. It was then that Gonzalo learnt of the death of his great friend and mentor, Martín of Alarcón.

Gonzalo learnt at the same time that, a month before, the Spanish ambassador in Flanders, Francisco de Rojas, had acted as proxy for Princess Juana and her brother, Prince Juan, in a marriage ceremony in Brussels for Philip and Margaret. Soon after, the Flemish ambassador, Monsieur de Baudin, Bastard of Burgundy, did the same in Valladolid for the two Spanish children, performing his duty with special powers granted by his liege sovereign, Maximilian. Fernando and Isabel issued orders for the preparation of an enormous fleet, the largest ever to be assembled in Spanish waters, to take Juana to Flanders and to bring Margaret back to Spain for Juan.

Reaching Castrovillari, seventy miles further north, in the spring of 1496, and now more than halfway to Naples, Gonzalo received word that Ferrante was encamped outside Atella, a fortified hilltop town inland from Naples. The French Viceroy had rashly withdrawn to there after being harried by Ferrante's forces. Ferrante asked for Gonzalo's help to take the town, since he had insufficient troops for a decisive engagement, although enough to surround the town.

However, before leaving his base at Castrovillari, Gonzalo decided to strike a further blow against the enemy at the fortified town of Laino. There, a mixed force of local partisans and French soldiers was waiting to rendezvous with the French commander. Brushing aside ambushes from the local partisans who opposed Ferrante, in what Gonzalo called 'the best day's hunting he had ever known', he reached Laino by dawn the next morning, after a twenty-mile forced overnight march across difficult mountainous and wooded terrain.

Before the inhabitants of the town were awake, the Spanish forces began a furious assault of the hilltop castle, but at that very moment a lantern was overturned and the castle caught fire. So sudden was the Spanish attack that the French had no time to dress. Grabbing their swords, they engaged the Spanish in close combat. The fiercest fighting occurred in the tunnel entrance to the main tower. Before sunrise, more than a hundred French knights, nearly all unclothed, were taken prisoner, much to the hilarity of the local people.

---

[3] Or harquebus, an early type of musket which was supported on a tripod or forked rest.

The news of the surprise attack and the rout of so many French noblemen quickly spread across Italy. Having received reinforcements from Spain, which boosted their forces by a hundred men-at-arms, 400 light horse and 2,000 foot, Gonzalo marched to Atella, a hundred miles away, where Ferrante was waiting.

When news reached Ferrante's camp of the Spanish approach, he rode out to welcome Gonzalo and to hold a council of war. They were accompanied by Venetian dignitaries dressed immaculately in red velvet, and by Pope Alexander's eldest son, Cardinal César Borgia, then in his twentieth year. Ferrante was amazed at the speedy advance of the Spanish and remarked, 'It is you who are retaking our kingdom for us from the French, and it is therefore for you to choose which parts of my kingdom you wish to possess.' But Don Gonzalo replied that his duty was simply to fulfil the mission of the Spanish monarchs and to restore to Ferrante those parts of his kingdom which had been invaded by the French king.

Ferrante's forces, including contingents from Venice and the Vatican, numbered 1,200 men-at-arms, 1,500 light cavalry and 4,000 foot. They were carefully placed to block the exits by which the French could flee Atella, which was situated in a broad valley, the swampy floor of which was a breeding ground for malaria-carrying mosquitoes.

Inside the walls of Atella dwelt the Viceroy and French commanders, as well as Italian princes and captains who had joined Charles VIII on his march south over a year before. So Atella was a prize worth winning, and Ferrante was more than content to leave the conduct of the siege to the Spanish general.

Gonzalo decided to start by attacking an outlying fort near the castle which protected vital water supplies and watermills. The French commander at Atella, Montpensier, knew how vital they were to his garrison, and sent out his Swiss pike men to oppose the Spanish advance. With the French already at the mills, a troop of Spanish heavy cavalry was ordered to prevent the enemy receiving further support, while the remainder of the cavalry cut off the line of retreat of the French on the far side. The Spanish swordsmen facing the phalanx of Swiss mercenaries covered themselves with their shields and dived under the pikes, cutting their way forward among the unprotected legs and thighs of the Swiss, a tactic which Gonzalo had devised and practised while at Reggio. As the pike men fell to the ground wounded, their long, unwieldy weapons fell among those still on their feet and destroyed the defensive line which was vital to the Swiss pike men's effectiveness. Then, to neutralise the French archers, Gonzalo spearheaded his attack with a company of infantry, who rushed forward to cover the advance of the Spanish pike men, who were now equipped with their new heavy weapons. After the French archers had fired just a single volley of arrows, the Spanish infantry were among them,

A Royal Invitation

leaving their own pike men to complete the rout. Those French archers who escaped threw their bows to the ground but were then cut down by the Spanish light cavalry. Meanwhile, while Gonzalo was destroying the water-mills and their machinery, the Spanish heavy cavalry withstood the charge of the French reinforcements. Gonzalo then withdrew his forces rapidly before more French reinforcements could arrive. The rout of the French at Atella was complete.

This whirlwind raid by the Spanish troops, so soon after their tiring over-night forced march from Laino, earned Gonzalo and his men rapturous praise from their allies. The Italians gave Gonzalo the title *Il Gran Capitano*, and it is as *El Gran Capitán* that he has become known to this very day.

Three days later, soon after Christopher Columbus had returned to Cádiz after his second voyage to the New World, a mixed force of Spanish and Italian troops took by storm the villages on the slopes of the hills to the north, thus cutting off the only means of escape for the remaining French forces. The French still garrisoning the town of Atella – tormented by hunger and thirst, and without any hope of relief – lost heart, and Montpensier sued for terms. These were agreed by Ferrante on 21 July 1496. The French were permitted to march off with their arms, while conceding to Ferrante their cannon and heavy cavalry horses.

The French, now in high spirits, since they were freed of the responsibility to do battle again, indulged their taste for the local wine and for fresh fruit, but many became very ill. In the heat of a blistering summer in a fever-ridden valley, and moving at the pace of the slowest soldier, many fell sick and died, including the commander-in-chief himself, Gilbert de Montpensier, plus four other commanders of the Swiss and German mercenaries. Of 5,000 who departed Atella, only 500 managed to return to France.

Soon after the surrender of Atella, Ferrante married his step-aunt, who was a niece of Fernando of Spain. The marriage festivities were barely concluded when King Ferrante himself succumbed to the fever and died before he could enjoy the fruits of his victory. He bequeathed his kingdom to his uncle, Federico. Federico was a mild, kindly man, but ill fitted for the task. He was no more than a child among the political wheeler-dealers like King Fernando and Rodrigo Borgia. Fernando was furious at Federico's accession – and not without reason, for Alfonso and Ferrante, when appealing for Fernando's aid the previous year, had promised him that Prince Juan, then seventeen, would be next in line to the crown of Naples. Now, eighteen months later, when Spain's *Gran Capitán* and Spanish soldiers had won back the kingdom, this elderly and ineffective Federico was occupying the throne. Worse still, he had been educated in France in the court of Louis XI.

Fernando sent Gonzalo written instructions to march on Naples forthwith, so that the fickle Neapolitans would see who their true saviour was. Unabashed, Federico asked Gonzalo to take the remaining towns occupied by the French, but before he could do so their Scottish leader withdrew what forces of his remained and marched off for France. With Gonzalo and his Spanish men able to relax and enjoy the autumn sunshine in the endearing city of Naples, hostilities closed for 1496.

With little to do, Pedro fretted about being away from Raquel and the children, particularly four-year-old Sara; but not so Mat. His new lady friend, Francesca, had returned to her home in Naples after the death of her aged aunt, and hardly a day passed without Mat meeting her.

XIII: Wedding Bells

August 1496

While Don Gonzalo and his Spanish army were marching towards Naples, final preparations were being made for the fleet which would take Juana to Flanders for her betrothal to the Duke of Burgundy, Archduke Philip of Austria.

Miriam and Raquel had been caught somewhat unprepared by the letter from Doña Ana of Beamonte telling them that August and not the autumn was the planned sailing date for the fleet then being assembled in Laredo. Laredo was a protected haven in north Spain, lying twenty-five miles west of the major maritime port of Bilbao. So Miriam hastened the completion of her Alhambra tapestry, with work proceeding during all the daylight hours. It was finished just a few days before Raquel and Agustín set off. Once pressed and suitably mounted, Miriam put the tapestry on display on the castle wall at Vélez Blanco so that the villagers could admire the handiwork of her needle-women. It was a beautiful and truly stunning piece of work, displaying the yellow sandstone walls and square towers of the Alhambra as if ablaze in the evening light, with the towering, snow-capped mountains of the dark and menacing Sierra Nevada behind providing a contrasting backdrop. Miriam was justly proud of it. 'Just two more tapestries to complete,' she sighed.

For Raquel, Ana's letter caused a flurry of activity as she assembled her wardrobe for the journey to Laredo and for the royal palaces of Flanders. The summer market stalls in the local villages and even in nearby Lorca could not provide her with the warm woollen clothes she would need for a winter in the Low Countries. She would have to buy these when she arrived there.

The direct journey northwards overland from Almería to Laredo was a daunting prospect, more than 700 miles across Spain, through the ancient cities of Toledo and Valladolid, on terrible roads and over several mountain chains. Agustín decided on a different route. Using Juan Chacón's contacts, he and Raquel boarded a boat that sailed up the Mediterranean coast to Tortosa, midway between Valencia and Barcelona. A couple of days' easy riding across country brought them to the Ebro, one of Spain's major rivers, which drained the northern heartland of the country. There, they followed the river valley through Zaragoza, the fine capital city of the kingdom of Aragón with its riverside Gothic cathedral, on through Tudela, the patronymic city of Pedro's forebears, to Bilbao and finally along the coastal road to Laredo.

Meanwhile, Queen Isabel had been staying in a village south of Soria, finishing her plans for Juana's voyage to Flanders. When she was informed that the ships were at last ready and manned for departure, she set forth for Bilbao and Laredo with Prince Juan and the Princesses Isabel, Juana, María and Catalina, following the same route along the Ebro valley which Agustín and Raquel had taken earlier.

The fleet which Isabel had put together was enormous. Under the command of Admiral Don Fadrique Enríquez, the 120 vessels included two immense Genoese carracks of 1,000 tons with crews of 500 apiece; two caravels of 500 tons with 500 men; two of 400 tons with 400 men; six of 300 tons with 900 men, plus eight other ships with 700 men. Among the total of 15,000 crew and passengers, there were dukes, marquesses and counts and 500 other high-ranking noblemen. Whether or not this veritable armada was expecting to be intercepted by French warships en route, there were also on board 250 arquebusiers,[1] 200 archers and 400 soldiers. The provisioning for these ships had been daunting: 20,000 two-litre flasks of wine, 400 oak casks of wine and 300 of water, 2,000 quintals each of dried beef and pork, 200 sheep, twenty cows, 1,000 chickens, 10,000 eggs, 100,000 pickled and salted herring and dried codfish, plus voluminous quantities of vinegar, olive oil, beans, chickpeas, salt and spices. To cater for the princess's every need, there was a chaplain, a master of theology, a royal butler, a chief cupbearer, a master of the horse, a carver, a chamberlain, a treasurer, a comptroller and an overseer, all of noble birth. Sons of gentlemen honoured her as pages. Juana was accompanied by three dames of honour, including Doña Ana of Beamonte, and nine ladies-in-waiting, of whom one was Raquel. All were wives or daughters of the grandees of Spain or Portugal, and most had served their time in the royal court. To escort Princess Juana to Flanders and return Princess Margaret to Spain for her wedding to Prince Juan, the Spanish sovereigns designated Doña Teresa de Valasco, widow of Admiral Enríquez, and their two sons, Fadríquez Enríquez, the current admiral of Castile, and his brother Juan. If poor Raquel had known of the illustrious company she would be keeping, she would surely have declined the invitation from Ana of Beamonte. Nevertheless, if she were ill fitted to even lace up the bodice of any one of these illustrious ladies on the journey, none of them could hold a candle to her for her sultry beauty, dark eyes, lustrous raven hair or her bewitching smile. She was a blazing Sirius in a firmament of very ordinary yellow stars, whether ennobled or not by fancy titles.

---

[1] Men armed with an early form of musket.

The crews and passengers were already boarding ship when Agustín and Raquel arrived at Laredo. There, the multitude of ships lay at anchor in the narrow haven, which was snug and protected between high, green hills. Queen Isabel and her children were still ashore when the couple arrived, relaxing in the sunshine in the garden of a cottage. Juana de Torres, sister of Antonio de Torres and governess to Prince Juan, was also there with her charge. She greeted Raquel warmly, recalling laughingly their dining together two summers before during the Tordesillas banquet.

'Ah! My good Captain López, if I'm not mistaken?' said the Queen. 'And your lovely stepdaughter, Doña Raquel. It's a pleasure to see you again, Captain,' she continued, noting his bronzed and smiling face. 'I must say, retirement in far away Andalucía evidently suits you. And how is Juan Chacón and your family in Vélez Blanco? We hear very little from Juan these days, so I assume all is well in Murcia and Cartagena?'

'Indeed, everyone is well, ma'am, and all send their loyal greetings to you and your family. Señor Chacón is in excellent health, as is his young son, Pedro Fajardo, who is showing a growing interest in the management of your estates.

'But most importantly, ma'am, before the fleet sets sail, we have with us Miriam's tapestry of the Alhambra. As she has reported to you in letters, the other two – of your receiving the keys of the cities of Almería and Granada – have still to be finished. But Miriam was very keen that one of the tapestries at least was finished in time for the Princess to take to Flanders. The ladies of Los Vélez have been working flat out this last month to get it finished.' He paused. 'Permit me to show you, ma'am.'

With the three royal princesses all bubbling with excitement, eighteen-year-old Prince Juan helped Agustín lift the heavy bundle off the packhorse which bore the precious tapestry. The five-foot-wide tapestry had been carefully rolled around a trunk of agave, the desert cactus prevalent in southern Spain, and then wrapped tightly in waterproofed canvas. Agustín and Juan rolled it out and found a peg on the outside of the cottage wall from which to hang it. There were gasps of astonishment. All stood back to view the work and then huddled around it to inspect the intricate stitching.

'Truly lovely, Captain, truly lovely,' enthused the Queen, gazing at it in awe. 'Please convey my gratitude to your wife and to all the ladies of Los Vélez. I will, of course, write to her. This beautiful work will be the equal of the illustrious tapestries of Jan van Eyck and the other great Flemish artists. I know that Juana will be thrilled. Yet she mustn't see it until it's unveiled in Brussels on her wedding day.'

The next day, the young Duchess of Burgundy bade a tearful farewell to her brother and sisters and boarded the galleon on which she was to depart from her country of birth. Because of contrary winds and a storm in the Bay of Biscay, Juana's departure was delayed for three days. Queen Isabel remained on the vessel with her daughter to the very last.[2] Finally, on the afternoon of 22 August, as the clouds began to clear, anchors were raised, Isabel kissed Juana goodbye, bestowed her maternal blessing on her, and went ashore in pensive mood to join her other children. Apprehensive about the treacherous waters of the Bay of Biscay and the English Channel, Isabel set off on the road back to Burgos with a heavy heart, offering prayers to God for the protection of the princess. As the great fleet glided out of the harbour and set course for the Low Countries, Juana stood on the high prow of the carrack and watched the last rays of the setting sun fade behind the Cantabrian Mountains. When a curtain of mist darkened the sky, she drew her robe around her, turned her back on her homeland and peered ahead into the gloom. She had finally embarked upon her fateful adventure, but she could not have guessed that it would be nearly six years before she would see her mother again.

And fateful it would be. Sadly, Juana was wholly unfit for what lay before her. Reared and educated in the cloistered austerity of the royal households of Castile, she often went for months on end without seeing her itinerant parents as they moved constantly around their kingdoms. Priests, tutors, and courtiers, all well meaning, cocooned her and her siblings from the realities of life. To Fernando, and one supposes Isabel, their children (and particularly their daughters) were pawns to be used in the power game of international relations in their bid to secure Spain's future destiny. France was the great foe, powerful and menacing. To fortify Spain, a marriage alliance with the House of Habsburg, whose territory extended from the Alps to the North Sea, was the perfect answer. With Emperor Maximilian coincidentally possessing a son and a daughter, Philip and Margaret, of similar ages to Juan and Juana, a golden opportunity arose to constrain France to east and west. While the beautiful and golden-haired Princess Margaret would soon travel to Spain to marry the apple of Isabel's eye, Prince Juan, sixteen-year-old Princess Juana was being despatched to far-off Flanders to consummate her marriage to Archduke Philip, two years her senior, a young man she had never met. Years later, Princess Catalina, six years younger than Juana, would be offered up in a strategic alliance with France's northern foe, England.

For Juana, her future was equally uncertain, as she was despatched to a country as alien to her as could possibly be imagined; to a land which spoke Flemish and Dutch; a future husband who spoke French, and a father-in-law

---

[2] A malicious rumour persisted in Spain for many years afterwards that such was the deep bond between the Queen and Don Gonzalo that he was by her side to see the princess off, but we know this to be untrue since he was at that time in Italy.

whose language was German. The Low Countries were cold and rainy, the sky seemingly always overcast, while the food was tasteless and monotonous to the Spanish palate. Sunshine, oranges and olive oil all belonged to a different world. Compared with Spain's open spaces and its austere values, Flanders was densely populated, and its customs notoriously lax and bawdy.

So what was the make-up of the country which Juana was approaching? Politically, unlike the stable kingdoms of Portugal, Spain, England and France, the regions of northern and central Europe comprised loosely grouped discrete states. Wars, treaties and marriage alliances changed these groupings continually, with their evolution into nation states only occurring centuries later.[3] Central Europe itself, mainly Germany and Austria, was dominated by Maximilian's Holy Roman Empire. This comprised the eastern half of what had been Charlemagne's vast ninth-century empire, of which the western half became France. But despite its grand title, the Holy Roman Empire never possessed the political unification of, for example, France or Spain. Even at the end of the eighteenth century, it was still composed of over 300 discrete states governed by kings, princes, counts and clerics. The Holy Roman Empire was not ruled by a hereditary king, but by an emperor elected by the member states. His powers were simply executive, and, in effect, the grandiose Emperor was little more than a puppet king.

Wedged uncertainly between France and the Holy Roman Empire was the House of Habsburg. This was made up of small provinces occupying the rich lands of the Low Countries, with French-speaking peoples in the Meuse valley to the south, and Dutch-speaking peoples to the north. Holland, Flanders and Luxembourg were the largest of the dozen or so provinces governed by the House of Habsburg.[4] These provinces were largely autonomous and were not ruled as a single unit until the advent of Juana's betrothed, Philip of Austria, known as Philip the Fair.

---

[3] The Holy Roman Empire was dissolved by Napoleon in 1806. The constituent parts were brought together by Bismarck to create the modern state of Germany when Wilhelm I of Prussia was proclaimed German Emperor. Around the same time, Garibaldi annexed Venice and the Papal States into the kingdom of Italy.

[4] Holland at that time was just part of what is now present-day Holland or the Netherlands, while Flanders corresponded with present-day Belgium.

XIV: *Flanders*

October 1496

Having returned from his second voyage, Christopher Columbus went to meet the monarchs at Burgos, where they received him cordially in the fine palace of Casa de Cordón.[1] He presented them with a good quantity of gold nuggets, and yet more parrots and carved wooden masks to add to those he had brought back from his first voyage. Anxious as ever lest his influence in the islands was wrested from him, the Admiral was keen to return without delay for a third voyage. Eight vessels were deemed necessary, six for carrying supplies and two for exploration. However, the new Governor of the Indies, Archdeacon Juan Rodríguez Fonseca, disliked and distrusted Columbus, and strongly opposed another voyage by him, finding every pretext to block it. Consequently, the Admiral, with time on his hands and keen to remain in the royal eye, followed the monarchs as they moved their court between the cities of Burgos, Valladolid, Tordesillas and Medina de Campo. He obtained various books from England, including one describing the voyage across the north Atlantic by the Venetian John Cabot, and he reassessed the dimensions of the Earth, calculating that its circumference was only some 4,400 miles.[2] He remained convinced that on his two earlier voyages he had reached Asia. He repeated Aristotle's assertion that the sea between the eastern border of Spain and India could be crossed in a few days!

After leaving Laredo, Juana's fleet crossed the Bay of Biscay in just a few days, with seven of the escorts scouting ahead for French marauders, managing to capture two innocent Breton fishing boats. As they rounded Finistère into the western approaches of the English Channel, the sky darkened and a fierce storm tossed the ships around like corks. Raquel and the other ladies stayed below decks, desperately holding on to whatever they could. But, undeterred, Juana posted herself on the bows of her high-prowed carrack as water crashed over them, the princess seeming oblivious to the tempest. She spoke very little,

---

[1] A plaque above the doorway of the Palace of Cordón in Burgos states that 'In this house of the Constables of Castile the Catholic Monarchs received Cristóbal Colón who returned from his second voyage to the New World and confirmed all his privileges on 23 April 1497.'
[2] Implying that the continent of America and the Pacific Ocean were absent. The circumference of the Earth is 25,000 miles.

only occasionally taking herself down to her small cabin below decks to eat the cold food set on her table, it being impossible in such weather to light the fire in the ship's galley.

Powerless before the storm, Admiral Enríquez was forced to seek shelter on the south coast of England, in the lee of Portland Bill. But even then, one of the unwieldy Genoese carracks snapped from its moorings and rammed into one of the smaller ships, sending it to the bottom. For the remainder of the storm, Juana and her attendants remained ashore, graciously receiving the many Englishmen and their ladies who came to pay their respects. Days later, after the storm had abated and the fleet reassembled, she and her party boarded ship to complete the rest of her journey.

Three weeks after leaving Spain, the fleet reached the low-lying coast of Flanders, where grey skies and shorelines merged. Juana and her ladies were transferred to flat-bottomed Biscayan boats, which ferried them across the shallow, sandy shoals to the harbour of Vlissingen at the mouth of the Scheldt estuary. In the swirling currents, one of the unwieldy galleons ran aground and sank and, although all its crew and passengers were carried safely to land, much of the bride's wedding trousseau and precious jewels were lost. For Raquel, as for most of the ladies of the court, the journey had been a nightmare, cooped up as they were with little privacy in the dimly lit and rat-infested bowels of the ship.

Juana was temporary lodged in a fine house in the nearby village of Middleburg, while what remained of her belongings were unloaded and carried ashore. The Flemish had been caught napping by the arrival of the Spanish party, and it was several days before the royal procession could be assembled to wend its way through the villages to Antwerp, fifty miles inland. All along the route, Juana was acclaimed by a vociferous crowd who struggled to catch sight of her. With her youthful, radiant and noble demeanour and her dark Spanish complexion, she proved a fascination to them. On her part, Juana was dazzled by the reception and tarried in each village they passed through to chat to the bystanders.

Raquel described the events in a letter to Pedro.

Antwerp, 20 September 1496

My Darling,

As your mother suggested when I left home in August, I'm keeping a diary of events here and what I've been doing. So this letter comes from the notes which I've made so far. When we next meet, whenever that will be, and for Sara and baby Antonio in years to come, it will allow me to recall things which, by then, I might have forgotten. To say that I that miss you and the children dreadfully would be an understatement, but your Don Gonzalo would answer that by saying, 'Duty, my dear, duty!' He's probably right, but it's proving hard at times.

We had a terrible journey from Laredo to here, being forced to stop in England to ride out a storm. I and the other ladies were confined to the lower deck of one of the bigger ships, with little privacy. We slept huddled together in twos and threes in what are best described as cots! You can guess the rest of the arrangements from your time on the Pinta *and* Niña *with Columbus. But at least we were partitioned off from the sailors and the other men aboard, which I suppose was one blessing.*

Princess Juana was aboard one of the two big Genoese carracks. This must have been even more uncomfortable for her than for us on our ship. These Genoese ships stand so high out of the water – with big wooden castles at each end – that they look as if they'll topple over at any time! In fact, at Portland one nearly did, and ran into one of the smaller ships which sank. Juana seemed to have spent a lot of time on deck peering into the gloom and rain. She seems inured to the cold and wet.

We have now been in Flanders two weeks, and I haven't spoken to the Princess once. She spends a lot of her time with a Flemish lady, María Manuel, who she knows from her time at the Spanish court. Our party of dames of honour and ladies-in-waiting are getting disgruntled that they see next to nothing of Juana. They wonder what they are here for! That applies to me, too. Maybe they're here to be married off to Flemish gentlemen! Talking of marriages, there's still no sign yet of Archduke Philip of Austria, whom the Princess is to wed and has not even met. Apparently he's on his way back from meeting his father Maximilian in Germany, but it's puzzling why he wasn't at Vlissingen to meet Juana. She must have been very disappointed. However, the Archduke's sister, Margaret, who is to wed Prince Juan, has arrived to greet her. I caught a glimpse of her when she arrived with her grandmother, Margaret of York, and she looks stunning, with golden hair, a full figure and a captivating smile. Prince Juan will be over the moon when he eventually meets her.

I still don't know what my duties for the Princess are to be; responsibilities for her toilet, hair, wardrobe, night attire, meals etc., have all been assigned to one lady or another. Maybe I'll be asked to help Francisco de Luján, who is Master of the Horse – of which I have seen none! It's all rather perplexing. Fortunately, Ana of Beamonte is very kind to me and has taken me under her wing. She is less haughty and prudish than many the others ladies who, as yet, I haven't got to know, all except Doña Aldara of Portugal, whose Castilian is as poor as mine! We spend a lot of time together.

The country around here is dead flat with water everywhere: rivers, canals and marshes. In the gloomy weather which predominates, it's sometimes difficult to know where the sea ends and the sky begins. The beech trees and oaks in the meadows are immense. It's no wonder they can build such big ships. Antwerp is an amazing city, and so different from anywhere I've seen in Spain. It's teeming with merchants of all nationalities. Hundreds of ships enter the River Scheldt daily, bringing spices from Ceylon, cotton from Egypt, camphor from Sumatra, grain from Greece, silks from Italy, musk from China, and all our lovely oranges, lemons, raisins and olives from Spain. Gold, ivory and ebony are all starting to arrive from Africa.

Accompanied by a couple of the gentlemen of the court, Aldara and I have had a chance to see a bit of Antwerp life during the light evenings, and we're amazed, yet frankly appalled, by what goes on. There are dark, smoky taverns everywhere, where men and women mingle freely together and drink a bitter brew called ale from enormous pewter tankards. Juan Vélez, who is the royal carver (but of what I'm not sure), bought us a glass of this ale and it tastes absolutely horrible – yet the people here drink it by the gallon! The streets are filled with bookstalls selling the most awful lewd books and pamphlets. Poor Aldara, who is unmarried, is truly shocked by what's on display. Mind you, that didn't stop her sneaking a look at them when she thought I wasn't looking! We've seen young men and women holding hands and, can you believe, openly kissing in the streets, and the low necklines of the womenfolk in the market and around the taverns don't leave anything to the imagination. One thing that happened was hilarious. We were walking past one fruit stall early one evening, where a middle-aged woman with straggly blonde hair and rouged cheeks was standing in front of her stall, serving an unshaven, weather-beaten sailor with rotten teeth. She was wearing a laced-up bodice and had huge, huge breasts. Well, as she leaned forward towards the fruit, her bodice burst open and her breasts flopped out. The sailor cupped then in his hands and said, 'I'll take these two pink pumpkins, if you please, ma'am. But leave the stalks on!' Everyone around roared with laughter, including the woman stallholder.

It being autumn here and harvest time, the market stalls are filled with vegetables, some of which I've never seen before, with a type of cabbage they call 'cauliflower' being very popular. I've eaten it raw and, in fact, I quite like it – crispy and sweet. But what's incredible is the size of the black and white cows which are brought to market! They're enormous, and each one delivers a huge amount of gorgeous creamy milk. The local wines we have in the palace are thin and tasteless, and the food is very bland, since they don't use pepper, saffron, salt, lentils, rice or almonds in their cooking. Apart from salt, none of these are evident in the markets either. Parsley, onions or even lettuce are only occasionally seen.

Well, my love, I think that's give you a taste of what life in Flanders is like. It's starting to get dark in the room I'm sharing here with Aldara, and the candles in the palace are now being lit. I'll write to you soon. I understand that there's a good postal service between Brussels and Milan, so hopefully you'll receive this in Naples before too long. My love to you, and to Mat and Don Gonzalo. I hope you are all safe and in good health. Please write.

Raquel

But Pedro never received her letter.

A few days after the Spanish army had taken Naples, and about the time of Juana's arrival at Vlissingen, Don Gonzalo had called Pedro into his room in the palace which he had taken over as his temporary headquarters. An immaculately dressed courtier was seated there.

'Ah, Pedro,' Gonzalo said, welcoming his aide-de-camp, 'do come in. I received a letter from Queen Isabel two weeks ago saying that she was on her way to Laredo to bid farewell to Princess Juana, who was preparing to leave for Flanders for her wedding to Philip of Austria. You've heard me talk about this before. What with the siege of Laino and our march to Atella, the letter had completely slipped my mind. Now Paolino Romero, Pope Alexander's envoy, has arrived here today to say that the Pope's sending his youngest son, Jofré, on his behalf to Juana's wedding in Brussels with a papal gift for the betrothed. Alexander asks whether I'd like to send a representative to travel with Jofré and, of course, I must. I'm wholly remiss to have overlooked this. Clearly, I can't go myself and I'm proposing to send you in my stead.'

With much on his mind, the Gran Capitán was speaking rapidly and in a businesslike way. Pedro's eyes lit up.

'Yes, I can see that already you've realised that you'll have a chance to be with Raquel for a while! An early departure is essential, Pedro, since time's already very short. Indeed, it's quite possible that the wedding will have taken place before you get there. So you must return with Paolino to Rome on the morrow. I'll arrange a wedding present for you to take. I've something rather nice in mind.' He smiled. 'Now, go and put your affairs in order and prepare yourself for the journey. I'll arrange an escort for you.'

With a posse of three Spanish horsemen accompanying them, Pedro and Paolino set off from Naples at dawn the next morning for the three-day ride north to Rome along the Appian Way. It being a warm morning, Pedro was dressed in his favourite white blouse with broad sleeves, woollen trousers and high riding boots, and he wore his Toledo sword at his side and his horn-hafted dagger on his belt. But their escort were encumbered by mail shirts and steel helmets and carried lances. The fine clothes Pedro wore for the Tordesillas banquet were carefully folded in one saddlebag, while a box on the other side contained Gonzalo's gift to the royal couple: a set of beautiful Venetian glass wine goblets. They were cherry red in colour and traced with gold filigree, and were packed carefully in cork.

The party reached Rome on the evening of the third day. Pedro had dreamed of one day visiting the Eternal City and seeing its fabled treasures. But sadly he had little time to tarry, as they passed through what remained of ancient Rome, past the immense ruin of Caracalla's thermal baths, then the elongated Circus Maximus with its central line of columns, through the arched Gate of Constantine, with the spectacular Coliseum some hundreds of yards to their right. Then on, below the Palantine Hill, concealing behind it the ruins of the old Forum; then around the circular, former pagan temple of the Pantheon with its colonnaded portico, finally reaching the banks of the River Tiber. There they crossed the Sant'Angelo Bridge to the west bank of the river, into the Pope's very own domain. Paolino led them through a doorway into the heart of the squat, round fortress of the Castle of Sant'Angelo. Half a mile beyond lay the walled city of the Vatican, enclosing Constantine's third-century basilica.[3] Nearby, the Pope's

---

[3] The present St Peter's Basilica was begun in 1546 and completed in 1589.

residence was connected by an underground passage to the Sant'Angelo fortress.

Guards armed with heavy pikes were everywhere. While the three escorting riders dispersed, their job now done, Pedro followed Paolino along a passage into the heart of the fortress, up several flights of stone steps and into a well-furnished room high in the castle with a window looking out over Rome. There, the Pope's youngest son, fifteen-year-old Jofré, greeted them cordially. Jofré was a handsome young man. He lacked his father's round nose and lascivious lips, but none of his father's charm. He was not quite Pedro's height but broader in the chest and had the soft hands of a cleric. Jofré was eager and ready to start, but he granted Pedro a night's rest after his three long days in the saddle, finding for him a sparsely furnished room deep inside the fortress. Jofré brushed aside the need for the Spanish riders to travel with them, since a six-man squadron of the papal forces was already deputed to ride as their bodyguard.

Pedro, Jofré and the six papal guards set off next morning at around the time that Juana's royal procession was on its way to Antwerp. The group had a daunting ride ahead of them, through the Apennine mountains to Siena, through Tuscany and Florence, then on to Milan, Zurich, Luxembourg and finally Brussels; some 1,000 miles in all. Even with no rest days, it would take them the better part of a month. Would they be in time for the wedding?

Soon after settling into his headquarters in Naples, Don Gonzalo received a message from the Pope, Rodrigo Borgia, requesting the Spanish general's aid against a Basque nobleman, Manual Guerri. Guerri had been placed in command of the French forces at Ostia, just ten miles downstream of Rome at the mouth of Tiber, and was cutting off supplies to Rome so that food and wine were almost unobtainable there. Every vessel entering the river was forced to lower sail while Guerri's men plundered them and then set them ablaze. Responding to the Pope's request, and just a fortnight after Pedro's departure, the Spanish general marched from Naples with all haste for Rome, which lay about 140 miles to the north.

XV: The Partisans

October 1496

Archduke Philip of Austria was still in Innsbruck on a hunting trip with his father, Emperor Maximilian, when news arrived of the arrival of Juana in Flanders. Accompanied by a handful of men, he immediately set forth from Austria to join his betrothed 500 miles away. Pedro and Jofré should then have been well on their way there themselves. It was not until the middle of the month that Philip rode wearily into the small Flemish town of Lierre, where Juana and her retinue were installed. Without delay, Philip changed his travel-stained clothes for those befitting a suitor and, ignoring protocol, hastened that very evening to Juana's abode. Brushing aside her perplexed servants, he rushed into her room, where to his amazement he was greeted by the alluring Archduchess, a maiden blessed with beauty and grace, whose eyes promised him unlimited happiness and whose full figure awakened within him a restless desire. He waited with growing impatience while, with punctilious formality, he was presented to all the Spanish grandees, their ladies, the retinue of tut-tutting clergy, and all those attending the princess, all of whom approached Philip, bowed or curtseyed before him, and kissed his hand.

The overwhelming, all-consuming passion which Juana developed for her mercurial husband started at that moment as they exchanged glances through the throng of sycophants who surrounded them. It would sweep her down into a spiral of darkness and depression as she surrendered herself to its pleasures and pains. The handsome prince would henceforth supersede all others in her life and would dominate her visions. From this moment on, her love for Philip was to be all-pervasive and unquenchable.

Raquel wrote in her diary:

I stood in line alongside Doña Ana, so I was able to study the Archduke's features as he approached me. I had on an expensive gown which I bought a week ago from a dressmaker in the city. The gown had been made for Princess Margaret of Austria, but she had to depart for the coast and I was able to buy it. It's gorgeous and made of a rich shade of rose-coloured velvet with narrow sleeves widening at the cuff to knee-length and which are then turned back to expose their fur lining. The waist of my dress is confined by a sash-girdle, and to expose the dark red silk underskirt I have to hold up the long trailing skirt with my left hand. It's a bit impractical, but all the ladies do the same. It's the current fashion! My headdress is of black velvet and reaches down to my shoulders. The round neckline is deep and poses a real risk of my doing what the woman in the market did when I curtsey! I was terribly nervous. Philip was clean-shaven and dressed immaculately in gold-coloured doublet and hose with a heavy gold chain and medallion hanging outside his doublet and a finer gold chain with an oval ruby also around his neck. He had a square blue cap on his head. He looked every bit a prince of the realm. He is tall and slim and athletic-looking, with blonde hair down to the nape of his neck. He has rather beady grey eyes, a high forehead and a long straight nose. But most striking is his enormous jutting jaw, which to me is almost disfiguring. Frankly, I don't find him as handsome as people make out. He looked at all the ladies-in-waiting ahead of me full in the face – searching for what, I know not. But when I curt-seyed before him, he paused and looked me up and down and smiled; to me, it was more leer than smile, and it sent a shiver down my spine. Then he moved on, all the time looking around and over the line of people at Juana, with whom he is obviously besotted. She looked as radiant as I've seen her. She can certainly switch the charm on and off at will!

After the formality of the presentations, the Archduke summoned the Chamberlain, who bestowed the Church's benediction on the couple. Then the couple hastily departed through a door into the princess's quarters. The door was shut firmly behind them. Their union was consummated that very night!

Two days later, on 20 October, the couple were married by the Bishop of Cambrai. Thereafter, they departed for Brussels along a route swarming with jubilant but curious townspeople who had prepared pageants and receptions in their honour. The royal couple made a triumphant entry to the palace of the Dukes of Burgundy, where all and sundry greeted them. Juana had never in her life experienced such lavish entertaining. Like a child at a birthday party, she was swept along by the gaiety of the moment, and her days and nights merged into a festival of pleasure and laughter. She was the central figure around whom the court and the people whirled.

Philip revelled in all the celebrations and commanded the merrymaking to continue without interruption while the court wined and dined and danced the autumn hours away. Enclosed in the fine Burgundian palace, with its fabulous treasures of gold and silver, its tapestries and porcelains, oriental rugs and Venetian mirrors, Juana became mesmerised by the glamour of the bizarre Flemish court life. She fluttered around the palace like a butterfly at last freed from its chrysalis but, like a butterfly, her freedom was short-lived. The restraints imposed by her attendants, carefully selected by her strait-laced mother, closed in on her, bringing to a premature end her brief but ecstatic flight. But it was the actions of Philip which most destabilised Juana. In an attempt to pry Juana free from what he considered was the adverse influence of the Spaniards around her, Philip summarily reorganised her household staff, putting in their place his own chamberlain, house steward, master of the horse and chief waiter, returning unceremoniously to Spain all those who formerly held these positions. Only Rodrigo Manrique, her ousted house steward, was permitted to stay as Spanish Ambassador to Philip's court.

As Raquel complained in her diary:

We don't know where we are! Many of the gentlemen who accompanied us here from Spain are being sent home, and although most of Juana's ladies of the court remain, we are being sidelined by the Flemish ladies who don't understand or care for Spanish ways and boss us around. They are all big and boisterous and tower over us. They boom at us in French, and neither they nor we understand a word of each other's language. It's terrible. Worse still, to protect herself from these overbearing women, the Princess is shutting herself away more and more, even from us, and we hardly see her. She is intoxicated by the Archduke and is a slave to his whims.

The lucky ones are those who are returning to Spain with Princess Margaret, my friend Doña Aldara among them. She's returning to her home in Portugal. I shall miss her, but I can, at least, spread myself out in our small bedroom in the palace now that she's gone. They and Admiral Radrique Enríquez have already left the Flemish court and are on their way to the port, where the Spanish fleet and the seamen have been waiting patiently to transport Margaret back to Spain to marry Prince Juan. But it's now nearly November, and frankly I don't envy the sailors and passengers making that awful journey by sea around France. I think I'm better off here, despite the unpleasant atmosphere! The one blessing is that the Spanish men and women who remain here are drawn much closer together by our isolation, although it only tends to polarise us even more from the Flemish. The Princess is so wrapped up with the Archduke I'm not sure she sees this.

Two days before leaving Naples to march to Rome in response to the Pope's request for assistance against the French, who were blockading the River Tiber at Ostia a few miles downstream of Rome, Mat sought an audience with Don Gonzalo.

'Have you heard anything of Pedro, sir?' he asked. 'It's three months now since he left with Jofré.'

'No Mat, we haven't. And it's a bit worrying. We might have expected to have heard by now that he'd arrived in Brussels or, at the very least, had a note back from him that he'd passed through Milan, Zurich or one of the other cities on the way. I did ask him to write to me with progress of his journey.'

'Do you think something might have happened to him, sir?'

'No, Mat, I'm sure not. He and Jofré are accompanied by six well-armed and capable lancers of the Pope's guard. In any case, nobody's going to harm the Pope's youngest son. No, Mat, I expect the party will have arrived in Brussels by now. They might even be on their way home. Have no fear, all will be well.'

But inwardly, the Gran Capitán was becoming concerned.

The Spanish forces entered Rome in February 1497, accompanied by prelates of the Pope and a bevy of cardinals in their scarlet robes. Their commander, Don Gonzalo Fernández, rode alongside the Pope's middle son, Juan, the Duke of Gandía, who was six years older than Jofré. Gonzalo and his men stayed in Rome for only three days and then set off to relieve the blockade of Rome at Ostia. His Spanish force comprised only 600 mounted men and 1,000 foot. He had remarked to the Pope that his men were so ill clothed and lacking in supplies that at least the enemy would not be tempted to attack them for the sake of loot! After attending mass in St Peter's, Gonzalo and his men set forth for Ostia. They were joined by many Spaniards living in Rome who sought action.

The Spanish infantry were tall and youthful but conspicuously few in number; the rigours of their forced marches – which, as at Atella, often finished with an assault against a precipitous stronghold and over fortress walls – demanded exceptionally fit and hardy men. They wore no steel armour, except basin helmets and steel knee guards. From the ankle to the waist, Gonzalo's foot soldiers wore close-fitting hose which gave them freedom of movement. In the summer, they often discarded their chain mail shirts and relied on their leather jerkins, softened by daily usage, which were stout enough to resist most blows, preferring to rely for their defence on their agility. To speed their marches further, they carried little baggage. Female camp followers, as always, were forbidden. So quietly and softly did they move in their calf-high Moorish boots of soft red leather that they seemed almost a phantom army. Booty had to be used to replace the pay which Fernando all too rarely sent from Spain. Led by a commander who took good care of them, the morale of the Spanish soldiers was high. Their mobility, desire for action and bravery earned for them a deep and grudging respect from their foes.

Guerri, the French commander at Ostia, refused to accept the terms of surrender offered by the Gran Capitán. Don Gonzalo started the Spanish siege by concentrating his engines of war on one side of the high-walled castle, thus drawing the enemy to that quarter, while at the same time ordering his scaling ladders and ropes to be carried at night to concealed points on the far side. Incessant cannon fire during the day opened a breach in the wall on one side.

On the eve of the assault of Ostia, Gonzalo addressed his troops as was his custom before an engagement: 'In this fight, we are all resolved to serve the Supreme Pontiff and to help please our ally King Federico. We also look to gain honour and fame for ourselves and to demonstrate before all nations the greatness of Spain.'

Gonzalo then turned to his standard-bearer, Londoño, and said, 'I know upon whom I can rely to place our standard on the battlements of Ostia castle,' and turning to Alonso de Sotomayor, one of his captains, said, 'Señor Alonso, I know who will bring the French commander, Manuel Guerri, to me alive.'

It was by such challenges that Don Gonzalo inspired his officers to lead their contingents with such conspicuous bravery and valour.

Everything was made ready for this assault, with barely a sound heard except the gentle tinkle of armour, the scuffing of leather and the whispered orders of the officers. That night, with the campfires extinguished, the Spanish columns felt their way forward. As soon as they reached their allotted places, Gonzalo moved among them, giving them their last orders. His force in front of the breach was to advance slowly to give time for the scaling ladders on the far side to be erected. Then, the whole attack was to be carried out rapidly.

Just before sunrise, the rekindling of Gonzalo's camp fire signalled the assault. Ascending the scaling ladders and clambering up the knotted ropes hooked over the tops of the walls, the Spaniards caught the French sentries posted along the wall by surprise and put them to the sword. Then, raising a loud cheer, and led by the lively Spanish ambassador in Rome, Garcilaso de Vega, they charged the French through the breach in the walls on the far side of the fortress. The French were sandwiched between the two Spanish columns and were easily overcome. Nearly all were either killed or captured.

Watching in safety from the protection of the central keep, Manuel Guerri, the French commander, saw all was lost and quickly surrendered. He was bound in chains for later public display. Gonzalo reprimanded him scathingly for surrendering himself so tamely after selling his forces short at such cost in lives, but the miserable man remained uncaring and unrepentant.

On the Ides of March, 15 March, with the French at Ostia defeated and Gonzalo's task in Italy nearly at an end, and accompanied by a sumptuously dressed Juan Borgia, the twenty-one-year-old middle son of the Pope, the Spanish general and his army entered Rome, passing triumphantly through the Ostia Gate into the city. The streets were thronged with cheering citizens, while the windows of the wealthy were draped with colourful rugs and flowers and burst with people eager to see the Spanish victor pass by. The clatter of the hooves of the cavalry on the cobbled streets drowned the rolling beat of

145

kettledrums, the fanfares of the Spanish trumpeters and the acclaim of the Roman people, who showered sweetmeats on the soldiers as they marched past. After the regiments had passed by, there came a hundred helmeted pike men bearing their heavy ten-foot weapons, then Gonzalo's standard-bearer, followed by dancers who twirled and twisted streamers high into the air. Next, a herald and three trumpeters proclaimed their victorious leader. Finally, fifty paces behind, rode Don Gonzalo himself, followed by members of his head-quarters staff, Mat among them.

But the celebration was cut short. As the procession reached its conclusion in the centre of the city, two riders galloped towards him, their horses almost spent. One was a cavalryman, armoured but bareheaded and clearly fatigued. The other rider was also clearly at the end of his tether. He was a young man. His fine clothes were torn and dishevelled. A week's stubbly growth gave testament to many days hard riding.

'Jofré!' exclaimed Don Gonzalo, as the two riders came to a stop in front of him. Mat rode forward to join him.

'My Lord Gonzalo,' panted Jofré, 'we bring terrible news… about your aide-de-camp, Pedro Togeiro… He… he—'

Don Gonzalo interrupted him, trying to calm the Pope's son. 'Come, Jofré, dismount, the both of you. Catch your breath and come into the palace and tell us what's happened. Mat, please run ahead and fetch some cool water for these men. They looked all in. And some brandy to rekindle their spirits,' he added.

'Now, young man,' said Gonzalo quietly, once they were inside and out of the sun. 'What happened? What's become of Pedro? Take your time.'

'We don't know what's become of him, or where he is. We don't know if he's alive or dead. We… we…'

'Calm yourself, Jofré, you're safe now! Tell us what happened from the beginning – after you left Rome in September.'

'I'm sorry, sir, I'm so ashamed. I… I…'

Tears ran down the youngster's face, his chest heaving in long sobs. Mat and the Gran Capitán exchanged anxious glances. Jofré's companion, the sergeant, looked at them both, shook his head slowly and turned away. He looked ashen.

'When we left Rome,' started Jofré, after taking a long draught of water, 'that is, Pedro, me, Giuseppe, my sergeant here, and his five lancers, we made good progress, riding forty or fifty miles each day.'

He took a sip of the brandy from a glass which Mat had passed to him. Giuseppe did likewise.

'It must have been about ten days after we left Rome. We had crossed the River Arno and were in the rugged Tuscan mountains beyond Florence, which we had passed through two days earlier.'

Jofré took another sip of brandy. He was a lot calmer now and his voice less shrill.

'It was a lovely day, as I recall. We were riding along a track through a narrow defile with high cliffs on each side and wooded mountains beyond. Trees and bushes lined the stream which ran along the middle of the gorge.'

He paused, bringing the scene back to mind. His face darkened. Giuseppe looked down at the floor, picking his fingers.

'Suddenly, out from behind the bushes ran a dozen or so men, screaming at us... death threats... and waving knives and clubs. We were taken by surprise. They were on us in a second, pulling us from our horses. Giuseppe here had the chance to strike one of them across the back with his sabre, and I saw Pedro almost remove the arm of one with that lovely sword of his. But we had little time, we—'

Giuseppe interrupted, as if by way of apology.

'We had little chance, my Lord. They came at us from all directions... My men weren't prepared... they couldn't reach their lances in time. They...'

'We were dragged from our horses,' continued Jofré, 'and driven into a clearing. They ransacked our horses and led them away. I explained to the ringleader who we were; that I was the son of Pope Alexander VI and that Pedro was a member of your headquarters staff, and that we were on our way north to Flanders for the wedding of Princess Juana of Spain and Archduke Philip of Austria. I had no fear about mentioning Pedro's allegiance to you, since you are here fighting the French who had invaded these people's country.'

' "We care nothing for your so-called *Gran Capitán*," the ringleader said roughly, spitting out the words. "We didn't invite him here, did we? We can deal with the accursed French ourselves, and the Spanish for that matter. We don't need their help. We didn't ask them to come here."

'The man was hideous, with a deep scar running across his face. His dozen or so men were a real motley group of cut-throats, dressed worse than peasants, with filthy matted hair and coarse beards. They brandished long knives, which they continuously honed on pieces of whetstone they carried with them, all the time grinning and showing how they would use their blades on us. I was terrified.

'Pedro's Italian isn't very good yet, but he was very spirited and told them what a great leader you were and how you had defeated the French in many battles. It did him no good. For his trouble, he was gagged and blindfolded and his hands were tied tightly behind his back.'

'We realised then,' said Giuseppe, 'that we were in the hands of Tuscan brigands or partisans. Outlaws, in truth. They live in the mountains of Tuscany and answer to nobody, not to the Pope, not to the Medici in

Florence, not to the Duke of Siena, nobody. They kill or hold to ransom all those who cross their path, and they are noted for their cruelty and mercilessness.'

'What happened then?' asked Don Gonzalo.

'Our hands were tied, like Pedro's, although we weren't blindfolded, and all our weapons and belongings were taken from us. Then, at the point of our own lances, we were led away, down through the ravine to a small village a mile away. The place was a ruin and scarcely fit to live in. The roofs of most of the ramshackle stone buildings had fallen in and others were crudely thatched. It was a place for pigs, not humans. The villagers came out of these dwellings to scoff at us. The children were filthy and had no clothes or shoes. They ran up to us and tried to beat us with sticks. The few women we saw were haggard and half-clothed, screaming abuse at us in a dialect I didn't understand. I suppose being the son of the Pope gave me some protection, but Pedro was beaten badly as we approached the village and eventually was dragged away bleeding and barely conscious.'

Jofré stopped and looked Don Gonzalo in the face.

'We have not seen him since,' he said quietly, after a pause.

'No,' added Giuseppe, 'we've no idea what became of him… has *become* of him,' he added, trying to be positive. 'Simply no idea.'

'We were then separated,' said Jofré. 'I was led off to a hut at the edge of the village. It was better than the rest, and had a roof of stone slabs and a stout door.'

'The rest of us,' said Giuseppe, 'were taken to the centre of the village. There couldn't have been many more than a dozen buildings there, all surrounded by cow dung and filth. Ugh! We were pushed into what smelt like a cowshed and locked up. And so we stayed there for nearly five months, until they… they—' Giuseppe's face darkened.

'Take your time, Giuseppe,' interrupted Jofré sympathetically, 'take your time.'

'We were well fed, I suppose,' he continued, 'and at the time we thought we were being reasonably well treated. The lumps of pork we were given were almost raw, but at least we were fed. But all the time we were worrying about Pedro… we still are.'

'We assumed by then that we were to be ransomed,' said Jofré. 'Did you receive any ransom demand for us, or for Pedro?'

'No, nothing. Not for you, nor Pedro,' replied Gonzalo.

'Hmm. That's worrying,' said Jofré pensively.

Giuseppe continued the story.

'Although it was generally the women who came with the food and water each evening, we could hear the men arguing noisily among themselves. We assumed they were arguing over what they were to do with us. Their dialect was so strong I could only make out occasional words. Then...' He paused, looking up from the ground before continuing. 'I saw young Prince Jofré being pushed into the open space in the middle of the village. Through the crack in the door I could see him standing there alone, confused, frightened.'

He glanced at Jofré, who nodded in confirmation.

'They took my five lancers out from our prison, leaving me behind.' Again Giuseppe stopped, reliving the horrible events. 'To the delight of the women, who cackled and egged them on, the partisans ordered my men to strip naked. These butchers then fell upon them, brandishing their knives. My men were dragged over to a wooden cattle trough, pleading and begging for their lives. But it was in vain. Knives flashed through the air as ears, noses and tongues were sliced off. They were held down as their hands were sawn through and thrown to the gaggle of women who ran around, hurling them into the air.'

'It was truly terrible,' murmured Jofré, 'I never thought human beings could do that to one another...'

'These people are not human, my Lord,' corrected the sergeant, pausing to think about fortunes of Pedro. 'Then,' Giuseppe said in a voice that was barely audible, 'my men were dragged to an upright wooden frame on the edge of the square, from which the farm animals were hung and slaughtered, and they were strung up by their heels.'

'By this time,' added Jofré, 'their cries had become no more than sobs. These were even more pitiful than their screams.'

'Finally and, I suppose, mercifully,' he said, 'their throats were cut, their blood flooding out over the ground. Then, paddling in their blood in their bare feet, the women set to, cutting up and making sport of their bodies. And there they were left, hanging from the slaughter frame, unrecognisable as men.'

Jofré and Giuseppe just sat there, the brandy glasses in hand, reliving the horrible scene. Don Gonzalo waited patiently for them to finish their story.

'The next day, all was quiet in the village,' said Jofré, 'the blood lust of these murderers having been satiated. Even the women had fallen silent, as if ashamed of their actions the previous day. Giuseppe and I were led to the village square, still with the naked bodies of our five lancers hanging from that frame. We were given our horses and handed back our swords. Giuseppe was given back the armour which he was wearing when we were ambushed.

'Without saying a word, the ringleader with the scar led us out of the village up through the defile, and pointed the way back towards Florence and Rome. After several days' hard riding, we arrived here, just as you were leading your forces in triumph into Rome. I regret, my Lord Gonzalo, that we have ruined what should have been a wonderful day for you. Please accept my sincere apologies.'

'That is of no importance, Jofré. What is important is that you and Giuseppe have returned safe and sound from your terrible ordeal.'

He turned to Mat. 'Now we know what happened to them, and why we'd received no news of their journey north to Brussels.

'I'm truly sorry for what happened to your men, Giuseppe, truly sorry. However, you are both alive and safe. So thanks be to God. Now we must think about Pedro and what we must do to find out what's become of him – and if he's still alive.'

'And f-f-for that, sir,' Mat said, 'if you will p-p-permit me, I have a suggestion to make.'

The Gran Capitán's entry into the city had been spectacular. He always had a sense for grandeur, for display, for timing. Moreover, he was a man with a deep sense of history, who could not ride victorious into Rome without thinking of other great commanders who through twenty centuries had done as he was doing. Riding alongside Gonzalo had been Juan Borgia, the Duke of Gandía, followed immediately by the captive French commander, Guerri, who was chained to Gonzalo's page. Guerri was a pitiful sight, his hair and beard uncombed, his eyes baleful; he was mounted on a scraggy mare to humiliate him further. In contrast, the Spanish knights following behind in order of rank with their swords drawn were wearing shining armour which they had confiscated in Ostia. The excitement of the populace following the violation of their city by the French two years before, the exuberance of the Spaniards and the dejection of their French prisoners, were consummated when Gonzalo entered the Vatican. There, the Pontiff and the College of Cardinals stood to receive him, with Rodrigo Borgia himself raising Gonzalo from his knees to present him with the Golden Rose, the highest honour a layman could receive from the sovereign pontiff. The Golden Rose, its origins lost in time, was a reward for prowess in the service of God and his Vicar on earth. It was a proud moment; now the highest authority on earth had honoured the Gran Capitán with an award which was granted to only a very few.

The Pope then gave an oration praising the Spanish general's valour and thanking him and his loyal Spanish soldiers in the name of Rome for having delivered the Eternal City from the blockade of Ostia. Gonzalo followed in fluent Italian, giving a typically modest reply. Meanwhile, the wretched Guerri was prostrate on the ground at the Pope's feet, begging for pardon. But it was Gonzalo, always merciful to the vanquished, who won for him his life, requesting clemency from the Pope as well as exemption from taxation for the people of Ostia and those who suffered at the hands of Guerri. The Pope accepted both petitions, and Guerri, who had defied him at the very gates of his own city, was allowed to depart for France.

XVI: Tuscany

March 1497

Deeply worried about what they had heard from Jofré and Giuseppe, Mat sent a note to his lover Francesca, in Naples, asking her to join him in Rome without delay. She arrived within the week.

For a few days, the Spanish veterans had enjoyed the delights of Rome in springtime, giving themselves over wantonly to every pleasure under the idle rule of the capricious Pope and his cardinals. The Spaniards, normally more reserved than the Italians, eventually gave way to unbridled and erotic ardour that astonished the most abandoned Roman libertines.

By Palm Sunday, 19 March, Gonzalo was in angry mood, with the conduct of his own men illustrating so clearly the debauchery into which the city had sunk. He declined to take a seat behind the Pope's throne in St Peter's and refused to carry a palm through the basilica when it was offered to him. Perplexed, Rodrigo Borgia sent his secretary to learn the reason for Gonzalo's inexplicable behaviour. The Spanish general replied that he was appalled by the wantonness of the Roman citizens and, not least, by what he'd leant of his son Juan's shameful treatment of his young Spanish wife, María Enríquez, who was a cousin of King Fernando.

So the Gran Capitán was in an angry mood when, a few days later, his Sergeant of the Camp Guard, Matute, came to see him, accompanied by his tough and strong-willed Neapolitan lady friend, Francesca. Events in Rome had pushed to the back of Gonzalo's mind what thoughts he might have had about Pedro's whereabouts.

'So how do you plan to find Pedro, Mat? If I thought it might have done any good, I would have despatched a force of lancers and Swiss pike men to find him. But where would I have sent them?'

'Francesca here, sir, comes from the very mountains in Tuscany where Jofré said they were captured by the partisans. She knows the area well and she understands and speaks the local dialect.'

'So?' chided Gonzalo. 'Do you plan to send her with my lancers?'

'No, sir,' replied Mat calmly, rather irritated by the commander's tone. 'What I'm planning is that Francesca and I take on the aspect of peasants escorting a humble donkey, and infiltrate the mountain region north of Florence.'

'Is that why you've been growing a beard, Mat?' laughed Gonzalo, feeling ashamed of his uncharacteristic sarcastic remark. 'I was wondering why you were starting to look so wild!'

'Yes, sir, that's it exactly. My plan is that we wander from village to village and see if we can find out what's become of Pedro. Where he is… if he's alive. Somewhere there'll be a clue as to his whereabouts, of that I'm sure.'

'Have no fear, my Lord,' said Francesca, in no way awed in the presence of the famous general. 'We'll be quite safe among my people, and I'm sure we'll find out what became of Pedro. Mat's Italian is good enough now for him to pass as my Sicilian husband, since the accent there is quite different from Tuscany's. It'll take us some time to get there, so we'll be gone for quite a while; but have no fear, we'll return with Pedro, or with news of what became of him.'

'An excellent idea, Mat,' replied a supportive Gonzalo. 'Your plan might just work. And there's nobody more resourceful among my officers who could carry it out.' He was silent for a moment, thinking.

'To speed up your journey, Mat, since time might be short, why don't I arrange a boat to take you up the coast to the city of Pisa? With the southerly wind now blowing, you could be there in days. Pisa lies on the River Arno, and from there you can take a boat upriver to Florence, where you can get all the things you need to pass as "peasants". What's more, if you're agreeable, I can arrange for a party of light cavalry to follow you overland and wait for you in Florence – just in case you need to leave rapidly.'

'That all sounds excellent, sir,' replied Mat. 'But please, it must all be very discreet. Nothing must blow our cover as peasants.'

'Of course not. Have no fear, Mat. By the way, yesterday I received this letter from Barcelona addressed to Pedro. It's from his mother, Miriam. Under the circumstances, I think you should open it.'

Mat did so and read it out:

'Vélez Blanco, 10 February 1497.

'My dear Pedro and Raquel,

'I am writing to you jointly, although to different addresses. The postal service to Italy is likely to be more secure and a lot quicker than to Flanders, which must be very uncertain, particularly at this time of year. We're surprised that we haven't received a letter from you, Pedro, for quite a while. But I expect Don Gonzalo keeps you very busy. But do please write and let us know how you and Mat are.

'Firstly, Pedro, our love and best wishes to you on your twenty-third birthday in two weeks' time. I hope you'll be able to celebrate it appropriately with your "men-at-arms". Nine years ago, you celebrated your fourteenth birthday entombed in the prison of the Inquisition at Jaén. I still tremble when

I recall your description of your ordeals there. At least now you're safe in the hands of Don Gonzalo. Praise be for that.'

Mat looked up from the letter and glanced at Don Gonzalo. The innocent remark of Miriam had hit home hard.

'All is well here in Vélez Blanco, and your young Antonio will shortly be two years old. He's growing into a lively little boy and dotes on your uncle Joshua, as did you. Joshua spends hours playing with him and telling him stories. Antonio helps him dry his herbs, which Joshua still collects from the mountains above the town and sells in the local markets, but he's looking a lot older now and gets out of breath very quickly. Sara's asthma seems to be getting worse and is becoming a cause for concern. She'll be five in April and we'd hoped by now she would be growing out of it, but it doesn't seem to be the case. Spring is the worst time for her, when the almond and olive trees are in blossom, and we'll be moving her bed to the top of the keep where the breeze is stronger. Joshua remembers that your father Abraham used to prescribe sage for respiratory problems such as asthma, and he has been collecting leaves of this plant which grows so prolifically on the rocky mountains around about. So we've been methodically infusing sage leaves in boiling water and giving the drink to Sara three times a day, but so far it's not seeming to do much good.

'In November, we finished the second tapestry showing the monarchs' historic entrance to Granada five years ago (for your mother's people, Raquel, it was a disaster, but for me it spelt freedom!). We despatched the tapestry to the Queen in Medina for forwarding to Princess Juana in Flanders. Queen Isabel is delighted with it, and we received a lovely letter of thanks from her. With all the matters of state with which she has to deal, it's remarkable how thoughtful and considerate she is. Raquel: has Juana hung our first tapestry of the Alhambra in the palace yet, and have you seen it? Please let me know.

'Well, my dears, it's time to press on with our third tapestry, which is now nearly finished. What a feat these three tapestries have proved to be!

'Pedro, I enclose a letter from your Indies friend, Antonio de Torres, which arrived last week from Seville. I expect he's there planning another voyage.

'Much love,

'Mama.'

Antonio's letter read:

Seville, January 1497

Dear Pedro,

How are you? How are you getting on with Don Gonzalo in Italy? We hear great reports of his successes against the French, and we hope his campaign will soon be over and you'll all be able to return to Spain.

As you may have heard, Christopher Columbus is trying to organise a third voyage and, although the King and Queen are supportive and have offered to contribute over eighty per cent of the cost, the voyage is being blocked by Archdeacon Fonseca in La Española. I've been put in charge by the monarchs of all expeditions to the Indies and I'm assisting the Admiral now in equipping a fleet of six ships. That's why I'm here in Seville. However, CC is experiencing problems in enrolling crews (as happened with his first expedition), since the seamen have heard such bad reports of his leadership from former crew members.

The monarchs are keen to stabilise things on La Española now, and to give the Indians more rights and better protection from exploitation. They want to send more monks and priests to speed up their conversion to Christianity, but in my experience they do more harm than good, and I've written to Their Majesties saying so.

They have been drafting various decrees while they've been in Medina del Campo for promulgating this summer, which will permit CC to distribute parcels of land on La Española to existing and new settlers, providing they work the land for four years, cultivate wheat, cotton or flax and construct sugar mills. These decrees will provide great opportunities for young family men like you. All lands with mineral reserves will remain in the hands of the Crown, while the rest will remain common land. CC will be instructed to construct new settlements close to the gold mines.

My sister, Juana, is in Burgos with Prince Juan, awaiting the arrival of Princess Margaret of Austria, who should have arrived by now. She says he's very excited. Juana sends her kind regards to you and Raquel, who I expect will already have met Princess Margaret. By all accounts, she's very beautiful.

With very best wishes,

Antonio de Torres

In fact, for two months the Spanish fleet had been waiting in Flanders to transport the Austrian bride to Spain, but the weather was so adverse that the princess chose to stay in nearby Zeeland in anticipation of fair winds and a calmer sea. However, the storms increased and the cold became more severe as winter closed in around them. Stricken by hunger and the freezing temperatures, hundreds of sailors of the armada sickened. As many as 9,000 may have fallen prey to pneumonia, flu and the pestilence that was endemic in the fleet. Not until the spring was the fleet ready to weigh anchor.

But already there were recurring rumours in Brussels about Philip's fickle conduct, since he had once again reverted to his adventurous bachelor ways, seeking happiness wherever a pair of enticing eyes might lead him. The novelty of possessing an enamoured Spanish princess was clearly wearing thin. Juana, on the other hand, remained a slave to his every whim and, although baffled by his swift changes of mood, continued to give him full measure of her love. She treated with contempt all those who sought to monopolise him, never feeling able to confide her vexation to her staff.

The months passed swiftly. In February, Philip entered the lists in Brussels and tilted in the jousts with great success before the fascinated, but frightened, gaze of his young wife. April and May saw Juana journey from one Flemish city to another, while the Archduke escaped more and more with his hunting parties. In June and July, the royal couple were ever restless, moving through the cities of Holland to the north, such as Delft, the Hague and Amsterdam, with Philip going off alone yet again to slake his thirst for pleasure throughout his territories. Inebriated by tourneys and banquets, and surfeited with dancing and fêtes, he would call upon his courtiers to play endless sets of tennis or to chase deer through the great forests. For him, life was brimming with every pursuit.

Mat and Francesca reached Pisa at the end of March, and decided to make that their base rather than Florence, some sixty miles upriver, where they feared they might be 'spotted' by partisans visiting the city. Francesca suspected that the stronghold of the partisans was in the wooded mountains north of Prato, and it was there that they headed. So, after passing Bonnano Pisano's famous leaning bell tower in Pisa, they followed the course of the Arno valley, acquiring a donkey in a village on the way for just a handful of ducats. With Mat dressed in worn and faded trousers, sandals and a fleece waistcoat, and Francesca in a brown woollen skirt and a wide-sleeved, loosely laced-up blouse, and with both donning broad-brimmed straw hats, they looked sufficiently like country people not to be conspicuous. The donkey had a rough saddle for Francesca to perch on when she chose, as well as saddlebags on each side to carry food, clothing and bedding. Leather water bottles hung from each side of the saddle. A yard-long sword was too conspicuous for Mat or the animal to carry, so for security he had to make do with his trusty ash staff, a couple of twelve-inch-long hunting knives concealed within the saddle and, of course, his own immense physical strength.

Taking their time, they left the wide valley of the Arno and headed up into hills. Francesca had no particular plan in mind; but she had a suspicion that the area where Jofré's men might have been murdered was around Montovolo, and it was to there that they headed. They wandered from one village to another, up hill and down dale, through fields and woods, along paths and hedgerows, through wide valleys and tight ravines, across stone bridges and through fords. The villagers and farmers they encountered met their enquiries with nods of the head or in stony silence. What were they concealing? After three weeks of passing through dozens of villages and hamlets, they were beginning to realise that their quest was hopeless. Pedro could be anywhere in these mountains – held captive in a cottage, a farm building or in a cave or even a mine. Since no ransom demand had been received after nearly five months, it was more than likely he was dead.

Tired and demoralised, and at the point of turning back, Mat and Francesca approached the village of Fanano on the foothills of the 7,000-foot peak of Mount Cimone. It was fiesta day, and a market was in full swing, with dozens of stalls selling fruit and vegetables, fresh meat, bread and cakes, spices and herbs, pots and pans, farm tools, boots and shoes, wicker baskets, crockery and glassware. Everything a countryman or woman could ever want. Mat and Francesca pushed their way slowly through the hubbub of people, all of whom were laughing and in high spirits. After all, it was the highlight of their year. Eventually, at the end of the market, the couple passed a stall selling clothes. Most were worn garments and hand-me-downs, and were piled unceremoniously one on top of the other. A dozen women in black were picking through the heaps.

Then something caught Mat's eye. Quite out of place, and hanging tidily on a wooden hanger under the canvas awning of the stall, was a fine high-waisted jacket made of blue velvet and laced at the front. It had seams under the arms and ample sleeves open at the shoulder and elbows. Beneath the jacket on the hanger was a white undershirt with a square neck, the edging of which had been embroidered in black silk thread. Pale blue woollen hose lay on the crosspiece of the hanger and protruded below the jacket and shirt. Alongside was a second hanger supporting a dark red cloak.

Mat recognised the outfit immediately. The clothes were Pedro's. They were those he wore at Tordesillas to meet the King and Queen!

Mat could barely control his glee, and fumbled in the saddlebags of the donkey in an effort to conceal his interest, but he was transfixed by the clothing.

'What are you doing?' asked a perplexed Francesca. 'Have you seen a ghost?'

Mat made some funny signs with his head as much to say, *Shut up, woman, and follow me!*

He led his bemused companion and the donkey out beyond the market to where all was quiet.

'Well! What's the matter? Have you lost your senses?' said the fiery Neapolitan.

'No, I haven't. I've just seen Pedro's clothes hanging in that stall!'

'What! Are you sure?' cried Francesca, stupefied.

'Absolutely, I would spot them a mile off. They are very distinctive, with his mother's black stitching around the neck of his silk shirt.'

'Thanks be to God!' exclaimed Francesca with a gasp. 'At last we've found him.'

'Not so fast, my love,' cautioned the bearded giant. 'They might be his clothes, but it doesn't follow that the stallholder knows where they came from.'

'So what do we do?'

'We'll wait until he's packing up. Then we'll offer to buy them.'

'What if he refuses?'

'He won't refuse a decent price. Why would they be hanging in his stall if he didn't want to sell them? But we must find out where he got the clothes from. That might be tricky.'

The couple hung around for an hour or so while the crowd dispersed and the stalls packed up. The clothes stall was free of customers when Mat and Francesca approached it.

'I'm interested in that blue doublet and hose and blouse you have there, and the red cloak,' he said to the stallholder as nonchalantly as he could.

'These?' he said, pointing to the hangers.

'Yes.'

'But they won't fit you!' he laughed. 'They don't make clothes like this for the likes of you!'

'They're not for me. They're for my son. He's been invited to court at Florence.'

'Fine story!' mocked the stallholder. 'But if they're what you want, then they'll be 500 ducats. Bearing in mind you're the father of a prince, you can have them for 550 ducats! The lot, including the hangers!'

Mat and Francesca exchanged glances. Was that a fair price? They didn't know.

The deal was struck at 450 ducats, and the clothes were carefully wrapped and placed in a box for the visitors.

It was now getting dark, and the village square was largely deserted, except for the stallholder's wife packing away clothes and some dogs scavenging leftover food from where the food stalls had been.

'Now, my man,' said Mat looking down on the stallholder from his great height. 'You've had the bargain of a lifetime selling us these clothes, so could you be so good as to tell us where you got them from?'

Although he spoke quietly, there was a menace in his voice which made the man tremble visibly.

'I bought them in another market, signore, not far from here... from another stallholder. I don't know the man's name... I'd never seen him before...'

Mat grabbed hold of the man's jacket and lifted him bodily off the ground, so that his reddening face was level with his own.

'No, you didn't! You know exactly who you got them from. So tell me, or I'll break you in two.' Freeing his right hand, Mat circled it around the man's neck and squeezed.

'I'll tell you!' he blurted out. 'I'll tell you. I promise I'll tell you!'

'So where?'

'From a village fifteen miles away, over those mountains yonder.'

'What's the village called?'

'Canevare.'

'And who sold you these clothes?'

'I don't remember his name… I-I…'

Mat tightened his grip on the stallholder's neck.

'Romano, Romano Latini.'

'Good, you will take us to him.'

'Oh no! I can't. Not Romano Latini. He's the—'

'He's the what?'

'I can't go,' the stallholder repeated. 'I've got a wife to care for. But I'll tell you where you can find him.'

'No, you'll take us there. You might be sending us on a fool's errand. No, you'll take us there yourself,' demanded Mat, letting the man down to the ground.

'Who is this Romano Latini anyway?' asked Francesca.

'He's – he's…' The stallholder stopped. He had frozen with fear.

The man's wife appeared from behind the stall and brushed her husband aside.

'Get out of the way. You'd be frightened of your own shadow! I'll tell you who he is,' she asserted forcibly. 'He's the leader of the partisans, here in these mountains.'

The woman was fair-headed, slim and sprightly. She must have been in her late twenties. Some twenty years less than her wimpish husband.

'Very well,' said Mat, addressing the man. 'You'll take us to this village of Canevare and you can point out to us where this scoundrel lives.'

'No. *I'll* take you there,' insisted his spirited young wife. 'I know exactly where he lives. My husband doesn't. Romano Latini's cottage is not in the village. It's a mile outside, down a track. The man's an animal, a pig.' She spat on the ground.

She spoke rapidly in a staccato voice and with a very strong local accent. Mat could not understand her, although Francesca could.

The young woman sat down on a box by the emptied stall.

'My name's Rosa,' she started in her staccato voice, clearly keen to explain things. 'My family lived in Canevare. It's a hillside village over that mountain. It's a very old village. Might even be Roman. It had silver mines. I suppose that's why the Romans were there. There are lots of old ruins. Some old mine buildings. When I was thirteen or fourteen, my parents and two sisters died when our house burnt down. I had nobody to care for me. This Romano Latini took me into his house. He didn't ask anybody. He just did. Nobody cared. That's the way with the people in Canevare. Nobody cares.' She looked up at Mat and Francesca.

'Yes, we're listening, Rosa,' said Francesca. 'Please continue your story.'

'Romano Latini's a big man, although not your size, signore. I've never seen anybody as big as you before! Even then he had a frightening appearance. He had lost an eye in a fight and had a deep purple scar running halfway across his face where his eye was. He's hideous, truly hideous. I was only a young girl – well, young woman, if you understand me – but having two sisters, I'd never seen a man before...'

She looked up at Francesca questioningly. Francesca nodded; she understood what she meant.

'Well, he did everything to me. Every vile thing under the sun. In effect, for five years I was his sex slave. Every day, I was humiliated and brutalised. The things he did to me, and the things he used on me, mean that I can never have a child. At twenty-nine, I'm a physical wreck. In constant pain. Sometimes my insides feel like they're being ploughed.'

Rosa stopped. She got up from the box and rubbed the palms of her hands down her skirt, as if washing away the hurt.

'I've said enough. Suffice it to say that you'll both understand that if this man were to die tomorrow, I'd dance on his grave. So, signore, I'll gladly lead you to his house. But I must warn you that the man's evil – a killer. You must be on your guard.'

'If my husband's son, Pedro, is alive, Rosa,' asked Francesca, 'is he likely to be held captive by this Romano Latini in his cottage?'

'No, I don't think so, signora. If your Pedro is still alive, then I think it's more likely he'll be somewhere in the village itself. There are so many ruins, there are all sorts of places where he could be hidden away.'

'Would you be able to help us locate him, Rosa? Or at least search for him, or for signs of him?'

'Yes, of course, signora, I already have some ideas. But first we must deal with Romano.'

Mat caught the gist of this last comment and nodded slowly, aware that he might well meet his match.

'Now,' said the stallholder, cheering up noticeably, 'you can't set off now since it's almost dark. With no moon tonight, you couldn't possibly find your way through the pine forest which covers the mountains. Please return with us to out humble cottage and you can set off at first light tomorrow.'

As they left, he turned to Mat. 'Whose clothes are these – if I might be so bold as to ask?'

'Have you heard of the Gran Capitán?'

'The Spanish general? Signore Fer-Fer—'

'Yes, Don Gonzalo Fernández of Córdoba. At the request of the King of Naples and Pope Alexander VI, Don Gonzalo is driving the French from your country. These clothes belong to his aide-de-camp. He's not my son, but a very close friend. You might say I am his protector.'

'So did you come here in response to the hostage demand, signore?'

Mat stopped in his tracks. The mention of a hostage demand came like a bolt out of the blue. '*What* hostage demand?' he roared.

'I picked up a conversation in the market two months ago that a hostage demand was to be issued by the partisans.'

'So you know about this?' thundered Mat.

'No, signore. Please believe me, I know nothing. I am not one of the partisans. They are a scourge among us. We villagers hate them. We're afraid of them. If we don't meet their demands, they burn down our houses, rape our wives and daughters, slaughter our animals.'

Rosa nodded her assent. 'What he says is true,' she said.

'As Rosa has explained,' continued the stallholder, 'this Romano Latini is an evil man. I heard some months ago that he killed several horsemen in a village to the east of here who were simply riding through. But I don't know what happened.'

'They were the Pope's lancers,' Mat said, 'and they were butchered in cold blood. My young friend, Pedro, was taken away separately, and we're looking for what became of him.'

'Ah! Now I understand,' said the stallholder slowly.

'So what about this hostage demand?' scowled Mat. 'What do you know about it? No such demand has been received by Don Gonzalo in Naples or the Pope in Rome.'

'I'm sorry, signore, I don't know any more than I've told you. Please, you must believe me. It was just something I heard in the marketplace.'

'Very well,' said Mat pensively. 'But it's worrying that we've heard nothing about a hostage demand. That makes me even more anxious about what has become of Pedro.'

The four walked in silence for a while, just listening to the hoof steps of the obedient donkey on the stony path.

'I can see that you're not carrying a sword, my friend,' concluded the stallholder. 'I've just the thing for you. Something someone gave me as payment for something he bought.'

'What?' asked Mat. 'A suit of armour?'

'No, something of far more use to you. A French cavalry sabre: long, curved and very, very sharp!'

XVII: The Cottage in the Clearing

January 1497

With the departure of Juana's fleet to Flanders the previous August, Queen Isabel had started to have doubts about the wisdom of sending her second daughter to a country which was so different from Spain. She was embittered by the hostility of the French that necessitated the dangerous sea voyage, and she grew restless by the day, owing to the lack of reports on the progress of the fleet and on how Juana was faring in Flanders.

To add to her woes, word was brought that her mother, sixty-eight-year-old Isabel of Portugal, had died in the small town of Arévalo on the high meseta of Castile. In truth, her death came as a blessed relief from the void in which she lived, but it initiated the darkest period in the Queen's life, from which she would never fully recover.

Gambling on a respite from the violent gales which were roaring through the English Channel, the Spanish fleet bearing Margaret had set forth from Flanders on 22 January 1497, two months before the Gran Capitán's triumphant entry into Rome. But the winds had not relented and the seas had become a mass of turbulent grey water. Then a great storm struck, forcing the ships into the safety of Southampton harbour on the south coast of England. Not until March did the seventeen-year-old Flemish princess reach the Spanish port of Santander. After the rapid unloading of the baggage, she and her retinue commenced the long ascent up to the 3,000-foot-high plateau on which Burgos sat. A group of horsemen, led by Prince Juan and his father, King Fernando, galloped out to greet the bride and to lead her into the city to meet the Queen. But the wedding was delayed by the forty days of Lent. In vain, Juan pleaded with his mother to waive the constraints imposed by this religious observance, the delay proving purgatory for the prince. He was two months short of his nineteenth birthday and had fallen head over heels in love with the blonde maiden. After a seeming eternity of self-denial and abstinence, his patience was rewarded and the connubial knot was tied on 3 April. A period of tourneys, bullfights, banquets and fiestas followed, during which the people of Castile rejoiced in the good fortune of their Prince Charming. He was the pampered darling of Queen Isabel, and her one and only son. Among the many nobles and scholars who appeared at court to render homage to the newlyweds was Christopher Columbus, Admiral of the Ocean Sea, wishing, as ever, to remain in the sight and favour of his principal benefactor and supporter, the Queen.

Margaret, eighteen months younger than Juan and just two months younger than her sister-in-law Juana, was a notable beauty. It was no wonder that Juan was completely smitten by her. Likened to Venus herself for her nobility, beauty and age, this lovely young woman was without any coquetry in her make-up or dress.

Meanwhile, in Flanders, gloom had descended on the Spanish party, as Raquel noted in her diary:

April 1497: It's now six months since we arrived in Brussels, and nearly eight months since we departed from Laredo. Most of us are very homesick, partly because of the continuous damp, gloomy weather, broken only by occasional days of sunshine which, even then, have billowing white clouds beating across the sky like great galleons, but mostly it's because we feel so far from home. One cannot travel overland to Spain across France because of the hostilities between our countries. The journey south across Germany and Switzerland is truly forbidding, and the sea journey past England is terrifying. I'm sure the Indies are more accessible from Spain across the Ocean Sea than Spain is from here!

I was honoured the other day when the Princess invited me into her quarters to show me Miriam's two tapestries of the glorious vista of the Alhambra from across the River Darro, and of the monarchs' entrance into Granada. They look truly stunning side by side on the Princess's wall, and a space has been left for the Vélez ladies' third tapestry. Juana and the Duke are thrilled with them and rightly so.

With the Duke away so much (and we all have our suspicions as to why), the Princess spends a lot of time on her own. Her evident loneliness would be relieved if she would only confide her feeling to her ladies – after all, that's why we're here. But she bottles it all up and shuts herself away from us. It's so sad, since she looks so forlorn and distant for much of the time. But she cheers up amazingly when Philip returns from his hunting (and we suppose his amorous adventures), and all is quickly forgiven and forgotten.

I feel particularly depressed and anxious. Miriam's recent letter saying that Sara is unwell and that her breathing is getting worse is worrying enough, but Ana of Beamonte, who's been wonderful to me, has just informed me that you, my dear Pedro, set off with the Pope's youngest son last October to come here to the wedding. Last October! Where are you, my love? What has become of you? I'm growing more anxious by the day. Even with all the delays which I know can occur and the enormous distance from Rome to here, you should surely have arrived by now. I pray every night that you are safe and that you'll arrive any day now. I am really at my wits' end.

With their donkey lightly laden, Mat, Francesca and fair-headed Rosa set off at first light for the trek over the mountain to Canevare. Around midday, with the village visible on the hillside a mile away, Rosa led them down a stony track through a wood.

'Romano Latini's cottage is not far from here,' she whispered. 'We must take care so as not to be seen. I suggest we leave the animal here among the trees. I'll scout ahead and you can follow a little way behind. Remember, this man's dangerous.'

'Yes,' cautioned Francesca, mindful of Mat's sense of fair play. 'If this Romano Latini's there, don't for one minute think you have to confront him in a fair fight, strong though you are. He's a killer and won't conform to Don Gonzalo's rules of chivalry. So no heroics, Mat. Is that clear?'

'Yes, my dear, it is. Have no fear. I'll be on my guard, but he won't get the better of me. That I promise you.'

The stone cottage came into sight in the middle of a small clearing. It was surrounded by long grass. Smoke spiralled slowly from the chimney in the still air. Logs were stacked against the side wall, which had a tiny window. Clucking chickens ran around pecking at the ground, looking for seeds. They might be a problem if they were to warn of the strangers' approach. Two horses grazed quietly in a paddock nearby. Several items of wet clothing hung from a washing line behind the house. One item, at least, was a woman's. Hmm!

The trio stopped at the edge of the clearing, remaining hidden among the trees. They exchange glances, uncertain as how to proceed. Mat drew from his scabbard the heavy, curved sabre lent to him by the stallholder. His ash staff was tucked into his belt. In his left hand, he held one of the long daggers which he had brought from Rome. Francesca held the other one in a fashion which suggested that she knew how to use it.

They waited, listening, watching. Minutes passed.

Then suddenly there was a cry from within the cottage, followed by a scream. The door of the cottage flew open and a young girl ran out, screaming. She was barefoot and naked except for a thin short cotton shift. Her tiny breasts made little impression on her flimsy attire, and her thin legs and undeveloped body showed that she was just a slip of a girl. Maybe eleven, maybe twelve? Her long brown hair streamed behind her. But the look of sheer terror on her small face was nothing as compared with the chilling sight of her blood-soaked shift and bloody hands.

The girl saw the three strangers as they ran out from among the trees, and she ran towards them, falling into Rosa's arms, crying pitifully and gripping the older woman closely to her. Rosa stroked her long hair and did her best to comfort her.

Mat and Francesca ran to the door of the cottage, not knowing what to expect. Mat gripped the sabre tightly as he rushed into the cottage. It was so dark inside that he could barely see anything. He knew he had made a great mistake in his precipitous haste. He fell headlong over something bulky on the floor, half expecting then to hear the swoosh of a sword descending on him. He rolled over in an instant and jumped to his feet.

What lay on the floor, now lit by the light from the door, was a gruesome sight. A big man lay spreadeagled, face down on the stone floor of the cottage; his trousers were open and halfway down his buttocks. The hilt of a knife stuck out of his back. There was blood everywhere. But worse, much worse, an axe lay embedded across the back of the man's neck. His head had been half severed. Blood was still spreading over the flagstones.

Romano Latini was no more. Mat's job had been done for him.

Francesca ran outside and told Rosa what they had found. How could such a slip of a girl have the strength to cause such terrible wounds?

Mat stayed inside and removed the knife and axe, tempted to complete the removal of the partisan's head and return it to Rome in a sack. But he thought better of it. He turned the inert body over; its half-attached head slithered around reluctantly. Mat shuddered as one open eye stared at him, the other obliterated by the deep purple scar running across his bearded face. Averting his gaze, Mat threw a rug over the corpse. What the young, blood-soaked girl and Rosa had gone through at the hands of this gruesome man was beyond comprehension. With Mat's sight now adjusted to the gloom, he looked around him. Hanging from a hook on the wall was Pedro's beautiful Toledo sword in its scabbard, with its distinctive haft composed of alternate red and white brass rings. His horn-hafted dagger lay on the table nearby. Both had been fashioned for Pedro's thirteenth birthday by a Toledo-trained swordsmith in Lorca.

Mat stopped. Was Pedro here? Was he imprisoned in another room? Was he lying dead inside the cottage? Was he buried outside in the wood?

Mat went from room to room. There were only two other rooms in the small dwelling. One was a dishevelled bedroom and the other a tiny kitchen with a wood-burning stove. Mat ran out through the back door. There was no sign of Pedro and no sign of recently disturbed ground. At least that was something. He ran up to the two horses in the paddock. One was Pedro's faithful chestnut mare, Indy. Mat was sure of it. The diamond blaze on the horse's forehead was so distinctive. Mat cuddled the horse's head and stroked her neck. The horse neighed and seemed to bodily relax. Did she recognise Mat? Apparently so, since the animal trotted behind him to the paddock fence.

Mat retraced his steps into the cottage and continued his search. There was nothing of note, nothing of value. A small, crudely made wooden box stood on the stone mantelpiece over the fireplace. Mat picked it up and slid back the lid. What he saw made his blood freeze. He stood there mortified, trying to work out the significance of the contents. He must keep this to himself. Still stunned, he stuffed the box into his pocket, out of sight.

Dismissing the idea of dragging the bandit's body outside to bury it, Mat screwed up a piece of paper into a spill, lit it from the grate in the kitchen and put it to the rug over the Romano Latini's body. He then threw the burning spill into the bedroom. He went back out to the paddock, and led Indy and the other horse out. By the time he joined the three women at the edge of the clearing, smoke was already billowing from the cottage.

'Let's get away from here,' instructed Mat. 'We'll talk when we reach the path to Canevare.'

With her arm wrapped around her new charge, who was still wearing her bloodstained shift, Rosa followed Francesca, Mat and the horses through the wood and back to where the donkey was tied. Francesca found some clothes for the young girl in the animal's saddlebags, and Rosa cleaned her up with water from one of the leather water skins. Eventually the girl calmed down and told her story.

'My name's Tina. I live in Canevare. My family's very poor. I'm the youngest of five children; all but one of us are girls. My father was caught stealing food for us. Romano Latini, who ruled the village like he's king, promised to get the charge against my father dropped, but only if one of us girls was given to him. My father chose me, since I'm more of a burden to the family than the others. That was three weeks ago.

'Romano brought me here to his house. I didn't know what to expect, what he wanted me for. I thought he'd want to me to cook for him and clean his house, all the things I do at home, but it wasn't for that. The man's an animal, and lives and eats like a pig. He's not interested in cooked food or a clean and tidy house. All he wanted me for was... my body... what little of it there is!'

She stood there with her arms out from her sides, as much as to say, *Well, look at me!*

'Every day he's abused me in the most horrible way until I couldn't stand it any longer. I hid a knife under a cushion and this morning as he undid his trousers to... to do it to me again... I thrust the knife in his back as hard as I could. Not knowing if he was dead or alive, I used the hand axe on him, which lay in the hearth.'

'And you very nearly removed his head!' interjected Mat.

'You're a very brave young woman!' said the stallholder's wife, Rosa, now warming to the thought of the young girl being the child she could never have.

'You must return with me to my home over the mountain,' she said tenderly. 'My husband and I will care for you. You'll have a good life with us. That I promise you. You see, I too have suffered at the hands of this terrible man.'

Mat and Francesca took the young girl's hands and nodded warmly at her in approval of Rosa's idea.

'Now, Tina, tell us what you know of Canevare. Do you know anything of a young man held hostage there?'

'Oh yes,' replied Tina in a totally matter-of-fact way, as if she were asked if there were a bread shop in the village. 'I helped feed him.'

Mat was lost for words. 'You mean he's alive and well?'

'Well, he was alive three weeks ago,' the girl replied. 'But he's very sick and has been brutally treated. If you like, I can take you to where he's being held.'

With Rosa and Tina riding Indy, the group hastened up the path to the village of Canevare. It seemed largely deserted when they arrived at the hillside settlement. Ruins lay everywhere. Leaving the animals in a walled enclosure, Tina scurried over broken-down walls and up stone-strewn alleys to a large ruin with thick, high walls and a tumbledown tower.

'This was an old Roman church. My father says it was one of the first in Tuscany. Please follow me. We're very close.'

A military field commander such as Don Gonzalo bears enormous responsibilities; for directing the course of his campaigns, for leading and inspiring his forces, for directing his officers, for maintaining discipline and morale in his army, and for feeding, clothing and arming his soldiers. And not least for tact and diplomacy in dealing with his allies, foreign kings and potentates, and – in this fading era of chivalry – his foes. Don Gonzalo Fernández's accomplishments in fulfilling all these duties with such aplomb rightly earned for him the title *El Gran Capitán*, a title which would reverberate down through the ages and illuminate the history of medieval Spain.

But now he was unsettled, on edge, tetchy. Normally a sound sleeper, he tossed and turned in bed, aware that something was troubling him. But in his heart he knew what it was. The letter to Pedro from his mother Miriam, which Mat had read out a few days before, had touched a sensitive spot. Although she was worried that she had not heard from Pedro in months, Miriam had, nevertheless, expressed her confidence that Pedro was in the safe hands of Gonzalo – who, after all, had been like a father to Pedro. Indeed, it was because of this that she and Raquel had reluctantly concurred with Pedro's wish to accompany Don Gonzalo to Italy as his aide-de-camp.

Don Gonzalo tossed and turned, unable to expel Miriam's innocent remark from his thoughts. However he tried to justify his decision to send Pedro with Jofré to the royal wedding in Flanders, his mind dwelt on the same point. He had let Miriam down. However brave Mat and Francesca were in their sally into the Tuscan mountains in search of Pedro, it was inconceivable that his aide-de-camp had not been killed by these barbarous, lawless partisans.

Don Gonzalo's thoughts kept returning to Pedro and his mother; how he had saved the fourteen-year-old from the hands of Tomás de Torquemada, the notorious Inquisitor General of Castile; how he had then nursed Pedro back to health in the castle at Porcuna, near Córdoba; how he had summoned his Moorish foe, the warlord known as El Zagal, who owed Don Gonzalo a favour, to conduct Pedro safely through Muslim-held territory to the coast in order for him to board a ferry boat home. But, more than anything, Don Gonzalo remembered the wedding reception held in Miriam's home after Pedro and Raquel's wedding in Vélez Blanco on a snowy November day four years before, and her expression of thanks to him for caring for Pedro as if he were the son he'd never had. Her charm and sincerity on that day brought a tear to his eye and, in his own way, he had become enchanted with this elegant and beautiful woman who had suffered for all those years during her long captivity in the Alhambra. The image of a radiant Miriam in her gorgeous, pale blue dress on that memorable day kept returning to his mind. What words could he use in his letter to tell her of the death of her son? Lying there in the darkness, he rehearsed over and over again what he might write, but nothing seemed adequate. No words would assuage his sense of guilt or provide comfort to a woman who surely had lost her only son and the last remaining member of her family.

It was in this agitated state of mind that, shortly after his triumphal entry into Rome, Gonzalo met the Pope in order to seek his leave to fulfil one final task against the French. Furious at what he had seen and heard while in the city, he addressed Rodrigo Borgia in forthright terms about the licentiousness rampant at the very heart of Christendom. Three days later, after leaving strict instructions to be informed immediately of any news from Mat and Francesca about Pedro, he marched on French-held Rocca Guillermo, a fortress on the upper reaches of the River Garellano, several days' march back towards Naples. The fortress at Rocca Guillermo was commanded by Andrea Doria, aged thirty, and garrisoned by only sixty men. Doria had been raiding as far as Gaeta. Warned of Gonzalo's advance, Doria had quickly raised and fortified his walls and had drawn within them the inhabitants of nearby villages to prevent them aiding the Spaniards.

The Spaniards' first assault failed, but the following day they gained the outer towers and walls, although not the inner keep. A truce was called, when Gonzalo invited the young French commander to dine with him in his tent. Doria was won over by the consideration and generosity of his rival, and next morning he surrendered the fortress. With Rocca Guillermo neutralised,

Gonzalo and his army marched southwards back to Naples at a leisurely pace, their work in Italy finally completed.

The Gran Capitán's return to Naples was no less triumphant than his entry to Rome. King Federico came out to welcome him and bestowed on him the title of Duke of Sant'Angelo, as well as the fiefdom of two towns and several villages in his kingdom from which Gonzalo would receive the dues. The people of Naples celebrated his return with triumphal arches and by dancing the high-stepping *tarantella* in the streets. The music and feasting lasted several days and nights.

After defeating the French at Seminara, Tropea, Laino, Atella, Ostia and finally Rocca Guillermo in May 1497, the Spaniards' three-year-long Italian campaign was finally over. But it would be a year before Gonzalo and his veterans would return in triumph to Spain.

XVIII: The Crypt

April 1497

Prince Juan and his young bride Margaret were married in Burgos on the third of the month, and were celebrating the union with spectacular vigour. With equal ardour, Archduke Philip was spreading his amorous favours far and wide, and Christopher Columbus was continuing to pester Queen Isabel in Medina del Campo for the go-ahead for his third journey. In Xiquena, Miriam was growing ever more anxious over the health of her granddaughter, Sara, and, for his part, Don Gonzalo was struggling in writing a personal letter to her.

Naples, 5 April 1497

My Dear Miriam,

I am writing this just before I return with my forces to Sicily, since our work here in Italy is nearly done. But I do so with a heavy heart, knowing that I have to convey to you some worrying news which is ever on my mind.

I have to inform you that Pedro is missing, and we're uncertain as to his whereabouts or even if he is alive. Of course, we're doing all we can to find him, and I pray daily that we will locate him soon and find him in good health.

In early September last, Pope Alexander VI, alias Spanish-born Rodrigo Borgia, contacted me to say that he was sending his youngest son, fifteen-year-old Jofré, as his representative to the wedding in Flanders of Princess Juana and Philip, Duke of Austria. You know all about this from your dealings with the Queen. Clearly I couldn't go myself, so I chose Pedro as my envoy to accompany young Jofré; firstly because Pedro conducts himself with gentlemanly decorum, and also because he'd have the opportunity to spend some time with Raquel. They must have been missing each other terribly. The group left Naples soon afterwards with a squadron of papal lancers under the leadership of an experienced sergeant. With a long journey ahead of them, which by necessity had to avoid the easier route through France, no time was to be lost, but I was confident that they would arrive in time in Brussels for the royal wedding.

Over the next few months, I waited with increasing anxiety for news of their journey, since I had asked Pedro to relay messages back to me of their progress northwards. We learnt nothing of their journey until Jofré and his sergeant appeared suddenly in Rome during my entry into the city on 15 March with my soldiers. The two men were in a bad way and told of their ordeal. Somewhere in the Tuscan mountains, north of Florence, they had been set on by a band of ruffians who call themselves partisans and seek independence, although from whom is not clear to me. Pedro was separated from the rest and ridden off. Jofré and the five others were imprisoned in a small village in the mountains. After more than five months, he and his sergeant, Giuseppe, were released but, sadly, not before his five brave lancers were put to death.

We have heard nothing of Pedro since then, neither have I received a hostage demand as is common in these cases. Your loyal gatekeeper at Xiquena, Matute, was as ever concerned about Pedro, whom he cares for deeply. He proposed after Jofré's return to set off in search of Pedro in Tuscany. This he is now doing. With his Neapolitan lady friend, Francesca, both dressed as poor peasants, they plan to infiltrate the partisan stronghold to learn what they can of Pedro's whereabouts and return him safely here. Mat's an amazing man, whose resourcefulness matches his size, and he is accompanied by a woman who grew up in the rough streets of Naples and is as tough as they come. They make a formidable couple. To speed his journey, I arranged a boat to carry them to Pisa on the River Arno, where they could get a river craft upstream to Florence. Mat and Francesca have been gone a month, and might well by now have located Pedro – and indeed may already be returning him safely here. Unfortunately, I am sailing to Sicily from Naples tomorrow, but I've alerted my soldiers who are remaining on the mainland between Rome and here to watch out for them. I have also lodged a squadron of light cavalry or lancers in Florence in case Mat needs help in his departure from Tuscany.

I can only say, my dear Miriam, that I am confident Mat and Francesca will be successful in their venture and will return safe and sound with your son. I pray with all my heart that this will be so.

Yours, as ever,

Gonzalo

Commander, Spanish forces in Italy

So, with Don Gonzalo and his Spanish forces already en route to Sicily, Mat and his three female companions arrived stealthily in the hillside village of Canevare. It was a small village and as old as the hills among which it lay. The sun-bleached stone dwellings were spread across the hillside and most seemed in ruins, with tumbledown roofs and no doors or windows. Few, if any, seemed to be occupied, and there was no sign of life, neither human nor animal. To Mat and Francesca, the whole scene felt distinctly eerie, if not scary.

Tina stopped in the centre of the ruins to which she had led the other three. She spoke in a whisper, although there was no need. Not a soul was to be seen.

'This was an old Christian church,' she said. 'You can still see some coloured floor tiles in the corners.' She pointed to them, then beckoned them to follow her.

'Is Pedro here?' Mat whispered anxiously, looking around at the low rectangular walls and the stones strewn over the ground. 'If he's here, where on earth can he be?'

'Come over here!' Tina called, running towards the tower.

She heaved back a stone slab which half-covered a hole in the ground some two feet across. Crouching on her knees, she peered down into it. Mat, Francesca and Rosa ran across the rubble and joined her.

'Are you there, signore?' cried Tina, her head stuck in the hole.

Mat knelt by her side.

'He's down there,' she said. 'My father thinks this must have been the crypt of the old church.'

'Pedro!' Mat called out. 'Are you there?'

He thought he heard a groan.

'Pedro, it's me – Mat. We've come to save you. Can you hear me?'

There was no response.

He peered down into the crypt, but after the bright light of day it was too dark to see anything. There appeared no sign of life, nor of any movement.

'How do we get into it?' queried Mat.

Tina scrambled to her knees.

'Follow me. Me and my sister fed him through this hole. The way into the crypt is barred, but come with me.'

She ran into the ruins of the tower, falling over blocks of stone lying everywhere. She tore into a low arched doorway and disappeared from sight. Mat, Francesca and Rosa followed. In the darkness and feeling their way against the side walls, they followed her down a flight of twenty or thirty steps which spiralled down until the stairwell opened out opposite an iron-studded door at the bottom. As Tina had said, it was locked. Clearly it had not been opened in months.

'Pedro's inside there?' asked Mat.

'Yes – well, he was three weeks ago,' replied Tina, breathlessly.

'How do we get inside? Pedro!' he shouted, banging on door with his fists.

'If he's there,' said Tina, 'I doubt if he'll hear you. The door is very thick and the walls themselves are six feet thick.'

'Who's got the key?' asked Francesca.

'Romano Latini had it, but I don't know where he kept it. It wasn't in his cottage. I looked everywhere for it.'

'We'll have to break it down,' cried Mat. 'There's no other way.'

'You'll never break this door down, signore, it's very thick and strong.'

But Mat had gone. He was already running back up the flight of steps into the daylight. For ten minutes, he ran in and out of the ruined buildings around the old church, searching for something with which to batter the door down. He ran into what must have been a mine building, since there was a rusty old winding frame and pulley. In increasing desperation, he scrambled over the debris, searching, searching…

'Ah!' he shouted as Tina caught him up. 'Just what I need.' He climbed onto some huge blocks of stone and yanked at an iron axle that straddled the mineshaft. The solid iron axle was as thick as his wrist. In its centre was a rusting iron pulley a foot across.

'You'll never remove that,' cried Tina, climbing up beside him and reaching up to touch it. 'It's fixed into the wall at each side.'

Mat climbed up the rough wall beside it, looking down into the void over which it sat. A stone which he dislodged fell into the mine shaft, falling for five or six seconds before hitting the bottom with a big boom. Getting what purchase he could with his knees, Mat lifted himself a bit higher and tried to pull the axle from the wall. But it would not budge. He climbed back down to the ground, found an iron spike nearby and climbed back up alongside the axle. At each end it sat in a stone bearing. With the spike, he worked the stone bearing loose and pulled it away from the axle.

'But you can't lift that axle out!' yelled Tina. 'It must weigh a ton. If you do, it will fall down into the mine – and take you with it!'

Mat had to try.

Leaning out over the void, his big right fist grasped the iron axle, reaching almost to the pulley at the centre. With the two older women, Rosa and Francesca, holding onto his legs, he pulled with all his might. Once, twice, three times, until his shoulders and arm muscles swelled mightily.

'One last heave!' he cried.

The axle came free from the stone bearing on the far side of the shaft, and the central pulley slid with a clank to the far end. Weighing between 200 and 300 pounds, the heavy mechanism immediately swung down into the mine shaft with Mat holding onto it like grim death with one hand. If the two women had not been holding his legs, he surely would have followed it down into the void. With all his might, he hauled it up until axle was resting on the edge of the shaft. He had done it!

After recovering his breath, Mat lowered it down to the ground beside Francesca and Rosa and climbed down from the wall. The two women tried to lift one end of the mechanism, but failed to move it. It remained rooted to the ground. They looked at Mat and shook their heads in disbelief and awe. How had he done it?

Mat heaved the axle and pulley onto his shoulder and the four of them retraced their steps to the tower. Francesca made a detour to the roof opening into the crypt to warn Pedro, if indeed he were there, that Mat was going to try and force an entry into his dungeon.

Mat carried the axle down the steps, manoeuvring it around the tight curvature of the staircase. At the bottom, in the widened stairwell, he lifted the massive axle and swung the heavy end with the pulley against the studded door. The force he exerted was enormous. Two, three, four times he swung the iron battering ram against the door. Then, *crack*, the door splintered along the line of the lock. Two more heaves and the door was shattered. Mat dropped the axle, and forced his way through the splintered door into the near-darkness.

On a stone bench on the far side sprawled Pedro. The three ran to him. Francesca ran down the steps to join them.

'Pedro, it's us – Mat and Francesca!'

He turned his head slowly and muttered some words.

Mat repeated what he said, lifting Pedro's head in his hands.

'Pedro, it's me, Mat, Matute. We've come to rescue you and take you home.'

'Mat?' Pedro croaked slowly, deliriously. 'Matute... Don Gonzalo... Raquel... Mama.'

'Yes, Pedro,' Mat said, relieved above all else that his young charge was alive. 'We've come to take you home. You're safe now. You're in good hands. Nothing more will happen to you.'

While Mat was talking to Pedro, Francesca had been studying him and the dungeon in which he had been incarcerated for five long months.

The man lying on that stone shelf was hardly recognisable as the Pedro she knew. His hair was long and matted, as was his beard, both filthy beyond words and now streaked with grey. His face, hands and feet were caked in grime and his nails brown and broken. His red-rimmed eyes were sunken in their sockets, distant, not focussing. What clothes remained on his body were just torn rags. He lay there inert, with just the odd twitch as his emaciated body fought to keep death at bay, if only for a few more days. As he tried to move his hands to touch Mat, the blackened rags bound around his left hand fell away, exposing a gruesome sight. His middle finger was missing and what little stump remained of it, as well as his whole hand, was swollen and purple and crawling with maggots. Mat jolted at the awful injury, knowing that he should have expected this after what he'd found in the box on the mantelpiece of Romano Latini.

But now he understood. Pedro's middle finger of his left hand, which used to bear Queen Isabel's jade ring, had been cut off as evidence to support a hostage demand from the partisans. But none had materialised. The gruesome blackened finger and ring had remained on Romano Latini's mantelpiece until Mat had discovered it.

As Francesca looked around, she could see that Pedro had been imprisoned in a dome-shaped sarcophagus, with the central round opening some fifteen feet above the floor. The lower part of the chamber was cut into solid rock, but the upper half comprised dry stonework formed into a round dome. There were benches on each side, and some ancient bones lay scattered on the ground below them. Across the dusty floor along one side ran a small trickle of fresh water emanating from the bare rock. Flies buzzed over decomposing food in the centre of the chamber, obviously dropped from the surface by Tina and her sisters.

All four realised that Pedro had to be removed from that living coffin immediately if he were not to expire there and then in front of them. So, easing the inert Pedro up to sitting position, Mat carefully lifted him onto his shoulders. He was as light as a sack of hay. He carried him carefully up the spiral staircase to the surface, Francesca shielding Pedro's eyes against the glare of the sun with her hand.

Answering Mat's unspoken question, young Tina said, 'I know where we can find some water for him to drink and for us to clean his body. Down the bottom of the hill there's a spring-fed pool. It's not far from here. Can you manage to carry him, signore?'

Mat just grinned. The question did not even warrant an answer.

At the pool, in the shade of the trees, the three women removed the rags covering Pedro's body while Mat got his charge to sip some cool water from a beaker. To Mat, every sip he swallowed was a triumph and one small step towards his eventual recovery. Using Mat's torn-up shirt soaked in the cool spring water, the three women worked their way slowly over Pedro's naked and emaciated form, cleaning the grime from his body, face and eyes, and washing his hair and rough beard as best they could.

Pedro's eyes remained glazed and unfocussed, and he continued to mutter the same words over and over again: *Mat, Don Gonzalo, Raquel, Mama.* He was barely alive.

'We must get him to my home as soon as we can,' said Rosa. 'Can you manage him, signore? We can't put him on one of the animals, the jarring would kill him.'

'Have no fear, my dear,' said the gentle giant. 'I can carry him. He's as light as a feather.'

And so he did, all the way.

Mat, Francesca, Rosa and eleven-year-old Tina arrived back at Rosa's village of Fanano in the afternoon of the next day. Rosa had ridden ahead on Pedro's mare, Indy, to advise them of their coming, and she and her stallholder husband had already made up a bed for Pedro in the cool of their veranda when the group arrived. Water was being heated to complete his clean-up; knives and a razor had been sharpened and honed to cut his hair and remove his beard. Food was being prepared for the invalid.

Fanano's weekly market was in full swing with its usual jollity. News spread of Rosa's return. With the rumour that the hated Romano Latini was dead, a loud cheer travelled from one market stall to the next like a touchpaper lighting a gunpowder fuse. The loathsome partisan leader who had terrorised them and made demands on them for years was dead. Men and women left their stalls and danced and rejoiced in the open spaces, hugging and kissing each other as if it were May Day, when old pagan customs decreed that all inhibitions were thrown to the wind.

'What?' they said. 'Butchered by a slip of a girl of just eleven years old!'

Tears ran down the faces of the women in the village, and some of the men too, when they heard of Tina's awful sufferings at the hands of the brutish Latini and her triumph over a man who had become an ogre to them all – terrible and untouchable.

'What?' they continued. 'And that giant of a man who passed quietly through our village last week has returned with this young girl and our very own Rosa? ...And they've rescued the Spanish man for whom the partisans were demanding a ransom! ...Oh! Thanks be to God.'

The rejoicing and merrymaking continued well into the evening. All wanted to see the four celebrities at the stallholder's cottage a quarter of a mile out of the village. In ones and twos, they crept to his cottage in the wood to see what they could see. But of Mat, Rosa, Francesca and Pedro, none was a greater celebrity than young Tina. She was Fanano's very own Joan of Arc. Her status in her new village was assured for life.

Before the market closed at dusk, the womenfolk had formed their own action group to return Pedro to health. Between them, they took to the stallholder's cottage fresh milk and cream, eggs, fresh fruit and vegetables and bowls of mutton broth, full of goodness. They organised a rota so that one of them was always by Pedro's bedside night and day. They were magnificent.

With his body freshly washed and dressed and his hair trimmed and his beard cut, Pedro's appearance improved considerably, but he was still like a scarecrow and the pallor of his skin was grey. He remained in a delirious state and was running a high temperature. His speech was incoherent and he appeared totally disoriented, unable to recognise Mat or Francesca. He just mumbled the same few words over and over again.

But what caused Mat the greatest concern was his left hand. Although they had cleaned the remains of his middle finger, it remained inflamed and continued to discharge pus. Moreover, his whole hand was red and swollen, and his other fingers were turning black. The village doctor, a portly, well-spoken elderly man arrived and shook his head.

'Signore,' he said to Mat gravely, 'your friend Pedro's hand is gangrenous. Unless we act rapidly, it will spread up his arm and then his whole body. In his weak, delirious state he will die in day or so, maybe even tomorrow.'

He shook his head slowly.

'What do we do?' asked Mat, although in his heart he knew what the response would be.

'I'm afraid, signore, that we'll have to remove his hand at the wrist. Otherwise tomorrow it will be his arm at the elbow. I'll go and warn the village butcher and get things ready.'

Mat's jaw dropped.

'Have no fear, signore! Luiz Delgado is an able surgeon and has performed many amputations in Fanano and the surrounding villages. He has all the right instruments and will know exactly what to do. I'll assist him, and everything will be done to minimise the suffering of your friend. But, poor fellow,' he added, 'he's suffered enough already. We'll do it this very evening. Time is short.'

By then, the villagers knew that Pedro was an officer of the famous Spanish general known as the Gran Capitán. Three lively brothers, aged fourteen, fifteen and sixteen – named Ham, Japeth and Shem after the sons of Noah – volunteered to ride post-haste to Florence with news that Pedro had been found and was safe and in Mat's good care. There they would aim to contact the Gran Capitán's riders, who could relay the good news to their commander in Rome or Naples, or wherever he might be.

Not one for the written word, Mat wrote a short letter for the three boys to take:

To General Don Gonzalo Fernández in Rome, Naples or Sicily:

Sir, I am pleased to inform you that Francesca and I located Pedro in a small Tuscan village called Canevare, and extricated him from the underground dungeon where he had been kept for the past five months. We are now in a nearby village among the mountains called Fanano, where Pedro is being cared for wonderfully by the villagers. He is delirious and in very poor health, and must remain here for a month or more to recover before he will be strong enough to leave. Even now, there is a risk he might die as a result of his incarceration. He has suffered terribly. Everyone is doing all they can. The Tuscan partisan leader, Romano Latini, is dead and there is much rejoicing here. There is much to tell you, but until we return, this must suffice.

Matute

Fanano, Tuscany, 20 April 1497

Mat thought it wise to omit any reference to the amputation of Pedro's hand. No doubt the Gran Capitán would write to Miriam and Raquel, and it was better that neither he nor they knew. There would be time enough later.

The three 'Sons of Noah' set off late that afternoon in high spirits. They had never gone more than a day's journey from their village, and the thought of visiting the famous city of Florence made them eager to start. While Mat and Francesca had spent a month travelling slowly through the Tuscan mountains with their donkey so as not to arouse suspicion, the three lads would ride from sunup to sundown, taking a little known and more direct route to Florence over the forested mountains, laughing and in high spirits as they raced each other along the narrow paths. They would accomplish the tortuous and difficult journey of well over 150 miles within a week.

That evening, an hour before sunset and while the light was still good, Luiz Delgado and the village doctor arrived. While Mat paced around fretting, Francesca and Rosa were much calmer, so they pushed Mat out of the house and turned their attention to what needed to be done.

For two hours before, Pedro had been sucking on a flannel imbibed with a herbal tincture which dulled the senses. So with the butcher-surgeon's instruments sharpened and cooling after being sterilised in boiling water, with tourniquets tightened above the elbow and at the wrist, and with the same tinctured flannel placed in Pedro's mouth to bite on, the two women held the patient's arm and body still while Luiz did his work.

Cutting expertly between the bones at the base of the hand and the ulna and radius bones of the arm, the surgeon removed Pedro's hand in seconds. He tied off the radial and ulnar arteries and several blood vessels, and in little time had closed the wound with a flap of flesh. The whole procedure took just a few minutes. Pedro cried out once and his eyes flashed into life for the first time, and then he was still and calm.

As the village doctor had forecast, Luiz Delgado had done his job efficiently and expertly. And if the amputation were in time, Pedro would make a full recovery. Without ceremony, the two women wrapped Pedro's severed hand in the tinctured flannel and cast it into the flames of the fire which was burning in the kitchen. Mat sought to do the same with the 'mantelpiece' box containing Pedro's finger, but, thoroughly perplexed, he could not find it.

Ham and Japeth, the eldest of the three 'Sons of Noah', would return to Florence within the year to claim as brides two sisters they had met on their first visit. These girls would bring welcome fresh blood into a closed, inbred community. The youngest of the brothers, Shem, would settle down and win the prized Tina for himself when she reached maturity. The village of Fanano would attain celebrity status as a result of the death of Romano Latini and the extinction of the partisans, and its small church would become a point of pilgrimage... because it housed, in a special screened niche, a box alleged to contain the middle finger of the left hand of a saint, martyred by the Romans.

XIX: Annus Horribilis

Summer 1497

In Burgos, Prince Juan was smitten by the beauty of his new bride and was consumed by his passion for her. The doctors and the King himself begged the Queen to intervene and separate the newlyweds to provide some respite in their incessant lovemaking, warning of the dangers that would ensue. Time and again, they called her attention to the paleness of Juan's face and his general fatigue, insisting that his sickness was eating away his very being. But all their warnings to the Queen were in vain. 'Man does not have the power to tear asunder those whom God has joined together,' was her reply.

The court divided into two groups in September, with Juan and his bride, Princess Margaret, departing for Salamanca, while the Queen and Fernando accompanied their eldest daughter, twenty-seven-year-old Isabel, as far as Valencia de Alcántara, just a few miles from the Portuguese border, to witness her simple betrothal. The widow of Prince Alfonso, after several years of being hidden away in a convent, had finally consented to become the wife of Alfonso's younger brother, Manuel, who had assumed the throne of Portugal. But the joyous occasion of their wedding was to be short-lived.[1]

Word was rushed to the King and Queen in Valencia de Alcántara of the desperate illness of Juan in Salamanca. Beside himself with anxiety, Fernando set forth to ride to his bedside. There, the King attempted to arouse his son and instil in him a will to live, but the Prince replied that he felt death near at hand and implored his parents and his sisters to resign themselves to the will of God. Soon after, on a brilliant autumn day in the first week in October, doleful wails from the Prince's hunting dog pierced the silence of the court, and proclaimed his having breathed his last.

Fernando sought to prevent the news from reaching the Queen, but she soon learned of the tragedy and declared stoically 'that the Lord had given and the Lord had taken away'. The premature death of the only male heir to the thrones of Spain – Castile and Aragón – rocked the royal family. Now the

---

[1] As a point of clarification for readers, there were four Isabels. The mother of Queen Isabel (husband of Fernando) was Isabel of Portugal. Queen Isabel's eldest child was also called Isabel and married Manuel, King of Portugal, after the death of her first husband, Alfonso, Manuel's elder brother. And lastly, Princess Juana's third child was called Isabel.

hopes of the monarchs centred upon the child that Princess Margaret was carrying. But again fate intervened. The baby was stillborn.

Upon hearing the news, the new Queen of Portugal, Fernando and Isabel's eldest child, set aside the colourfully embroidered gowns of her trousseau and once again attired herself in black. Thus, garbed in robes of mourning similar to those she had worn during the previous years, she entered Lisbon with her new husband, Manuel. Isabel did not stay there long. As the next in line to the thrones of Castile and Aragón, she was hurriedly summoned to Toledo to be sworn in by the Cortes of Castile. Representatives from seventeen Spanish cities – from Córdoba to Segovia and from Murcia to Zamora – unanimously accepted Princess Isabel as heiress apparent without reservation. But not so Zaragoza, the capital city of the kingdom of Aragón. There, tradition demanded a male successor to Fernando, and the Aragonese Cortes voted to await the birth of Isabel's expected child before arriving at a decision.

In Flanders, meanwhile, in the latter months of 1497, life maintained its usual pace with royal banquets, tourneys and provincial tours, not even pausing for the lengthy period of mourning over Juan's death that protocol demanded. Upon the Prince's death, Archduke Philip reacted in a predictable way by adopting for himself the title of 'Prince', believing that all the sons-in-law of Fernando were entitled to this appellation. But, very promptly and in no uncertain terms, he had his knuckles wrapped by the monarchs and he withdrew his claim.

Philip's father Maximilian, the Holy Roman Emperor, was visiting the Low Countries at this time and expressed his delight to the Spanish Ambassador of having Juana as his daughter-in-law, considering that she and Philip were well matched. But Maximilian's attempt to change Philip's attitude to his governance of the House of Flanders was rebuffed, and Maximilian departed Flanders in a huff, never to return.

Pedro did not arrive back at Don Gonzalo's encampment in Sicily until July 1497. Mat and Francesca and the villagers of Fanano in Tuscany had nursed him back to health, but only when Pedro had regained his strength did Mat, Francesca and he set off for Florence and the ensuing river and sea journey south. By then, Don Gonzalo was resident in a palace in Messina, on the flanks of the smoking Mount Etna. Most of his Spanish forces had already returned home.

'I'm delighted to see you looking so well, Pedro,' he said, welcoming him and Mat on the steps of the palace, 'and you Francesca, you clearly had a big part in Pedro's rescue and return to health. My sincere thanks to you both. I can't tell you how worried I was about Pedro. Despite your good intentions in setting off in search of him last year, I never thought I'd see him alive again.'

Turning to Pedro in party mood, he went on. 'I must say, after your months in the dungeons of the Inquisition years ago, I thought you'd finished with being incarcerated. Obviously not! But seriously, Pedro, tell us what happened to you after you were separated from Jofré and his men. We'd like to hear your story.'

'You're right, sir, to say that I do manage to get myself into some awful scrapes! But this latest ordeal was worse than my months in the cells of the Inquisition in Jaén. There, I was at least getting fed each day, and I just lived in terror of what awaited me in the Chamber of Confessions. In the underground crypt of Canevare, surrounded by the bones of the long dead, I knew that nobody could ever find me, not in 1,000 years, and that I'd slowly die and my bones would join those around me. How Mat and Francesca found out where I was hidden is a true wonder. Not for the first time, Mat, I owe you my life.

'However, Don Gonzalo, to answer your question: when I was separated from Jofré and his six lancers ten days into our journey to Flanders for Juana's wedding, I was dragged from Indy and blindfolded and my hands were tied. Why I was singled out I don't know, but in the light of what happened to Jofré's lancers maybe I was lucky. But, before they bound my eyes, I did catch sight of the ringleader, a big man with a terrible purple scar running right across his face. He rode ahead of me along a dusty path, with me being pulled behind him at the end of a tether, half-walking and half-running. Frequently I stumbled and was dragged along as I tried to keep up with him. The path wound its way up hill and down dale and across streams, until I was too exhausted trying to stay on my feet. In the end, I was just pulled along the ground through the dust and stones and puddles until the rider stopped in an open space near an old church. By then, my blindfold had fallen from my face so I could see that I was in a hillside village, although I couldn't see any sign of life. However, I'd little time to look around, since I was pushed down a flight of stone steps into the underground chamber where Mat and Francesca later found me. The man with the scar thrust me into the old crypt, which was as black as pitch, freed my hands and left, bolting the door behind him.'

'Did you ever see him again?' asked Don Gonzalo.

'I'll come to that, sir. The next day, a stone was pushed back on the roof of the crypt and for the first time I could see where I was. Each day, two young girls came with food and lowered it down to me on a string, and for a while lowered down a pitcher of water. A small trickle of water seeped from of the rock wall of the crypt and flowed across the floor before disappearing the other side. I scooped the dust away to make a little channel, and when the mud had settled it provided me with a small supply of water. This kept me alive.

Eventually, the supply of food and water from the two girls became less and less frequent until it ceased entirely.

'It was days, maybe weeks, later that Mat and his three companions burst into my prison. One of them, I learnt, was Tina, who was one of the young girls who fed me, and I'll be eternally grateful to her and her sister for keeping me alive. Later, I learnt what Tina had been through at the hands of that monster with the scar, and I'm delighted that she's settled down with Rosa to a new life in Canevare.

'You asked if I ever saw Romano Latini again. Yes, once. A month or so after my incarceration, I heard him and another man clattering down the steps outside and the door being unbolted. My pulse raced at the thought of being released. But instead, without speaking, they set upon me. The second partisan, even more powerful than Romano Latini, grabbed me and held me as in a vice. Before I knew it, my left hand was splayed out over one of the stone benches covered in old bones, a knife was placed across my middle finger bearing the Queen's jade ring, and the blade was struck with a stone which lay on the floor. You cannot believe the pain. I screamed in agony and fell to the floor as the bigger partisan released me from his grip. While he took my finger from the stone bench and pocketed it, Romano Latini pulled out a rag from his pocket and bound my hand to stop the bleeding. When he was satisfied that he'd staunched the flow of blood, the two men quickly departed and I never saw either of them again.

'The rest you know. When Mat and Francesca and the two others found me, I was obviously delirious and close to death. In fact, I barely remember anything until they laid me on the bed in Rosa's cottage.'

'But you knew what had to be done about your h-h-hand?' asked Mat.

'No, not really, Mat. I knew my hand was swelling up weeks before you arrived, but I was too far gone by then to realise it was becoming gangrenous, and it had long since ceased hurting. It was just like a piece of dead meat on the end of my arm. I somehow thought it wasn't part of my body any more. Even when Luiz Delgado, the village surgeon, came to do his work – so expertly, it turned out – I was too delirious to know what he was doing, or feel much pain when he removed my hand. Now I know that if he hadn't acted as quickly as he did, I wouldn't be alive today.'

'Well, thank the Lord, Pedro, that you are alive and that you survived this terrible nightmare,' said Don Gonzalo. 'Without your incredible will to live, you could never have survived such an ordeal.'

The Gran Capitán gently took Pedro's left arm in his hands. The stump at his wrist had healed well in the ensuing months since the surgery, and, apart from still sensing that he had a hand there, Pedro did not feel any pain, just an occasional throbbing.

'So, now that you're a one-handed soldier,' Gonzalo laughed, though with no trace of mockery, and relieved beyond measure by Pedro's return, 'you'll be able to recount to your children and grandchildren your life-and-death adventures in Tuscany! And what adventures they were!'

Mat placed his hand on Pedro's shoulder.

'Didn't the old soldier who t-t-taught you how to use a sword only have one hand?' he asked. Mat's stammer was always worse in the presence of his commanding officer.

'Marco Arana?'

'Yes, M-M-Marco.'

'Yes, he did. I was only thirteen then.'

'Didn't he lose it when the T-T-Turks took Constantinople from the Christians forty years ago?'

'No, it was years later during the civil war in Cataluña.'

'But, it didn't s-s-stop him teaching you to use that lovely Toledo sword of yours, did it?'

'No, it didn't, Mat. Marco was expert in the use of all sorts of weapons, and taught me to defend myself against all of them. He was an amazing man, and I loved him dearly.'

'So there you are, Pedro,' said a relaxed Don Gonzalo. 'Losing your hand, particularly your left hand, is not the end of the world. The streets are filled with people and old soldiers with missing hands and arms and hobbling around on crutches without a foot or leg. There are people missing an eye, an ear or even a nose if they've been caught stealing, and pitifully disfigured from the pox and other diseases. You're not a cripple as they are. You have a good right hand which now bears your Queen's ring. You have all your wits about you, which I will continue to need here, and you have a beautiful wife and children and a loving family. So look on the bright side and a new life ahead of you.' He paused.

'What's more, Pedro,' he continued thoughtfully, 'I'll arrange for something to be made so that you can use your hand. The Italian armourers here are incredibly skilled, and can make almost anything from their bright steel. Just look at the intricacy of these steel gauntlets of mine! They're as flexible and as comfortable to wear as woollen gloves. So let's see what they can fashion for you.'

'Have you told my mother about my hand, Don Gonzalo?' asked Pedro tentatively.

'Yes, Pedro. I wrote to her in June after I received Mat's letter from Fanano. I told her what had happened and that you were making an excellent recovery. I impressed on her that losing a hand for one reason or another is commonplace, and that you would soon get used to coping with just one hand. I thought it best to write to set her mind at rest, since in my previous letter to her I had to tell her that you were missing and we didn't know what had become of you. In fact, she's written very recently and I've got a letter from her to give you. The envelope's dated late in May, so she won't have known about you losing your hand when she wrote it.'

It was some weeks later in September and Raquel was sitting with Princess Juana, as well as the remaining six of the Spanish ladies who had accompanied her to Flanders the previous year. This gathering was a rare event and helped dispel the gloom which had descended on the close-knit group; they were homesick for their loved ones at home, for bright blue skies and Spanish ways. On this blustery evening, Juana was the life and soul of the party, joking and laughing with her ladies, proudly showing off the third and last of the tapestries which had just arrived from Miriam in Vélez Blanco. It depicted the handover of the keys of Almería to Fernando and Isabel inside the city's Pechina Gate by the mercurial Mohammed Abú Abdalá, known as El Zagal, the Valiant One, as well as Ibn Salim Ben Ibrahim al-Nagar, the Prince of Almería, and his lascivious son, Cidi Yayha al-Nagar. Raquel held the rapt attention of the Princess and the Spanish ladies as she told of her meetings with the Muslim lord, who had been blinded and unjustly cast into the streets as a beggar by Sultan al-Wattasi; how, in the driving rain a year or so later, she and Pedro had fortuitously met El Zagal's daughter, Jadicha, at her father's graveside in Tlemcen.

Juana listened very attentively to Raquel's experiences. She recounted that her parents, Fernando and Isabel, talked with grudging admiration about this great warrior who caused them so much anguish during the ten-year Granada campaign to oust the Muslims from al-Andalus. Juana was thrilled to hear of Raquel's experiences and thereby comprehend better the significance of the tapestry.

With the wind howling outside, rattling the shutters as early darkness settled over the palace in Brussels, Juana's buoyant mood infected the other ladies. While they sat in a circle in front of the blazing fire, doing their needlework or playing chequers, there was much gossip and much ribald banter and sauciness about the sexual proclivities of the Flanders womenfolk, whom they considered resembled the huge Friesian cows in more ways than one. Juana in particular was very merry, since Archduke Philip was returning later that very evening with some of his courtiers from a hunting expedition in the Burgundy forests to the south. Much behind-the-hand mirth and chortling passed between the Spanish ladies as to what he had been hunting. It was a homely occasion and all were in high spirits.

Around ten, Juana left her Spanish ladies and retired to her room to prepare herself for her lord. Her passion had remained undimmed from the day of their first meeting, and she intended this night to be special. The Spanish ladies themselves retired to their rooms one by one. Raquel was pleased to seek the quiet cosiness of her small round room in a turret at the end of a passageway and a floor above Juana's chambers. As the wind whistled outside and the shutters banged against the small widow, Raquel shaded the night candles on the wall, turned the key in the lock and placed the key on her dressing table. She then slipped off her heavy woollen clothes and slid into bed naked, as was the custom at that time. Pulling the down-filled quilt over her, she was soon asleep, giggling to herself over the earlier tittle-tattle of the ladies-in-waiting and, as always on such occasions, longing for the company of Pedro. With a smile flickering across her lips, Raquel dreamt of the sunlit riverbank among the bulrushes near her former home in the Alpujarras where, as a fifteen-year-old, she gave herself over to Pedro for the very first time before he set off on the last stage of his journey across al-Andalus.

It must have been in the early hours of the morning when Raquel was abruptly wakened as she heard a key turn in the lock of her door. Startled, she sat up in bed, and as she did so two men burst into her room and fell upon her. One put his hand over her mouth to stop her crying out, while the other ripped the bedclothes from off her. Positioned on each side of her, they pinned her arms and legs down. Raquel struggled and twisted, but nothing she could do would free her from their strong grips. They prised open her knees as, as if on cue, a third person burst into the room. Quickly dispensing with his drawers, he fell upon her. She tried to cry out as he thrust into her. Just for an instant, her father's leering face appeared in front of her. She was just eight years old then, just a slip of a girl. Later, her father would die in agony from a scorpion's sting. Nobody grieved for his death; he was a brute. But the face was not her father's.

Raquel managed to free a hand from one of her assailants and grabbed at a pendant brushing against her breasts, tearing it from around his neck. The rapist thrust deeper and deeper inside her. She twisted and turned, trying to bring her knees up to throw the man off, but she was pinned down too strongly. The rapist would not yield until, jetting his seed deep inside her in his lustful climax, he pulled himself from her. He scooped up his clothes from the stone floor and was gone. The two men holding her down followed him through the door, withdrawing their key as they closed the door after them.

Oblivious to the stabbing pain inside her, Raquel leapt furiously from her bed, pulling her dressing gown from the hook on the door. Flinging open the door, she looked down the passageway, which was dimly lit by night candles at each end. Her attackers had already vanished.

XX: The Sorceress

Pedro left Don Gonzalo, who had been in an effusive mood, and found a quiet corner to open the letter from his mother which the general had passed to him. The letter, and that sent to her by Gonzalo telling her of Pedro's recovery, had crossed in the post. Pedro's happy mood was quickly extinguished.

Xiquena, Vélez Blanco, Almería

20 May 1497

Dear Pedro and Raquel,

As before, I am writing to you jointly, although to your different addresses, and hope that it will find you both. But oh, how you must wish that you were together. It seems such a long time since you went your separate ways in the service of the King and Queen, and everyone here wishes to see your return soon.

It is with terrible sadness, though, that I have to tell you that your dear Sara passed away on Sunday last. In the end, her difficulty in breathing got too much for her, and despite everything and all the care we could lavish on her, she passed away peacefully in the night. I and Raghad were by her bedside holding her hands when she expired. I had written to you previously of our concern over her worsening health, and I don't think anything more could have been done to relieve her wheeziness or make her breathing easier. Joshua tried all the herbal remedies which Abraham used for bronchial conditions with such noted success, and the doctor in the village, Ibn Mullah Omar, who is as good as any Jewish physician, made repeated visits here and tried all the things he knew. But in the end it was to no avail.

I know that you will feel guilty at not being here to care for her, but you must try not to feel this way. As your lively young son, Antonio, is loved to death by all of us, such was the case with Sara and, although she greatly missed your parental love, I don't think there is anything more you could have done to relieve her suffering or prevent her untimely death. However, whatever malady afflicted poor Sara, it certainly hasn't affected young Antonio. He's 2½ now and is always asking when Papa and Mama are coming home. He scampers up and down the steep path to the gatehouse if he hears Joshua and Raghad or Abel and Eva arrive, and the other day we saw him leaning over the parapet of the gatehouse. Agustín rushed down the path, but the rascal was already coming out of the doorway looking as innocent as a lamb! He's a right little scallywag, but he keeps us all young.

He and all of us miss you both, and pray that your various royal duties will soon come to an end and permit you to return home.

With much love,

Mama

Setting aside the temptation to run down the passageway screaming to raise the alarm, Raquel removed the shades from the candles on the wall, used one of them to light three more on her dressing table, soaked a linen cloth in the water basin and quickly washed herself, rubbing off vigorously the rapist's semen from her stomach and inside her thighs, where it was flecked with blood. In so doing, the pain inside her subsided – although not her shame, humiliation or inward fury.

Donning her dressing gown, she slipped her feet into her soft felt slippers and tiptoed down the corridor to the door of Doña Ana of Beamonte who, from the time of their visit to Tordesillas, was Raquel's good friend and confidante.

'What is it, Raquel?' murmured the Queen's dame of honour and the most senior of the Spanish ladies in Flanders as she peeped around her door. 'Oh, do come in,' she said seeing the young woman's distress. Ana removed the shades from the night lights in her room.

'Ana,' sobbed Raquel, now in floods of tears, 'I've just been accosted by a man! Two brutes burst into my room using a spare key and held me down while another forced himself on me.'

'Oh no!' gasped Ana. 'Did he... did he have his way with you?'

'Y-y-yes!' cried Raquel, her distress now flooding out. 'I couldn't stop him... I did all I could, but he was too strong for me... The other men held me down... I couldn't move... and...'

'Did you recognise him, my dear?' asked Ana, putting her arms around Raquel.

'I caught a glimpse of the two assailants in the dim candlelight as they burst in my room. I think I recognised them from court. They were part of the Archduke's hunting party. But they covered my eyes, and I didn't see who it was who raped me. But...'

Raquel held out the pendant and chain which were still in her hand. For the first time, she saw that the fine gold chain bore the distinctive oval ruby which Archduke Philip always wore around his neck.

'Oh, my God!' exclaimed Ana, drawing back, putting her hand to her mouth. 'Oh, my God!' she repeated, lost for words, her nimble mind racing through the implications of what Raquel had said. Calmly, she asked, 'Are you all right, my dear? Are you in pain?'

'No, not now,' the young woman replied between sobs, but now shaking as a reaction to her ordeal. 'Just numb from being so forcibly assaulted.'

Ana comforted her charge and was silent for a minute.

'Raquel,' she said firmly, 'there are things we must do – and do quickly. Firstly, the pendant and chain must be returned to the Archduke as soon as possible. You've shown me the evidence that it was Philip who raped you. Of that, there can be no doubt. If you'll give me the pendant, I'll see that it's returned to his dressing table as soon as possible without him knowing.'

'But the gold chain's broken, Ana! He'll see that, and know he didn't just leave it in his room.'

'I know, my dear. That's why your life is in danger. But he'll hope that by having the pendant secretly returned to him, his indiscretion won't be disclosed to Juana. To do so would mean the end of his marriage and the end of his ambitions in Spain. Nevertheless, you are in danger. We need to act quickly and get you out of the palace. We must do so before the morning. But first things first, Raquel. We should summon Enid Haas here forthwith to try and prevent the Archduke's seed from lodging inside you. You won't want to carry his child, although how many other poor girls there are in Flanders made pregnant by him is anybody's guess.'

'Who's Enid Haas?' asked a perplexed Raquel, not able to take in Ana's speed of thought.

'She's a midwife in this city who is said to have special knowledge of the inner workings of us women. Some say she's a sorceress…'

'A *witch*!' gasped Raquel.

'No, not a witch, but she's said to have special powers… no, more a deep understanding of how our female bodies work. She has a reputation as a brilliant midwife but, moreover, as someone who prevents unwanted pregnancies. I assume you won't want to carry the Archduke's child, will you, Raquel? Some girls might, I suppose,' Ana remarked as an afterthought.

The look on the victim's face gave her the answer. 'Have you met this Enid Haas, Ana?' Raquel asked, still very uncertain about Ana's suggestion.

'No, I haven't. But I've heard her spoken of in glowing terms.'

'Is she Flemish?'

'I'm not sure. I think she's Dutch or German. She comes from the Jewish quarter in Amsterdam.'

'So she's a Jewess?'

'Yes, I think so, but it seems all the best doctors are of that faith – as was Pedro's father, from what you've told me, as well as the Queen's physician, Salomón Byton.'

'That's true. Very well, Ana,' concluded Raquel, now feeling fortified by her friend's action plan. 'Send for this Enid Haas and let's see what sorcery she can perform on me! In the meantime, I'll go back to my room and scrub off what remains on me from this royal ram… Ugh!' She grimaced.

Ana summoned a trusty maid in the palace and handed her a note she had quickly written.

'Do you know where Enid Haas lives in the city, Betty?'

'Yes, ma'am.' Betty looked perplexed and was about to speak.

'No questions, Betty, please. Just do what I ask, and not a word to anybody. You'll be rewarded for your discretion.'

'Yes, ma'am. Thank you, ma'am.'

'Good, now leave by the back door of the servants' quarters, and bring Enid Haas in the same way. Give her my note and ask her to come as soon as she can. Speed is of the essence. She'll understand why.'

'Yes, ma'am.'

'Good for you, Betty. Now, not a word to anybody – now or later! Do you understand?'

'Yes, ma'am.' And she was gone.

Raquel returned to her room once more, threw herself on her bed, beating it furiously with her fists with the shame of what the Archduke had done to her. Eventually she pulled herself off the bed and repeated, almost as a ritual, the cleansing of her body. An hour later, Ana called her back to her room. Enid Haas had just arrived, bearing a canvas bag which clattered and rattled with the miscellaneous paraphernalia and concoctions inside it, although no scaly creatures crawled out of the bag when she eventually opened it. Betty was immediately sent to fetch some hot water.

Enid Haas was in her seventies, stooped and wrinkled with a wickedly hooked nose. But she soon dispelled any anxieties Raquel might have nurtured about her being a witch, for she was calm, businesslike and understanding.

'Now, my dear,' she said quietly, 'tell me what happened.'

Without declaring who her assailant was, Raquel narrated briefly the assault she had suffered, and answered the midwife's many questions about her life and general well-being.

'Hmm,' the midwife answered, pensively. 'From what you've said you're in the middle of your monthly cycle, and therefore at risk of becoming pregnant by this man. It doesn't always work,' she said, 'but it's always worth a try. What I'm going to do is try and flush out of your body the man's seed which remains inside you. Now, lie on the edge of the bed over this basin and put your feet up on this chair.'

With Raquel watching with some trepidation, and Ana with wide-eyed curiosity, Enid Haas inserted a hollowed-out length of thin animal bone, smoothed and rounded at the end, deep inside the young woman. She connected the free end to a tube made of something Raquel could not even guess at, and pushed the other end of the tube over a spout emanating from the bottom of a jug placed on a nearly shelf. Enid filled the jug with warm water. She added some drops of an aromatic tincture from a small bottle she had removed from her travelling apothecary kit, and the process of internal flushing started as the basin on the floor beneath Raquel started to fill.

The midwife inspected the messy, blood-specked emission flowing into in the basin, commenting bitterly, 'He was a virile scoundrel, whoever he was.' The process was repeated two more times, until the water discharging into the basin was clear.

'That will do, my dear,' the midwife said. 'Time will tell whether we're successful. Now dry yourself and get dressed. We'll discuss what else we can do.'

The three women settled into the soft chairs which Ana had in her room, with Raquel and Enid Haas sharing the sofa.

'What more can be done?' asked Ana.

'Well, there are things we can do and remedies we can try if Raquel were eventually to carry the child of this man, but that's many weeks away and we hope we don't have to get that far. There are some herbs – for instance, tansy and pennyroyal – which can precipitate an abortion, but they can be dangerous and I only advise them in desperate cases. At this stage, we just want to stop Raquel getting pregnant. There are several herbs, much milder, which will interfere with a woman's reproduction cycle. We'll try these, although not today. It would be best, Doña Ana,' the midwife added, 'if Raquel returns with me to my home so I can care for her for the next week or two and do what I can to prevent any foetus from developing.'

'That's a good idea, Señora Haas,' replied a much relieved Ana, aware how her own position in the palace could be put in jeopardy by what had happened. 'In the light of who her assailant was,' she confided, 'Raquel needs to leave the palace this very night. If she were to come with you, señora, for you to care for her, it would be the perfect solution. Are you agreeable, Raquel?'

'I suppose so, Ana,' she replied uncertainly, unsure of leaving the fold of the Spanish ladies.

Ana played her trump card.

'In two weeks' time, Raquel,' she said with a glint in her eye, 'a large papal delegation of high-ranking clerics and scholars is leaving Brussels to return overland to Rome. There'll be many coaches in the party and many horsemen in support. Why not join this party, Raquel, where you'll be very safe, and join Pedro in Italy? Even if he's not in Rome itself, you'll easily be able to join him in Naples or Sicily. This delegation will be under the control of Rome, and even the Archduke has no authority over it. You'll be able to travel incognito in one of the coaches.'

Raquel's eyes lit up at the thought of being reunited with her husband.

'Right, it's agreed, then. Pack what you need now, my dear, and leave with Señora Haas. I'll send the rest of your things on to you tomorrow.'

So that night, before the break of dawn, Raquel and Enid Haas quietly left the royal palace by the servants' entrance and zigzagged their way through the backstreets of the city to Enid's small house.

Raquel stayed with Señora Haas until the delegation finally assembled and departed the city. As Ana had hoped, she was given a place in one of the dozen coaches which rattled out of the south gate, heading for Reims and Lyon, taking a route which would skirt the Alps lying to the east. Although relations with France remained fragile, dispensation had been granted for the papal entourage to travel through it.

Earlier, true to her word, the ageing midwife had prescribed for Raquel a mixture of nettle, marigold and yarrow which she had suffused in boiling water from the leaves of these plants. For several days, Raquel had been ill, as the potion – several times given – rumbled in her belly, causing sickness and diarrhoea, all of which Enid Haas anticipated. Then, on the seventh day, a week ahead of time, Raquel's monthly bleeding had occurred, violent and effusive, expelling from inside her, it was hoped, the Archduke's semi-implanted seed.

'Now you can relax, my dear,' Enid had said, 'and get over the nasty few days you've suffered. We won't know if the herbal remedies have succeeded yet, but in the light of the pain you've had during your bleeding I'm hopeful they have been.'

So, for the week remaining before the delegation departed, Raquel had relaxed under the midwife's care, cheering up immensely now that the treatment was over, and in anticipation of a change of scene from the claustrophobia of palace life and the excitement of the journey south.

On the day of her departure, Enid Haas had handed Raquel two small glass phials containing coloured liquid. One was of tansy and the other pennyroyal.

'You are only to consider using these, Raquel,' she had said sternly, 'if you're certain that you are with child. Is that clear? Even then, you must place yourself in the hands of a physician who knows what these herbs are and how they are to be administered. Remember, in reality they are poisons; but they're highly effective.'

Two days after the party set off for Rome, Miriam's letter arrived at the royal palace in Brussels telling her of the death of Sara. It was as well that Raquel was not there to receive it.

XXI: Scandal and Intrigue in Rome

In June 1497, an infamous scandal occurred in Rome, the circumstances of which have taxed historians and novelists to this very day. Alexander VI had called a convocation of cardinals to approve the investiture of Federico as King of Naples after Federico's nephew, Ferrante, had died without leaving an heir. On the eve of his investiture, the Pope had submitted to the Holy College of Cardinals a recommendation for the transfer of the title of Duke of Benevento to his middle son, twenty-one-year-old Juan Borgia, as a means of strengthening Juan's candidature for the much coveted crown of Naples, and thereby aligning the kingdom to the Borgia dynasty. As we have seen, the Kings of Spain and France both claimed ancient rights to Naples, which had precipitated the Gran Capitán's military campaign in Italy, now nearing conclusion. Juan Borgia had been in Rome for little more than a year, and he already held the titles of Duke of Gandía in Spain, Captain General of the Vatican, Prince of Tricarino and Count of Laurci and Chiaramonte. The majority of the cardinals approved the Pope's proposal for his son Juan, but several opposed it, including the Spanish ambassador, Don Garcilaso de la Vega, since he believe it prejudiced King Fernando's rights.

The day after Federico's investiture on 8 June, the College of Cardinals met again to choose the papal legate who would accompany Juan Borgia to Federico's coronation in Naples. Nobody was surprised when Juan's elder brother, César, the Cardinal of Valencia, was nominated for this honour by their father. Inevitably, much envy and dissent surrounded them.

The afternoon before their planned journey south, the two sons met their mother, Vannozza Cattanei, near the church of Saint Peter-in-Chains in Rome. In a private court enclosed by high walls and bushes, several other people arrived. These included Vannozza's cousin, Juan, who was also a cardinal; the Pope's youngest son, sixteen-year-old Jofré, recently returned from his harrowing experience in Tuscany; and Princess Sancha, Federico's daughter-in-law. This extraordinary gathering was convened by Vannozza to celebrate Juan's new title of Duke of Benevento and the imminent departure of the two brothers, César and Juan, to Naples.

At sunset, Juan, César and their cousin, the Cardinal De Monreal, accompanied by various servants, set off on horseback to the Vatican, which lay nearby. Passing close to the palace of Cardinal Sforza, they reached the

Sant'Angelo Bridge over the River Tiber, which led directly into the round bastion of the castle. There, Juan, Duke of Gandía, stopped and declared sheepishly that he had another engagement, letting the others believe that he had planned an amorous adventure. César and De Monreal insisted he should not go unaccompanied since Rome was so unsafe, especially at night. The Duke agreed and left with another man. After separating from his brother, Juan headed towards the Plaza de los Judios, but then ordered his servant to wait there until midnight and, if by then he had not appeared, to return alone to the Vatican.

At two in the morning, Jorge Schiavone, who kept a boat close by on the Tiber, saw two men approach the Sant'Angelo Bridge. These individuals looked around furtively to see if all was quiet and were then joined by two other men, who were accompanied by a third leading a horse with a heavy bundle draped over the saddle. This bundle was cast into the river at the spot where rubbish was customary dumped. The next morning, a body was recovered from the Tiber covered in human excrement and filth. It was that of the Duke of Gandía. The unfortunate Juan had nine knife wounds in his body and deep gashes in his neck. After washing and cleaning the body, Juan was dressed in his ducal robes bearing his noble insignia. At midnight, a cortège formed and filed in torchlit procession to the church of Santa Maria del Popolo, where Vannozza Cattanei had a family vault. There the Duke was interred.

The general populace of Rome could not conceal its glee at the demise of the Borgias, who generated much contempt and revulsion; for, by then, the Borgia dynasty had become synonymous with nepotism, sordidness and deviousness. Juan had accrued many enemies because of the many honours bestowed on him during the year he had been in Rome, and not least because of Rodrigo's scheme to align his family to the throne of Naples.

The death of Juan scandalised Rome. Pope Alexander remained inconsolable, retiring to his rooms and crying bitterly. From Wednesday to Saturday, he remained in his room, neither eating, drinking nor sleeping. Despite an intensive investigation, nobody discovered what exactly had transpired that night, or even who it was who accompanied Juan when he separated from his brother and Cardinal De Monreal at the Sant'Angelo Bridge; but the allegation took root that César was implicated in the death of his brother. For this he still stands accused.

In August 1497, soon after Juan's assassination, seventeen-year-old Lucrezia, Rodrigo's youngest child, announced that she could no longer maintain the shame of her married life with Juan Sforza due to his impotence. She provided a certified statement that in their four years together their marriage had never been consummated. Consequently, she requested that their marriage be annulled, and declared her willingness to be subject to medical examination. Despite Lucrezia's husband, Juan Sforza, demonstrating his potency naked in front of a panel of prelates, the commission decided to annul the marriage, and Lucrezia was set free. Three days later, she entered the convent of San Sixto. Sforza later claimed that before her marriage to him Lucrezia had maintained sexual relations with her father and César, even though she was barely thirteen years old. False or true, this rumour fed the public's craving for scandal surrounding the Borgias.

Such was the agitated state of the populace that the people saw auguries everywhere. The gunpowder store in the Castle of Sant'Angelo exploded, destroying the winged statue on its apex which crashed to earth, scattering fragments all around. Soon afterwards, César rode to Naples with his entourage for the coronation of Federico. On the way, he picked up what had then been dubbed 'the French pox' after an brief affair with María Díaz Garlón, the daughter of a count. By then, the pox was spreading as an epidemic among the armies across the whole continent, as it was among Columbus's colonists in La Española. No medication could cure it, with the sufferers carrying repugnant sores on the face and hands for the rest of their lives. In public, César habitually wore a mask, by which he became identified.

At the end of 1497, the 'apples in the barrel' started to jostle again. The Holy League fragmented when Emperor Maximilian appropriated the city of Gorizia, while the Republic of Venice, always ambitions, occupied much of the Adriatic coast. New battle fronts opened up between Holy Roman Empire and Venice, and Venice and Naples. In the meantime, without consulting their allies, the Spanish monarchs deviously agreed a treaty with France.

Rumblings of discontent were afoot against Rodrigo Borgia. In February 1498, a move was set in motion in Florence by Friar Jerónimo Savonarola, inviting the kings of Spain, France, England, Hungary and Germany to convoke an assembly to depose the Pope. Never slow to react, the Pope responded by proscribing the city of Florence, prohibiting the taking of the Sacrament and burials in consecrated ground, and curtailing commerce with other cities. At his trial, Savonarola was declared a heretic and schismatic. The very same day in May 1498 he and two of his supporters was taken to a high scaffold and bound to stakes. Faggots were piled high around their feet and legs. Although it was common for victims to be strangled before the flames took hold, this time the cord around their necks and the stake were barely tightened so that their suffering was greater. As the flames licked around their ecclesiastical habits, the executioner broke Savonarola's neck. His body slumped into the flames, provoking a chilling gasp from the multitude. The victim's ashes were scattered on the River Arno.

During the trial of Savonarola the month before, Charles VIII of France had died at the age of twenty-seven with no male heir, and he was succeeded by the Duke of Orléans, who took the title Louis XII. Like his predecessor, Louis coveted the crown of Naples. He pressed Pope Alexander for the annulment of his marriage so that he could wed Charles's young widow, Ana of Brittany. Seeing this as an opportunity to stifle Louis' ambitions, Alexander acceded to Louis' request and his marriage was annulled in December. At the same time, Alexander VI persuaded Louis to grant César a French dukedom and thereby put an end to César's uninspiring ecclesiastical career. This was all part of his father's scheming to link César in wedlock to the French royal house. Fernando in Spain opposed this, foreseeing that it would prejudice his own historic rights to Naples. Nevertheless, César was conferred the Dukedom of Valentinois in central France, and in October 1498 he left Rome for Marseilles in a flotilla of six ships donated by Louis for César's personal use. All the costs were born by the French king. Nothing was spared in the riches and splendour which surrounded his departure.

Wearing a white damask tunic and black bonnet and cloak, César impressed the French when he arrived in Marseilles as being very handsome, slim and muscular in body, and well-featured. His obsession remained to increase his domains and influence at whatever price. In this, he was little worse than the monarchs of the age – Louis XII, Fernando of Aragón or Henry VII of England. César rapidly became one of the most coveted personages in Italy.

With César now a layman and free of his ecclesiastical bonds, Alexander, forever wheeler-dealing, sought a match for him with the daughter of the new King of Naples, but she was repelled by the very thought of the pox-scarred César. Instead, the French king offered César the hand of sixteen-year-old Carlota d'Albret, sister of the King of Navarra, a small, independent mountain kingdom located in the Pyrenees between Spain and France. They were married in May 1499. So amazingly, in a few months, César had been trans-muted from being an Italian cardinal to a French nobleman. But the happy union of César and Carlota lasted just a few months, for Louis XII was in haste to leave France and ride forth to take the Italian possessions which he believed were his, starting with the Duchy of Milan. César returned to Rome in November 1499. He had remained in France and Navarra for just a year, and yet returned to his country of birth a duke, husband of the sister of a king, and friend of the most powerful monarch at this time. César and Carlota's daughter, Luisa, never got to meet her father. When César later died in a battle, Carlota remained in Navarra, and died at the age of thirty-six, having lived a discreet and austere life.

XXII: Columbus's Third Voyage

Spring 1498

Christopher Columbus had been kicking his heels for over a year, desperate to begin his third voyage to the New World. The governor of La Española, Juan Rodríguez Fonseca, continued to block the return of the Admiral to an island which he considered his personal domain. Having been present at the burial of Prince Juan in the royal monastery of Saint Thomas[1] in Ávila, Columbus hoped that a third voyage would provide some solace to Isabel in her grief over the Prince's death. But he was thwarted when the master-at-arms from his second voyage, Pedro Fernández Coronel, was put in charge of two supply vessels which departed for La Española. However, by April five ships, all constructed in Palos, had been assembled for Columbus by Antonio de Torres; but such was the demand for berths that a sixth caravel had to be chartered. Finally, on 30 May, Columbus departed Sanlúcar, Palos's twin town upstream, with more than 200 men, among them eight men-at-arms, nearly fifty crossbowmen, and seventy seamen. Administrators, farmers, miners, priests and twenty women were among the remainder. Columbus had his former rights in the island confirmed by the Queen in a document which authorised him to assign his lands between his family members. The rights of the natives were not considered, any more than had been those of the Muslims in the defeated Nazarí kingdom of Granada during the carve-up of their lands, which followed their overthrow six years before.

Yet the Admiral and the Crown had conflicting ideas about how colonisation of the Caribbean should proceed. Columbus saw the island of La Española as no more than a trading colony where Spain could exploit its gold, cotton, dyes, spices and slaves, while the monarchs set a higher ideal of the island serving the Lord's wishes and of expanding their possessions in the Indies. Consequently, while they wanted Columbus to distribute the lands between the colonists and to initiate the cultivation of sugar cane, they also wanted him to treat the indigenous population 'benignly in the name of the Lord so that in due course they might partake of the Holy Sacrament'.

---

[1] Where the notorious Tomás de Torquemada, the first Inquisitor General of Castile, is also interred.

So Columbus set off, dividing his fleet in two, with one group heading directly for La Española under the direction of Pedro de Arana, the cousin of the Admiral's lover in Córdoba, Beatrix. The second group, under his direct command, sailed to the islands off the coast of Africa, moving between the Canaries, the Azores, Madeira and Cabo Verde before setting off across the Ocean Sea, reaching the island of Trinidad at the end of July. Sailing south from there, he encountered the vast flow into the ocean from a river[2] which clearly could only have emanated from a large landmass. Off the coast, the ships nearly capsized in a huge standing wave where the freshwater flow from the river met the sea. Although he planted a cross on the shore, the Admiral failed to realise that he was anchored off what was a new continent – South America – persisting with his belief that he had reached the coast of Asia.

Confused by directions given by the natives to various islands which he believed he knew from previous voyages, the Admiral reached the conclusion that the Earth was not round but shaped like a pear, with a nipple-like protuberance existing in the Atlantic Ocean to the east and south of the equator. Furthermore, he was convinced that one of the four arms of the huge river corresponded to that which watered the Garden of Eden, and that he had therefore found the Earthly Paradise.

Although belonging to the warlike Cariba tribe, the natives were, in fact, very friendly and used a network of irrigation channels to cultivate maize, manioc, sweet potato, pumpkin and hot pepper. With bows and arrows made of cane, they hunted porcupine, rabbits, squirrel, tapirs, cane rats and turtles, all of which formed part of their diet, as well as birds such as pigeon, ducks and partridges. They distilled a form of palm grape and beer from maize, the first alcoholic beverage which Columbus had encountered in the New World. Their villages comprised some 200 round huts with roofs of bark or split palm leaves disposed around a central compound. They slept in hammocks and lit fires through the night to ward off mosquitoes. The men decorated their penises with strips of cotton, although some had loincloths which reached their knees or wore aprons like the women. Like the men, the women wore necklaces of teeth; also bracelets, earrings of pearls, coral or flowers and little else. Sometimes they painted their bodies and attached head plumes with resin. Like the Tainos Indians in the islands to the north, the natives of the coast of South America used canoes, which they propelled with great rapidity. Their liberal customs accepted homosexuality. Widows were adopted by the brothers of the deceased. The elderly were respected. Village chiefs were sometimes elected and sometimes hereditary. Drunkenness was common, and

---

[2] The Orinoco of Venezuela

dancing was accompanied by flutes, bells and drums, with some of the men sitting around smoking. They divided the year into lunar months.

Adamant that he had not found a 'new world' and was in the Orient, Columbus set off once more with his three caravels, sailing along the north of present-day Venezuela until he reached an island he christened 'Margarita', where he found pearls. This was to be the most important discovery of Columbus's third voyage. After landing on Margarita, he continued on to La Española, arriving at the end of August. Since Columbus's last visit to the island, his brother Bartolomé had established a new town called Santo Domingo on the more protected southern side of the island, with a church, town hall and governor's house set around a central square, and he started to move people there from his brother Christopher's very first settlement of La Isabela to the north of the island. The mayor of La Isabela, Francisco Roldán, was furious that his town was to be relegated in importance, and fomented a rebellion with seventy of his settlers. This developed into a long and bitter feud between Roldán and Diego and Bartolomé Columbus, whose action in imprisoning a friend of Roldán just made things worse. Although seen as an agitator and troublemaker, Roldán had shown more sympathy towards the natives and had accorded them more benefits and rights. Christopher Columbus was adamant on his return to La Española that power had to revert to him. He tried to arrest Roldán, who was in possession of most of the island's arms. Roldán refused to be deported to Spain as demanded by the Admiral.

Two months after Columbus's arrival, five ships set sail for Spain with 300 disaffected settlers, each of whom Columbus permitted to take a slave. When the fleet arrived in Cádiz on 10 December 1498, the Queen was furious that Columbus had permitted them to bring slaves, and ordered that all were to be freed and repatriated to the Indies. She was growing tired of his ways. But still the Genoese failed to take heed of her changing mood. He claimed that he could send 4,000 slaves to Spain each year and sell them for 1,500 *maravedís* in the marketplace of Seville.

In Brussels, Raquel's frustration grew, as it seemed to take an eternity to assemble the delegation which was to leave for Rome. Mobilising the scarlet-clad Cardinal of Flanders, three purple-clad bishops – of Amsterdam, Utrecht and Luxembourg – plus all their many acolytes dressed in clerical grey, took several weeks. Who should travel with whom, where they should sit, which of the eight carriages travelled first and in what order, consumed hours of debate and argument. Papal bulls were fruitlessly scanned for guidance. Each carriage would carry the heavy, iron-hooped, barrel-topped chests of its passengers, containing their day-to-day clothing and toiletry needs, while ten wagons would travel behind, transporting the remaining baggage containing the heavy religious vestments of the clergy, their miscellaneous reliquaries to bewitch the laity on the way, as well as hundreds of intricately fashioned gifts of gold, silver and ivory in the form of altar crosses, chalices, candlesticks, lecterns, and incense boats – all of which would quickly disappear into the dozens of churches in Rome or be cast into the vast Vatican treasure hoard, the repository of over 1,000 years of papal gifts or peace offerings.

Three other ladies were to travel with the party as well as Raquel, and she was paired with one of them, a staunch, elderly Frau. Two innocent young curates destined for five-year secondments to the Holy See, their future in the Church secure, and bubbling with enthusiasm and religious zeal, made up Raquel's coach party of four. Forty uniformed and armed riders accompanied the delegation, the purpose of which was to attend a quinquennial assembly of cardinals and bishops to review ecclesiastical law. Cardinals and bishops were already on their way to Rome from every corner of the Roman Catholic Church.

For Raquel, the journey was a nightmare, alleviated only by the knowledge that each day took her further south into warmer climes and each mile brought her closer to her reunion with Pedro. Frau Magdalena Berkel, beefy with purple-veined cheeks, enveloped in blankets from head to foot, spoke only Flemish, and she quickly abandoned any attempt to converse with the young, tawny-skinned, dark-eyed beauty sitting opposite her, who seemed distant and withdrawn. The two young priests, although courteous and charming, mixed their Flemish and some French with giggling and prattling to one another in perfect Latin, undoubtedly practising their datives and ablatives for their scholarly duties ahead.

The long line of carriages and wagons, each drawn by two or four horses, set off on icy roads in February 1498, with the normally glutinous mud now frozen into sharp ridges and furrows which the vehicles shook and rattled over. The outriders, well wrapped up against the cold with mittens, woollen surcoats and headscarves, had the freedom to circumvent the most rutted parts of the road and could stop at their leisure to chat or sip from their spirit kegs.

Two weeks into the journey, a rider arrived with mail from Brussels. It included Miriam's joint letter to Raquel and Pedro telling them of Sara's death three months before; it had arrived in Brussels after Raquel's departure with the delegation. Raquel was standing in the cold outside the coach when she opened and read the letter. Expecting a nice homely letter from her mother-in-law, Raquel gasped and fell to the icy ground in a faint when she read the terrible news. Still mentally numb from her ordeal in the palace, the news was more than she could bear. She was lifted gently back into the coach. With the two curates genuinely distressed and offering all the comfort they could, Frau

Berkel took charge. Unwinding her woollen blankets from around herself, she wrapped them around her co-traveller and listened sympathetically but with only partial comprehension to the sad tale which Raquel told of her young daughter's long battle against the asthma which finally took her life. Raquel's tears eventually gave way to sobs as the train of coaches got underway, catching her breath as the sobs caught in her throat. Tears ran down the cheeks of the two clerics as they languished in their helplessness in offering comfort to the young woman.

However, a second letter had been handed to Raquel by the courier, but had fallen on the ground when she fainted. Fearful of its contents, one of the curates held on to it as they resumed their places in the carriage. That afternoon, when Raquel was calmer, he passed it to her, praying that it would bring good tidings.

It was from Don Gonzalo in Sicily:

Messina, Sicily, 20 November 1497

My Dear Raquel,

I am writing this to you while you are in Flanders in the hope that you might receive it in good time, since the courier system linking the main European cities is now well established and pretty reliable. I have both good and bad news to relay to you. The good news is that our task is nearly done here in Italy, and I am making plans to return to Spain with the remainder of my forces next June or July. Some things still remain to be done here. I am not sure how much you know or might have already been told by Miriam, but Mat located Pedro in an isolated village in Tuscany (north of Florence), where he had been incarcerated in an underground crypt by Tuscan partisans. Mat rescued him and after a long period of convalescence brought him back here, and he is now resting in an adjacent room of this palace. How Mat located him is a story he will enjoy telling you. Suffice it to say that Mat is an amazing man and his lady friend, Francesca, is just as tough and resourceful. However, because of injuries Pedro received while he was in the crypt, his left hand became gangrenous and the surgeon in the village where Pedro had been recovering had to remove it surgically. Pedro has made an excellent recovery and has returned to good health. I am delighted and relieved that he is back here safe and sound. I know that it will upset you to learn about the loss of his hand, but you must be brave and accept this as a consequence of warfare. Being one-handed need not stop Pedro living a perfectly normal life.

I'm told that the Cardinal of Flanders and his bishops are due to set off in January or February to journey to Rome for a quinquennial gathering of cardinals and bishops and, if this letter reaches you in time, you might be able to gain release from the Archduchess Juana and join the delegation. It would be lovely if you and Pedro could be reunited here and return to Spain together.

Ever yours,

Don Gonzalo Fernández

Commander, Spanish forces in Italy

The two young curates in the coach watched Raquel's face closely while she read the letter, looking for a smile or a sign that she had received good news. She looked up from the letter with a watery smile, trying to imagine her husband with just one hand. But the thought that she might meet him soon and return home with him swamped her worries, and she nodded a seal of approval to the young men, who settled in their seats feeling happy and reassured.

That evening, during their overnight stop in Nancy, she wrote to Pedro via Don Gonzalo, saying briefly that she was on her way with the cardinal's delegation so as to be with him and return home with him and the Spanish party. Later that week, a courier would pass through the city delivering and collecting mail to and from the next city down the line, Lyon, from where it would be forwarded in stages. But would the letter reach Pedro in time?

So, following a route through France which skirted the Alps, the delegation passed through Dijon and Lyon and headed for Grenoble, Turin and Genoa. At over 1,000 miles, it was a well-worn and much-travelled road to the Eternal City from Flanders. Travelling between twenty and forty miles per day, and staying several nights in each city to savour the bounteous hospitality offered en route, the weary travellers arrived in Florence on 23 May 1498, passing through the Al Proto Gate in the city wall. They were met by a tumult.

As the coaches headed towards the heart of the city and the Piazza della Signoria, their way was blocked by thousands of excited citizens, shouting and waving their arms, all pushing and shoving their way towards the central square, from which columns of smoke were rising upwards into the midday sky. Raquel descended from her coach and immediately was caught up with the swirling mob, some in high spirits at the rare spectacle ahead of them, but others waving their fists and shouting, '*Viva Savonarola, la pena di morte al Papa!*' Caught up in the frenzy, an arm tightened around Raquel's shoulders, holding her firm. It was the burly sergeant of the guard accompanying the delegation who had earlier befriended her. He was now on foot, helmeted, armoured and armed.

'Stay close to me and you won't come to no harm. This is no place for you!' he shouted to her.

The crowd swirled into the central square, by then blocked by thousands of revellers. A hundred yards away, over their heads, Raquel could see three blackened figures tied to stakes, consumed by flames which reached high over their heads, and now slumped forward in their bonds.

'Who are they?' shouted the sergeant to a bystander.

'It's our Archbishop, Savonarola, and two archdeacons,' he replied, coughing in the smoke. 'They dared to oppose that bastard Borgia in Rome, and now they're paying with their lives.

'*La pena di morte al Papa!*' he shouted in unison with the crowd, waving his fist.

A gasp went up from the square as the central of the three figures disappeared in a burst of sparks as he slumped to the ground among the flames, his bonds having being burnt through.

'Come, signora, this is no place for us. Let's get back,' said the sergeant, guiding Raquel back through the jostling crowd.

He led her by a back street to the famous Ponte Vecchio across the River Arno to await the coaches, wagons and riders.

'You're on your way to Sicily to meet the Gran Capitán?' the sergeant asked. 'In that case,' he said, without waiting for a reply, 'you're as well to go by boat from here. It will be a lot quicker than travelling overland. Follow me.'

He led Raquel over the bridge to the left bank, where several boats were moored on the downstream side. On one, a waterman was slouched against the mast, asleep with his arms folded and a cap over his eyes.

'You there!' shouted the sergeant. 'Do you go downriver?'

The seaman sat up startled.

'Aye,' he said gruffly, 'and if you don't believe me, you can ask them three strangers I took down to Pisa recently.'

'Who were they?' shouted Raquel, her interest aroused.

'I don't know, signora,' he replied. 'One had his arm in a sling, one were a woman – a Napolitana, I'd guess by her features – and the other were a huge fellow with fair hair. My God! I'd hate to tangle with him!'

'That would be Mat!' shouted Raquel, jumping for joy and clapping her hands together. 'And my husband, Pedro. *Oooeee!*' She danced up and down on the spot in glee.

For Raquel, after three months on the road, the sun was shining at last.

XXIII: The Baron of Montecorvino

Messina, Sicily, June 1498

'Pedro!' exclaimed Raquel in astonishment, as she steered herself down the wobbly gangplank from the daily ferry which she had boarded at Naples early the previous day. Two young sailors were lifting Raquel's heavy chest of belongings onto the quayside. It was a lovely warm summer's evening and, in a golden glow, the sun was backlighting the huge mass of Mount Etna beyond the city. She fell into his arms, hugging and kissing him with tears of joy running down her face. It was three years since Pedro and Mat had left Xiquena one snowy day to travel to Málaga to join Don Gonzalo, and two years since she herself had travelled with Agustín to rendezvous with Juana's fleet in Laredo.

'But how did you know that I'd be on this ferry?' she asked, perplexed.

'I didn't. A week ago, I got your letter, so each day I've come down here to meet the evening ferry to see if you were aboard... and today you were! Welcome to Sicily, my love. Very soon now we'll be going home to Spain.'

They stayed hugging one another as the remainder of the passengers drifted past with their bounty from their shopping expedition to the then second largest city in Italy. As the couple separated, Raquel noticed for the first time that the sleeve of Pedro's left arm was folded up. She caught his eye as he grinned sheepishly at her, and she raised her eyebrows and nodded her head slightly in recognition of his disfigurement. Pedro had not been certain whether she'd been told of his plight, and he was relieved that she already knew. He had been worrying for weeks how she would accept it.

'Come on,' he said. 'I've a trap to take us up the hill to the palace.'

Pedro helped her up onto the bouncy front seat, jumped up easily beside her and, with Raquel's chests strapped securely at the back, the horse set off at a lively pace through the town. The animal clearly was enjoying the outing. The upward afternoon air currents circulating over the island, and particularly over the bare volcanic rocks of Etna, were drawing a cool breeze in from the sea, scuffing up white horses which danced over its surface. At the steps of the palace overlooking Reggio on the Italian mainland, across the Straits of Messina, Don Gonzalo was there to meet her, together with Mat and his lady friend, the widowed Francesca, whom Raquel had not yet met.

Raquel and Francesca could have been sisters, so alike were they. The latter was senior by three or four years and was an inch taller, but both had flowing raven hair, dark eyes and full figures, with Raquel's hourglass form being the more eye-catching. Both women had tawny skins, one a shade more golden from her Neapolitan blood and the other a shade more dusky from her Arab blood. Both were spirited and full of zest, although Francesca's upbringing in the slums of Naples, surviving as an alley cat, gave her a toughness which one needed to master someone like Mat. And finally, for both women, Castilian was a new language to learn, although Raquel had six years' advantage over the Italian woman. Their chemistry could have been a recipe for competition and conflict, but luckily the two women got on famously, and their friendship would flourish in the years to come until they were as sisters.

It was a lovely reunion, but with so much news to tell and savour later at their leisure, the small group were content to make small talk and simply enjoy the occasion. The Gran Capitán, bareheaded and wearing a simple white cotton blouse with broad sleeves and a loosely laced neck – as was Pedro – was the first to break the revelry.

'Raquel,' he said, gripping her around the waist, 'I can't say how delighted I am to see you. From what I've heard, you and Juana's others Spanish ladies of the court haven't had the easiest of times, and I expect you were only too glad to get away…'

Raquel did not reply, but her assent was evident.

'Your long journey here must have been like torture to you. But you're here at last. We'll all catch up on news later. But first, you'll want to freshen up after your long trip. Pedro will show you to your rooms, where a warm bath is being made ready for you. When you're refreshed, please join us down here for a welcoming glass of wine. You can put all your clothes from your journey out for washing and pressing. Pedro and Francesca went to Naples last week and bought a new wardrobe of light summer clothes for you, more suited to the climate here… Oh, and by the way, tonight we're celebrating your return to the fold with a modest banquet. But take your time. We're best not to eat until well after sundown since it's so warm.'

While Pedro scrubbed Raquel's back as she sat in the tub relaxing in the warm soapy water, both were in a withdrawn mood. Both had so much to say but neither knew quite where to start, nor somehow felt that bath time was entirely the right occasion. After three years apart, they realised they were almost strangers to one another. Neither wanted to raise the pain of the death of their Sara. Indeed, neither was sure that the other had received the letter from Miriam. How would either of them, therefore, broach the subject? Pedro was now fully reconciled to the loss of his hand, but Mat and Francesca fully deserved to tell Raquel of their exploits in finding and rescuing him themselves, and he did not want to steal their glory by describing their incredible exploits in the Tuscan hills. And lastly, Raquel chewed over when, or even whether, to tell Pedro of her being raped by Archduke Philip. Now a long way away from the suffocating atmosphere of the Brussels court, she had pushed the assault to the back of her mind, and she did not want to relive the painful memory of it by answering Pedro's inevitable questions about what exactly happened. In any case, how would he react? Would he seek to exact a husband's retribution? Knowing Pedro, he would want to ride all the way to Brussels to settle the score; but it was the last thing he should even contemplate doing, since Archduke Philip was a gifted swordsman. And Don Gonzalo? The Gran Capitán, so honourable and just, would be truly appalled to hear of the Archduke's assault, and would ensure that Queen Isabel learnt of it. And there was no knowing then what might follow from the prissy Queen. No, it was better that Raquel kept her counsel regarding this matter.

So, while she soaked in the warm water, she decided that she would not speak of it to Pedro. Circumstances might arise in the future when she might tell him, but she could not for the moment think what those circumstances might be. To her, it was sufficient that Enid Haas had successfully prevented her from becoming pregnant, and she was glad enough of that. Nevertheless, she must write to Ana of Beamonte and tell her of her journey south across Europe. It would be a shame to lose contact with such an inspiring woman who had been such a good friend.

So, still in sombre mood, they descended the white marble staircase to the palace foyer, floored in the same pure Carrara marble, and out into the cool of the veranda. The sun had set and dusk was descending rapidly. The onshore breeze had abated and the sea had become calm. The scene was beautiful and romantic, and no doubt would rekindle their desire for one another that night.

'Come and join us!' cried Don Gonzalo, rising from his chair to greet the couple. Mat and Francesca sat alongside him at a low round table on which a decanter of red wine and glasses sat on a white tablecloth. Pedro recognised the glassware. It was the same fine, cherry-red Venetian glass with gold filigree tracery which he had taken as the Gran Capitán's wedding gift to Flanders with Jofré almost two years before.

'Ah!' laughed the military commander. 'I see that you recognise the glassware, Pedro! Now, that sounds like a prompt for Raquel to learn from all three of you what happened on that fateful journey north!'

Don Gonzalo rose, filled the glasses with wine, passed them around to the other four and sat back in his chair.

'Start at the beginning, Pedro, when you, Jofré and his six lancers set off from Rome.'

So Pedro started the tale, skipping what he had learnt from Don Gonzalo of the barbarous killing of Jofré's lancers. But the tale really belonged to Mat and Francesca. With the excitement of the storytelling and the effects of the wine and cordial mood, Mat lost his stammer, although it took Francesca's interruptions to fill in the story where Mat's innate modesty prevented him describing how his superhuman strength retrieved the pulley from over the old mineshaft, enabling him to smash down the massive door of Pedro's living sarcophagus. Don Gonzalo enjoyed hearing yet again of the discovery of the crypt, while Raquel was spellbound listening to the couple's incredible exploits, but truly horrified by what Pedro must have endured. So she just sat there, glass in hand, shaking her head in disbelief. When their tale was done, she got up, went around the table, put her arms around Mat and kissed him long and tenderly, for without him she knew she would now be a widow.

It was dark when the story was completed. Candles had already been set on the table and on the steps into the palace behind them.

'I think it's time to partake of the banquet which has been laid on for us – but particularly for you, Raquel,' he said, turning to Raquel. 'You won't believe how many sleepless nights I suffered worrying if Pedro was safe or even alive. So this is to celebrate his survival at the hands of the Tuscan partisans, your arrival here after nearly two years in the Flemish court, Mat and Francesca's wondrous exploits and... well... maybe other things besides.' He smiled broadly. 'Curio, my loyal manservant, has laid our banqueting table on the veranda so we can celebrate with a candlelit supper. Let's be seated.'

They took their places around the carved mahogany table, lit by several candles sitting in engraved holders. In a zephyr of a breeze, the flames flickered gently, adding to the homely ambience which Don Gonzalo was so keen to effect.

'So what shall we have?' he jested. 'As you might know, last year, following the assassination of his middle son, Juan, which I'm not going to sully the occasion by describing, Rodrigo Borgia decided to remedy his reputation for gluttony, extravagance... and goodness knows what else. In addition to reducing the number of cardinals to twenty-four, and insisting that they live a more godly life, he stipulated that their lavish banquets must be more frugal and comprise a first course of pasta, and main course of meat, either boiled or roasted, followed by fruit. We will take his lead, but I will spare you the reading of the Holy Scriptures while we eat!'

Don Gonzalo was in expansive mood. It reminded Raquel so vividly of his joviality and effervescent humour at her and Pedro's wedding five years before on a snowy November day in Vélez Blanco. How he graced that wonderful day with his presence! Then he was dressed in heavy, richly ornate clothing, while today he was clad simply to match the climate. But his sunburnt features and slimmed-down figure glowed with health in the candlelight. His re-nowned marital fidelity must have been challenged on many, many occasions by the hot-blooded Neapolitan beauties who were there for the taking. If only Archduke Philip were a fraction of the man Don Gonzalo was.

'So, like a bevy of compliant cardinals, we'll start with spaghetti *con salsa di accuigas*, a Sicilian speciality.'

'It looks g-g-gorgeous,' said Mat. 'What's it made with?'

'Freshly made spaghetti, of course, Mat. Then tomatoes, fillets of anchovies from Reggio, green olives, garlic, capers, ground ginger from the Orient, chopped parsley, plus a pinch of salt and a generous helping of olive oil. What would we do without our olive oil?'

Washed down with wine, both red and chilled white, and cool water from the deep palace well, they ate in silence, the visitors in particular being ravenous.

'So while we await the next course and let our spaghetti settle,' said Don Gonzalo, as their plates were being cleared away, 'perhaps you'll be so good, Raquel, to tell us of your life in Flanders in the service of our Castilian princess?'

'Yes,' agreed the other three. 'We can't wait to hear.'

The wine had loosened Raquel's tongue, and she was less inhibited than she might otherwise have been.

'There's much to tell. But it's best if I start with our journey from Laredo and the terrible storm we hit which required our seeking shelter in England. Juana was incredible. While we ladies-in-waiting stayed below decks out of the weather, we could see the Princess on the prow of her huge galleon across the water, holding on to the mast and facing the howling gale and driving rain...'

And so during the meal Raquel did her best to describe her time in Flanders; its near-continuous cloud, incessant drizzle, but above all the awful gloom; the flat, monotonous landscape with rivers, canals, lakes and wetlands all round; the tasteless and repetitive food; the inability of the Spanish contin-gent to communicate with the Flemish-speaking courtiers; the huge people there, particularly the buxom, red-cheeked womenfolk; their slack mores, with open kissing in the streets, even between strangers; their consumption of vast quantities of a brew they called ale in dark, noisy alehouses; of Juana's deep love for, and total infatuation with, her lord; of her terrible moods, which swung between kindness and joviality to deep depression and isolation lasting days on end, and which were getting progressively worse; of the amorous adventures of the Grand Duke, which were the talk of the court but of which Juana seemed wholly oblivious; and of the way the Spanish ladies were separated and isolated from their princess, with the Archduke quite intentionally planting his own appointees and spies from the House of Austria to oversee Juana's every needs. She was powerless to prevent this and subsequently had become even more isolated and withdrawn as a result.

'So, Don Gonzalo,' she concluded, as the main course was placed on the table, 'I was more than glad to get your letter inviting me to join you here – although, of course, I was distraught to learn in it of Pedro's plight. But one thing I've forgotten to mention – Miriam's three tapestries. These were well received, and Juana is thrilled to bits with them. She's placed them side by side in the main banqueting hall of the palace. They are truly stunning, and rival the famous tapestries by the Dutch masters which hang in other parts of the palace. It's such a shame that none of you has seen them, or are likely to now.'

'No, that's a shame. But what an adventure for you,' commented Pedro.

'Yes, I suppose so, but please don't send me back!' she pleaded. 'I'm not going to be separated from you again.'

'I concur with what Pedro said,' commented Don Gonzalo. 'It must have been a great experience for you, despite the open hostility of the Flemish court.' He paused. 'Anyway, now for our main course, which I expect you're all ready to eat.'

'What we now have in front of us is *saltimbocca*. It's a Roman speciality. It's made with escalopes of veal on which thin slices of Parma ham are secured with thin splinters of pine. These are cooked lightly in a little olive oil with sage leaves and salt and pepper, with some red wine sprinkled over each escalope. Some butter is added to the resulting sauce, which we then pour over the escalopes. And it's served, as you can see, with boiled rice from the Po delta coloured with a touch of saffron from Egypt.'

'And afterwards, *in conformità con el Papa*, we'll enjoy some fresh fruit!' he chuckled.

When the meal was finished, as the church bell in the town below chimed twelve for midnight, they moved to some softer comfortable chairs to savour the cool night air.

'I know, Raquel, that you'll be tired from your travels, but before you retire to your bed, I have a few announcements to make.

'Firstly, you'll be delighted to know that next week we'll sail for home. Eight ships are due to arrive from Naples, and once my veterans who have remained here are on board, we'll ourselves join them and set sail when the wind is set fair.

'Secondly, I promised you, Pedro, that I'd see if the armourers here could fashion a device which could be attached to your hand.'

Don Gonzalo reached across and picked up a wooden box which lay on an adjacent table.

'I see you flinch, Mat? Why so?'

'I'm sorry, my Lord, but my memory flashed to the wooden box, much the same size, on Romano Latini's mantelpiece, which contained...' He paused, looking sheepishly at Raquel. '...I'm sorry, my dear, I shouldn't mention it, please forgive me; but it contained Pedro's finger.'

Don Gonzalo understood Mat's embarrassment and tried to make light of it. 'Well, this box contains a hand – or something resembling one! As you will already have found, Pedro, you can't do everything with one hand. You need to hold things with one while you do things with the other... although you seem to be managing remarkably well.'

He opened the box and withdrew its contents.

'What the armourers in Naples have made for you is this device, like a claw or turned-over fork, comprising two steel prongs which are separated by a wedge-shaped space. You can use the fork to hold things, like the reins of a horse, or hold things fast by jamming them between the two prongs, such as plates or documents. I know it's crude and a poor substitute for a real hand, but it will help you. The device fits over your wrist and can be made firm with this strap. However, there will be many occasions when you'll want to conceal your disability, for instance when you are in court, so leather craftsmen have made this pair of suede gloves which are now the fashion. The left one, stiffened as with real fingers, fits snugly over your left wrist and should be comfortable to wear. Nobody in court will need to know of your disability.'

Pedro looked at the metal claw and the gloves in disbelief and tried them both on. What had been conjured up by the craftsmen was magical.

'And I have one last announcement to make, as well. The last such announcement I made, if I recall, was at your wedding in Vélez Blanco. Then, on behalf of the King, I conferred on you the title Don Pedro de Gozco, being the hamlet outside Granada where you saved the monarchs from the encampment fire.

'During our successful campaign against the French these last three years, I have been granted many awards and privileges, and many lands and titles. So many, in fact, that I can't possibly enjoy them all or even administer them. For many of them, I've the right to honour others who have served me, and therefore it is my wish, in recognition of your service to me during this Italian campaign as aide-de-camp, to give you title to lands not far from the port of Salerno. This, as you know, lies some thirty miles down the coast from Naples, and is therefore easily accessible. You'll have the right to the title of Baron of Montecorvino, and the lands and several villages around will be in your domain. More importantly, you'll own an attractive, thirteenth-century stone manor house in sight of the sea. This has a shady central court and a high-walled enclosure containing gardens, a vineyard and ponds. Three watermills lie on the River Tusciano, which passes below the hilltop town of

Montecorvino and feeds into ponds which rear trout commercially and belonged formerly to a Dominican monastery. You'll receive the rents and dues from these, and from all those living within your fiefdom. These will provide you with a modest income to live in reasonable comfort with your family. King Federico of Naples, whom you've met several times, has expressed his pleasure with this appointment. You're not, of course, obliged to live there, neither would you be expected to; but as with all my many possessions here now, the bankers in Naples or Rome will see your financial dues are transferred annually to you wherever you abide. The charter according you title to this land and the right to bear the title Baron of Montecorvino is now being prepared in Naples, although it may not be completed before we depart next week.

'So, Pedro, please accept this gift of mine, not just for your service to me in the last three years, but for your friendship and loyalty to me over many more years, which I treasure.'

'If Pedro's a baron, my Lord,' quizzed Raquel, 'does that make me a—?'

'A baroness?' interjected Don Gonzalo with a roar of laughter. 'Yes, it does, Baroness Raquel!'

Everyone laughed.

Raquel was speechless. While much handshaking and kissing followed, Mat raised himself to his full height and declared, his stammer returning in full measure, 'I also w-w-would like to m-m-make an announcement,' he started. 'Fr-Fr-Francesca and I are g-g-going to get m-m-m...'

'Oh, stop it, darling!' his partner interjected mockingly, placing her hand on his arm. 'What Mat is trying to say is that we would like to announce that we are to wed!'

All were jubilant.

'We are to wed in Naples in two weeks' time. Therefore we'll not return with you to Spain directly.'

'Will you stay and live there, Francesca, since Naples is your home town?' asked Raquel tentatively. She had taken a real liking to Mat's spirited fiancée.

'No,' she replied, anticipating the future. 'Spain is Mat's home and as his wife I will travel to the ends of the earth with him. How else will manage to I lift heavy pulleys off mineshafts! So after we're married I'll return with him to Vélez Blanco. With the mountains around, it sounds such a lovely place, and I'm longing to meet Pedro's mother, Miriam.'

'If you're journeying to Naples to wed, Francesca,' offered Don Gonzalo, 'why not spend a few weeks afterwards in Pedro's manor house in Montecorvino? It's less than fifty miles away, and you could get there in a chaise via Salerno in a day. At this time of year its gardens will be delightful.'

'Oh, what a wonderful idea!' said Baroness Raquel. 'You can tell us all about it when you return to Spain.'

'That sounds a wonderful idea, my Lord,' replied Mat, recovering his tongue.

Don Gonzalo's fleet was delayed for two weeks in departing owing to storms in the eastern Mediterranean. By then, Mat and Francesca were in Naples arranging their nuptials. This was to be a simple affair, since Francesca, back in the city of her birth, had so few living relatives. Don Gonzalo and his 1,000 remaining officers and battle-hardened men disembarked in Barcelona, learning there that Fernando and Isabel were in Zaragoza, some ten days march away. So they set off on a triumphal march to Aragón's capital city, lying on the banks of the River Ebro. However, although invited to join the celebrations there, Pedro and Raquel chose to board another ship heading for Cartagena, Almería and Málaga. Travel-weary, they simply wanted to get home.

Don Gonzalo could not have arrived at Aragón's main city at a worse time. The monarchs had remained there all summer with their eldest daughter, Isabel, awaiting the birth of her baby. The Aragonese Cortes had deferred recognising the young Isabel as the heir to the Aragón crown for the same reason. Their dilemma was solved when another tragedy struck. The gentle Isabel died in childbirth in the middle of August, leaving a son, Miguel, upon whose infant head rested the future of the Spanish as well as the Portuguese crowns.

So within two dark years, Queen Isabel had suffered four bereavements: her mother; her only son, Juan; Margaret's stillborn child; and now her eldest daughter. Predictably, the Queen was distraught and inconsolable. All she and Fernando had striven for all their married lives was in ruins: the destiny of Spain so diligently pursued and hard won was broken in pieces around their feet. Spain's future now lay in the hands of a frail newborn babe and their third child, Juana, whose mental instability was growing day by day. The strength which had propelled Isabel forward throughout her glorious years was ebbing from her, and she could not withstand any longer the blows which beset her. Condescendingly, the Aragón Cortes agreed to acknowledge the baby as its heir, and the Queen herself took the child to rear, her heart reaching out to meet the frail Miguel's need of a mother.

At this juncture, the Gran Capitán arrived from Sicily. The fame of his victories in Italy had preceded him, as had the news of the titles and honours and lands given to him in Naples, and the Golden Rose bestowed upon him by Rodrigo Borgia. But inevitably, Don Gonzalo's arrival was a quiet affair. On the outskirts of the city, he was met by nobles, prelates, courtiers and a great multitude who escorted him to the palace. King Fernando was waiting, and ran down the main staircase to receive him, a departure from normal protocol.

'Duke,' said the King, 'we owe you more than we can ever hope to repay for the great honour you have brought to us and our kingdoms. Let us go to the Queen, who has been waiting. She has a longing to see you and it is already late.'

The Queen, the brightness gone from her, and seeing them coming, descended from her dais and advanced with all her ladies as far as the landing to meet them. Gonzalo bowed one knee to the ground and kissed her hand. He was the only man beside her husband, it was alleged, who had been her lover. Raising him up and holding him in a long embrace, she said tearfully, 'Be thou very welcome, Gran Capitán.'

XXIV: The Granada Revolt

January 1499

Letter from Ana of Beamonte

Royal Palace, Brussels, 10 October 1498

Dear Raquel,

I was delighted to receive your letter from Messina, and to hear that you had arrived there safely and were awaiting transport back to Spain. I was shocked to hear of the loss of Pedro's hand and of the horrors he experienced in Tuscany, but it sounds like he's taken it very well. I'm also reassured to hear that you've pushed to the back of your mind your awful experience in February. You're a gritty young woman.

I've purposely delayed writing to you until now while we awaited the birth of Juana's first child. Thanks be to God, four days ago she was delivered easily and safely of a baby daughter who has been christened Eleanor in memory of Maximilian's mother. Celebrations and jousting in the market square are planned for next week, with the Archduke challenging selected courtiers. Such things don't change!

It would be nice to think that the arrival of the child will lead to a change in Juana's behaviour, but I doubt it. Queen Isabel has sent several envoys from Castile to report back to her on the rumours she's received about her daughter's conduct. Friar Tomás of Matienzo has been here for many months and has interviewed me several times to learn of what's been happening, and he's despatched several letters to Isabel. In these he's confirmed Juana's lack of devotion, her refusal to take confession and her general indifference to religious duties. This has been apparent for a long time to me. It's already evident that, since the birth of Eleanor, Philip has doubled his efforts to isolate Juana from her Spanish contacts and from her religious advisors. The frivolity of the Flemish court has particularly shocked Friar Tomás, as it did us when we arrived. The coolness of Juana towards her Spanish advisors is also clearly evident to him. The friar has also reported to the Queen on the mismanagement of Juana's funds by the treasurer appointed by Philip, and he's appalled by the low allowances allotted to us, despite the fact that only myself and six of the original contingent of ladies-in-waiting remain. Some of us have been reduced to veritable poverty, as you'll remember all too well. I've impressed on the friar that Juana is permitted no word in the running of her household, and is clearly intimidated by Philip, by the Council and by the people surrounding her.

One can only sympathise with her. The young woman is still only twenty. She's living in an alien land and in an alien culture, and is confronted by the might of the House of Austria and the Holy Roman Empire. What were Fernando and Isabel thinking of in arranging this match with the Archduke? Poor Juana is no more than a tool in their power game. I hope they've not prejudiced the future of their kingdoms. At least poor Juan, God rest his soul, was permitted to remain in Spain attached to his mother's apron strings. Juana unselfishly and passionately adores Philip, and she subordinates her desires to his dictates and he plays on this.

I'm glad to say that Friar Tomás recognises that I've always remained faithful to the interests of Fernando and Isabel and, as a result, he's able to speak freely with me. Sad to report though, due to our forced isolation from our duties assigned by the Queen, too many of my ladies have taken the easy way out and sided with Philip and his ministers in matters of domestic policy. The physical condition of our group is deplorable, and we all complain of hunger due to our reduced spending money and the exorbitant prices levied upon us for their everyday needs – and worse, of the scorn and despicable treatment shown to us by the citizens of Brussels.

It's sad that I should have to report such things, although little of this will be news to you. I do hope that you have settled back into home life at Xiquena. Please do write again soon.

Love and best wishes,

Ana

Worried beyond measure by the reports from Friar Tomás and other envoys and spies who she had sent to Flanders, Queen Isabel was preoccupied with deciding what course to follow in dealing with her recalcitrant daughter. Juana was showing worrying signs of following the mental instability of the Queen's late mother. Still recovering her health from the blows which fate had dealt her and bowed down by worries over Juana, the Queen was prostrate.

By the time Ana's letter was received by Raquel in Xiquena, Mat and Francesca had returned from their brief honeymoon in Montecorvino and were happily installed in the gatehouse. It was a little cramped, and Mat was busy adding several rooms facing into the castle grounds. He was barely in time, for early in 1499 Francesca was delivered of a baby boy. Just a week afterwards, Raquel followed with a daughter. One was baptised Carlos, after Francesca's father, and the other Elena.

Although there had been much kissing, hugging and celebrating on the return of Pedro and Raquel to Spain, and much celebration over the safe delivery of the two infants, the couple quickly detected an undercurrent of unease in their home in the castle of Xiquena. Unknown to them, disquiet among the Muslim communities in Los Vélez and the surrounding villages had been growing. Although there were few outward signs of this, it was clearly a reflection of the growing antipathy between Christians and Muslims far to the west in Granada, which was soon to break out as a major rebellion. Already Pedro's family was showing signs of strain. Pedro himself had grown up in Vélez Blanco, a Muslim town, and although the son of a Jewish father

and Christian mother, his only real friend had been Yazíd, so brutally murdered four years before. Moreover, in his wanderings across Muslim al-
Andalus as a boy he had been befriended by dozens of wonderful people, from
the Mullah and Sabyán in Oria to Sultan Boabdil and his warrior uncle, known
as El Zagal. Pedro had developed a deep respect and affection for these
peoples, and he had always made clear where his sympathies lay. And of course
the same applied to his wife, Raquel, who although she had adopted the
Christian faith was still Muslim at heart.

Miriam's stance was mixed. She had been deprived of nine years of her life
during her captivity in the harem of the Alhambra. Although the establishment
there of her renowned tapestry school had freed her from the lascivious
attention of the sultan, she could not forgive her loss of freedom – during
which she had lost her husband, Abraham, and her beautiful young daughter,
Cristina, when they were both brutally slain by soldiers of the Inquisition in
search of her husband's alleged hidden wealth. She had got on famously with
her team of needlewomen from the village, but even they had grown cold to
her in the last year. Why? What had she done?

For her husband Agustín, things were a lot clearer. He had served
twenty-five years as an officer in the service of Queen Isabel and had seen
much bloodshed and cruelty on both sides during the ten-year Granada
war. Since moving to Xiquena, he had worked hard to establish cordial
relations with the mayor of Vélez Blanco, Mohammed Adbuladin, with
whom he had worked closely, but even he was starting to distance himself
from Agustín. Raghad, Raquel's mother, always uncompromising, always
outspoken and always quick to complain, wore her heart on her sleeve and
clearly believed, albeit unfairly, that she was not welcome in the Xiquena
household. And for her husband, Joshua, Pedro's loving and loveable uncle,
whom young Antonio worshipped, his debilitating rheumatism from a
lifetime in the cold and damp mountains was taking its toll. Having turned
fifty, he just wanted to see out his few remaining years in reasonable
comfort and free of strife.

And lastly, what of Mat and Abel and their wives, Francesca and Eva? Both
men had served as soldiers of the Queen and had seen or heard how harshly
their fellow soldiers had treated their enemy, especially in Málaga eleven years
before, when most of the population was put to the sword or sold into slavery.
Mat had just returned after three years of active service in Italy with a young
and doting Christian wife, while Abel's wife was a local Mudejar woman.
Consequently, Abel was torn both ways; yet he secretly longed for a little
freedom and action.

So as news filtered across Andalucía of the growing unrest, sides were
starting to be taken in the Xiquena household, as was happening in many

homes across the land – even in the royal court, then resident in Seville. Such is the consequence of civil war.

For some time past, the Spanish Inquisition had been growing in power so that conversion to Christianity by force was almost inescapable and the condition of the Muslims was almost intolerable. Nevertheless, the tens of thousands of Muslims who remained in Granada and the surrounding mountains continued to live on reasonable terms with their Christian neighbours due to the benign stewardship of the city by its governor, Count of Tendilla, who was a friend of Don Gonzalo, as well as the city's archbishop, Fernando de Talavera, himself of Jewish descent. Being charged by the King and Queen to bring about the conversion of the Muslims in Granada, Talavera set about the task in a sensible and humane way. He learnt Arabic and had scholars make an Arabic translation of the entire Bible. However, his methods were too temperate for many zealots, who wanted conversions by the thousand. In 1499, the Archbishop of Toledo, Jiménez de Cisneros, came to Granada to bolster Talavera in his mission who, in December of that year, following his sermons and gifts to the converted, held a mass baptism of 4,000 Muslims.

Cisneros, Isabel's former confessor, a brilliant man but an ascetic who lived a life of strict obedience, saw the numbers of converts as a sign of divine approbation, and demanded that the process should be speeded up. He had the church bells rung day and night, a sound which the Muslims abhorred. He had the libraries in the city ransacked for copies of the Koran and other sacred works, and these priceless manuscripts were burnt on a great bonfire in the city. Its Christian inhabitants begged Cisneros to stay his hand and use greater forbearance, but the fanatical Archbishop of Toledo replied that it was no time to hold back when Islam was close to eradication. The inevitable happened. Muslims in the city marched on the Archbishop's palace in the Albaicín, the populous hillside lying directly opposite the Alhambra across the River Darro. Only the venerable Talavera was able to quell the passions of the mob, which knelt around him, kissing the hem of his robes.

Rumours of the attempted Muslim revolt reached Seville, where the court was spending Christmas. Fernando, who opposed Cisneros as being too fanatical, taunted the Queen by saying, 'So it seems we must pay dearly for your Archbishop, whose rashness can lose us in a few hours what took us years to acquire!'

Isabel summoned Cisneros to Seville, but he held his ground, insisting that his course of action was right. Isabel and Fernando acquiesced. On his return to Granada, he offered the Moors the alternative of baptism or trial for high treason. Mass conversions of 50,000 ensued.

The inevitable rebellion followed, spreading into the Alpujarras, a valley system to the south-east of Granada, lying between high mountains and stretching across the regions of Granada and Almería. At its Granada end, the River Guadalfeo drained westwards and then turned southwards to the sea, with white villages flanking the south-facing mountain side, while at the dryer Almería end of the Alpujarras the River Andarax drained eastwards to Almería, with the villages flanking the north-facing side.

The Muslims in the Alpujarras were a tough, hardy people who were used to poverty and hardship. With their strong traditions, and being deeply religious, they despised their compatriots in Granada for caving in so readily to the Christians. They proceeded to attack the fortified mountain passes and towns along the 100-mile-long valley system. From Morocco, nightly raids on Spanish coastal towns and villages were made by fast lateen-rigged dhows, and rumours of a major invasion from across the Mediterranean were rampant. Fernando, furious over the developments precipitated by Cisneros, decided to settle the issue once and for all. He determined to nip the revolt in the bud by sending a punitive expedition into the Alpujarras.

Don Gonzalo was his obvious choice as commander since he knew the area intimately. He spoke fluent Arabic and had proved himself an outstanding military leader. But the Gran Capitán was already assembling a force in Málaga for a second military campaign in Italy. Instead, the King turned to Gonzalo's second cousin, Diego Fernandez of Córdoba. Like many members of the Córdoba-based Fernández family, he was experienced in the art of war, and like his cousin spoke fluent Arabic. The conflict had now become a purely military campaign, with soldiers on the march, guerrilla battles, and attacks on towns and fortresses.

In January 1500, the Muslim rebellion in the Alpujarras broke out in Castell de Ferro, a town on the Mediterranean coast, set in a tight re-entrant leading northwards into the Alpujarran mountains. There was rebellion too in Albuñol, higher up the slope, and in the bustling port of Adra, from where Sultan Boabdil had fled to Morocco in the autumn of 1493. In the eastern Alpujarras, in the headwaters of the River Andarax, the Muslims in the villages of Terque, Huécija, Alicún and Alhama rebelled, fortifying their hilltop stronghold of Marchena, which lay across the river from Terque. Messengers were sent to the city of Almería, which sought immediate help from Lorca and Murcia to the east, informing them that the rebels had put to death eighty soldiers of the guard in Adra and were threatening to fall upon Almería itself.

Now twenty-two, Don Pedro Fajardo, son of Juan Chacón, was spending his honeymoon in Murcia with his young wife, but quickly mobilised a force, setting off with 130 cavalry and over 800 foot soldiers.

'What's that noise?' asked Raquel, sitting in the sun on the steps of Xiquena castle. 'That rumbling sound?'

'Ah!' answered her stepfather, Agustín, cocking his ear to the side. 'Sounds to me like a large force of soldiers on the move. Probably passing through Vélez Rubio and heading for Granada. But why?' he puzzled.

He had little time to wait. Approaching the castle along the Lorca road was a squadron of riders, a detachment from the main force, with the lead rider holding aloft the standard of the Fajardo family. They stopped at the bottom gatehouse. Mat invited inside the leader of the party, whom Agustín, who was on his way down from the castle, immediately recognised as Pedro Fajardo. He had assumed the day-to-day governorship of Los Vélez from his father and, in effect, was now Agustín's lord and master. It was a rare visit from the Murcia-based appointee of the King. He had matured into a tall, robust man and was very much his father's son: purposeful and forthright.

'Greetings, Don Pedro,' said Agustín cordially, as they climbed the steps up to the keep. 'From the sounds we hear from over the hill, it seems that this is a visit with a purpose?'

'Thank you for your welcome, Captain López. It's always a pleasure to visit you here in these glorious surroundings. But indeed you're right. There is a purpose in my visit. You may not know, Captain, but the Moors have risen in revolt in Granada and in the Alpujarras. They've taken many of our towns and are threatening Almería. I've just received a desperate letter from the mayor there, seeking my immediate support to defend the city. So, breaking off my honeymoon, I've hastily marshalled a force of cavalry and infantry. They're at this moment passing through Vélez Rubio.

'But I'm desperately short of experienced officers,' he continued, 'men who know the country around Granada and know the ways of these damned Moors. More, in fact, than I do. I'm here to ask you to join me in this venture.' He looked Agustín in the eye. 'So will you ride with me, Captain? The campaign can't last long, and there'll be bounty to be had, no doubt.'

Agustín needed no second invitation. Life had become a little fractious in the household of late and he needed to get away, if only for a few months.

'Yes, that I will!' he said with alacrity.

'Good man!' Don Pedro said with glee. 'I'll put you in charge of half my force. I need an officer I can trust. Other forces might join us later. My men are heading for Chirivel, twelve miles on from Vélez Rubio, where there's abundant pasture and water to be had for the horses, and where we can encamp for the night. I'm riding there now. If you can join me before night-fall, it would raise the spirits of the men no end. Many will still remember you.'

'I will, Don Pedro, I will. Have no fear, I'll be there by sunset!'

Matt, surprised by the turn of events but not hankering to join the fray, hastened down to the stables next to the gatehouse to saddle Agustín's horse and make it ready. Agustín, now thoroughly energised by the turn of events, ran to the armoury on the ground floor of the keep and assembled in a pile his sword and armour – breastplate and backplate, helmet, gorget, greaves, gauntlets and kneecaps, all of which he kept burnished, more through pride than ambition for the fray.

Miriam, startled by all the commotion, intercepted her husband running up the steps to the main hall. She guessed something was afoot.

'It looks like you're preparing to leave!'

Agustín explained what had happened. Miriam was a little relieved.

'How long will you be gone?'

'Just a few months, I imagine,' he replied. 'The Moors can't hold out for very long. For one thing, we confiscated all their weapons long ago!'

'Well, take care, my dear,' proffered Miriam. 'Let the young soldiers win the medals for bravery. You did your fighting years ago to earn your pension from the Queen.'

'Yes, I know. Have no fear. I shall return very soon.'

With kisses and handshakes all round, he set off. The sun had already dipped below the limestone massif to the south-west. Loath to admit it to herself, Miriam felt some relief in Agustín's departure. Arguments in the household over the rights and wrongs of the Muslim cause had led to a coolness between them and, moreover, Agustín's work on behalf of Juan Chacón had gone stale, not least because of the growing involvement of Pedro Fajardo in the management of the estate.

Then, quite out of the blue, the day after Agustín's departure, Raghad decided that she would return to her home in Mecina Fondales in the valley floor of the Guadalfeo River. This hamlet lay an easy day's ride from Lanjarón, itself less than thirty miles south of Granada.

Raquel was staggered by her precipitate decision.

'But there might not be anybody there, Mama,' she pleaded. 'The village might be deserted and the houses in ruins! When Pedro rescued us and baby Sara after his return from the Indies seven years ago, every single villager was trooping out of the village in the rain with all their possessions on their backs, heading for Adra and a boat to Morocco! If Pedro hadn't arrived when he did, that's where we'd be now! You are likely to be going back to a totally dead and deserted village!' Raquel was flabbergasted.

'That's as it may be,' her mother replied sharply. 'I've been thinking about this for months. With Agustín's departure yesterday to fight with the Christians, I've made up my mind. My place at this time is with my own people. There's nothing more to say.'

'But what about Uncle Joshua?' asked Raquel, still shocked by her mother's announcement. Raghad just shrugged her shoulders and turned away.

Abel, a little jealous of Mat's three-year sojourn in Italy, and desirous to spread his wings, agreed to accompany Raghad to Mecina on his way to Granada, hoping to enlist with the King's men and see a little action. He was still a soldier at heart. Nevertheless, he asserted quite clearly that whatever the state of the village, whether deserted or ruined, he would leave Raghad there and carry on to Granada to rendezvous with his old comrades. Raghad concurred.

Raquel never saw her mother again.

Joshua, now too infirm to live on his own, would move down from the family home in Vélez Blanco to Xiquena, where he would be made more than welcome. The family home could be securely locked. With Agustín's and Raghad's departures, the mood in the household warmed noticeably.

Within the month, Pedro Fajardo's and Agustín's Murcian force had seized the hillside town of Alhama and encircled the mountain-top fort of Marchena, thereby relieving the situation in Almería. King Fernando, then in Granada, decided to take the field himself and in March marched with a large army upon the town of Lanjarón. It lay a short distance to the south and was the western gateway into the Alpujarras. Don Luis de Beaumont, Constable of Navarra and Count of Lerín, continued on to the towns and villages in the headwaters of the Andarax, leaving behind a trail of blood and fire. Within eight days, Lanjarón fell. Fernando adopted the merciless ploy he had used many times in the Granada war in order to send a lesson to other towns resisting siege. There, in Lanjarón, he put to the sword 3,000 men and, shamefully, blew up the mosque in which 600 women and children had sought refuge. The Muslim rebels in neighbouring towns and villages capitulated, and in just four days they relinquished all their defences and agreed to abandon their rebellion, in addition forfeiting 50,000 ducats as a payment of war indemnity.

In the autumn of the same year, 1500, the Muslims in the Taha[1] of Níjar, a town twenty miles north-east of Almería and tucked up tightly against the mountains, as well as in the 6,000-foot Sierra of Filabres to the north, rose in rebellion. Níjar had long been a focus of unrest, and it would continue to be for many decades to come. The rebels were led by a tall, dark-skinned Berber leader, Walid of Huebro, who was noted for his bravery, and he was proclaimed king. The Catholic Monarchs, who were still in Granada, sent Diego Fernández of Córdoba to capture the town. He was joined by forces from Lorca and Murcia. He commenced his campaign on 20 October from Tabernas, the *alcazaba* twenty miles from Almería, where El Zagal had studied

---

[1] *Taha* was the Arab name given to a group of towns and villages forming an administrative and defensive alliance.

the surrender documents for Almería eleven years before. Aware of the fate which befell the citizens of Lanjarón, the rebels in the Taha of Níjar surrendered and for their pains were obliged to pay 25,000 ducats to obtain their liberty. Those who refused to pay, such as Walid of Huebro and Gomerí of Níjar, had their possessions confiscated. To dilute the Muslim influence there, the monarchs ordered the repopulation of these villages by Christians, and in the following year the King agreed to the creation of a town council comprising a mayor and four councillors to be elected annually in August.

Meanwhile, well to the north, in the mountains of the Filabres at Velefique, the rebels strengthened their stronghold. The mayor barricaded the gates of the town and strengthened its defences, and for months Pedro Fajardo's forces used artillery and battering rams to try and break them down. But each night the defenders repaired their defences, so that the following morning the Christians found that they were faced with the same defences which they had earlier destroyed.

A week into the siege of the town, Agustín was overseeing the firing of one of their several artillery pieces, a lombard, placed some fifty yards from the walls. The lombard's eight-foot-long barrel with a three-inch bore was made from lengths of square iron bar secured along their lengths by iron hoops. The barrel was tied with rope to a wooden frame which could be directed roughly at the target. The cannon was breach-loaded, with the breechblock inserted after a ball had been pushed into the barrel and after powder had been placed into the cavity inside the block. The gunner pushed a stone ball inside the barrel, carelessly not having previously tested its size through a check-hoop. He inserted the breechblock with its charge of black powder, and hammered in a wedge to hold the block tightly in place. When all was ready and the signal was given by Agustín, the gunner touched the powder hole with a light. There was an enormous explosion as fire and black smoke engulfed the men around the cannon. Screams rang out, and as the smoke cleared, and to the loud cheers of the villagers manning the wall above, a scene of bloody carnage emerged. The gun was no more. Three soldiers who had been standing nearby lay on the ground moaning and holding their faces as blood poured between their fingers. The uniforms of two were on fire. Of the gunner, there was no sign. Agustín lay a few yards away, the whole of his right shoulder and arm having been blown off by a lump of iron. In a disaster by no means uncommon, the stone ball, cut by masons, had jammed in the barrel and the whole gun disintegrated, shooting out red-hot lumps of iron and splinters of wood in all directions. Through loss of blood and shock, Agustín died within minutes.

Don Pedro Fajardo appeared on the scene soon after, appalled by what had happened. He had grown to respect Agustín in his administration of Vélez Blanco, and had been delighted that he had joined him in the campaign. Out of respect for his being retired from active service, and especially for Miriam, he tried to ensure that he was kept out of the firing line. Now he had died and his body was horribly mutilated. That evening, he wrote a letter of condolence to Miriam explaining what had happened and despatched a rider with it the next morning. He had Agustín's body wrapped in cloth and then in a thin sheet of lead sealed with a hot iron. Using this simple coffin, he returned Agustín's body to Xiquena. There was nothing more he could do. The coffin was placed in the recently consecrated Christian graveyard alongside that of young Sara, who had died two years before.

Diego Fernández, in overall command, could see that their artillery and engines of war were having little effect and decided to mine beneath the *aljibe*, the town's sole underground water reservoir. Within a week, he had drained it dry. Although the Moors melted snow from the roofs of their houses, they remained without water for eight days. With little option, they surrendered and placed themselves at the mercy of the King. Hernando de Zafra, the monarchs' secretary, who Pedro and Raquel had met some years before in Medina del Campo, arrived in the name of the King and formalised a surrender document. On the orders of the King, Diego Fernández rounded up the 200 ringleaders and they were thrown to their deaths from the tower of the mosque. The rest of the inhabitants of Velefique were pardoned. With great fortitude, the people of the town had held out until January 1501. The assault had lasted three months and employed more than 3,000 men and three siege engines. Many there, citizens and soldiers alike, died of the cold, losing hands and legs through frostbite. The cost of the assault exceeded 4 million *maravedís*.

Yet even with the surrender of Velefique, the calm did not return to the Almería region, and many remained under arms, particularly the Moors in the communities around Macael in the valley of the Almanzora. The citizens of Mojácar, on the coast to the east, threatened an uprising, but were constrained by the presence of Pedro Fajardo's forces in nearby Vera. Finally, Adra, where the rebellion had started, rose up again.

Several months later, quite out of the blue, another Muslim uprising erupted in the Sierra Bermeja, south of Ronda, over a hundred miles or more to the west of Granada in an area previously free from trouble. Its high mountains were thickly wooded and incised by deep ravines. With Gonzalo now abroad, his elder brother Alonso, Lord of Montilla, stationed not far away, was ordered by Fernando to march against the rebels. Worried that he had been allocated grossly insufficient forces for the task, Alonso led his men into the mountains against the rebels, who had been fired up by a young leader. Rashly, a company of Alonso's men were drawn to higher ground as the Moors feigned a retreat, which was one of their oldest tricks. The chance of rich pickings tempted the Spanish men ever higher, foolishly stopping to load themselves with gold and silver trinkets. Some, besotted by these temptations and blind to the danger, threw away their weapons so that they could carry away more loot.

Night closed in on the mountains, and the Moors began to attack. Rocks were hurled from the craggy limestone peaks around. In the darkness, the Spanish units separated, and in the passes and narrow defiles they were slaughtered by the score. Bravely, Don Alonso and a small band of faithful followers, his son Pedro among them, held a rocky ledge while the main body of Moors continued hunting the dispersed Spanish soldiers, loaded down as they were with their booty, hurling them bodily into the ravines below, the remainder falling under Moorish scimitars.

'We must retreat!' entreated one of Alonso's small band.

'The banner of Aguilar never fled the battlefield!' Alonso cried defiantly. But seeing his son Pedro severely wounded in head and thigh, Alonso begged the boy to save himself 'lest the hope of our house be lost this day'. However, Pedro would not budge until some men-at-arms forcibly carried him away. Fighting to the last, with the slain enemy lying at their feet, the little band died one by one, Alonso of Aguilar last of all.

The Moors respected the Lord of Montilla so much that they sent his body to Córdoba to receive a Christian burial. He was buried there with much ceremony in a special tomb in the Church of San Hippolyte. For days, the citizens of the city filed past to pay their respects to one of their greatest lords.

By the middle of 1501, the Muslim revolt was finally over. On 30 June, under a new agreement with the Moors, the King exempted from the payment of war indemnity those who had been baptised, returning to them the land which had been confiscated, including the hereditary rights of those who had died in the rebellion. With the Moors being allowed various other privileges, many finally converted to Christianity. In the district of Almería alone, nearly 5,000 became Christians, and in the Taha of Marchena over 2,000. Nevertheless, despite this and the adoption of Christian names, many of them continued to practise the religion of their birth.

Weary after nearly twenty years of ceaseless conflicts with the Muslims in their former kingdom of the Nazarí, a royal decree the following February obliged the Muslims in the whole of Castile to be baptised or exiled.

Loyal to his memory and to their happy times together, Miriam mourned Agustín's death. But, guiltily, she was not overly sad. She had now been widowed twice, and at forty-five, her fair hair dulling to grey, she was content to devote herself to Pedro and Raquel and to loveable Joshua, and above all to her two grandchildren – six-year-old Antonio, who was a little rascal, and baby Elena who, judging by her cries during the night, had a sound pair of lungs and did not suffer from the ill health which had taken poor Sara from them.

XXV: Affairs of State

February 1500

The start of the Granada revolt by the Muslims a year before had found the Flemish city of Ghent in the throes of uncontrolled excitement. Juana was expecting a second child. Fireworks had been set on the spire on the church of Saint Michael in anticipation of the announcement of the birth of a boy, which would secure the inheritance of the Habsburg dynasty for Emperor Maximilian. As the date of the birth drew near, the townspeople, freed from their labours, filled the taverns and boisterously celebrated in the streets. Other eager citizens clustered around the palace gates, waiting for the news of a boy child they craved to hear. Inside the palace, a dance was in progress beneath the lights of a thousand candles flickering in their crystal chandeliers, with the courtiers dressed in elaborate costumes of velvet and brocade. All were in a state of high anticipation for a male heir.

Juana did not disappoint them. On 25 February 1500, she was delivered of a son. The child was christened Charles and was accorded the title Duke of Luxembourg, previously held by Wenceslaus IV, King of Bohemia. Charles's baptism in March was a lavish affair attended by city burgomasters, princes and prelates in their hundreds from Flanders, Luxembourg and France. After the baptismal ceremony had been performed, and to the music of clarions, sackbuts, flageolets and trumpets, the people disgorged into the streets, illuminated by row upon row of flaming torches. The ensuing days were filled with celebrations, with Ghent hosting a gigantic crossbow tournament to which surrounding towns and villages sent teams to compete for prizes. One award of a thousand florins was for the best turned-out team of archers, another for the best bowman, another for the best-decorated fishing boat on the river. After weeks of exhausting celebrations, the Archduke and Archduchess declared themselves 'well pleased' with the fêtes held in honour of their firstborn son.

Juana and her two children remained in Brussels during the summer months which followed, while Philip toured his territories or spent long hours in the nearby woods and hills, hunting with his favourite hounds. Taking advantage of his absence, the newly appointed Spanish ambassador, Gutierrez Gómez de Fuensalida, spent many days with the Archduchess trying to substantiate the reports which he had received about her mental state, since

Gutierrez was under orders from the Queen to furnish a detailed report on the physical state of Philip and Juana and of their two children. Juana complained to him that under penalty of dismissal her own servants had been forbidden to address her in her native Castilian, and that her every word and deed had been divulged to her husband through his spies at court. While Philip gallivanted around the country with his dissolute companions, pursuing their every whim, Juana had become a virtual prisoner in her own quarters. In his reports to the Queen, the ambassador said that the Archduchess was completely dominated by her husband, and that her self-consuming love for him was so powerful that she wore it submissively like a hair shirt, suffering the resulting tortures.

Upon being informed of the birth of Charles[1] in Flanders, Queen Isabel turned to Fernando and said, 'Mark my word, Sire, this child is to be our heir, and fortune has smiled upon our kingdom.' Sadly, her words were prophetic, for in April, two months after the birth of Charles, her grandson, infant Miguel – her eldest daughter Isabel's surviving child – died in Granada aged just twenty-three months.[2] Everyone's hopes for an eventual unification under one throne of the Iberian kingdoms of Castile, Aragón and Portugal were dashed. Queen Isabel was devastated and would never fully recover from the shock. Their joint monarchy now rested precariously on the uncertain shoulders of Juana.

Messengers were sent at once to Brussels on the death of Miguel with urgent pleas for Juana and Philip to hasten to Spain to be sworn in as heirs apparent. Their reaction to the summons was negative. Time passed and no answer was forthcoming. As weeks turned to months without any signs of compliance or even interest on the part of Philip, others were sent to force the Archduke into action. Archbishop Fuensalida notified the sovereigns in a secret letter that the Archduke was doing all he could to resist the journey to Spain. This was despite his father Maximilian's encouragement to submit himself to the Spanish monarchs and accept the oath of loyalty from their future subjects. Pressed further by the monarchs, Philip vacillated once again, declaring that he could not possibly leave his lands or his children, and that he had many pressing matters in Flanders to resolve. Besides, winter was upon them and it would be impossible to undertake a sea voyage. Instead, he would send his roving ambassador, Besançon, to Spain to check the lie of the land. He asserted that neither he nor Juana would set foot in her homeland until the emissary had returned with the information he required. Smugly, Philip rested his case. Isabel and Fernando knew they had been tricked.

---

[1] Later Charles I of Spain and Charles V, the Holy Roman Emperor.
[2] Miguel's small coffin lies in the crypt of the Royal Chapel, Granada, alongside those of Fernando and Isabel and Juana and Philip.

That winter, ambassador Besançon journeyed south to Spain and was received generously by Isabel and Fernando. They impressed on him that it was imperative that Juana and Philip became acquainted with their inheritance and their future subjects. Artfully, Besançon gave the monarchs a false sense of hope. But again, their pressure came to naught when it was learnt that Juana was again with child.

Back in Brussels, Philip's attitude to his wife was becoming contemptuous, and he treated her – the heiress to the kingdoms of Spain – with a manifest lack of consideration. Again and again, he tried to bend her to his will, meeting her acts of defiance with impatience and intolerance until their arguments were the talk of the palace. Once, when she was unable to travel due her advanced pregnancy with a third child, he ranted and screamed at her like a pampered child, unable to bear the defiance of the usually compliant Juana. For beneath the outward docile appearance of the Archduchess lay dormant a strong character, stifled by her submission to her parents and to her petulant husband. As the prospects of a return trip to her homeland drew near, there flickered a reawakening of her self-confidence, with her emerging briefly from her shadowy existence.

With the revolt by the Muslims in the Alpujarras still raging, Fernando, back in Granada in April 1500 after seizing Lanjarón, had been faced with an urgent request from the Venetians for assistance in expelling the Turks, who had invaded Venice's possessions along the Adriatic coast. The King had issued orders for Don Gonzalo Fernández to lead a new expedition to join forces with the Venetians to fight the Turks. On 4 June, Gonzalo set sail from Málaga with a huge fleet comprising four mighty heavily armed Genoese carracks, thirty-nine cargo ships, eight galleys and four lateen-rigged caravels. With a fair wind, they reached Palma in Majorca in two days. Here the knights and soldiers, dressed in fine new uniforms, processed proudly through the streets. From Majorca, they sailed across a placid sea via Sardinia, reaching Messina in Sicily in July. It was almost exactly two years since he had left there after his first Italian campaign. In Messina, Gonzalo was joined by a young military engineer from the Pyrenees named Pedro Navarro. He was to play a vital part in the Turkish campaign and later in Italy, where he earned notable distinction for his undermining and destruction of fortifications and fortresses.

The Ionian Islands, situated along the eastern Adriatic coast, then belonged to the Republic of Venice, but they had been commandeered by the Turks; so it was to the islands of Corfu, Zante and Cephalonia that Gonzalo sailed to join Venice's magnificent war fleet of eighteen galleons and twenty-five galleys. The Gran Capitán and the Venetian commander decided to focus their first assault on the island of Cephalonia, where a force of 700–800 Turks had captured the almost impregnable coastal fortress of Saint George. Gonzalo sent a message to their commander, warning that if they did not surrender immediately they would receive no quarter. The Ottoman Empire, then at the height of its power, disdained to even respond to Gonzalo's offer, and the Turks withdrew their force into their fortress, making preparations to withstand the combined Spanish and Venetian assault. Gonzalo advised caution against a hasty attack, and waited while the Venetians landed several huge bronze siege guns. Once in place, these discharged iron cannonballs with such forces that they penetrated the eight-foot-thick outer walls of the fortress and, with a deafening crash, destroyed much of the inner defences. Undismayed by mounting losses, the Turks continued to repair their damaged walls under the barrage. They hurled down fireballs onto the assaulting Spaniards, fishing for them over the walls with iron hooks which lodged between breastplate and belt, hauling the unfortunate soldiers high in the air to be killed by arrow or lance.

Stung by letters from King Fernando, who could not understand the delay in taking the Saint George stronghold, Gonzalo devised a new method to protect his men from the hail of arrows raining down from above. A siege engine was constructed with a sloping roof which moved forward on wheels to batter the gate of the stronghold. The Turks, secretly tunnelling towards the Spanish lines, were caught unawares by a counter-mine dug by Pedro Navarro, and hundreds of them were blown to bits or buried when gunpowder exploded beneath them. Many were taken prisoner and brutally impaled on stakes by the Venetians in front of the walls as a warning to the others.

The Turks held out bravely for four months, and it took until Christmas Eve before Gonzalo was ready to assault the stronghold itself, with five points chosen to straddle the wide moat. At dawn, to the sound of Gonzalo's trumpeter, a deafening cannonade provided the signal for the Spanish and Venetians to storm the outer walls across pontoon bridges. In half an hour, the castle was theirs, with nearly every Turk slain. Only eighty were taken alive. Such was the starvation inflicted on the plucky garrison that only sixty sacks of biscuits were found in the store and not a single barrel of gunpowder.

So great was the defeat inflicted on the Turks in Cephalonia that the peace made between them and Venice lasted a generation. In appreciation of Gonzalo's superb generalship, Venice sent him a fine stud of Turkish horses, gold and silver table services and costly furs. Sadly, his victory was barely celebrated before a courier brought news of the death of his elder brother, Alonso of Aguilar, in his heroic action against the Moors, when single-handed he had tried to rescue some of his men who had foolishly attacked a force much stronger than his own.

With the defeat of the Turks at Cephalonia barely over, Gonzalo was perturbed when he was informed that the French were preparing to attack Naples, and he was ordered by Fernando to move his force to Sicily forthwith. King Federico of Naples, as well as Gonzalo, was appalled to learn from Pope Alexander VI in Rome that the Kings of Spain and France had signed an agreement, the Treaty of Granada, with the intent of dividing his Kingdom of Naples between them. This was only three years after the French had been so roundly defeated by his and Spanish forces and expelled from Italy. How could this be? How could the Spanish King, his cousin, contemplate such an action? Gonzalo was disgusted by the action of Fernando in making an alliance with the French King which required the Gran Capitán to fight his good friend, Federico. For Gonzalo, it was a dishonourable demand by the unscrupulous King, but he could do little else but to obey.

Returning to Sicily across the Adriatic Sea, Gonzalo at once relinquished the lordships of the towns and villages which had been granted to him by Federico, and he begged Federico to release him from the homage he owed him as the King of Naples. Generously, Federico refused to take back from Gonzalo the gifts which he had bestowed on him when they were allies. But knowing Gallic treachery as well as he did, Gonzalo began preparing for the day when the French would overstep the mark and give him the opportunity to gain the Neapolitan kingdom in its entirety.

The French were in league with the Pope's eldest son, César Borgia, who had returned to Rome from Navarra leaving behind his new wife, Carlotta, to take command of the Papal army. César started his own military campaign by offering a truce to Capua, a Neapolitan city twenty miles inland from Naples. But César's men, true to form, put 7,000 of Capua's defenders to the sword, raping the women and pillaging the place down to the very last coin. Poor King Federico, demoralised by the loss of his former ally, the Gran Capitán, was obliged to surrender to the French the strategic port of Gaeta, fifty miles north of the city of Naples. Humiliated beyond measure, he had little choice but to also relinquish his city of Naples.

Events in the Indies were also moving apace.

Letter from Antonio de Torres

Seville, 10 December 1500

Dear Pedro,

Thank you for your letter at the turn of the year. It was good to hear from you, but I was sorry to hear about your horrifying experiences at the hands of the Tuscan partisans. I had heard that they were savage and brutal, but hopefully the death of their leader, Romano Latini, may see an end to them. Your compatriot Matute sounds a remarkable man and I'd love to meet him.

With everything that's happening with regards to 'affairs of state', it's difficult to keep track of things. Fernando and Isabel still seem to be up to their ears in the Moorish revolt in the Alpujarras. It's like a cushion: you press down one end and the stuffing rises at the other! Your man, Don Gonzalo, was clearly the man to deal with it sensibly and sensitively, but he was whisked off to Italy in June on a fool's errand fighting the Turks along the Adriatic. Inexcusably, after the three-year war against the French in Italy, Fernando is now in league with them and looking to Gonzalo to turn on his friend and former ally, Federico, and carve up his Kingdom of Naples between Spain and France. What perfidy!

My sister Juana who, as you know, was Prince Juan's governess, tells me that the death of Isabel of Portugal's baby, Miguel, on top of those of Juan and Isabel herself, has hit the Queen very hard indeed, and the news from Flanders hardly brings joy to their lives. Maybe the birth of Charles, Juana's second-born, will turn the tide of misfortune. We'll see.

Knowing your interest in the New World, I thought I'd bring you up to date on Columbus's activities, which are never straightforward. He must have very big feet the way he tramples over people's feelings! I've just returned to Seville from the Canaries where I was governor for a year, so much of what I tell you comes from my sister, who maintains regular correspondence with CC.

A war of words erupted between CC's brothers, Bartolomé and Diego, and Francisco Roldán, the mayor of La Isabela, the town near the north coast which was the very first settlement on La Española. Roldán wrote to Cisneros, accusing the three brothers of wanting to cede the island to the Genoese! (i.e. CC and his brothers). On his return to the island, CC has been obliged to sort out the muddle and has conceded territory in the centre of the island to Roldán and his so-called rebels. This seems a sensible solution, since Roldán understands the Indians better and gets more out of them. To get to the bottom of the dispute, the Queen has appointed Francisco de Bobadilla to discover who was in the wrong and to take appropriate action to resolve the dispute, which was severely hampering developments on the island. Bobadilla is a member of the influential military Order of Calatrava and mayor of the monarchs' new city of Santa Fe[3] outside Granada, and if this isn't enough he's brother of the Queen's confidante, Beatriz. Having said all that, the man is an efficient public functionary with many years of experience.

So Bobadilla was made governor of the New World, and CC was instructed by the monarchs to follow his instructions. Juana told me that the monarchs had got tired of receiving complaints about CC and his brothers, and decided that a new face there was needed. Maybe the fact that CC had been sending slaves to Spain was the turning point, since 600 slaves arrived in Seville at the end of May. I've also picked up a rumour here that CC was keeping much of the gold which has been found on La Española, but I doubt this to be true since, for all his faults, I know the man to be honest. In appointing Bobadilla to the governorship, the Queen was evidently much influenced by Cisneros, the Archbishop of Toledo, whose influence over her is awesome. In fact, he's undoubtedly the most influential man in Spain, and the Queen reveres him for his alleged wisdom, saintliness and

---

[3] Santa Fe is a small walled town nine miles from Granada, started by the Catholic Monarchs in October 1491 after their encampment fire in July during their long siege of Granada. The town remains much as it was then.

asceticism. Personally, I found his predecessor, Cardinal Pedro González de Mendoza, a far more rounded and balanced character.[4] Francisco de Bobadilla departed for Santo Domingo from Seville at the same time Gonzalo was leaving Málaga with his fleet, and he returned hundreds of slaves on the Queen's orders.

But you should not think that CC and his brothers are the only ones exploring the New World. Far from it. Expeditions seem to leave our ports by the day for distant places. The first was in May 1499 under the command of Peralonso Niño, who set off from Palos to search for pearls on the northern coast of what is clearly a vast new continent; a second left Cádiz in the same month under Alonso de Hojeda to explore to the north; a third left Palos seven months later under the leadership of Vicente Yáñez Pinzon; a fourth left Seville under Diego de Lepe, and a fifth under Rodrigo de Bastidas left earlier this year to explore the coast to the north of Cuba. In July, Alonso Vélez de Mendoza left Palos to explore south along the eastern seaboard of the new southern continent, but he was obliged to turn back, since this lies in the Portuguese domain, based on the Treaty of Tordesillas, and all captains are under strict orders to comply with this agreement.

The Portuguese have been even more adventurous than us, and have no intention of being constrained by this treaty. You'll remember at the time the treaty was negotiated in Tordesillas we discussed between ourselves whether the Portuguese were playing a subtle game with our negotiators in not disclosing what they knew of the Ocean Sea. They've always considered the Ocean Sea down to Cape Verde and beyond as their domain. As you might have heard, Vasco de Gama has just returned from an incredible three-year voyage, in which he followed the African coast right around the southern cape and crossed another ocean to reach India. What a feat! In March this year, we understand that another Portuguese, Pedro Alvares Cabral, set off with a number of ships with the intention of reaching India via the coast of Brazil, where he intends to explore the hinterland. We'll learn in due course whether he's been successful. But there's no doubt the Portuguese are intrepid and fearless explorers. Poor Christopher Columbus has barely got beyond Cuba and La Española, and still believes they lie off the coast of China! Even the King and Queen don't believe that any more.

Anyway, to return to more mundane matters, by the time Bobadilla reached Santo Domingo in August, it appears that CC and Roldán had resolved their difficulties and, moreover, over 2,000 natives had been baptised. Bobadilla presented his letter of authority to CC and showed him the powers that he'd been given to investigate the conduct of him and his brothers. As a starter, he clapped CC, Diego and Bartolomé in chains and imprisoned them! He then conducted an investigation into their activities, the most serious charge being that CC had executed various settlers without authority. After several weeks, Bobadilla had the three brothers placed aboard ship and despatched back here, where they have just arrived. So CC's third voyage, lasting seventeen months, ended in humiliation for him. It's very sad and I feel very sorry for him. I will try to go and see him shortly.

Disgracefully, the three brothers remained in chains throughout their voyage to Spain. After they reached Cádiz three weeks ago, CC wrote to the Queen complaining about his

---

[4] Interestingly, portraits of Mendoza and Cisneros, arguably Spain's greatest cardinals, lie side by side in the chapter house of Toledo Cathedral, where portraits of all the archbishops of Spain are displayed around the walls.

treatment. My sister Juana said that the monarchs, who are still in Granada, were amazed that their appointee Bobadilla had gone so far, and ordered that the Columbuses be freed and present themselves before them in Granada. Christopher Columbus, incandescent over the indignity to which he had been subjected at the hands of the monarchs' very own appointee, refused to be freed from his chains and turned up at court unkempt, unshaven and dressed in the filthy clothes he had worn from the day he was imprisoned! He continued to plead his innocence and told the Queen of the actions of the rogue Roldán. Isabel and Fernando were disgusted with the treatment meted out to the three brothers by Bobadilla, particularly since they have been CC's keen supporter for nearly twenty years and had backed him in his voyage of discovery – something which the Kings of France, Portugal or England had not been prepared to do. It had become clear to them that for all his qualifications, Bobadilla did not have what it took to manage the affairs of the Indies, and they have dismissed him from his post. We'll see who they appoint in his place.

One last thing of interest: when CC set off on his third voyage, he was given power to assign lands on La Española to settlers in order to encourage them to stay and develop the mineral and agricultural resources of the island. I'm flattered that because of my involvement in organising his fleet in Palos and his friendship with my sister he has granted us title to two contiguous plantations with fertile soils and ample water – one to me and the other to Juana. I must try and go over there and see where they are and what they're like, although neither of us have any plans to settle there.

Well, Pedro and Raquel, I must close, as the light is drawing in very early on a cold, overcast day. I know that my sister Juana will wish to join me in sending her love and best wishes.

Kind regards,

Antonio

Princess Juana bore her third child in Brussels in July 1501. The baby was christened Isabel after her mother. But Philip's every fibre rebelled against their projected journey south. He realised all too clearly that once he set foot in Spain he would have to play second fiddle to his wife, who would receive all the honours and attention. Moreover, he had been warned that the court of the Catholic Monarchs, with its endless religious services, its stifling atmosphere, its days and nights devoted to business rather than diversion, would be pure purgatory for him. In addition, he would have to curtail his extramarital exploits and behave like a model husband. He dreaded the thought of being marooned in the endless expanse of Castile.

So Philip was overjoyed when he received an invitation from the French King to journey overland to Spain through France by way of Blois. A guard of 400 lancers was promised. He accepted the invitation with alacrity, since it would not expose him to the rigours of the sea journey in winter. Finally, after almost eighteen months of prevarication, the couple's departure was scheduled for the beginning of November 1501.

In September 1501, the monarchs named Friar Nicolás of Ovando as governor and proconsul of La Española. He was the Commander of the Order of Alcántara, one of the three military orders alongside those of Calatrava and Santiago. Nicolás was fifty-two and noted for his honesty and frankness, and came from an illustrious lineage stretching back to the old kings of Leon and Castile. The monarchs wanted someone who was mature, competent, law-abiding and discreet. His area of control did not extend to continental South America, controlled by Vicente Yáñez Pinzon. Furthermore, he was prohibited from carrying to the Indies any Muslims, heretics or Jews. His salary was doubled.

By then, other voyages were underway, with orders to establish four settlements on La Española with fifty colonists in each one. These families would receive no money but would have free passage, and after five years the land they occupied would become theirs. Gold mines were reactivated in the centre of the island, and in 1501 they produced over 600 pounds in weight of gold. This went some way to pay for the wars in Italy and against the Turks. Finally, as a new measure, the Indians of La Española were declared free vassals of the Queen, meaning that they could be employed by the colonists but had to receive a wage. Roldán and his rebels were pardoned. At last, the colony was showing signs of sound governance.

XXVI: Home at Last

Autumn 1501

With the death of Agustín at Velefique during the Granada revolt, Pedro took over his administrative role for the towns in and around Vélez Blanco; Vélez Blanco itself, the largest town, Vélez Rubio, now growing, plus María, Chirivel and other small communities around. This suited Pedro Fajardo admirably. Pedro Togeiro, having just turned twenty-seven, was more his age, being four years his senior. Moreover, Pedro Togeiro had grown up in the area, knew the people and their customs well and spoke Arabic fluently. So Pedro Fajardo was delighted to appoint his namesake as his district administrator.

Pedro was not surprised when he received a letter from Don Gonzalo from Italy sounding him out as to whether he would like to resume his duties as aide-de-camp in the Spanish commander's new Italian campaign. Flattered to be thought worthy of fulfilling the role again, he nevertheless politely declined the offer; but Mat, with Francesca's encouragement, offered to serve the Spanish commander. Francesca saw this as an opportunity to return to her homeland, if only for a limited time.

'If you go,' she said, 'I can come, too – and bring Carlos?'

'But the child's only eighteen months old!' complained Mat. 'And where would you stay? I'm likely to be with Don Gonzalo, laying siege to a town or on a march across country.'

'That's easy, Mat,' she replied, her eyes lighting up. 'If Pedro's willing...' She giggled. 'I mean, of course, Baron Pedro of Montecorvino,' – Francesca continued to pull his leg about his fancy title – 'I can live in his country house in Montecorvino with Carlos, and you can come and stay when Don Gonzalo can release you.'

'Hmm,' huffed Mat, 'you've obviously been thinking about this, haven't you? But it sounds a fine idea,' he admitted after some thought. 'We'll speak to Pedro and Raquel. I suggest I go out there and join Don Gonzalo, and let you know when it's safe for you to come over. Montecorvino might be in enemy territory.'

'Ah!' replied Francesca nonchalantly, 'that won't be a problem. After all, I'm Neapolitan and I'll just be another villager.'

'Yes, but living in a grand mansion with servants!' quipped Mat.

But it was agreed. The Gran Capitán wrote back to say that he was delighted that Mat was willing to join him, and asked Mat to resume his duties as sergeant of the camp guard and also to assist him in his headquarters as aide-de-camp.

According to the Treaty of Granada with France, the southern part of the Kingdom of Naples was assigned to Spain. So in July 1501 Gonzalo crossed from Sicily to the toe of Italy as he had done in his first campaign seven years before. After securing all the towns in southern Calabria, he then marched on Taranto, an important port some hundred miles away. This was situated on the underside of the heel of Italy. Among his forces were companies of Basque archers and two squadrons of heavy cavalry. The ancient fortress of Taranto occupied an island connected to the mainland by a causeway and was defended by Federico's fourteen-year-old eldest son, the Duke of Calabria. With the defenders having strengthened the island's seaward side, Gonzalo was prepared for a long siege. But not for the first time his troops were disgruntled, since Fernando had failed to send the moneys needed to pay them.

By midwinter, the high pay offered by César Borgia and boredom during the long siege was causing Gonzalo's men to desert to the other side. A fleet of French ships was caught in a storm in the Adriatic, and Gonzalo sent galleys to intercept them and conduct them safely to Taranto. Being now his allies, he generously provided the French crews with new clothes and provisions; but this so incensed his own soldiers, who lacked warm clothing, that it aroused serious discontent among them. The ringleaders of the mutiny gathered around Gonzalo's tent, demanding their back pay. One of them thrust his lance at Gonzalo's chest. Gonzalo defused this situation with a humorous remark and managed to persuade the men to disperse. The next morning, the body of the ringleader was found hanging by a rope from a window. The mutiny was quashed. Two days later, by good fortune, a Turkish ship was spotted sailing close by in the Adriatic across the narrow peninsular. It carried a cargo of iron and general merchandise worth hundreds of thousands of ducats. Gonzalo had little compunction in seizing the ship, selling the merchandise and paying his men.

Perfidious as ever, the French persuaded the young Duke of Calabria holding Taranto to surrender the town to them and not to the Spanish, although the town lay within the agreed territory of Spain. Recalling an ancient ploy of Hannibal, the Gran Capitán had twenty rafts made and moved them overland on rollers into the inner lagoon. There, to the sound of trumpets and the beating of drums, they were launched across the water. Taranto lacked fortifications on that side, and with little to oppose the Spanish soldiers the weary Neapolitan garrison surrendered. The Spanish entered Taranto on 1 March 1502, after a formal armistice had been drawn up. Annoyed by the underhand dealings of the Duke of Calabria with the French, Gonzalo sent him to Spain as an honoured captive. In Spain, the youngster was well treated and later became governor-general of Valencia. Until his death, Gonzalo continued to express deep remorse for his precipitate treatment of the young man, the son of his friend and former ally, King Federico.

Inevitably a dispute arose between the Spanish and the French over the division of the Neapolitan kingdom, with the Pope, Alexander VI – so bounteous in his praise of the Gran Capitán five years before – now siding with the French, as did most of the Italian states. The French had an army of over 8,000 men led by the veteran Everard Stuart, Sire d'Aubigny, and reinforced by many of the French nobility. Against them, Gonzalo had less than 5,000 soldiers, who were ill paid, ill equipped and ill supplied. By the beginning of June, the French began attacking the Spanish in all parts of the country.

Gonzalo hardly needed Fernando's warning that the French intended to grab whatever territory they could when the opportunity arose; he instructed Gonzalo to consolidate his hold on all the towns within the Spanish domain. However, the Spanish general, unable to disperse his slender forces, had little choice but to concentrate them at Barletta on the north coast some thirty miles from Taranto. Here he made his headquarters. The small port there, albeit exposed to northerly winds, would allow him to be reprovisioned. This did not stop Queen Isabel writing to Gonzalo, criticising him for retreating to a town which the French could blockade; but the Gran Capitán replied curtly that it was for the local commander to decide what was best in the circumstances, declaring that 'time will testify to the wisdom of my decisions'. Meanwhile, the French marched south to occupy the southern part of Calabria and the Gulf of Messina, so recently in Gonzalo's possession, while a separate French force besieged Barletta. The towns to the north, even Cerignola just twenty miles away, also surrendered to the French, so that only the Spanish bases at Barletta and Taranto remained in their hands. Gonzalo's situation had become precarious.

In September 1502, Fernando wrote to say that he had revoked the treaty with the fickle French and had formally declared war on them. Consequently, 200 knights, 200 light cavalry and 300 infantry were on their way to Italy from Cartagena. Thousands more, many mounted, were to follow from Asturias and Galicia in northern Spain. The tide was about to turn.

The besieged Spanish at Barletta were strengthening their defences daily. Then, choosing his own time for an attack, Gonzalo made a sortie against the enemy. Using a tested Moorish ploy well known to Gonzalo, the Spanish withdrew in apparent disorder, drawing away the French rearguard to be confronted by the Spanish commander himself leading the main body of infantry. The French were routed. As the Spanish cavalry cut off their retreat, the French were killed or taken prisoner to a man. Gonzalo was so delighted with the action that he ordered a month's extra pay for all his men. In a typically chivalrous gesture of the age, the captured French and Italian nobility were entertained at dinner that evening.

Gonzalo's supplies were still short, but fortune shone on the Spanish when two Italian ships laden with corn, clothing and general supplies happened to put in to Barletta. The situation was further helped by the capture of a supply ship destined for the French, and the arrival of seven Sicilian ships with grain.

On 2 November 1501, the royal party finally left Brussels on their overland journey to Spain. Its exodus was full of noise and confusion. Ana of Beamonte described what happened in a brief letter to Raquel.

Letter from Ana of Beamonte

Paris, 30 November 1501

I am writing this from Paris, where Philip and Juana's party (but more a travelling circus) has just arrived on our way to Spain. Although the weather's cold and murky, Paris lives up to all our expectations, with the grey waters of the Seine, boosted by autumn rains, swirling around the lovely cathedral of Nôtre Dame sitting on an island in the river. It's an impressive scene. The buildings and palaces on the right bank of the river are all very grand and show off the wealth and historic grandeur of France's capital city.

But to start at the beginning. The departure from Brussels was as shambolic as you might have expected. The mobile court assembled in the courtyard of the palace was filled with loaded wagons which were so top-heavy that a gust of wind would have toppled them over. Wooden crates of silverware and boxes of porcelain jostled with paintings by the Flemish masters, while furniture and tapestries were jumbled up with woven carpets and kitchen utensils. Countless trunks, overflowing with robes and dresses, were carried out of the palace and stacked upon the remaining royal drays allotted to personal belongings. The ring of coopers hammering new iron treads on the wheels of carriages, the clop of horses' hooves and the screech of chests being dragged across the cobblestones vied with the cacophony of the multitude there. Half of the wagons, it seemed, were given over to the accoutrements of the Church. There was also a huge, ornately carved altar and I even saw a silver-lined font. I'm sure that if the archdeacon organising all this paraphernalia could have taken church pews and a pulpit he would have done so!

In the midst of the tumult, trumpets heralded the arrival of the Archduke and the Archduchess. When farewells were made to all and sundry, Philip signalled the caravan to form in line. Like a long, wriggling millipede, the two-mile-long wagon train joined the highway leading out of the city. Of more than 200 people in the retinue, well over half were courtiers of noble birth and knights of the Order of the Golden Fleece, not counting the bishops and archbishops and their retinue. Our own small Spanish contingent was loaded with yet more Flemish gentlemen and noblewomen, the only genuine Spaniards being some clergy, myself and six of my ladies-in-waiting who made the voyage north four years ago with the young bride. The remaining half of the huge cortège was composed of maids, cooks, grooms, servants and workmen to keep the whole wagon train on the road.

In the French towns and villages we passed through, we were met by fanfares, pageants, bonfires and the celebration of Mass. Prisoners were set free in honour of the son of the Holy Roman Emperor. At Louvres, the Prince of Orange was waiting to escort Philip and Juana into Paris. There, we were conducted to Nôtre Dame to hear Mass sung in our honour. That afternoon, the couple received members of parliament and professors, stepping out onto the balcony from time to time to wave to the crowd who were clamouring to see them. It was all pretty heady stuff.

Yesterday, Juana scorned the official engagement in honour of Philip, and chose to take me and several Spanish gentlemen, who happened to be in Paris, to meet the Count of Cabra who is returning to Spain after accompanying Juana's youngest sister, Catalina, to the court of Henry VII of England[1] for her marriage to Arthur. This took place two weeks ago. Arthur is a year younger than Catalina,[2] and I'm told by the Count that he's a very sickly boy, unlike his robust brother, ten-year-old Henry. Catalina, who's still only sixteen, is a very pretty young woman and I'm sure will make Arthur a very loving and devoted wife. She's the last pawn in Fernando and Isabel's power game, and I hope will fare better than Juana has done so far. But now I must close, since tomorrow we set off again for King Louis's court in Blois.

Trusting that you are all well in Xiquena, and my love to Pedro.

Ana

On 28 November, the caravan left Paris and rumbled on through Orléans to Blois in the Loire valley. Already the party had doubled in size. There they were greeted by the King of France, Louis XII. French-speaking Philip bowed low and embraced the King three times, as was customary, thereby declaring his homage to the French king as his liege lord. Juana, who was instructed to do likewise by the Lord Chamberlain, shrank back from this act of subservience and only acquiesced after the Bishop of Córdoba pressed her. This determination by Juana to sidestep the acts of obeisance expected of her was a sign of her aversion to French protocol which had been instilled in her by her parents. But she continued to attend the ceremonies out of duty, maintaining her poise and her status. Philip, on the other hand, was bedazzled by the sumptuousness of the French court, giving himself over during the day to hunting with falcons, tilting at jousts and playing tennis with the King, and at night to banquets and dancing with the ladies of the court.

---

[1] Henry VII (1457-1509) – as Henry Tudor – was the first Tudor king, who won the English crown from Richard of York (Richard III) at the Battle of Bosworth in 1485. The Tudor connection lay with Henry being the grandson of Owen Tudor (1400-1461), who secretly married Catherine of Valois, the widow of Henry V. Owen Tudor was related to Owain Glyn Dŵr (c.1355-c.1415), who was the hereditary Welsh prince and led the last Welsh uprising against the English between 1500 and 1508.

[2] Later known as Catherine of Aragon, Henry VIII's first wife and mother of Mary Tudor, Queen of England, between 1553 and 1558.

One day, after matins, a French lady handed Juana a silk purse to make a symbolic gift to the French Queen, Queen Ana, the young widow of Charles VIII, Louis' predecessor. Juana refused to accept the coins, declaring that any such act on her part would demonstrate an act of vassalage, and she returned to her rosary and prayers. The French Queen, provoked by such a rebuke, rose and stormed out of the church, but Juana intentionally prolonged her prayers for fifteen minutes before calmly returning to the vestibule where the Queen had been obliged to wait. Without a word or undue haste, Juana passed her by and went to her rooms. Hastily, early next morning the Flemish party departed Blois, passing through Tours and Poitiers. Christmas was observed in Saint Etienne.

By early January, they reached the great port of Bordeaux, but declined the official welcome because of the plague which was raging in the city, altering their route to be ferried across the Gironde estuary upstream. Soon they entered the small independent kingdom of Navarra, which straddled the mountainous border between France and Spain. With snowbound passes ahead of them, their boxes and trunks were loaded onto pack mules and they and the heavy wagons were shipped back to Flanders. On 26 January 1502, in the midst of icy gales blowing from the Bay of Biscay, Juana once again set foot upon the frozen soil of her homeland, six years after leaving Laredo.

Fernando and Isabel, still in Seville after the Granada revolt, issued instructions to all cities in Spain on how the Archduke and Archduchess were to be received and pampered while they were in Spain, overturning an earlier standing instruction to towns and cities on the need for thriftiness and frugality in their civic ceremonies. Meanwhile, in the Spanish border town, a frozen delegation of Castile's nobles jostled to be the first to kiss the hands of the Archduke and their very own Princess. The Flemish retinue looked forlornly at the towering, snow-topped mountains which hemmed them in on all sides, and shrank from the austerely dressed and long, sombre faces of the haughty grandees of Spain. With the mules in tow, the party laboured strenuously up the long ascent to the 3,000-foot-high plateau on which Burgos sat with its fine gothic cathedral, the city of El Cid. There, they recovered their energies for ten days before reaching Segovia, passing beneath the granite arches of the Roman aqueduct which dominated the beautiful city.

By now it was the end of March, and spring was bursting forth all around them; the mountain streams were roaring torrents of meltwater, almonds and cherry trees were ablaze with pink blossom, and yellow and purple wild flowers bordered the highways. They crossed the bleak granite massif of the Guadarrama mountains and carried on down to the central plateau of Madrid, where they awaited news from the Catholic Monarchs, who had finally reached the cathedral city of Toledo. But before reaching there, Philip contracted measles. Fernando rode out with his physicians to attend the bedridden Archduke, firstly greeting his daughter with great affection, and then his son-in-law. Philip was disarmed by the friendly manner of the King, which was contrary to what he had expected. Juana acted as translator, and she was overjoyed that the first meeting between her father and her husband had proved cordial.

When Philip had recovered from his illness, Fernando led the Flemish party to the ancient city of Toledo, lying on an elevated high spur of the River Tajo, passing through its gates on 7 May 1502. At last, they had reached their goal.

The new governor of La Española appointed to replace Francisco Bobadilla, Friar Nicolás de Ovando, left Sanlúcar on 13 February of this same year with twenty-seven ships, the largest fleet ever to leave Spain for the New World. Sanlúcar, lying at the mouth of the River Guadalquivir, had replaced Seville as the port of embarkation, since Seville lay more than fifty miles up the winding river. Aboard the ships were 2,500 colonists, priests, women and craftsmen, plus sufficient shoots of white mulberry from the Alpujarras to establish a silk industry, as well as cuttings of sugar cane from the Canaries. Of the ships' complements, most were very poor and sought to escape from the ailing economy in Spain, particularly from Andalucía and Extremadura, and from the privileged status of sheep rearing on the mesetas of Castile. Ovando's deputy was Pedro's friend, Antonio de Torres, a mariner of extraordinary experience who had sailed the Ocean Sea several times and had recently relinquished his post of governor of Grand Canary. Twenty-year-old Hernán Cortés,[3] a relation of Ovando, should have gone too, but he had broken a leg after jumping from a window of a woman in Seville whom he had tried to seduce. There were also seventeen Franciscan priests aboard.

As an ominous portent for the voyage, a week after setting sail and halfway to the Canaries, the fleet met a terrible storm. One ship sank with the loss of over one hundred passengers and crew. The remaining ships, heavily loaded as they were, had to jettison objects over their sides. The boats were scattered far and wide. This disaster just added to the calamities which surrounded the monarchs and added to their despair. Ovando regrouped the major part of his fleet in Grand Canary and set off again for La Española, arriving there in the middle of April, at the time Juana and Philip were on their way to Toledo. The remainder of the expedition under the command of Antonio de Torres arrived two weeks later.

Ovando found that the Spanish population of the island amounted to just 300 souls who were concentrated in the new capital, Santo Domingo, and

---

[3] Later the conqueror of Mexico

several small mining communities inland, such as Concepción de la Vega and Santiago. Columbus's very first settlement at La Isabela, located near the north coast, had largely been abandoned, but already buildings of stone were being constructed in Santo Domingo. Many of the settlers had taken native wives and several had mixed-blood children, *mestizos*. Power largely remained in the hands of the native chiefs, the *caciques*, although Columbus's friend and ally from the first and second voyages, Guacanagarí, had died. Gold and cotton remained the main products of the settlers.

Ovando started his governorship by investigating the activities of Bobadilla, who under Spanish law was permitted to remain in his house for thirty days. Ovando was keen to remove him from the island. Although newly arrived, Bartolomé de Las Casas[4] believed there was little substance in the charges against Bobadilla. By the end of June, Antonio de Torres was ready to depart with Bobadilla and several of his supporters with all the papers relating to his conduct as governor. While they were preparing the ships for the voyage, Ovando was perturbed to hear that Christopher Columbus was sailing along the coast with four ships. Columbus had been instructed by the monarchs to make a fourth voyage and explore the coast of the new continent, searching out new lands for Spain, although Columbus was still consumed by the idea of discovering a route to the Spice Islands, and even of encountering Vasco de Gama on the way. Columbus had departed Sanlúcar with his two brothers, Bartolomé and Diego, as well as Fernando, his intelligent son by Beatriz Enríquez of Córdoba.

Knowing the unrest which Columbus caused on the island, the monarchs had instructed him to avoid Santo Domingo, but he nevertheless entered the harbour on 24 June after visiting the neighbouring island of Puerto Rico and sailing along the southern coast of Cuba and La Española. Antonio de Torres was due to set sail on 29 June with the former governor, Francisco Bobadilla, an Indian chief called Guarionex, the rebel Roldán, the documents surrounding their alleged crimes, plus a famously large nugget of gold found years before. Angrily, Ovando refused Columbus permission to go ashore, and rejected a written plea from the Admiral that the departure of Torres' fleet of twenty-five ships be delayed because of a pending storm in the Caribbean. Ominously, the fleet set sail on 30 June. More experienced than any other sailor in these treacherous waters, Columbus found a sheltered cove for his four ships and dropped anchor to sit out the impending storm.

---

[4] He, with Cisneros, did much in later years to try and alleviate the hardships suffered by the native population and the injustices inflicted on them by the colonists.

XXVII: Nobility and Peasantry

If we are to understand better the years of hardship and suffering which are soon to smite Spain, we must pause a while and take stock of the 'health of the nation'. For while wealth and opulence were exhibited in the courts of Brussels, Rome, Paris and to a lesser extent London and Burgos, or wherever the peripatetic Catholic Monarchs of Spain were temporary resident, the countrymen of Spain – the peasants – lived in grinding poverty. Small in stature through constant toil and lack of nourishment, their life expectancy was low. Few reached forty, and infant mortality before the age of one exceeded 30 per cent. Smallpox, measles, chicken pox and later syphilis scarred their faces, while a poor diet and non-existent health care twisted and crippled their bodies. With pockmarked faces and rotting teeth, few except the young could have had a pleasing countenance. Allied with inbreeding in small, tightly knit communities, with the resulting imbeciles and cretins, with premature death through childbirth, with farming injuries and the consequences of war and rebellion, life was harsh and unforgiving. For many, death must have been a blessed relief.

Spain at the turn of the sixteenth century was a vast open space with some 7 million people occupying close to 200,000 square miles of Castile, Andalucía and Aragón, four times the size of England. On average, there were fewer than five households per square mile. Isabel's kingdom of Castile was six times more populous and wealthier than Fernando's kingdom of Aragón. In contrast, France and Germany had over twice Spain's population, Italy a little less, England half as much as Spain, and Portugal one-fifth. Then, as now, the climate of central Spain, the second most elevated country in Europe after Switzerland, was brutal, with searing summers, freezing winters and winds which scoured the goodness from the soil.

In 1500, 80 per cent of the people lived off the land – of which the nobility, making up just 1 per cent of the population, owned 97 per cent directly or indirectly. A third of this was owned by the three military orders and therefore, in effect, by the Crown and the Church, while in Old Castile a quarter was held directly by the monarchs. With the cities in the hands of the Church, ecclesiastical orders and the aristocracy, it meant that between them the monarchy, the Church and the high nobility controlled Spain.

Spain was still largely a feudal country, where the peasant worked his piece of land at the behest of his lordly but generally absent landowner. With a holding so small as to barely provide enough to sustain himself and his family, the peasant existed in dire poverty and austerity, and he was tied to his smallholding for life. The lack of mobility was a noted feature of feudalism. Communication was slow and journeys were to be avoided. Where you were born was where you died. For soldiers and merchants alike, fifteen miles was about as much as was travelled in a day, although royal couriers could manage sixty miles with a change of horses.

Lordly dues accounted for nearly 30 per cent of what the peasant grew or reared, and to that was added a 10 per cent Church tax. With the tenant farmer having to set aside a quarter of his produce as seedcorn for the following year, what was left over provided the tiniest margin for survival. Rarely could the peasant save anything, and in times of drought or famine they had little choice but to consume the precious seed they had set aside. Starvation was always around the corner. The rents paid in kind went to finance the lords' manors and their high living. What returned to the land to improve it, drain it, fertilise it, or ameliorate living conditions, was minimal. On occasions, in times of severe duress, the smallholder had to buy back from his landlord his very own corn from his lord's granaries. On top of this, the peasant was subject to the whims and abuses of the gentry. To object to the landowner dallying with his wife or daughter possibly meant being turned off his land and beggary. Soldiers, friend or foe, were always a threat. Carefully tended crops could be trampled underfoot by passing feet or hooves, livestock slaughtered to eke out scant military rations, draught animals commandeered to pull wagons or cannons, dwellings occupied for overnight accommodation, womenfolk molested and precious reserves or food taken with no recompense. Even a simple journey to sell vegetables, fruit or eggs in a nearby village market was fraught with the threat of robbery or worse at the hands of marauding gangs. In short, the majority of peasants, smallholders or tenant farmers – call them what you will – toiled their lives away for the benefit of a handful of absent land-owners. There was no escape.

This rigid feudal system arose after the so-called 'Reconquest' by the grant of lands recovered from the Muslims, who were being driven ever southwards across Spain by the Christians. This process started after the crucial Battle of Covadonga in Asturias in northern Spain in 722 and continued up to, and even after, the conquest of Granada in 1492, when the Muslims were dispossessed of the lands which they had nurtured with such care for 700 years. The acquisition by the Catholic Monarchs of the desert and mountainous land of al-Andalus, rich and fertile as it was, watered and administered by a sophisticated irrigation system, was not simply a matter of religious zeal. The Christians coveted their carefully terraced farms, their olive groves, their vineyards, their fields of mulberry trees in the Alpujarras on which silkworms were reared, their orange groves, figs and other exotic produce. In short, the Catholic Monarchs looked enviously at the wealth of Muslim al-Andalus. But in truth, they coveted all its produce, since for 200 years the Muslim Nazarí kingdom of Granada had been forced to hand over up to half its wealth annually as tribute to the Christians in order to be left in peace. By 1481, the Catholic Monarchs decided enough was enough, and laid siege to al-Andalus. The ten-year war ensued. Yet within decades, after the Granada revolt and the resulting ingress of people from distant regions of Spain with different farming traditions, much of the land was desolate.

Economically, the richest areas in Spain were the two mesetas and Andalucía. The vast plains of the southern meseta in the Tajo basin of Toledo were the breadbaskets of Spain and had been the granary of ancient Rome. The cooler, wetter northern meseta of the Duero basin of Valladolid and Zamora was given over to grazing and pasture. There was little development in relation to crops or farming techniques; neither had changed much since Roman times. One advance had been the substitution of oxen with mules as draught animals, since they were stronger beasts and less demanding of pasture.

However, the dominant factor in the economy of Spain was the rearing of sheep for merino wool and the production of cheese. Merino wool, unequalled in Europe, was the most important commodity in Castile and a vital money-earner for the monarchs, both as exported wool and as woven fabric. Several well-defined sheep droves ran across the heartland of Spain from Extremadura in the west, from the Guadarrama mountains in the centre and from Leon in the north. These droves ran for hundreds of miles across the country, carving out wide swathes across the land. At this time, nearly 3 million animals took part in this annual migration, with the drovers, powerful and empowered by law, possessing ancient rights of passage across the country and through towns and cities.[1] Inevitably, their interests conflicted with the villages through which they passed and the farmers over whose land they led their flocks. But always the rights of the drovers were dominant. Once again, the peasants' needs were sacrificed.

Wool was therefore the most important commodity. It furnished the textile industry with exports to Flanders from Bilbao in northern Spain and to Italy from Barcelona. By law, up to two-thirds could be exported, with the Crown benefiting from the tax imposed. While the city of Burgos, lying on the rim of the northern plateau, was the hub of wool exports, Segovia became a major centre for woollen cloth.

In 1501, when Spain suffered a failure of the corn harvest following a dry winter and spring, the monarchs, desperate to fund their wars in the Alpujarras and Italy by expanding the wool trade, dramatically exacerbated the problems caused by the famine. For instead of increasing the amount of arable land available for cultivation, they issued new laws which strengthened the rights of the sheep drovers, reserving for them exclusively their routes across Andalucía and Extremadura. This caused much anguish among the farmers, since it reduced even further the land at their disposal for growing their crops. Spain would suffer dearly for Isabel and Fernando's avarice in the years which immediately followed.

---

[1] Sheep being driven through the streets of Madrid was a common sight until as late as twenty-five years ago.

XXVIII: Caribbean Catastrophe

Autumn 1502

Pedro and Raquel had settled in well in the two years since their return from Italy. Pedro saw little of Pedro Fajardo and even less of his father, Juan Chacón, and was left to administer that part of the estate which was his responsibility. Things had quietened down in the Muslim community after the Granada revolt, and most of the Muslims who were left in the villages had resigned themselves to convert to Christianity and adopt new names. Some had left, but this was as much due to the famine which was spreading across the land after two dry winters. Crops had failed due to a lack of rain, and the price of food in the markets was causing real hardship. But even if the corn harvest had been bounteous, it would have counted for nothing, since river and stream flows were so low that the watermills were largely inoperative.[1] Only trickles emanated from the normally bounteous springs at Vélez Blanco and Huebro, north of Níjar, where, in the latter case, a dozen or more mills shared the normally copious flows which were channelled along the *acequia* or water carrier running down the valley. Raquel and Miriam were not spared the problems of feeding the family, and it was fortunate in many ways that Mat and Francesca were away in Italy, where things were a lot better. Mat had been able to get away a couple of times from Barletta to visit Francesca, two days' ride away, and had written to Pedro and Raquel to say that she was in her element as 'Contessa di Montecorvino'. It was a far cry from the squalid slums of Naples where she had grown up.

In the late autumn, Pedro picked up a rumour in Chirivel from a Granada merchant that a catastrophe had occurred in the New World, with a fleet bound for Spain. He thought little more of it until three weeks later a letter arrived from Toledo bearing the name of Señora Juana de Torres on the back of the envelope. Recalling the rumour, he turned pale at the possible implications of the letter, the first he and Raquel had received from Juana, as they opened and read it.

---

[1] At this time, windmills were a thing of the future in Spain. In fact, they did not reach La Mancha from northern Spain until *after* Cervantes' Don Quixote tilted at them around 1600!

Letter from Juana de Torres

Toledo, 25 October 1502

My Dear Pedro and Raquel,

It is with great sadness that I have to tell you that Antonio has perished in a terrible storm which struck La Española in June soon after a large fleet he was commanding set sail for Spain. Only one ship, the Aguja, *the smallest among them, managed to return home. I have spoken to Sánchez de Carvajal, Christopher Columbus's agent on board the* Aguja, *when he came to Toledo to tell Fernando and Isabel of the calamity. The Queen is truly distraught at yet another disaster which has befallen their monarchy in recent times. She is inconsolable and has not left her quarters for days. The loss of ships, of crew and passengers, and the precious cargoes the ships were carrying is beyond belief. I'm heartbroken, since Antonio and I were so close. I know he would have wanted you to hear from me what transpired, since he always spoke with such affection of you both and of the fun you had together at Tordesillas when the Portuguese ran rings around our haughty delegates. So this is what Sánchez told me.*

The fleet of twenty-three ships left Santo Domingo on 30 June. Soon after leaving La Española, as they passed through the dangerous straight of Mona between La Española and Puerto Rico, they were struck by a hurricane. Twenty-three or twenty-four of the thirty ships foundered, including those carrying my brother, the ex-governor Francisco Bobadilla, the rebel Francisco Roldán and the native chief Guarionex. Only three ships made it back to Santo Domingo, which was also flattened and destroyed in the hurricane. They lost 200,000 gold pesos which had been struck on the island, the famous nugget of gold which was to have been a gift to the Queen, and, of course, all the papers relating to the investigations of Bobadilla and Roldán. Only one ship, that of Sánchez de Carvajal, arrived back in Spain with just 4,000 gold pesos. It was truly a calamity.

Sánchez told me that two days before the fleet sailed, Christopher, who is an old friend of mine, had sent a letter to the new governor, Friar de Ovando, urging him to delay the departure of Antonio's fleet since he feared a severe storm was brewing. He himself took shelter in an enclosed and protected bay, and all four of his small flotilla survived. Antonio was hoping to take a look at the plantations for which we hold title, but I've no idea whether he managed to do so since he was there such a short time.

Please excuse the brevity of this letter, but you'll understand that I'm too upset to do more than convey this information and send my cordial greetings to you both. My apologies for my shaky hand and the tear stains on the page where the ink has run.

My love to you both,

Juana

Despite this disaster, Nicolás de Ovando wasted no time in reconstructing Santo Domingo, starting with twelve stone houses. He imposed a new tax of one ounce of gold for every three extracted, which was very severe to those dedicated to mining. This coincided with the higher costs of supplies and the precariousness of communications with Spain. Most of the new colonists were sent to the gold mines in the centre of the island. Working enthusiastically under difficult conditions and high temperatures, many died of dysentery due to the change in diet. Often they returned to the capital sixty miles away with little more than a grain of the precious metal to show for their efforts. The initial euphoria soon evaporated due to the heat and fatigue from working up to their knees in soft ground. Then, at the end of 1502, they were hit by another wave of syphilis. Hundreds of the new arrivals died and hundreds more were sick, leaving only 1,000 colonists on the island. To try and arrest the deteriorating situation, 300 of Columbus's veterans from the earlier voyages took hold of the situation and established a systematic approach to the mining and smelting of the gold. A new alluvial goldfield was discovered around Santo Domingo, and its production of 60 million *maravedís* of gold annually equalled that obtained in the older centre at Concepción de la Vega. After the initial reverses, the new policies of Ovando started to bear fruit. At last, it seemed, Spain's first colony was getting established.

Although mining was seen as crucial by the Catholic Monarchs, agriculture was in fact more valuable, with manioc, garlic and pigs the main products. Yet, even by then, only the central valley axis running across the island was occupied by the colonists. At the end of the year, Ovando despatched a party to explore the extreme east of the island but, after a bull mastiff belonging to the Spanish killed an Indian chief, a rebellion broke out, which was put down with much bloodshed. Later, in a show of strength using 300 soldiers and seventy horsemen, Ovando's victory was total, although fifty Spaniards died. Several of the Indian leaders were strangled to death. In the end the Indian chiefs, faced with overwhelming force, had little option but to accept a state of vassalage.

By 1503, Santo Domingo boasted a governor's palace and a hospital, and a cathedral was being planned. The new port established on the northern coast at Puerto Plata facilitated communication to Spain and provided a ready exit for the island's produce.

Francesca was revelling in her time in Montecorvino with young Carlos, now three years old. As poacher turned gamekeeper – in the sense that she was brought up in poverty and was now the Lady of the Manor – she suffered no qualms about giving orders to her servants; but at the same time was the first to roll up her sleeves and help out when, for instance, the roof fell in on the pigsty or the underground water cistern needed cleaning out. She was well liked and respected by those around her. Late one afternoon, she was sitting on the stone-flagged terrace of the manor house, enjoying a cool glass of water from the deep well in the courtyard. Carlos was playing quietly on his own in the garden below, with the vineyard and fish ponds to the side and the red roofs of the village of Montecorvino below peeping over the manor's boundary wall at the bottom of the garden. All was tranquil and peaceful.

In the still, hazy air of the late afternoon Francesca noticed a swirl of dust several miles away on the plain running down to the sea. She watched it with no more than curiosity, since such eddies were a common sight in the summer. But she watched more intently as the column of dust thickened and moved slowly across the plain towards the village below. Soon flashes illuminated the dust in the blue sky, accompanied by the rumbling of thunder, and Francesca realised that it was not an impending storm but a squadron of cavalry in shining breastplates that was riding her way. Eventually, long, forked pennants could be seen streaming from the lances of the lead riders, and a hubbub arose in the streets below as the agitated villagers identified the sound of horses' hooves in the distance. They knew from long experience that nothing good ever came of soldiers and a column of cavalry.

Francesca also stirred. These were not a contingent of Don Gonzalo's well-disciplined men. These were French and the enemy. One of her gardeners, Fabio, a lovely old man, came running up the steps of the terrace, and her maid, Claudia, ran out of the house on hearing the commotion. With screams and cries coming from the streets below, Fabio ran and gathered up young Carlos in his arms as a shepherd might a lamb caught in a storm, and started up towards the terrace. As he did so, a French lancer burst into the house. With jangling spurs and sabre clattering on the stone floor, he strode onto the terrace, his plumed helmet and burnished breastplate ablaze in the sun. Fabio turned away and, with his hand over the boy's mouth to stop him crying out, scuttled off into the sanctuary of his beloved garden. Claudia, just thirteen and as nimble as a mountain goat, hitched her skirts up to her knees, skipped across the terrace and ran down the steps as quick as lightning to join Fabio, urging the old man along in the process.

'I'm Gaspar de Villeneuve, Captain of King Louis' horse,' announced a tall cavalry officer as he spotted Francesca. 'We're—'

He didn't get a chance to finish. 'I don't care if you're the Pope himself!' screamed Francesca, running at him. 'Get out of my house!'

'We're commandeering your manor for officer accommodation, and…'

'Oh no, you're not!' bellowed the Neapolitan woman. 'Get out of here! This is my house!'

Francesca ran at the man with all the fury of an alley cat. She was a practised street-fighter. The French officer, tall, handsome and moustachioed, was taken aback. Using fists, elbows, knees and feet, she knocked the man to the ground, kicking him with all her might in the one place his breastplate did not reach and tearing his face with her nails. De Villeneuve's helmet went skittering across the floor and his long, heavy, curved sabre swinging on his belt caught on the floor as he fell back. The round steel pommel on the end of the sword hilt jolted up and struck him hard on his temple, stunning him. Hearing the commotion on the terrace, two other lancers ran out of the house and dragged Francesca off the officer as she kicked him on his head for good measure. It took the two of them to pull her off de Villeneuve and push her back into the house through the terrace's double doors. Francesca was like a wild animal, with flailing arms and legs aimed at anything in uniform. The lancers managed to subdue her, and eventually they dragged her into a small outhouse in the courtyard and threw her onto the pile of straw in the corner. A gag was tied across her mouth and her hands were tied tightly behind her back.

'Now, ma chéri,' leered the first lancer, casting off his sword belt and unbuckling the side straps of his breastplate, 'let's see what you're made of.'

Francesca wriggled and twisted as he pulled open her loose blouse and roughly fondled her ample breasts. By this time, the second lancer was unbuttoning his trousers, exposing his erect shaft, almost bursting in lustful anticipation.

'You can put that away, Claude,' sneered the first lancer. 'This one's mine! You had first go yesterday.'

'But she was only a girl of ten… hardly worth bothering with. This one's worth coming all the way to Italy for.'

'Well!' snorted the first lancer, pulling his own trousers down to his knees. 'You're not going to do this Italian beauty much good with that little thing of yours. It was barely fit for the ten-year-old!'

He went up close to Francesca, who was now on her feet, and waved his huge protuberance at her, veined like ivy around an oak tree.

Despite the gag around her mouth, Francesca snorted and guffawed as much as to say, *Huh, not worth the bother!*

'No?' replied the lancer, understanding clearly what Francesca's facial expressions meant. 'You'll soon find out what I can do with this,' he retorted.

But he was to be disappointed.

His eyes looked down to see the blade of a razor-sharp sabre resting lightly on what he held most dear. Startled, the lancer turned to face his moustachioed captain grinning at him. His face was badly scratched and he stood with a stoop, obviously still feeling the effects of Francesca's assault.

'Put that away, François, or I'll cut it off and feed it to the pigs. Now, both of you, clear off. This lady is not for scum like you.'

Muttering to themselves, the two lancers hitched up their tunic trousers and slouched off out of the building.

'You've got a lot to answer for, Contessa,' sneered Gaspar de Villeneuve, holding his groin. 'But payback time is not now. I'll return in a few days' time. And I'll bide my time until then in glorious anticipation.'

The captain searched around the outhouse and pulled out from beneath the pile of straw an iron chain which was attached at one end to a ring in the wall. It was substantial and used to tether animals.

'This will do fine,' he said.

He returned to his horse in the yard, and came back with a pair of fetters to shackle her ankles. He pushed Francesca backwards onto the straw, his eyes sparkling at the delights he beheld beneath her skirt as she fell back. One of the fetters he attached to the free end of the chain and, despite Francesca's kicking and vocal protests through the gag, he placed the other around her ankle. He snapped both shut and locked them with his key. He got up and stood over her for a few moments, anticipating the pleasures of his return.

He disappeared outside and returned in a few minutes with two pails, one full of water from the well, and the other empty. 'Well, you can guess what that's for,' he said.

Ensuring there was a key in the lock of the outhouse door, he pulled the gag from Francesca's mouth.

'I'll be back in a few days' time,' he said. 'In the meantime, you can starve. You can earn your next meal on my return.'

With that, he bent down, forced her shoulders into the straw and kissed her. He got up and departed, locking the door behind him.

XXIX: The Orphan Girl

May 1502

Toledo is an ancient Roman and Visigothic city situated in a perfect defensive position, where a tight meander in the River Tajo skirts a high granite hill on nearly all sides. When Philip and Juana finally reached Toledo and crossed into the city through the double Moorish archway of the Puerto de Sol, they were greeted by banners embroidered with the Burgundian and Spanish coats of arms. Preceded by trumpeters and 150 archers, they climbed the narrow streets to the cathedral. The streets were festooned with flowers, flags and richly woven tapestries hanging from the balconies of the houses. When the royal couple reached the cathedral, the deep tones of its thundering heavy bells drowned out the treble tones of the surrounding churches. After receiving the blessing of Archbishop Cisneros on the cathedral steps, they processed up the long nave to the main altar to the accompaniment of the *Te Deum*. Then, without delay, they were ushered to a nearby palace where Queen Isabel greeted them affectionately before whisking her daughter off to her chambers for an hour's audience, although nothing ever emerged as to what was said between them. The new arrivals lunched with the King and Queen. Fernando was dressed in his usual sombre woollen garments while, in contrast, Philip was bedecked in gorgeous violet satin trimmed with sable, and Juana in cloth of gold. Of her remaining siblings, Isabel and Juan having both died, Catalina was in England, while Maria, her second youngest sister, was domiciled in Portugal after her marriage to King Manuel, the widower of her late sister Isabel.

In the midst of the celebrations, a courier arrived with news of the sudden death of Prince Arthur in England before the consummation of his marriage to Catalina. Setting aside the planned festivities, the palace mourned Arthur's death for three days. Philip resigned himself to drifting around the dreary palace on his own or to accompanying Juana to Mass every few hours, sung for the repose of the young prince's soul. Finally, not being able to stand the stifling routine any more, he broke free to enjoy the May sunshine, the orange and pomegranate trees, the olives and figs, all in glowing blossom. Following a programme laid on specifically for the benefit of the Flemish party, the spring and summer months passed with jousts, tournaments, banquets and hunting deer in the forests across the river; but Philip was aghast at the state business which consumed Isabel's every waking hour. Both in awe and overwhelmed by the illustrious Queen, he began to cast longing eyes towards his homeland.

Not surprisingly, Philip's Flemish followers were also becoming more and more restless, and found themselves totally at odds with Spain and Spanish ways. For them, Spain was a world apart. They found the dry summer heat oppressive and were unable to sleep; to them, the Spanish noblemen were inscrutable and unapproachable; the food cooked in olive oil was unpalatable; illnesses struck them down with unfailing regularity, and they were suffocated by the monotony of court life. Inevitably, tempers began to wear thin and arguments flared up between the two groups.

In the autumn, with Juana pregnant once more, she, Philip and Fernando set off on the week's journey to the Aragonese capital of Zaragoza, for Juana to receive the approbation of the Aragón Cortes as the legitimate heiress to the crown. Three previous supplicants to the throne of Aragón had been rejected by the all-too-choosy council. This time, Juana was acclaimed as Fernando's legal successor, but – significantly as it turned out – it was on the proviso that he did not have a future male heir from a legitimate marriage. The Aragón Cortes could not have guessed the implications of this caveat.

On the following day, Fernando received a message that Isabel had fallen ill, and he set out post-haste for the long journey back to Madrid. Philip followed soon after, having received a summons from Isabel to attend her. Juana stayed behind in Zaragoza, brooding as anxiously as ever over the changing moods of her husband. Then, on receiving a curt letter from Philip declaring his intention to return to Flanders via France, she rushed back to Madrid. Everything was in chaos. Philip's utter indifference to Juana's feelings was again manifest. He was determined to escape from this alien land and leave Juana behind until after the birth of their fourth child. Juana begged him to remain with her over Christmas, but he had made up his mind. Desperate to get away, he left Madrid on 9 December for southern France, accompanied by his full panoply of sycophants, who all the way complained of the treatment they had received in Spain.

Deserted, Juana fell prey to depressions, sobbing her heart out or moodily fixing her eyes on the ground and refusing to talk or be entertained. The Princess was uninterested in riches, power, kingdoms or family, and thought only of the sudden departure of her husband. She had done her utmost to attract him, lavishing great love on him, but it was all in vain. He had escaped to distant lands and left behind a frustrated wife awaiting the birth of another child. Fruitlessly, Queen Isabel tried to rouse her daughter, who spent her days alternatively weeping and wailing or blindly staring into space in a state of trance. With Fernando again absent in Aragón, Isabel was left alone to appease her daughter. Even now, Isabel grieved for her only son Prince Juan, whose premature death had exposed the insecure future governance of her many kingdoms. Frustrated that at every step she was met by defiance from Juana, Isabel changed tack and packed her off to Alcalá de Henares and Archbishop Cisneros, who had founded a university there and was noted for his counselling of troubled souls.

Francisco Jiménez de Cisneros was born of noble but impoverished stock sixty-seven years earlier. Showing great aptitude, he was sent to the University of Salamanca, where he gained a degree as a Bachelor of Law and followed that with six years in Rome as a consistorial lawyer. From the time he was appointed Archbishop of Toledo in 1495 on the death of Cardinal Mendoza, the austere Cisneros was a constant source of inspiration and comfort to the Queen. The combination of Cisneros and Isabel was an incomparable one, and together they reformed the Church and the prestige of the religious orders. Now he was to give her strength to face the crisis concerning Juana with the same patience and tolerance which she had shown in critical moments in the past.

Juana gave birth to her fourth child and second son on 1 March 1503. He was christened Fernando. But with his birth, no miracle took place to bring Juana back to her senses. She found no solace in her child and entrusted him to a wet nurse, assuming that it was enough that she had produced the baby and that the road to Flanders was now clear, but forgetting that Spain was now at war with France and a journey overland was impossible. As one possessed, she selfishly sought to wear her mother down by staging daily scenes with tears and moans and jumbled threats.

Isabel ordered the court to move to Segovia in June, but Juana was not fooled by her argument that Segovia was nearer the port of Laredo, and she became even more difficult to manage. Exhausted, Isabel took to her bed, racked by pains. Doctors reported to her that Juana's physical condition was worsening. She slept badly, ate little or nothing, was melancholic, had become extremely thin and was rarely moved to speak to anybody. She lived in her own fantasy world in which she imagined that Philip was by her side.

Philip's conduct in France had also caused consternation in Spain. He had maligned all he had seen in Spain, forgetting the honours bestowed on him, and he had showed undue friendliness to France, with whom Spain was at war. On crossing the border and arriving in Lyon in March 1503, shortly after receiving news of the birth of his second son, he had immediately entered into negotiations with Louis over an accord with France. Ignoring the advice of Fernando's representative that he should consult with the Spanish King first or delay the discussions for ten days to permit a courier to acquaint Fernando with the details of the pact being plotted, Louis had pressed the young upstart to sign the document, and the Treaty of Lyon had been signed on 5 April. By the provisions of this pact, concocted by Philip and Louis, Fernando was to renounce all claims to his part of the Kingdom of Naples in favour of the French, and hand over his territories in Naples to the Flemish Archduke.

Fernando refused to ratify the treaty and denounced it as a complete travesty. He demanded that it be torn up and he sent despatches to Maximilian in Germany and Henry VII in England, warning them that such a concordant could and would not be tolerated while he was King of Spain. Deviously, Philip had written to Gonzalo declaring an end to the hostilities in Italy. But such an underhand move was to blow up in his face. Fernando, sensing the situation, had previously advised the Gran Capitán to ignore any instructions emanating from Philip, and the Spanish commander had judiciously complied with his sovereign's wishes. The outcome was an intensification in the attacks by the Spanish, which would lead to a resounding defeat of the French at Ruvo and Cerignola.

Although fettered to a chain, it was sufficiently long for Francesca to move freely around her prison, and she soon found something with a rough edge to cut through her bonds. But as much as she tried, there was nothing she could do to free herself from the chain. Its iron ring in the wall had been there for donkey's years, and the manacle around her ankle was tight and impossible to shift.

It was nearly dark when her maid, Claudia, whispered to her through the door.

'Are you in there, Contessa?'

'Yes,' replied Francesca, dragging the chain to the door. 'But I'm chained to the wall and cannot escape. The French officer said he'll return in a few days.'

'What? To let you go?' asked the young girl innocently.

'Not quite, Claudia, no. To do what French soldiers normally do.'

The remark went over the youngster's head.

'Is Carlos safe, Claudia?'

'Oh yes, Contessa, Fabio and his wife, Lola, are looking after him in their cottage in the village. He's quite safe with them. They're lovely people.'

'Oh, that's a great relief. I've been so worried about him. Are there many French soldiers around?'

'Most of those who passed through the village earlier have moved on. But not before ransacking the house. It's terrible! I've just been in there. Everything's in an awful mess. Tables overturned, chairs broken, bottles lying around on the floor. All your lovely Florentine china smashed. There are about twenty men billeted all over the house. They're no better than animals. They've emptied your wine cellar and larder. There's tunics, helmets, armour, swords and boots scattered over the floor everywhere. They're all drunk and asleep, either half-dressed or wearing your clothes. It's awful. That's why I was able to come here without being noticed to try and find you… But what about you, Contessa? Have you got any food?'

'No. No food, just a bucket of water. But that's all I need.'

'I'll try and find what food I can in the kitchen and push it under the door. There's a small gap. Can I fetch help?'

'I think that's impossible for you, Claudia,' replied Francesca. 'My husband Matute's a long way away in Barletta with the Gran Capitán. It's several days' ride from here.'

'But I can go there, Contessa! I know the way. I went there before, when I was small.'

'But it's through the forests and over mountains, and everywhere between here and Barletta is occupied by the French.'

'But I can go. I know the way,' she repeated. 'I know these mountain paths like the back of my hand. I can do it, Contessa. I know I can.'

'I know you mean well, Claudia. But you'll never get there and return with my husband in time. The French captain will return in a few days, and I've no idea what will become of me then.'

'But I'll go now, Contessa,' she persisted. 'There's a bright moon tonight and I'll ride my pony, Sorrel. He knows the way better than me! If I go now, I'll be there by tomorrow evening, and your husband can be back here in another day if we ride back through the night.'

'Well, if you're sure…'

What Claudia was proposing sounded impossible. And for a girl of thirteen? She was like a waif as it was; more like a boy of ten. But Francesca remembered Tina in Canevare. She was only eleven, and managed to nearly decapitate Romano Latini with a chopper.

'Well, all right, Claudia,' resolved Francesca. 'Please go. You are a brave girl. Here, take this ring. It's the ring Mat gave me when we were betrothed.'

Francesca removed the ring from her finger and pushed it under the door.

'Oh, thank you, Contessa, thank you! I'll be gone in a jiffy. I'll be back with your husband before you know it. Have no fear.'

Claudia was an orphan. Her parents had been killed when she was nine during a storm when water swept through the village, taking their house with it. Claudia was the only one in the family to survive. She lived with her aunt for a while, but she was spiteful and beat the young girl and she ran away. Afterwards she lived off scraps that she could find and she slept in the empty chicken house of the equally empty manor. That was until Francesca arrived. She found the half-starved and filthy girl and, remembering her own childhood, took her in. Since then, Claudia has been her housemaid and was devoted to the 'contessa'.

Claudia found some lumps of cheese, carrots and a few crusts of dried bread and pushed some under Francesca's door. With what remained she ran to the stables, put reins on her pony Sorrel, threw a fleece onto the animal's back, led it out of the side gate and galloped off.

While earlier, in March 1503, Louis and Philip were hatching their Treaty of Lyon, the French in southern Italy had led a successful, punitive attack against the town of Ruvo, twenty miles from Barletta. Ruvo had sought deliverance by the Spanish after the French had dishonoured their womenfolk. Spurred by the plight of the town, Gonzalo marched with the whole of his force upon the Ruvo stronghold, reaching it in a single night. Early the next morning, after a short cannonade, he breached the walls in two places, personally leading one column of the assault while Diego Garcia de Parades led the other. The French fought bravely, but were compelled to surrender. There, the Spanish found a huge quantity of food and arms, which they triumphantly took back to their base. Many of the French soldiers who had acted so despicably in the town were condemned to the galleys, such was the baseness of their conduct against the town's womenfolk. The raid on Ruvo was the turning point in the fortunes of the Spaniards in Italy. Reinforcements arrived from Spain, as well as seven regiments of Germans, who were sent by Emperor Maximilian at Gonzalo's request. They soon showed their mettle and fought magnificently, to the delight of the Spanish.

Incensed by Archduke Philip's attempt to inveigle him to his side after signing the Treaty of Lyon, Gonzalo marched out of Barletta at the end of April to resume the offensive, and he targeted the French-occupied fortress of Cerignola, just sixteen miles inland from Barletta. The Spanish commander chose high ground a few miles from the town to draw up his army, and there he awaited the French, who had a long march ahead of them in the blazing sun. Gonzalo took the precaution of issuing double water rations and insisted that every mounted soldier carry a foot soldier behind him to lessen fatigue, himself lifting onto his horse a young German standard-bearer. At the foot of a vine-clad slope, beneath the village where the Spanish were marshalled, ran a small stream, and Gonzalo ordered that this natural defence be widened and deepened. He bordered it with stakes and mounted his artillery of thirteen guns out of sight just over the brow of the slope behind.

Disregarding the tiredness of their men, the French officers had overruled their able commander, the Duc de Nemours, and demanded an immediate attack. Several thousand highly disciplined and trained Swiss pike men made up the centre of the French force of 8,000 men; 400 knights and light horse held the flanks. On his part, Gonzalo, with an equal force, put his Germans in the centre, with the Spanish infantry on either side under two able leaders.

There, at Cerignola, for the first time in medieval warfare, Gonzalo created standing battalions of foot under the command of colonels who remained in charge of their units after the battle. Long absent from Spain and conventional patterns of warfare, Gonzalo was thus able to remodel his forces into new formations, which would be copied for centuries to come as free-standing regiments. Each unit of 3,000 men was made up of swordsmen, pike men and arquebusiers. These were supported by cavalry and artillery using their mobile lombards or their more static and bigger siege guns. This arrangement, comprising infantry, cavalry and artillery, became known as the *tercios* or 'thirds' and would for ever be associated with Spain's greatest military commander, Don Gonzalo Fernández of Córdoba.

The Spanish artillery, under the command of Pedro Navarro, was trained on the French heavy cavalry on the right. The Spanish cavalry was drawn up on the flanks, with a third group in reserve behind the Germans, ready to go into action at a moment's notice. As the afternoon light faded, the flower of knighthood of three nations was poised to engage on the field of battle, with the honourable conduct of medieval chivalry then still the byword. From that time forward, the dominance of firearms and artillery would bring it to an end.

After Claudia had left Francesca chained up in the outhouse at Montecorvino, she rode all night along little-used tracks through and over the wooded Picentini mountains. Under a full moon, she and her sure-footed pony found their way without difficulty, and by dawn she was through the 5,000-foot peaks and down onto lower ground beyond. Fording as necessary the numerous tributaries of the Bradano River, which drained to the Gulf of Taranto to the east, she skirted Mount Vulture, avoiding the large town of Melfi overlooking the broad coastal plain, which extended to Barletta on the sea.

Claudia still had more than fifty miles to ride, and from now on she was unsure of the way. But would Francesca's husband, Matute, be at Barletta when she arrived there? Only now had such doubts entered her mind. She stopped to eat from her meagre rations and to rest her pony while he drank from a stream and munched the luscious grass on its bank. She surveyed the plains ahead. The sun was now well up in the morning sky, and despite the haze which was forming she could see dust rising into the still air beyond several low hills – and not just a swirl resulting from a few riders, but from hundreds of soldiers on the move. But which soldiers? Spanish or French? Tired and exhausted, she climbed back onto her equally weary pony and headed off to find out.

The sun was several hours beyond its zenith when the noise of battle reached her. The shouts and cries of soldiers summoning up their courage, the crash of cannons and the beat of drums came from over the hill ahead of her. Claudia's instinct was to find somewhere to hide, if only in a nearby dense thicket. But the plight of Francesca was ever on her mind. She must press on and find Signore Matute, the contessa's husband.

Quelling her growing fear, the young girl urged her pony to one final effort. But the poor animal was almost spent. Half an hour later, leaving the beast by a shaded pond where it could drink its fill and rest, she dragged herself up the grassy slopes of the low hill ahead of her. The noise ahead was terrifying and the earth shook with the concussion of the guns being fired. Claudia breasted the hill and fell to her knees in both terror and awe at the sight of what lay on the slopes below. Scores of colourful campaign banners appeared through swirling smoke, but whose were they? Had she come out behind the Spanish lines or the French? Close by along the ridge, a line of cannons were firing over the head of a phalanx of pike men, their steel helmets flashing orange as they reflected the fire of the guns behind them. Ahead of them and at the bottom of the slope, Claudia could just make out a newly dug earth bank with sharpened stakes driven into it. Behind this defensive line, riding a huge white horse, a general in dazzling silver armour dashed back and forth, urging his men on, oblivious to the danger from the enemy sharpshooters lying within easy range. Beyond, on the far side of the bank and the ditch which lay beyond it, thousands of men and armoured cavalry on their chargers were moving forward, rousing their spirits by hurling blood-chilling threats at their foes. Crouching behind a dead horse and wincing at the discharge from each gun, a terrified and awestruck Claudia could only watch as the battle unfolded before her.

As the French advanced with their commander, the Duc de Nemours, in the lead, the wind blew smoke from the Spanish cannons into their faces and they were unable to see what they were doing. So, on arriving at the ditch which was then nigh invisible to them, the French cavalry was brought to a standstill. At close quarters, a murderous fire was poured into them as they endeavoured to climb over the Spanish breastworks and between the sharpened stakes. In vain, the French kept urging their horses past the obstacles. Their hardy Swiss pike men made attempt after attempt, but to no avail.

The Gran Capitán, spectacularly clad for once in his full suit of resplendent armour, rode along his ranks calling individual officers and men by their names, encouraging them by words of praise. Mounted on his giant horse, Santiago, so full of power and fury, Gonzalo lead the charge. He captured the first enemy standard of the day, that of a Burgundian company. The battle raged and the sun had nearly set when the French commander was killed by a shot from a Spanish arquebusier. Soon the field was won, with the fleeing enemy only saved in their flight by the growing darkness. In the battle, the

French lost 4,000 killed and the whole of their baggage train and colours, while the Spanish lost just a few hundred. In near darkness, Gonzalo ordered a general advance across the whole battle front, while the cavalry dashed upon the flanks of the enemy.

Claudia had watched all this from her vantage point on the hillside, praying that the general on the white horse was none other than the famous Spaniard whom she had heard about. As the conflict drew to a close, the smoke started to clear, and the cries of the dying and wounded in the floor of the valley could be heard as the clamour of battle abated. A group of soldiers reached the brow of the hill bearing several others who were pitifully injured. Claudia ran to them.

'Are you the soldiers of the Spanish general?' she asked breathlessly in her own language.

One soldier, swarthy and taller than the rest, picked up the word 'spagnolo'. He nodded his head in assent, and pointed to one of the injured men who was being laid carefully on the grass. Claudia ran to him.

'Yes,' the injured man replied in Italian, grimacing with the wound in his leg, from which blood was gushing. 'We're Don Gonzalo's men. The Spanish have won a great victory. They're great fighters. I'm a Neapolitan fighting on their side.'

'Do you know of one of them named Matute?'

The first soldier picked up the name. 'A huge man?' He gestured with his hand above his head. 'With hair the colour of dry grass?'

'Yes, yes!' replied Claudia. 'Do you know where I can find him?'

'Down the hill,' the injured Neapolitan man replied. 'He'll be with the general. Find the Gran Capitán and you'll find Sergeant Matute.'

'Come with me,' offered a third soldier whose arm had just been bandaged. 'I'll take you to look for him. At least he's easy to spot! You don't want to be wandering down there on your own. Come on, follow me.'

Claudia ran after him, down past the cannons, through a melee of sweating and dust-covered soldiers, now in boisterous mood and draining their water flasks. Soon they would have something better with which to celebrate. The soldier and Claudia ran among them, searching out the camp sergeant. At last, after twenty minutes, a mop of fair hair stood out like a beacon among a bevy of swarthier souls. Mat turned as she ran to him and called his name, her exhaustion forgotten. She had found her man! It took Mat a few moments to recognise her. He had just met her the once when he was with Francesca a month before.

'Claudia! What are you doing here?' he stammered in his broken Italian.

The thirteen-year-old fell into his arms, crying with relief and joy at finding him. She held out Francesca's wedding ring in her hand. Oh! He was so big and strong. Her explanation poured out of her, the words all jumbled and confused. The other soldiers standing around listened intently, trying to make sense of the girl's utterances. But Mat quickly understood the message she brought. How could this slip of a girl ride well over a hundred miles, over mountains and through forests, in the space of just eighteen hours? It beggared belief. Even now, from what she said, he had little more than a day to rescue Francesca before the French officer returned. Although she was not really in a fit state to return to Montecorvino, Claudia insisted that the few hours' rest she had got while watching the battle on the hilltop, and the food the soldiers had given her, were all she needed. Mat instructed an orderly in his unit to notify the Gran Capitán of the reason for his hasty departure, and called for a volunteer to accompany them. Many came forward eagerly, pressing to be chosen. Among them was a local soldier, Fausto, who knew the terrain as well as Claudia. So, collecting several water skins and filling some bags with food from the mess tent, they ran to the corral where fresh horses were saddled. Claudia climbed on Mat's horse in front of him and they galloped off. But would they be in time?

The news of the cataclysmic defeat of the fleeing French soldiers travelled ahead of them, as they found towns and villages bared to them and supplies of food unobtainable. Naples itself was in a state of ecstasy at the defeat of the French invaders. Gonzalo's soldiers pushed on well beyond the city, which they skirted, stopping only at the formidable French-occupied fortress of Gaeta on the western coast, a third of the way to Rome itself. Exhausted by their pursuit, they halted to await further orders. Gonzalo himself began his march to Naples, which lay over a hundred miles to the south-west of Cerignola and across the central mountain spine of Italy – the very mountains which Claudia had crossed the night before.

Back in Lyon in France, when Louis learnt of the resounding defeat of his army at Cerignola and the death of his general, the Duc de Nemours, he angrily turned on Philip and called him a naive bungler for precipitating Don Gonzalo's angry response to his foolish intervention when he instructed Gonzalo to cease hostilities in Italy. Reacting petulantly like a spoilt boy, Philip succumbed to a strange fever, which confined him to his bed for two months at the home of Margaret, the Duchess of Savoy, the widow of Prince Juan who had died six years earlier. Not until November 1503, eleven months after he left Madrid, did Philip reach Brussels, from where he promptly wrote to Juana, requesting her to join him.

XXX: Action on All Fronts

May 1503

Mat, Claudia and Fausto reached Montecorvino late the following evening. It was almost dark, but they were in time; the French lancer had not yet returned. It took just a minute or two for Mat and the young soldier to break into Francesca's prison. Her relief at his arrival and gratitude to Claudia for her epic journey were, of necessity, brief. With Fausto standing guard outside in the yard, Mat inserted the thick ash haft of his lance into the ring on the wall to which Francesca's chain was anchored. But with all the huge leverage it afforded, it would not budge. Likewise the shackle around her ankle was too tight to even think about breaking or levering it open.

'What can do we do?' whispered Claudia. 'Won't we just have to wait for the Frenchman to return with the key?'

Mat shook his head. 'Not if I can help it!' He knelt on the ground, placed the chain around his back and pulled it across his forearms. Then he straightened up and pulled his shoulders back, taking up the slack by looping each end of the chain twice around each hand. Then, girding his colossal strength and taking a long, deep breath, he hunched his shoulders, pulling them into his chest, at the same time bracing his forearms to tighten the chain. The muscles on his neck bulged and his face reddened under the huge force he exerted. But the chain would not give.

Claudia looked on in disbelief at the Herculean strength of the man. He seemed oblivious to the deep red weals being imprinted on his arms and back by the heavy chain. Francesca also shook her head in disbelief, but she had seen Mat in action once before at Canevare, when he had hauled the iron pulley from the mineshaft to break down the door to Pedro's crypt. Mat released his grip for a moment and took a couple of deep breaths. Then, taking up the slack on the chain again, and with the muscles of his chest and arms now fully braced, he rounded his shoulders once more. Seconds passed as he maintained the huge force. The chain bit deeper into his body and his fists turned white as the blood was squeezed out of them by the grip he maintained. Then, all of a sudden, there was a loud *ping*, and the chain burst asunder as a link gave way. Francesca was free.

They were only just in time. Fausto came running into the outhouse at that very moment.

'The Frenchman's coming!' he said excitedly. 'I can hear a rider entering the courtyard. But have no fear,' he added with unconcealed glee, 'I'll deal with him.'

Panting and physically drained, Mat got to his feet and went to the door. He could see Fausto concealed in the blackest of shadows across the open space just a few yards away. He had his sword ready in his hand. Mat could only guess at the grin on his face.

Quickly! Mat mouthed the words to Francesca. *Get back on the ground as if you're still chained up.* He pushed the door to and he and Claudia hid behind it. The Frenchman would see the broken lock, but that could not be helped. The three could hear the sound of a horse clattering to a stop on the flagstones outside and the jangle of bridle, stirrups, spurs and sabre. The visitor approached, fiddled with the lock and swung open the door. In that instant, Fausto issued a blood-curdling cry and thrust the point of his sword into the French officer's back, while Mat jumped out from behind the door and grabbed him around the neck in a bear-like hug. The man was too startled even to cry out. He already had in his hand the key to the fetter around Francesca's ankle, and in no time Claudia had released her from it. She held up the free length of chain like a trophy.

'What shall we do with him?' asked Fausto.

'Let's have some sport!' cried Francesca, remembering what the Frenchman promised to do to her on his return. With Fausto's sword pricking the man's neck, she undid his belt and dropped his thick tunic trousers to the ground. Claudia looked on aghast with her mouth wide open at Francesca's clear intent. The French lancer flinched. He knew what was coming.

'Oh no you don't!' scolded Mat, constraining her hand. He knew what was in her mind. 'I've seen a man castrated before and the loss of blood is unbelievable. He doesn't deserve that.'

'Let's string him up then,' offered Fausto, looping a rope over a crossbeam above him.

'No,' commanded Mat in a loud voice. 'Not that, either. We'll take him with us to Naples and let Don Gonzalo decide. His justice is fair.'

Mat gathered up the loose chain and pulled it tightly around the man's arms and chest, securing it with the shackle padlock. Francesca lit a lantern and she and Claudia went into the manor, which was now deserted. The whole place had been trashed. There was not a single item of furniture or piece of crockery left unbroken. Paintings, chandeliers and mirrors had all been wilfully smashed, and human excrement lay everywhere. Appalled by the shear vandalism perpetrated by the French soldiers to this lovely old Montecorvino manor house, Francesca put a spill to the lantern and threw the lighted end among the debris. Quickly the flames took hold.

Mat nodded his approval to what Francesca had done. Pedro was Baron of Montecorvino in name only now. But what was done was done.

'Let's be on our way,' he said, gathering the horses together.

'But what about Carlos?' cried out Claudia.

'Oh, heavens!' exclaimed Francesca. 'I'd totally forgotten that the gardener Fabio is looking after him. It's lucky you spoke, Claudia!'

'And what about me?' the thirteen-year-old lamented, her head downcast. 'What shall I do now? Where shall I go?'

What home she had had was now ablaze.

'Can I come with you, Contessa? You're all I have. Oh, please let me come with you, please!'

'Of course,' comforted Mat, putting his arm around her narrow shoulders. 'We wouldn't dream of leaving you behind. You're one of us now. Isn't that right, Francesca?'

The Neapolitan woman took Claudia in her arms and kissed her warmly.

'Of course she is,' she said. 'Welcome to the family, *cara mia.*'

'Fausto,' ordered Mat, 'you go ahead with this French officer. Tie his hands behind his back and then to the saddle. We'll stay here until the morning, when we'll collect Carlos from Fabio. And then we'll come on to Naples.'

'Very well, Sergeant Matute. I'll see all of you some time tomorrow.'

The Gran Capitán was already en route himself to Naples with the remainder of his Spanish force when Fausto set off. From some twenty miles away, Don Gonzalo saw the night sky to the south lit up by the flames of Montecorvino. In his entry into Naples at the head of his troops on 16 May, he was received with royal pomp. The streets were strewn with flowers and a canopy of gold brocade borne by six of the sons of the principal nobles was held over his head, with the sound of saluting cannons and the city's bands accompanying the procession of the rejoicing soldiers and citizens. The French veteran commander, D'Aubigny, had little choice but to surrender the city, and he was held in captivity while the rest of the French army were allowed to go free. Only the harbour fortress of Castel Nuovo in Naples itself and the city of Gaeta to the north remained in French hands.

Mat, Francesca, Claudia and young Carlos arrived in Naples during the festivities, some hours after Fausto and the French cavalry officer he had had in tow. Don Gonzalo wasted little time in committing the prisoner to the galleys, as he had done with many of the disgraced French prisoners taken at Ruvo. Francesca was truly ecstatic at being back in her hometown, and left Mat with his army unit while she skipped off with Claudia and Carlos to her old haunts.

The reduction of the almost impregnable Castel Nuovo – with walls 100 feet high and a moat twenty yards across – was entrusted to Pedro

Navarro. He quickly began undermining the fortifications by tunnelling and bombarding it with the Spanish siege guns. Meanwhile, Gonzalo gave very strict orders to his army billeted in Naples not to harm the civilians: those who did so out of greed, lust or insolence would be punished by death. On 12 June, while Fernando was still in Aragón and Isabel was moving her court to Segovia to assuage the petulant Juana, the undermined wall of the castle at Castel Nuovo collapsed. Then, watched by the inhabitants of the city from their rooftops, including Francesca and Claudia, the outer keep was carried. Gonzalo, who was taking a siesta in his billet in the palace of the rebellious Prince of Salerno, was roused from his bed and, dressed only in blouse and breeches, was one of the first to leap into the fortress, armed only with his sword. The French retreated to the doors of the keep, intent on raising the drawbridge, but before they could do so two of Gonzalo's men reached it and crossed over, while another leapt onto the second bridge as it was being raised and cut the ties with his sword so that it fell open again. The French were left with only the inner keep. They hurled stones, fire and quicklime down onto the Spanish, who were smashing at the doors of the keep and fighting with great fury. Under covering fire from archers and arquebusiers, nimble-footed Spanish soldiers scaled the walls on all sides, putting the defenders to the sword.

The booty was immense: gold, jewellery and plate, vast stores of grain and a full treasury. Three years of provisions, a great quantity of artillery, and many hundreds of thousands of ducats and much else was found. To their delight, the soldiers were rewarded at once. That night, after the spoils had been divided among officers and men, Gonzalo slept with his men in the castle. Two days later, on one of the hottest days ever remembered, the Spanish, fully refreshed, headed in good order northwards towards Gaeta, barely three days' march away. But even then some of the bitterest fighting of the Italian campaigns lay ahead of them.

Communication with La Española had now become a matter of routine, with twenty to thirty ships sailing annually from Seville or Sanlúcar to Santo Domingo or to the new port of Puerto Plata on the north coast. Each year, the governor, Nicolás de Ovando, sent native chiefs to Spain to learn Spanish and remain there for two years. The fleets bound for the Indies transported a wide range of manufactured goods, including the best fabrics from northern Europe and London, linen from Holland and velvet from Flanders.

After the disastrous hurricane which had hit Antonio de Torres' fleet, Columbus, now on his fourth – and what would be his last – voyage to the New World, left La Española two weeks after the Spanish took Castel Nuovo in Naples. He sailed along the south coast of Cuba and then headed 600 miles southwards across the Caribbean Sea to what is now Honduras and Nicaragua, encountering terrible storms and lightning on the way. Incredibly, he was convinced that he had reached the land which Marco Polo called Cochinchina, and was only ten days from the River Ganges! The Indians whom he encountered on these new lands were much more refined than the Tainos and the Caribes of the islands to the north, and lived a more settled and untroubled life.

Columbus then made an unfortunate decision. Instead of sailing northwards along the coast to the yet undiscovered Mayan people on the Yucatan peninsula, he sailed to the south-east to Panama, where he learnt of a narrow isthmus which separated two oceans. Ever searching for gold, he discovered a little in a river in Panama before crossing the Caribbean once more to Cuba, stopping over in Jamaica. Without food, he and his crew were forced to live on rats, rabbits and manioc bread. Another rebellion of his crew ensued, with the men demanding to return forthwith to Spain. Incapacitated again from gout, most of his party deserted him, killing most of their native helpers in the process, and headed off overland across Jamaica, hoping naively to reach Santo Domingo – which, in fact, lay a hundred miles away across a treacherous stretch of water. Finally, Diego de Escobar arrived in Jamaica from La Española, charged by Nicolás de Ovando with getting to the bottom of the latest rebellion against Columbus; but instead he was confronted by its leaders.

In the early autumn of 1503, desperate to break away, Juana left her mother and moved to Mota Castle, the family retreat in Medina del Campo. On hearing that Juana had received a letter from Philip pressing her to join him in Flanders, Isabel put her daughter in the restraining hands of the Bishop of Córdoba, who had accompanied Juana on her return from Flanders. Cunningly, Juana feigned willingness to await the return of her father from Zaragoza. But unaware of the constant surveillance of the Bishop, Juana made secret plans to depart. On a bleak day in November, she fled from Mota Castle on foot, clad only in a flimsy nightdress, and dashed towards the gate and to freedom. Unfortunately for her, the Bishop had been tipped off about her intention, and the outer portcullis of the barbican wall was lowered to prevent her escape.

Juana clung to the iron bars and refused to let go. Neither would she allow anyone to place a shawl around her shoulders to protect her from the biting wintry winds blowing across the plain, nor listen to the Bishop's pleas to return inside. In a frenzy, she lashed out with her tongue at the cleric, shocking all around her with the foul words she uttered. There, clinging to the bars, she stayed a day and a night before being persuaded to take refuge in the kitchen of one of the guard's huts. She remained there for five days in the same state of undress, refusing to heed the words of Cisneros, who had appeared by her side. In the end, Isabel was forced to rise from her sickbed in Segovia and hurry on horseback to Medina, some sixty miles away, to pacify her daughter. Juana delivered a foul-mouthed diatribe at her mother using the vilest language. Gradually, Isabel was able to calm her and lead her back to her rooms, promising that as soon as Fernando returned and the weather improved a fleet would be made ready to transport her to Flanders.

From that moment on, a legend arose about the attempted flight of the Princess from Medina. She was nicknamed by the peasants *Juana la Loca* – Joan the Mad – by which appellation she has been known through the years. This incident became the first clear sign of the abnormality of her mind. It left the Catholic Monarchs, Philip, the Cortes and the populace in general, to speculate on what the future held in store for the Spanish realms under their hereditary queen.

In Andalucía to the south, an investigation was initiated into the loss of gold arriving from the Indies. A sum valued at 150 million *maravedís* was unaccounted for, and the loss was thought due to the activities of the Genoese merchants who dominated maritime trade in the Old World. To exercise control, a chamber of commerce, called the Casa de Contratación, was established in Seville to control and account for all the gold and silver arriving from the Indies. This established Seville as the principal centre for communication with the Indies. From then on, all trade was sanctioned and registered there, although ships could use other ports. Although Cádiz on the Atlantic coast had a deeper and more secure harbour, it was rather isolated; while Palos, from which Columbus's first journey to the New World had departed, was too small and deemed too close to Portugal for comfort. So while Seville was handicapped by the sandbar downstream at Sanlúcar, it remained the centre of trade for over 200 years more.

The first fleet to sail to the Indies under the control of the Casa de Contratación left in November 1503 under a new law prohibiting the sending of Berber, Negro or Muslim slaves to the Indies. In a welter of new laws issued from Madrid, it was decreed that the Indians should receive education and be Christianised; the children would be taught to read and write; they would dress modestly; be prohibited from swearing; be baptised; and be prevented from bathing naked. Pagan items were to be prohibited, and they would live in their own communities.

But even after ten years of contact with the indigenous peoples of the Indies, the Spanish could not distinguish between the various tribes. They could as easily mistake a friendly and compliant Taino for a headhunting Caribe and, if he did wrong, declare him a slave. The treatment of the Indians – regarding the working conditions in the mines – disregarded the decrees issued in Spain. As a consequence of the brutal and inhuman treatment meted out by the settlers, there began a decline in the native population.

With Gonzalo triumphant at Naples in June, and the agreement with Louis rescinded, Fernando instructed Gonzalo to complete the conquest of Italy without delay. However, facing a humiliating defeat, the French King resolved to strengthen his force in Italy. He raised new French infantry divisions, financed 8,000 Swiss pike men, enrolled Italian mercenaries and called for volunteers for the cavalry. By July, the new French army was crossing the Alps, where it was joined by the Swiss and Italian levies. With a formidable French naval and military force now assembling at Gaeta and causing mounting casualties to the Spanish forces outside the fortress, Gonzalo decided to withdraw and set up base nearby.

On 18 August 1503, Pope Alexander VI died at the age of seventy-two. Spanish-born Rodrigo Borgia had been pope for eleven years. If his papacy had been mired in intrigue and suspicion, so was his passing. Some say he was poisoned with arsenic during a banquet two weeks before, which nearly also put an end to his eldest son, César, and Cardinal Adrian de Corneto. Some say he died of a fever, probably malaria, during a sweltering hot summer in a fetid and stinking Rome, where contagion was rampant. Nobody knows for sure. One month later, a friend and ally of the Borgias, Cardinal Piccolomini, was elected as the new Pope, taking the title Pius III. Three weeks later, on 18 October, he was assassinated and succeeded by Julián della Rovere, a bitter rival to the Borgias. He took the title Julius II. Within days, Rovere had arrested César Borgia.

The French force had now reached 22,000, by far the largest force mustered by either side during the Italian campaigns, while, despite his new recruits, Gonzalo could only muster just over half this number. With the French army marching south through central Italy, Gonzalo abandoned his base near Gaeta and marched inland to confront the French at Montecassino, some twenty-five miles inland. Some 200 French were stationed in the famous cliff-top monastery, and Gonzalo ordered it to be taken and blown up because of its strategic importance. However, after believing he saw a vision that night of the black-robed figure of St Benedict rebuking him, he changed his mind. The Spaniards harried the French as they moved across the fertile plain south of Montecassino in search of food. Bogged down in glutinous mud in atrocious autumn weather, the French avoided an engagement and headed to the coast where they expected to be further reinforced. But Gonzalo, moving quickly, blocked their route to Gaeta and took up a position facing the French across the swollen River Garigliano, fifteen miles from their coastal fortress at Gaeta.

Both sets of forces moved upstream looking for a place to bridge the brimming river, each testing the other with cannon fire. By early November, the French had completed a pontoon bridge capable of bearing artillery, and the next day they launched a furious attack against the Spanish. More than 1,000 Spanish soldiers perished in their waterlogged trenches under the first French assault, and many more deserted their posts. With casualties mounting, Gonzalo ordered a direct assault on the pontoon bridgehead, which was crowded with French soldiers and cavalry unable to move forward or back. The two heaviest cannons ever cast were stranded in their midst and unable to fire, surrounded as they were by their own men. Hand-to-hand fighting between the two sides followed, with many of the French falling into the river and being swept away. Many threw off their armour to escape by swimming downstream. The bridge was ruined by Spanish cannon fire and by the weight of the retreating French soldiers and horses.

Not deterred, two days later the French commander brought up boats from nearby Gaeta and constructed a new bridge over the river with a double carriageway for infantry and cavalry, but all attempts to move forward from the bridgehead were checked by the deep water-filled trench built earlier by the Spanish along the river. With the mid-November weather worsening into snow and sleet, the ground in front of the bridge became a morass of thick mud, with neither horse nor cannon able to move, and it was impossible to 'dig in' in the waterlogged ground.

Gonzalo refused the pleas of his officers to retreat to higher ground. He constantly moved among his men, who were living in abject conditions along the river, finding ways to provide them with hot food every day and means to dry their clothes. Thereby he maintained morale and discipline. With a drenched and sullen army, Gonzalo held this position for six long weeks through one of the worst and wettest winters ever remembered in southern Italy. In even worse plight, the French were in a state of open mutiny, retreating in droves to the nearby villages, where they indulged their tastes for wine and women in such an abandoned and orgiastic way that stories of their behaviour have been repeated down the centuries.

XXXI: Shock Waves across Spain

December 1503

The weather worsened even more during December, driving both sets of mud-caked forces further inland as the river surged out over the plain. Their tents were now unable to keep out the rain and their cuirasses, swords and cannons were rusting. The clothing of the men, the coats of the animals, tents and food, were all sodden, and more and more men were taken ill. Under a Christmas truce agreed in the bitterly cold weather, Gonzalo's men constructed a pontoon bridge five miles upstream of the French position on the Garigliano River. Just before dawn on the second day after Christmas, in a driving snowstorm, 3,000 men of the Orsini division stealthily crossed the bridge. The plan worked better than expected, with many of the French still lying with their women when the Spaniards broke into their quarters. Pedro Navarro came across the bridge next and was quickly followed by the heavier armed knights, and finally by Gonzalo and the rest of the cavalry and the German regiments.

The noise of the approaching Spanish cavalry was the only notice the French garrison received of their doom. The French, caught totally unawares, were put to the sword. Many fled, unable even to recover their cannons sited near their abandoned bridge. The Spanish light cavalry harried them in their flight, with Gonzalo in the van of the pursuing squadrons, until finally they reached the coast, just across the bay from Gaeta. Approaching from several directions, the Spanish reached the impregnable walls of the Gaeta fortress, with its immense round towers at each corner. The French had lost 3,000 men, with an equal number taken prisoner and wounded, plus all their cannon and baggage. Once their strength had been over 20,000, but now the two sides were almost equally matched. Worse followed when news arrived that part of the French army escaping by sea had met disaster in a storm off the mouth of the Tiber, and all the men had perished.

The French commander at Gaeta surrendered. Under the convention signed on 4 January 1504, all his remaining forces were permitted to depart by land or sea, provided that all fighting by French forces in Italy ceased. All prisoners were returned. Most of the French chose to return home by sea, with the remainder taking the overland route through Rome. In the end, scarcely a third of the French army arrived home, nearly all in rags, without arms or anything of worth except the memory of the valour of the Spanish soldiers. Gonzalo was praised for his merciful treatment of prisoners and for preventing his own soldiers from robbing and looting the vanquished French. With the French finally routed, the Gran Capitán broke camp and marched for Naples.

Like many of his officers and men, Don Gonzalo fell sick. He was worried above all else with the news coming from Spain that Queen Isabel was now at death's door. Moreover, he was worried about his future at the hands of the fickle and temperamental Fernando. By the middle of February, he was sufficiently well to enter Naples. The Kingdom of Naples, so long targeted by the Kings of France and Spain as well as the Pope, was his for the taking. At last, he could recognise the achievement of his officers and men, and he set about rewarding them, some with castles and fiefdoms and others with annuities and sums of money. No one was overlooked. Consumed by jealousy of Gonzalo's military success in Italy, Fernando believed that the Gran Capitán was intent on assuming the kingship of Naples for himself. For while Fernando was King of Aragón, he was only regent of Isabel's larger Kingdom of Castile – while Gonzalo was now Viceroy of Naples and, importantly, a blue-blooded Castilian to boot.

With the fighting now over, Mat obtained Don Gonzalo's permission to return home to Spain with his family, which now included Claudia. He was not overlooked in the recognition of service. After the experience of Montecorvino, a fiefdom in Italy was deemed inappropriate, but Mat was elevated to the rank of captain, for which he would receive a pension. In addition, he was awarded a bounty of 20,000 ducats, the ducat being the most widely used currency across Europe.

César Borgia, then twenty-six and in wretched health with his face all covered in pustules beneath the mask he habitually wore in public, was held in custody by the new pope, Julius II, while the handover of the Borgia possessions was arranged. But César escaped from prison and was thus free to pursue his own brand of mischief. Gonzalo knew that the new pope favoured the French, and he took the precaution of putting César under close arrest when he discovered him to be in Naples. Learning of this good fortune, Fernando wrote to Gonzalo expressing disquiet about the role of César in Italy, and instructed Gonzalo to send him to Spain. This he did. On 20 August, César Borgia was despatched to Spain in a fleet which was large enough to repel a French attack. There, he was imprisoned in La Mota Castle on the outskirts of Medina del Campo, where Isabel lay terminally ill.

The situation across Spain was getting desperate due to the failure of the wheat harvest, in consequence of which the price per bushel had trebled. Hunger was rife in towns and villages, where peasants had turned to begging.

People were dying of hunger by the score and bodies were left in the fields unburied, for, after two years of drought, the ground was brick hard and people lacked the will or energy to dig into it. The regions of Galicia, Asturias and Vizcaya in the north had never been self-sufficient, but now Castile itself, once 'the breadbasket of Rome', had become dependent on the import of cereals from northern Europe and Italy. This state of affairs was due in no small measure to the 1501 law which set aside lands on the *meseta* for sheep in their annual migrations across Spain. In Andalucía and Extremadura, in particular, huge tracts of good farmland became unusable for agriculture. Consequently, the need to increase wool production to fund Spain's overseas ambitions caused ruination and starvation across the land.

Because of the unpredictable weather in Castile, Juana's departure for Flanders was postponed until March 1504, one year after the birth of her second son. With young Fernando left in the care of Isabel, yet more severe weather was encountered by Juana's party as they headed northwards to Laredo, the port of her departure eight years before. For two long months, Juana waited as the waters off the Cantabrian coast beat against the shore. Not until the middle of May did the small squadron of ships leave harbour. But in just nine days they reached Bruges. After packing her Spanish ladies off to their residences, Juana was met by Philip, who had sped to the port. Momentarily she was in a state of rapture to be with her husband once again after eighteen months apart. Together they rode to Brussels. Doña Ana of Beamonte was with her again, and wrote to Raquel of the happenings.

Brussels, 4 July 1504

Dear Raquel,

This will be my last letter to you from Flanders. I'm returning home! I and my ladies have had enough of this turbulent Princess. All was sweetness and light when she arrived in Bruges at the end of May and was met by Archduke Philip. For a couple of weeks, they enjoyed a second honeymoon. But of course it didn't last. Quarrels and daily disputes became increasingly more recurrent, with Juana ever more selfish, wilful and consumed with jealousy of the women in the court, whether ladies in attendance or parlourmaids, all of whom she fears dally with Philip (but it has to be admitted many do!). Philip grew ever more indifferent, bored and disinterested in her as a consequence, but finally Juana has realised that her fears about his promiscuity during her absence in Spain were true.

Two weeks ago, she picked on a blonde and very pretty young Flemish lady in the court as the focus of Philip's attentions and attacked her physically, scratching her face and demanding that her long blonde tresses be shorn. I'm sure that the young woman was quite innocent and undeserving of Juana's suspicions. Philip reprimanded her sharply for her disgraceful behaviour, and in front of the whole court made her apologise to the woman in question. For days, he refused to speak to her. The sensitive Princess, scorned and isolated in court, has been beside herself with despair and fell sick.

From the outset, she has distanced herself from me and the other Spanish ladies – that is, the few of us who remain here – and now, to cap it all, Philip has, in effect, barred us from Juana's chambers. I don't want to worry Queen Isabel further with reports on Juana's behaviour, since I know that she's been growing weaker by the day, and in any case she receives regular reports from others here. Nevertheless, there is now no role for me and my other ladies, and I've decided that we'll return to Spain on the next ships which leave here. It's very sad that it's come to this after all the loyal service we've given the Princess. More worrying still, though, is what will become of Spain (and I really mean Castile) when Isabel passes away.

I do hope you and your family are well. I hear terrible stories about the famine which is afflicting Spain and the people who are dying of starvation. Oh! It's all so distressing, and my heart bleeds for Isabel in her terrible suffering.

My love to you all,

Ana

The scandalous story of Juana's attack on the young woman in the court mushroomed through the courts of Europe. When the story reached Spain, both Fernando and Isabel were sick in bed with fevers. The noble Isabel, fifty-three years of age, lacked sufficient strength to rally from such an insidious struggle with adversity and became weaker and weaker. Yet still tales of Juana's conduct continue to pour forth from Flanders.

By the summer, the Queen's health had deteriorated further, with tumours over much of her body. In continual attendance, her physicians could do nothing to relieve her constant pain. Confined to her chambers, Isabel was dying while the reins of government slipped from her fingers. But no strong hand was there to receive them from her. Her only son had died in his youth, her eldest daughter and her child had both preceded her to God's tender mercy, and the actual heirs to her many realms, so hard won, were wrangling in Flanders. For her daughter was on the verge of madness, and her son-in-law was an immature sapling and in league with the French. Even on her deathbed, the grandees of Castile hovered over her debating how the country should be governed in her absence. Should Fernando be despatched to Aragón? Should he hold the reins of Castile until Charles was of age? Or should they throw their lot in with Philip?

After arriving in Santo Domingo from Jamaica, where Ovando finally conde-scended to provide him with lodgings, Columbus and his constant companions, his brother Bartolomé and son Fernando, left La Española for Spain on 12 September. He arrived in Sanlúcar to learn that the Queen, so long his benefactor, was on her deathbed. During his two-year-long absence on his fourth voyage, the Crown had come to consider the New World its own

– not any more Columbus's personal domain, or even belonging to the native population. Amazingly, the Admiral of the Ocean Sea never ceased affirming that in his four voyages across the Ocean Sea he had been to India, Malaysia, China and Japan. He continued to enjoy his fame as the great explorer and navigator, although as a governor and leader of men he had been a disaster.

On 1 November, Isabel received a blow-by-blow account from Flanders of the daily quarrels in the Flemish household. Each word drove a dagger into her heart as the fury between Philip and Juana grew. Philip had demanded the expulsion of all her Spanish retinue who served her so faithfully and devoutly, and had bolted the doors of her chambers to prevent their access to her. Bored beyond measure by her conduct and demands, Philip escaped to the nearby forest to pursue the chase of hart and heart alike. All this and more was relayed to Isabel. It was the last report that she would receive. Astutely, Fernando had been advised in a letter from the monarchs' ambassador in Brussels that 'if Juana and Philip could not run a household in peace and harmony, they would scarcely be able to rule with wisdom the great realms they would inherit.'

Almost as a harbinger of her death, a violent earthquake in Andalucía on 4 November shook Spain to the very core, reverberating as far as Medina, over 200 miles away. Stories of the loss of life and devastation caused quickly travelled north.

The Queen's health continued to deteriorate as the cancer eating her body took hold. At midday on Tuesday, 26 November 1504, Isabel, aged fifty-four, mercifully passed away, with her husband, her confessor and closest friends grouped around her. So ended the life of Europe's greatest queen. Fernando ordered a stand built in the market square of Medina del Campo, and there he processed with all the members of the court and with Cisneros, the Archbishop of Toledo. Preceded by heralds blowing trumpets, the Duke of Alba mounted the stage and raised the standard of Queen Isabel on high three times, proclaiming in a loud voice, 'Castile, Castile for our Sovereign Lady, Queen Juana!' Archduke Philip's name was not mentioned. Humiliatingly, Fernando, after thirty years as joint monarch with Isabel, was forced to relinquish the title of King of Castile, and became instead Governor and Administrator of the Castilian territories. Enduring much sorrow, he left Medina and sought asylum in a nearby monastery to recover from the depression which consumed him.[1]

---

[1] The sad music written by Juan de Encina (1469-1529) entitled *Triste España* in David Munrow's lovely compilation of *Music for Ferdinand and Isabella* is thought to have been a lament for Isabel's death.

In her lengthy, carefully prepared will, signed by her a month before, Isabel asked to be buried in the Franciscan church now established in the former Nazarí palace of the Alhambra in Granada. She stipulated that no mourning be mounted and any moneys donated be used to provide for the poor and needy.[2] Acutely aware that Juana's mental state might make her unfit to govern her kingdom, Isabel had very carefully referred in her will to Fernando as 'King' and instructed that he should assume the Governorship of Castile as sole regent until Juana's eldest son, Charles, reached the age of twenty and could take over the reins. No mention was made of Archduke Philip. Nevertheless, this did not stop him – on 12 January 1505, in Brussels – declaring himself King of Castile, Leon, Granada, Prince of Aragón and Sicily, as well as Archduke of Austria, Duke of Burgundy and Count of Flanders. Without any ado, he elevated himself to kingship.

In the turmoil surrounding the last days of the Queen, César Borgia escaped from La Mota and fled to the independent Kingdom of Navarra to join his young wife, Princess Carlotta. He died soon afterwards, leading an assault on a rebel position in the Pyrenees.[3] Undoubtedly gifted, César was nevertheless one of history's most notorious characters. Through an incestuous relationship with his sister Lucrezia when she was thirteen years of age, an alleged similar relationship with his mother Vannozza and, it is claimed, the arrangement of the murder of his younger brother Juan, César brought disgrace to the name of Borgia, itself shamed by the nefarious conduct of his father Rodrigo.

---

[2] Her body now lies alongside that of Fernando in the Royal Chapel of the cathedral in Granada.
[3] On 11 March 2007, César Borgia, 'the infamous son of Cardinal Rodrigo Borgia', was honoured when a Requiem Mass was held at the Santa Maria church in Viana, just outside Lograno, northern Spain, where he was killed 500 years before (*Daily Telegraph* report).

XXXII: Forces Unleashed

The earthquake on 4 November 1504, felt in Medina del Campo in the north, was one of the most severe ever experienced in Spain.[1] Its epicentre was near Seville, 250 miles to the south, where the town of Carmona was severely damaged. One hundred people died, and religious and military buildings were destroyed.

Pedro, Raquel and their nine-year-old Antonio were outside in the grounds of Xiquena Castle, and Miriam was reaching the bottom of the castle steps with four-year-old Elena and Francesca's Carlos, also four, when the earthquake struck at midday. Joshua, not so nimble, was coming down the steps behind, while Mat, Francesca and Claudia were up in Vélez Blanco, five miles away, buying provisions in the market, ever more difficult to come by because of the food shortages.

For half a minute, the ground shook. Dogs barked and the children screamed as the ground quivered beneath them. Pedro had been five miles away from the city of Almería when the 1487 earthquake struck and left most

---

[1] Seismologists assign magnitude 9 to this earthquake, and believe it as great as the Lisbon earthquake of 1 November 1755, which is considered the worst earthquake experienced in Iberia in recorded history. Amarie Dennis's reference in her lovely book *Seek the Darkness* to a huge earthquake in Andalucia on Good Friday 1504, which was felt in Medina, is questionable, since no reference to this is made in technical references listing sixteenth-century earthquakes. (Maybe confusion arose over the use of *santos* in Spanish, between *El Día de Todos loss Santos*, All Saints' Day, on 1 November, and *Vienes Santo*, Good Friday, or *La Samana Santa*, Holy Week.) Historical references do exist to an earthquake in 1504 affecting Almería province, but most believe that these erroneously referred to the 1552 earthquake which totally destroyed the city of Almería and was its worst ever. No historical reference exists to the November 1504 earthquake affecting Vélez Rubion or Vélez Blanco, but it is fair to assume that it did. Vélez Rubio lies on a major east-west structural fault, one of many which traverse Andalucia and which between them have a horizontal displacement westwards of 200 miles, resulting from Africa squeezing southern Spain against the Iberian crystalline massif. This Vélez Rubio fault is associated with thrust and extension faults running westwards to Carmona. Pedro's castle residence at Xiquena lies directly over the Vélez Rubio fault, and the rocky outcrop on which it sits is a chunk left over from the movement. The fault isolates a wedge of reddish-brown Devonian sandstones and marls between older Palaeozoic rocks and younger, massive Jurassic limestones which form the mountain wall behind Vélez Blanco; indeed, Xiquena Castle was constructed using this reddish-brown sandstone. Lastly, it seems more than coincidence that Pedro Fajardo started the construction of the magnificent castle at Vélez Blanco in 1505, soon after the November 1504 earthquake.

of the city in ruins. Much of it still remained so. But this time the tremors were less intense, and he sensed that the earthquake was centred a long way away.

But Xiquena did not escape its effects. As the ground rumbled beneath them, a huge invisible hand grasped the castle around its midriff and shook it back and forth like a rag doll five or more times a second. Raquel was staggered by the sheer power of the earth forces released. All four watched from the path down to the gatehouse as the top of the high tower slowly wavered and came crashing down onto the steps leading up to the castle entrance. Poor Joshua, seeing stones from the parapet above falling around him, tried to retreat back into the building, but he was too late and he was crushed and buried under tons of masonry. As the rumbles continued, vertical cracks opened up in the castle walls and Pedro could hear thunderous crashes from inside as ceilings came down. The gatehouse below them did not escape, and one side of the tall tower came crashing down onto the stone gateway. Amazingly, Mat's recently completed small extension on the inside wall was undamaged. It was indeed fortunate that he and the others were safe in the nearby town. Or were they?

Young Elena scrambled to her knees, tugged his father's sleeve and pointed to the hill to his right. A cloud of brown dust was rising from Vélez Blanco as, at that same instant, the deep rumble of the destruction of the Moorish *alcazaba* struck them. As the dust settled, Pedro could see that the top of the massive main square tower was missing, and a smaller one had taken on a dangerous tilt.

Pedro and Raquel raced up the path to the castle. They had seen Joshua start to descend the flight of steps as the earthquake struck. But the steps were now invisible and buried under massive blocks of stone. Dust was even now settling over them. They called Joshua's name, but silence had descended over the tragic scene. Pedro clambered over the stones and worked his way into the castle. The steps up to the main hall were intact, but several columns and beams had given way. With several walls rent by cracks, it was clear that their home was unsafe to live in.

Abel and his Mudejar wife, Eva, arrived from their cottage down the road at the same time as Mat, Francesca and Claudia returned from Vélez Blanco, where only the Moorish *alcazaba* had suffered damage. It took the menfolk two days' hard toil to uncover the remains of Joshua's body, and he was buried that day in the town cemetery alongside Agustín and Sara. Uncle Joshua was a lovely man, and Pedro and Miriam were greatly upset by his tragic death. With Xiquena uninhabitable, Pedro, Raquel and Miriam moved down temporarily to Abel's cottage, while Mat and Francesca squeezed Elena into Claudia's small room in their gatehouse extension. Later, with as many of their belongings as possible recovered from the castle, Pedro and his family moved back to the family house in Vélez Blanco, which had remained empty but secure since their move to Xiquena. Likewise, Joshua and Raghad's small house across the square had remained locked up, and Mat and his family moved there. For all of them, the moves were far from ideal, but they sufficed.

If the forces released by the Carmona earthquake were felt as far as Medina del Campo, those released by the death of Isabel would threaten to fracture the very heart of Spain and release pent-up forces of dissent.

On the eleventh day of 1505, representatives of all the cities and towns of Castile, Leon and Granada met and resolved to adopt the Queen's wishes. They took the oath of allegiance to Juana as the legitimate ruler and to Philip as her husband. At the same time, they recognised Fernando as governor and administrator of the kingdoms in the absence of Juana. Later that month, Fernando brought the fragile state of Juana's mind to their attention. In a confidential letter, he explained the meaning behind Isabel's coded message in her will which stated that due to her wild outbursts and fits of melancholy – which had got steadily worse – Juana might 'not being able to govern'. He asked them to take a solemn oath to keep this matter secret. But, of course, the cat was now out of the bag. The fears of the people were given substance: the new Queen of Spain was unfit to rule. The way was now open for subterfuge and plotting by the most powerful magnates in the land, who had had their wings clipped by the monarchs as they wrestled in their early days to bring unity to Isabel's divided inheritance. The Crown was now balanced precariously on an unsound head, and several hands were ready to topple it – notably the ever-mischievous Duke of Medina Sidonia, who dreamed of his own realm in Andalucía centred on his dispossessed fortress of Gibraltar. Many of the upstarts, seeking personal advantage, joined the growing ranks in support of the young upstart from Flanders. Others bided their time to see which way the wind would blow.

Meanwhile, in Flanders, Philip lost no time in gathering the discordant dross around him. Juana was kept under lock and key in her quarters, and only her chaplain was allowed to see her. Guards were doubled at her door as she beat with her fists upon it in a frenzy. The Spanish ambassador reported to Fernando that Philip passed from banquet to banquet and woman to woman, and that affairs were in a deplorable state. He believed the Queen was pregnant again but was extremely thin, showing signs of being consumptive as a result of being confined to her room since her return from Castile. Philip continued to canvass support for his bid for the Spanish Crown. He pressured Louis of France to invade Spain, but the wily French King was content to bide his time and watch Spain disintegrate before his eyes. And not for the first time, the Gran Capitán in Italy rejected Philip's overtures for support. Loyalty to the

Crown was one of the great man's virtues, and he was not going to be swayed by an interloper wearing his enemy's clothes.

For Fernando, Castile and Aragón had to remain united. Cognisant of a clause inserted by his Aragón Cortes, which adopted Juana as his legitimate heir subject to Fernando himself not having a legitimate male heir, a strategy formed in his mind to stabilise the situation. He was only fifty-two. What if he were to take a bride? Without delay, a secret mission was despatched to France. In no time an alliance had been arranged, and Germaine, Louis XII's niece, was chosen as his bride. Eighteen years of age, Germaine was no beauty. She was chubby, somewhat lame in one leg, and given to banquets and fiestas. No matter; a Queen she would be and a male heir she would provide. A treaty with Fernando followed. For the astute King of France, with Spain about to fall into the hands of Philip of Austria, one less enemy on his borders was vital.

During the summer of 1505, Juana remained in solitary confinement, spending endless hours removing, then rearranging, beads on her dresses or reordering the stones of her jewellery. Always alone, with no one to serve her, she would sit in the corner of her room in the darkness and softly sing to herself for hours on end. Meanwhile, Philip hunted.

On 13 September, Juana gave birth to her fifth child, María, the future Queen of Hungary. Shortly afterwards, Philip announced his intentions of departing for Castile to claim for himself what rightfully belonged to his wife. To prepare the way, he issued a mountain of decrees to Spanish governors and appointed the Duke of Medina Sidonia as Captain General of Granada and Andalucía. These decrees were signed jointly by Juana and Philip, but there is little doubt that Juana's signature was forged. Moreover, he instructed them to ignore any and all decrees issued by Fernando and to withhold rents and taxes until he and Juana returned to Spain.

With his hand forced, Fernando accelerated his marriage plans to Germaine and, on 19 October, just eleven months after the death of Isabel, the marriage took place by proxy. The battle lines over who was the legitimate ruler of Spain intensified, with Louis siding with Fernando. Henry VII warned Philip that he would blockage any armada that attempted to sail south from Flanders, while Maximilian, Philip's father, urged Philip to reconsider his position. On 24 November, almost exactly a year after Isabel's death, an accord was signed in Salamanca, confirming Juana as the sovereign Queen, Philip as King, and Fernando as perpetual governor of the realms, with half the revenue going to the sovereigns and half to Fernando. Fernando and Philip would alternate in appointing members to the vacancies in the three military orders.

As Gonzalo's popularity increased among his forces and in Naples, Fernando became more and more jealous and suspicious of his motives. On Fernando's marriage to Germaine, Louis agreed to withdraw his claim to the throne of Naples, provided the kingdom was secured by way of a dowry to Germaine and her heirs in perpetuity. On his part, Fernando agreed to reimburse Louis for 1 million ducats over ten years for the cost of the Italian campaign, and to return all the forfeited honours and estates. To Gonzalo's men who had been fighting in Italy on and off for ten years, this was pure treachery, and was compounded when Gonzalo was instructed to hand over his hard-earned viceroyalty to the Archbishop of Zaragoza, one of Fernando's bastard sons.

After four years of drought and famine, the heavens opened in 1505, deluging much of Spain with intense rainstorms. With the ground rock hard, the water could not soak into the earth and flooded out over vast tracts of land. Where shrinkage cracks had opened up on clayey hillsides due to the drought, rainwater seeped down into them, lubricating their sides and causing huge landslides which carried away roads and buried houses and villages. No part was worse hit than in the Alpujarras, south of Granada, where landslides in the soft, unstable shales blocked the only access into the valley for months. The few crops that had managed to get established during the spring were flattened and ruined under the deluge. Rivulets became streams and rivers became raging torrents, sweeping soil, leaves, trees and even unburied human and animal carcasses before them. Many bridges were carried away. Others became blocked by the debris and the waters spread out over the land, causing further flooding. Farms and villages on the plains of the *mesetas* were inundated and disease spread as water became contaminated. Watermills which had lain virtually idle for years, owing to a lack of river flow to drive them, were ruined as the banks of their carefully tended *acequias* or inflow channels were broken and the mills' horizontal turbines, lying in deep chambers below the millstone assemblies, were smashed by boulders and choked by debris.

The mills located on the springhead of the River Vélez, set in the ravines which bounded each side of the spur on which Vélez Blanco was located, were similarly damaged. Pedro, as Pedro Fajardo's estate administrator, had his work cut out to mobilise the town's menfolk to repair them. But early September showed some respite from the rains, and the sun appeared through a watery sky.

It was on a warm morning that Pedro gathered all his family and friends together beneath the shade of the awning he had erected in the same small square, between his and Mat's house, where his father Abraham used to set up his tables to sell his herbal palliatives and medicines. The business at hand was a letter which Pedro had received. All those present had already read and studied it.

Letter from Juana de Torres

Seville, 15 August 1505

My Dear Pedro and Raquel,

I've just returned from Santo Domingo on La Española and have much to tell you. I went there this spring to honour the memory of Antonio and to cast some flowers into the sea off the island where he perished during the hurricane. After his death, I simply could not settle, but now I'm content that I've helped laid his soul to rest. Equally importantly, it turned out, I was able to see a little of the island which he'd grown to love.

While there, I met Friar Nicolás de Ovando, the new governor. I was impressed by what he's doing to establish a proper, long-lasting foothold in 'New Spain'. He handed me a letter which he should have sent to me last year. In many ways, it constitutes Antonio's last will and testament, since he took the precaution of getting the friar to sign and witness it. Most of its contents, or course, concern only me. In it, he passes to me the piece of land on the island for which he holds title. But he requests that if I should decide not to take up the rights to the adjacent landholding, which is in my name, that his piece of land be ceded to you. You know that he always held you in the highest regard and this is his way of recognising your mutual friendship. It was never my intention to emigrate to La Española to take up my concession, and consequently I would like to fulfil Antonio's request by passing to you his landholding, but at the same time make over to you mine also. That is, of course, if you were to consider moving to the island with your family to live. Spain has been going through difficult times in the last couple of years, and I don't expect you've been spared the effects of the terrible famine which has afflicted us. So you might find this offer to be opportune.

I didn't get the chance to visit the two land concessions, but Nicolás tells me that they're in the low-lying and fertile centre of the island. One concession constitutes some 300 acres and the other a little less and they are contiguous, lying either side of a river. The Tainos Indians there are friendly, and although inclined to laziness they're willing workers if directed properly. Timber abounds in the forested hills around, as do fish in the river. It all sounds rather idyllic!

Please let me know what you think. I shall be in Seville until the spring and would love to meet you again if you were to travel this way. As a matter of information for you, the autumn fleet is now assembling in Sanlúcar, downriver from Seville, and is due to sail in the first week of October.

Love and best wishes,

Juana

'Well, Mama, what do you think?' asked Pedro, after he had read the letter out loud.

Miriam looked a little startled by the suddenness of Pedro's question. At forty-nine, her fair hair had turned silver but, as slim as ever, she was still strikingly handsome.

'It all sounds very interesting, my dear. With the terrible famine we've suffered for four years, then last November's earthquake and now the floods, it might even be a sign from the Almighty. If the Bible's anything to go by, we're due for a plague of locusts! But you're head of the family now. It's for you to decide.'

'But I'd like to have your opinion, Mama.'

'Maybe afterwards, Pedro. I'd like to hear what the others think first.'

Their views were not long in coming.

'I think Mama is right,' said Raquel. 'Juana's letter might be a sign from God. Rather like the four riddles of the hermit which guided you in your journey across al-Andalus all those years ago… and,' she added with a giggle, 'which led you to me… and eventually to the Indies. I think you should treat Juana's letter in the same fashion – like a signpost, pointing you to your destiny.'

'Hmm…' murmured Pedro, nodding slowly. Maybe Raquel was right. There was a certain similarity between the hermit's riddles and Juana de Torres' letter arriving totally out of the blue.

'And what about you, Mat? What do you think?'

'It sounds a great opportunity,' burst forth Francesca, never short of an opinion. 'None of us has been able to settle since we moved up here from Xiquena after the earthquake. As Baron of Montecorvino, it's for you to decide, Pedro!' She never ceased to pull his leg. 'But I'd be willing to give it a try.'

'I-I-I agree,' stammered Mat. 'What have we got to lose? We c-c-can keep these houses here, just in case we need to return.'

'Abel?' asked Pedro.

Abel was sitting across the table from Pedro. He was just a year younger than Miriam, but in contrast to her he was dark and stocky. Born in Galicia of farming stock, he had travelled south as a young man in search of adventure and had enlisted in the army, where he saw much action during the Granada campaigns to oust the Muslims from Spain. Pedro owed his life to Abel, for it was Abel who, eighteen years earlier, had tipped off Don Gonzalo that Pedro was imprisoned by the Inquisition in Jaén. Without Don Gonzalo's forceful intervention, Pedro would not have survived the ordeal at the hands of Torquemada. Alongside Abel sat Eva, formerly a Muslim who, like Raquel, had changed faith, although with little conviction. A little darker of skin than Raquel and several years older, she sat with Abel, looking rather plump.

'Our first reaction, Pedro,' said Abel, 'was to dismiss the idea. But the more we've thought about it since you showed us the letter, the more we've come round to Francesca's view. I'm getting a bit long in the tooth, but… well, why not give it a try? It might not have escaped your notice,' he added, gently patting Eva's belly, 'but Eva's expecting a child, and the New World might be a good place to bring him up...'

'...or her!' interjected Eva.

'Yes, or her!'

'Claudia?' asked Pedro.

'Me?' asked the youngster in her fast-improving Spanish. 'Do I get a say?'

'Of course. You're one of us now. What do you think?'

'I'll go where the contessa goes...'

Everyone laughed.

'And what about you, Antonio?' asked Pedro, turning to his son. Ten-year-old Antonio had sat quietly next to his father throughout the whole discussion. The boy remained in deep thought for a few moments, his imagination working overtime.

'Can I play in the forest and fish in the river, Papa?' he enquired.

Everyone laughed again. Antonio's remark brought the discussion to a nice conclusion. The unanimity of opinion had taken everyone by surprise.

'But now, Mama,' said Pedro turning to his mother, 'you've been very quiet. What do you think? Nobody's opinion is more important to me than yours.'

'The last few years here have not been good years, Pedro,' she said very quietly, her eyes fixed pensively on her hands resting on the table. 'Too many tragedies, too many deaths. Firstly the awful murder of Yazíd on the hills above Chirivel. Then the tragic loss of your little Sara after all her suffering. How we cared for her while you were away! Then the death of Agustín five years ago in the Muslim revolt in the Alpujarras, and Raquel's mother's precipitate decision to return to her home village. We've no idea what became of her, have we? And finally the death of poor Joshua under the rubble at Xiquena in the earthquake. There have been too many sadnesses here for me to hold this place dear to my heart any more. On top of that, there have been the years of famine we've endured, and then the floods...'

Miriam's voice trailed away. She looked up, her voice lightening.

'I think we need a change of fortune, my dear. Maybe a total change of scene and a new challenge is what we all need.'

'Pedro,' said Abel, while Miriam and Raquel went to refill the water jugs in the fountain. 'If we're serious about migrating to La Española, wouldn't it be sensible if you went to explore the island first to see what it's like and where we would settle?'

'Yes, Pedro,' interjected Miriam, returning to the table, now buoyed up and incisive. 'You should go there and see the island for yourself – although didn't you visit it with Columbus?'

'Yes, but only along the north coast. By that time, Martín Pinzón had sailed off in the *Pinta* and the Admiral was desperately worried that he was sailing back to Spain to claim the discovery of the Indies for himself. Then the *Santa María* foundered on a sandbank and was lost. Columbus left forty or so crewmen from the stricken ship to establish a small colony, and soon afterwards the rest of us sailed back in the *Pinta* and *Niña*. So La Española was barely explored.'

'But would you go?' asked Miriam.

'Yes, it's a good idea.'

'Can I come, too?' asked Antonio cheekily.

'Why not?' interjected Francesca. 'He can go fishing in the rivers there!'

'But what about your work here for Pedro Fajardo?' asked Raquel.

'Well, actually,' replied Pedro, 'I'm becoming a bit surplus to requirements. Pedro Fajardo, now the first Marqués de los Vélez following the death of his father two years ago, is bringing in new people from Cartagena. As you've seen, workmen are already dismantling the *alcazaba* after the damage caused by the earthquake, and the plans for the new castle are already well advanced. From what I've seen of them, it will be fantastic. Construction's due to start very soon. No, the new *marqués* won't miss me.'

A thought crossed Abel's mind. He was thinking of Eva and Raquel.

'In a recent proclamation, didn't the Queen ban Jews, Berbers, Muslims and slaves from emigrating to the Indies?'

'…And people with only one hand!' chided Francesca, concealing the fist of her left hand in her sleeve and holding it up in front of Pedro.

Laughing, Pedro leant forward and tweaked her nose with the steel-pronged device fitted to the end of his wrist. Acting like a forefinger and middle finger bent over and partly opened, it allowed him to hold papers, documents and such things as plates, but it had proved little help to Mat and Abel in removing the blocks of stone from Joshua's crushed body after the earthquake.

'I carry a special letter of dispensation from the Queen,' he replied in a high, affected voice, waving a blank piece of paper. 'This is my passport to board ship to wherever I wish to go!'

Francesca pointed her tongue out at him.

So, after much leg-pulling all round, it was agreed. No time was to be lost if Pedro was to join the Indies' fleet leaving in little more than three weeks' time.

XXXIII: A Kingdom Pulled Three Ways

October 1505

The uncertainty in Castile after Isabel's death left Governor Ovando a free hand on La Española. The success of his harsh but efficient government saw the Spanish population rise from 300 to several thousand. With famine and general disquiet rife in Spain, more and more sought a new life in the Indies[1] with Andalucía, as the gateway to the islands, being the principal source of the colonists. The herds of cows on La Española grew rapidly in the open pastures, as did the number of horses and the herds of pigs. Yuca tubas dug from the roots of the manioc tree, which was native to the region and could be harvested at any time of the year, provided a staple diet as a form of fibrous potato, and when grated could be made into bread.[2] Oxen were yoked in pairs to transport ore from the mines to ships at Santo Domingo and Puerto Plata on the north coast, and to construct the base for new roads. As an added bonus, a deposit of copper was thought to have been discovered on the island.

Nevertheless, instability was always around the corner, and a new conflict broke out with the natives near Higüey, close to the south-eastern promontory, but the Spaniards were too strong with their arms and guns and captured the last of the chiefs, whom they strangled in the square in Santo Domingo. The majority of the Tainos prisoners were reduced to slavery, and a fifth of them were sent to Spain as slaves of the Crown. To maintain a local presence on the island, Ovando established new settlements close to the old Tainos villages which he called 'villas'. These were located in the mining zones along the central valley of the River Haina, where foundries were established in Concepción de la Vega and Buenaventura. All the new villas were given coats of arms as if they were old Spanish cities. Councillors, judges and notaries were assigned to each of them. The settlements were all laid out in a square grid around a central plaza containing a governor's residence, a town hall, church and, inevitably, a prison. The villas were the focus for the country

---

[1] The term 'America' did not emerge until 1507, when Martin Waldseemüller's printed map of the world christened the new continent 'America' after his friend, the explorer Amerigo Vespucci.

[2] Cassava (*Manihot esculenta*) is also known as manioc, for which the yuca (or yucca) root provides a low-protein, starchy staple made into a dough and cooked on a griddle as cassava flatbreads. Tapioca is made from the purified starch derived from the roots.

around. Families could cultivate the fields around them, and many chose to live within the community. Ovando retained the right to name all the officers of the towns.

Pedro and Antonio reached Seville near the end of September after a week of easy riding. The roads were dry, the weather warm and sunny and the roadside inns pleasant and commodious. The two enjoyed every minute of the journey. For Pedro, it was like old times. But from Granada onwards, the signs of the Carmona earthquake increased progressively. No town or village had escaped the destruction, with houses in ruins, roofs collapsed, walls rent by cracks, and stone gateposts toppled over. For the small villages, the caving in of their wells and *aljibes*, their barrel-vaulted underground water cisterns, was the most serious of all. Carmona, through which they passed, was a ghost town, with at least half the buildings no more than piles of rubble. What remained of the town was deserted save for scavenging dogs. More pitiful, though, were the small mounds, some fresh, some grassed over, which bordered the fields outside the towns and villages, giving silent witness to the scale of the famine which had ravaged Spain, and not least Andalucía. Pedro counted hundreds and hundreds of these shallow, hastily dug graves. Across Spain, tens of thousands must have perished.

Seville, just twenty-five miles west of Carmona, had not escaped the destruction, with parts of the former poorly constructed Muslim city wall fallen down, as well as the top-heavy coping stones crowning the arched gateways. It was fourteen years since Pedro had last been in Seville, but he quickly found his way to Juana de Torres' house in the heart of the city, near the huge Gothic cathedral alongside the towering, square Giralda Tower, the former Muslim bell tower. It was almost as many years since he had met Juana during the banquet in Tordesillas after the signing of the treaty with the Portuguese. She had now turned fifty. The death of her brother Antonio, as well as the untimely death of her former charge, Prince Juan, for whom she had been governess, and then Queen Isabel, had taken its toll, and her features were etched by fine lines. But she had lost none of her sparkle. Chatting over a glass of pomegranate juice in her garden, they relived the fun they had had at the banquet and with the fabulous French menu.

'What's happening in the Plaza de Triunfo by the Royal Palace, Juana?' Pedro asked after a while. 'There are rows of seats and stands being erected all around it – enough for thousands.'

'It's for an auto-da-fé next week.'

'An auto-da-fé? The Spanish Inquisition?' checked Pedro.

'Yes. It's awful, isn't it? I shudder just to think of the horror of it all and the suffering of all those poor people. But what's the matter, Pedro? You've turned pale.'

'Like you, Juana, I shudder when I hear about the Spanish Inquisition.'

'You were held by them, weren't you?'

Yes, when I was fourteen – for five months in Jaén. I still have nightmares about what happened to me.'

'Jaén? Wasn't that where that butcher, Diego Rodríguez Lucero, was the inquisitor?'

'Yes. He started there but later moved to Córdoba, where his reputation for cruelty flourished.'

'He must be a horrible man.'

'Yes, he is. An absolute monster. But even worse for me was Tomás de Torquemada, the Inquisitor General of Castile. Tall and gaunt, his sunken eyes beneath his black cowl were like death itself.'

'Isabel's appointee? You know, Torquemada died some years ago.'

'Yes, I heard.'

'So you met him, Pedro?' asked Juana.

'Yes. He interrogated me with Lucero in the chamber of examination.'

'The torture chamber?'

'Yes.'

'Is that where you lost your hand?' For Juana's benefit, Pedro was wearing the leather glove over his missing left hand, so cleverly fabricated by the Italian leather craftsmen. But he need not have worried. So many adults were maimed or disfigured through poor health, disability or injury that missing limbs were a common sight.

'No, that was due to the Tuscan partisans in Italy,' he replied. His nightmare in the church crypt was now just a bad dream. He explained what had happened.

'How truly awful! But how did you come to escape the clutches of the Inquisition?'

'It was while I was being tortured on the *strappado*.'

'What's the *strappado*, Papa?' asked Antonio, listening intently to the conversation. He had heard of the Spanish Inquisition.

'It's a hook on the ceiling. A pulley hoists you up by your wrists, which are tied behind your back. In no time, your shoulders are dislocated and you can end up crippled for life. Luckily for me, after I'd been lifted off my feet and dropped to the ground a few times, Don Gonzalo Fernández burst into the chamber and at the point of his sword demanded my release. Torquemada and Lucero had no option but to let me go. Don Gonzalo took me to Porcuna, which is a small castle on the way to Córdoba, and his wonderful doctor there healed my wounds.'

'Gonzalo's an amazing man,' commented Juana. 'How did he know you were there?'

'One of the soldiers who took me to Jaén, Abel Jiménez…'

'Our Abel?' interjected the youngster.

'Yes, Antonio. Our Abel. He saved my life, as has Mat on more than one occasion. Abel got a message to Gonzalo and he wasted no time in riding to Jaén. He hated Torquemada and had crossed swords with him before. No one in Spain will be sorry about his death.'

The couple sat in thought, contemplating the auto-da-fé the following week. Several people were to be burnt at the *hoguera*, including the Bishop of Cádiz, whom the Inquisition had discovered had a Jewish grandfather – as, in fact, had Torquemada. Luckily, Pedro and Antonio would have left Seville by then and might even be en route to La Española.

'Seville and Toledo seem to have more autos-da-fé than any other city in Spain, Juana,' observed Pedro.

'That's true, Pedro, and from the very outset in 1482 when the Inquisition was established. But it's not surprising really. The Archbishop of Seville, the Dominican friar Diego de Deza, is the new Inquisitor General of Castile. In league with Lucero in Córdoba, upriver from here, they burnt 120 poor souls two years ago and twenty-seven in May this year.'

'And more now?'

'Yes, it's awful, isn't it? But I've heard on the grapevine in the city that a recent study by the Chapter House in Córdoba has found that Lucero falsely fabricates evidence against his victims, and he's to be accused of robbery and unlawful killing. Moreover, they've found that Diego de Deza has repeatedly failed to respond to complaints lodged against Lucero. So maybe their rule of terror will at last come to an end.'[3]

'I hope so, Juana, I do hope so,' commented Pedro with feeling.

Juana passed to Pedro copies of the parchment maps attached to her and her brother's concessions in La Española, which showed where they were located. There was little to go on, but the bends in the river dividing the lands, the location of Tainos settlements and distinctive landmarks would be sufficient to locate them. Pedro thanked her for her generosity in making over the concessions to him, and, after fondly embracing her, he and Antonio left the next morning for Sanlúcar on one of the river ferries which plied the fifty or so miles down the Guadalquivir. The river was in spate after the heavy rains, and much of the low-lying land below Seville was under water.

Due to onshore winds, the departure of the autumn fleet from Sanlúcar was delayed until the middle of October. Pedro had no difficulty obtaining berths for them on one of the eighteen ships making up the armada. Between

---

[3] In 1508, the Supreme Council of the Church voted to detain Lucero, who was conducted in chains to Burgos while his victims in Córdoba were freed. He died in Seville the same year.

them, the ships carried several hundred new colonists, mostly poor people escaping from impoverished Andalucía and Extremadura, plus woollen fabric and made-up clothes, grain, and seeds and plants for sowing. Pens had been constructed on the decks of several of the caravels to hold horses, donkeys and cattle, with pigs housed below decks. More would be collected in Gomera in the Canaries, the usual stopping point for ships bound for the Indies. Chickens on all the ships provided fresh eggs and would add to the island's poultry stock.

'Don't I know you?' asked the fleet's commander when Pedro enrolled himself and Antonio for the voyage. He was a burly man, now in his fifties, and as true a sea dog as ever sailed the high seas. He sat behind an upturned barrel outside the quayside tavern at Sanlúcar, a tankard of ale in his huge calloused fist.

'Juan Quintero?' responded Pedro, laughing and clapping the man on the back. Fancy the fleet commander being Juan Quintero!

'Aye, lad,' he replied. 'I recognise your face now from long ago. You were a young slip of a boy, if I remember correctly... shy... bullied by other cabin boys... a cut above the rest... could read and write... always seemed to be on the wrong side of—?'

'Martín Pinzón.'

'Of course! Now I have it. The first voyage from Palos. You joined the *Pinta*... late... some confusion over your name?'

'Yes, Juan. Pedro Togeiro's my real name, and this is my ten-year-old son, Antonio. And you were the ship's bo'sun who saved me once from a good beating...'

Pedro hugged the powerful man around the shoulders. How wonderful it was to meet the old rascal again.

'But then you had two hands, Pedro. What happened?'

Pedro joined his former shipmate for a glass of ale and explained. Antonio sipped his father's ale and spat it out. Ugh! Horrible! Juan and Pedro laughed.

'Are you going to be a cabin boy, Antonio, like your dad was?' asked the former bo'sun.

'No, I'm going to be a fisherman,' replied the youngster.

'A fisherman!'

'Yes,' replied Antonio spiritedly. 'I'm going to catch fish in the rivers in Sp-Sp-Spanla.'

'Española?'

'Yes, there.' Antonio pretended to hold a rod and line in front of him.

Juan roared.

The adults reminisced over Columbus's historic first voyage across the Ocean Sea, laughing and chuckling, forgetting the bad times, the storms, the rotten food, the becalmings, the mutiny of the crew. Briefly, Pedro explained what had become of him after the *Pinta* and *Niña* had returned to Palos; his time as royal ambassador in Morocco; his role as aide-de-camp in Italy to Don Gonzalo, who was now a household name across the breadth of Spain; and how he had lost his hand.

'Well, I never!' was all the old bo'sun could say. 'And all I've done is sailed the high seas... back and forth, back and forth. 'You, a friend of the great man himself... well, I never!'

The sun had set across the estuary, now at low water, when Pedro finished his tale and explained why he was returning to La Española.

'Well, Pedro, you're doing the right thing,' said the fleet commander. 'There's no future here. I don't know what's going to happen to Spain, I really don't.'

Snowstorms and bad weather caused the sailing of Philip and Juana's fleet from Flanders to be delayed, but the armada of fifty vessels did manage to set off from Middleburg on 10 January 1506. 1,500 German soldiers embarked as Philip's personal guard. Caught in a fierce storm, a shattered yardarm and its rigging was swept off the royal galleon, which took on a strong list. Philip and his courtiers huddled together on the poop deck to await their fate in the swirling storm. With the fleet scattered across the sea and blown back from the north coast of Brittany, the battered vessel crawled into a small port on the Dorset coast. Three vessels failed to reach shelter on the English coast. With repair of the damaged ships put in hand, Philip accepted Henry VII's invitation to meet his son, the Prince of Wales, the future Henry VIII, in Winchester. Juana refused to accompany her husband and stayed behind in the port. Only under pressure did she respond to the pleas of her sister Catalina, already dubbed Catherine of Aragón, and finally show herself in the royal court at Windsor. But then only for one night.

On 2 March, Philip bade farewell to the young Henry, and with six replacement ships arriving from Spain at the Cornish anchorage of Falmouth, the fleet resumed its voyage in the middle of April. Aiming to join his new ally, the Duke of Medina Sidonia, and his army-in-waiting in Andalucía, adverse winds forced the fleet to make for the harbour of La Coruña in Galicia, northwest Spain. Meanwhile, Fernando had moved from Segovia to Valladolid, where on 22 March he married Germaine. Soon afterwards, he moved to Burgos to await the arrival of Philip and the inevitable confrontation.

Philip's fleet arrived on 26 April and was met by cheering crowds, but the petulant young Queen Juana, seized by one of her perverse moods and irritated by the attention shown to her husband, refused to join in the celebrations, to the astonishment of the townsfolk. Within no time, the nobles and prelates who had deserted Fernando swarmed around the twenty-eight-year-old Philip, complaining of the taxes levied by Fernando and of his remarriage so soon after the death of Isabel. Almost immediately, Philip dismissed the mayors and constables of the towns he passed through, replacing them with his own Flemish lackeys. Chaos followed. Attempts by Fernando to reach an accord with Philip over their joint administration of Castile were repelled. Philip was determined to rule his new domain alone. With the nobility torn hopelessly between the two parties as they manoeuvred for advantage, and with the growing jealousies between the Spanish and Flemish nobles, the country was on the verge of open conflict and civil war. Fernando's position became more and more precarious.

Throughout this whole period, while her father and her husband measured swords, Juana was relegated to the background and held under surveillance, subject to the mercy of Philip. None of Fernando's ambassadors was allowed in her presence. Sensing the danger, she refused to affix her name to any document without first consulting her father. Philip was caught in a cleft stick as nobles and prelates did an about-face and returned to their former king on bended knees; and for the sixth and last time Juana was with child.

Almost unnoticed, Christopher Columbus died in Valladolid on 20 May 1506, aged fifty-six. His gout had finally taken its toll. His successes were substantial. He had convinced the Crown to support his first voyage of discovery when other monarchs rejected him, and he had conducted the conquest and the colonisation of half the new lands for his adopted Spain. Yet, perversely, he died still stubbornly holding the view that the vast continent, later called the New World, was part of Asia. But whatever his shortcomings as an administrator and governor, he was, above all else, an exceptional sailor and navigator, with vision and determination.[4] Columbus did not die poor, since his properties on La Española were considerable and he had enjoyed the income proceeding from many concessions. On 26 November, Fernando wrote to Columbus's son, twenty-seven-year-old Diego, lamenting the difficulties which his father had experienced and reiterating the esteem in which he had held him.

While Fernando approached from the south with his followers, Philip moved his retinue to Santiago de Compostela, with his German mercenaries

---

[4] It is worth recording that on his first voyage of discovery in August 1492 he assessed by dead reckoning the distance of his landfall on Samana Cay as 3,200 nautical miles from the Canaries, compared with the correct distance of 3,100. Moreover, despite what he thought was a defective quadrant, he determined the latitude of Cuba as 21°N, compared with the true value of 21°18'N. Columbus' body was buried in Valladolid but was transferred to Seville in 1509. It was later sent to Santo Domingo but returned to Seville, where he is buried in the cathedral.

marching in battle array. The roads were appalling, and every night brigands descended on the convoy to pillage and steal what they could. Many wagons toppled over on the stony tracks. Cisneros urged Fernando to withdraw to the safety of Toledo and create a stronghold at the heart of the kingdom. Fernando refused to give ground in his own county. Encamped close to the Portuguese border in the Sierra de Cabrera, Philip's forces were situated at the town of Sanabria and Fernando's at Asturianos, just eight miles away. They were scarcely a hair's breath away from what would be the first battle on Spanish territory since Fernando, as a twenty-one-year-old, had saved Isabel's then precarious kingdom from Alfonso V of Portugal's bid to claim the crown of Castile for his niece, the illegitimate Juana La Beltraneja. That was at the Battle of Toro, fought in the teeming rain in 1475; by chance, it was only fifty miles from their present positions. To avert what would have been a calamity, Fernando and Philip agreed to meet midway between their camps with minimum retinues. They met on 20 June.

On the morning of the meeting, Fernando, unarmed and mounted on a mule, set off early, accompanied by his secretaries, officials and gentlemen of his court, totalling some 200. All were unarmed. Then, wafting over the hill came the sound of drums and high-pitched fifes, announcing the impending arrival of the self-proclaimed King. Philip had sallied forth with all the panoply and fanfare of an advancing army. 1,000 German mercenaries were sent ahead to reconnoitre the countryside, while Philip was surrounded by over 2,000 horsemen, archers, bodyguards, lancers, pike men and grandees. As the multitude reached the oak grove, the appointed neutral meeting place, the turncoat nobles who had joined Philip's side rode down to pay their haughty respects to Fernando. Beneath their colourful tunics, they were in full body armour.

Soon after the appearance of Philip, the two kings retired to a nearby hermitage, followed at a respectable distance by Cisneros and Juan Manuel, the King of Portugal, who, as Fernando's former son-in-law, had sided with him. But Fernando had been wrong-footed and was unable to obtain an agreement even to see his daughter who, to all intents and purposes, was held hostage by her husband. A week later, Fernando accepted a concordat in which, incredibly, he agreed to give up Castile, Leon and Granada to Juana and Philip. He would receive during his lifetime half the gold arriving from the Indies and the revenues accrued from the three military orders. Fernando soon realised that he had been hoodwinked by the young pretender and had conceded too much. He wrote a circular to all his kingdoms and all his ambassadors seeking to justify his acquiescence to the demands of the new king. But it was too late; he had conceded too much. The die in favour of Philip was cast.

Unaware of all these machinations, Juana went riding in a nearby park with some of her courtiers when she suddenly veered off, galloping for all she was worth to freedom. But a ring of mercenaries loomed over the brow of a hill ahead of her. Not to be thwarted, she wheeled around to elude the soldiers, taking refuge in the first house she found. But it was to no avail; Philip had been told of her flight and had returned. Juana threw a tantrum, demanding to see her father, whom she knew was in the locality. But Philip was well versed in her threats and left her alone until the morrow. By then, she was quiet and acquiescent, and thoughts of her father had departed her.

A second and last brief meeting took place between Fernando and Philip in July. The meeting lasted only one hour, and once again the younger man refused to let Fernando see his daughter. When the interview was over, Archbishop Cisneros, the lubricant of power, was summoned into the chapel to hear the outcome, and farewells were said. Fernando set off for his own kingdom of Aragón but faced disdain and aversion in the towns through which he passed. Later, slighted and humiliated by his own people of Aragón, he set sail for Naples with his young wife, Queen Germaine.

With his father-in-law out of the way, Philip stepped into the role of undisputed King of the three kingdoms. Calling the members of the Cortes to Valladolid, he anticipated that Juana would be malleable in the demands he planned to make of them. He was in for a surprise. The dark embers of Juana's life flickered and ignited, and the moment was at hand. She demanded that she rode ahead of Philip into the city with her own standard held high. But the spectacle of the female figure dressed in black with her face covered in a black veil caused the townsfolk to shrink before her in trepidation, and the crowd fell silent. In her funeral robes, she seemed more the precursor of death and sorrow than the long-awaited Queen of Castile. Philip made one last attempt to push through a vote in the Cortes to sequester Juana, but again he was thwarted by those who remained convinced that Juana was sane and of sound mind. Not for the first or the last time, Philip realised that when the chips were down, the bickering nobles of Spain would shy away from an interloper from a foreign land.

Juana persisted, and in an audience with the assembled lawmakers she lucidly demanded and obtained their recognition that she was the legitimate heiress of the dead Isabel. Philip and his cohorts sat in stony silence while the Queen held centre stage. He knew that her temporary sanity would soon evaporate; but for once he was wrong. At a ceremony on 12 July, she was recognised as Queen of Castile, Leon and Granada. Charles, her six-year-old prince, was recognised as her heir, and Philip as King and Governor. But as suddenly as she saw reason, she relapsed into her passive state and sought refuge again in her life of darkness.

Poor Isabel would have turned in her grave. Her loyal husband of over thirty years had been roundly trounced and had run off with a new bride to Italy; Juana was 'unfit for purpose', as she had recognised all too clearly in her will; and the philandering upstart from Flanders had triumphed. Worse still, the united kingdom of Castile which she and Fernando had forged in hot metal over a lifetime was divided and seemingly in ruins, with the nobility looking to recover their lost rights and privileges.[5]

---

[5] In 1520, the Holy Roman Emperor Charles V (Charles I of Spain) recognised sixty lineages of high nobility in Spain; twenty-five in the category of grandees and the remainder as titled nobles. The grandees were privileged to receive official documents, while the remainder were considered as 'members of the royal family'.

XXXIV: Spain in Turmoil

August 1506

Spain was now in desperate straits. The coffers of the treasury had been emptied by the cost of Philip's journey south from Flanders and by Fernando and his close advisors, who had been funnelling most of the moneys into their own pockets and had grown opulent as a result. Discontent was rampant among the old guard of the Spanish nobility. With Philip having assigned fortresses to his Flemish followers, scarcely any now remained in the hands of their former owners. Even his closest Spanish ally, the Duke of Medina Sidonia, had abandoned him.

Pedro and Antonio returned home to Vélez Blanco during the month. The seven other prospective adult colonists – Miriam, Raquel, Mat, Francesca, Claudia, Abel and Eva, nursing her new babe in arms, Rafael – gathered excitedly to hear his news. The six-year-olds, Carlos and Elena, as close as brother and sister, were playing nearby. A handsome, dark-skinned boy with shining white teeth and a bewitching smile sat alongside Antonio.

'So what did you discover, Pedro?' asked Abel, always to the point and eyeing the newcomer.

'I'll tell you in a minute, Abel, but firstly, I'd like to introduce Behechio to you all. Behechio is the sixteen-year-old son of the Taino chief Guarionex. Tragically, along with Antonio de Torres, Guarionex was drowned in the hurricane which took so many ships and so many lives five years ago. We met Behechio in the new settlement of Santiago. He wanted to do what his father was hoping to do and visit Spain and learn our language. Behechio will return with us to help us settle down in his country.'

The young Taino nodded keenly. He guessed the sense of what Pedro was saying. The Tainos were the indigenous race in much of the western Caribbean. They were good-natured and had been well disposed to the settlers there from the outset, despite the awful cruelties and indignities they suffered at the hands of the Spaniards.

'And he's going to teach me how to fish, aren't you, Bechy?' giggled Antonio.

The two boys clearly got on well together. Already each was picking up the other's language, while Pedro spent an hour each day with the youngster doing the same.

'Unfortunately,' continued Pedro, 'Nicolás de Ovando wasn't there when we arrived in Santo Domingo. He was in nearby Jamaica sorting out problems. We spent two weeks in the city. It's very impressive and growing rapidly. We were very fortunate to meet Francisco Tostado, who's a notary, and he showed us around the city. Being a lawyer, Francisco will prepare the title deeds for the two concessions which Juana has made over to me. He'll have them ready for when we return there.'

'So what's the city like?' asked Francesca impatiently. 'Is it like Naples?'

'Oh no!' laughed Pedro. 'Naples has been there for hundreds of years and has tens of thousands of people. Santo Domingo was only established ten years ago! But let me start at the beginning. Here,' he said, unfolding a piece of paper. 'I've traced a plan of the city from one Francisco has made, so you can see what it's like.'

Raquel helped him spread it out on the table and everyone gathered around to examine it.

'You can see,' he explained, pointing with his finger, 'that Santo Domingo lies at the mouth of the River Ozama, where it flows into the sea.'

'And the river's as big as the river through Seville,' claimed Antonio, not wanting to be left out of the narration. After all, he had been there too. What an adventure it had been for a ten-year-old.

'Well, nearly!' corrected Pedro. 'It's a hundred yards wide at Santo Domingo, and with all the rain the island gets it flows very quickly. Eight years ago, Bartolomé Columbus – that's Christopher Columbus's younger brother, who, by the way, makes brilliant maps – established a colony on the other side of the river. But Nicolás de Ovando decided that the right bank would be better suited for the settlement, and Bartolomé's small wooden fort was abandoned. It's already rotting away and overgrown by vegetation.

'Antonio de Torres' hurricane destroyed the wooden buildings in the new settlement, and Ovando made a ruling that all new buildings had to be of stone. The new city rises to a low plateau made of an old coral reef, and this is being quarried to provide the stone needed. A city wall has been marked out and this encloses an area of about 1,000 yards square. Quite a lot of it's been built, particularly along the river frontage. The city's first construction was a stone fort at the river mouth called the Ozama Fortress. It looks like it's made of solid stone and must be nigh on impregnable. A square called the Plaza España has been laid out above the main gateway into the city from the river, and it looks down onto where the ships moor.'

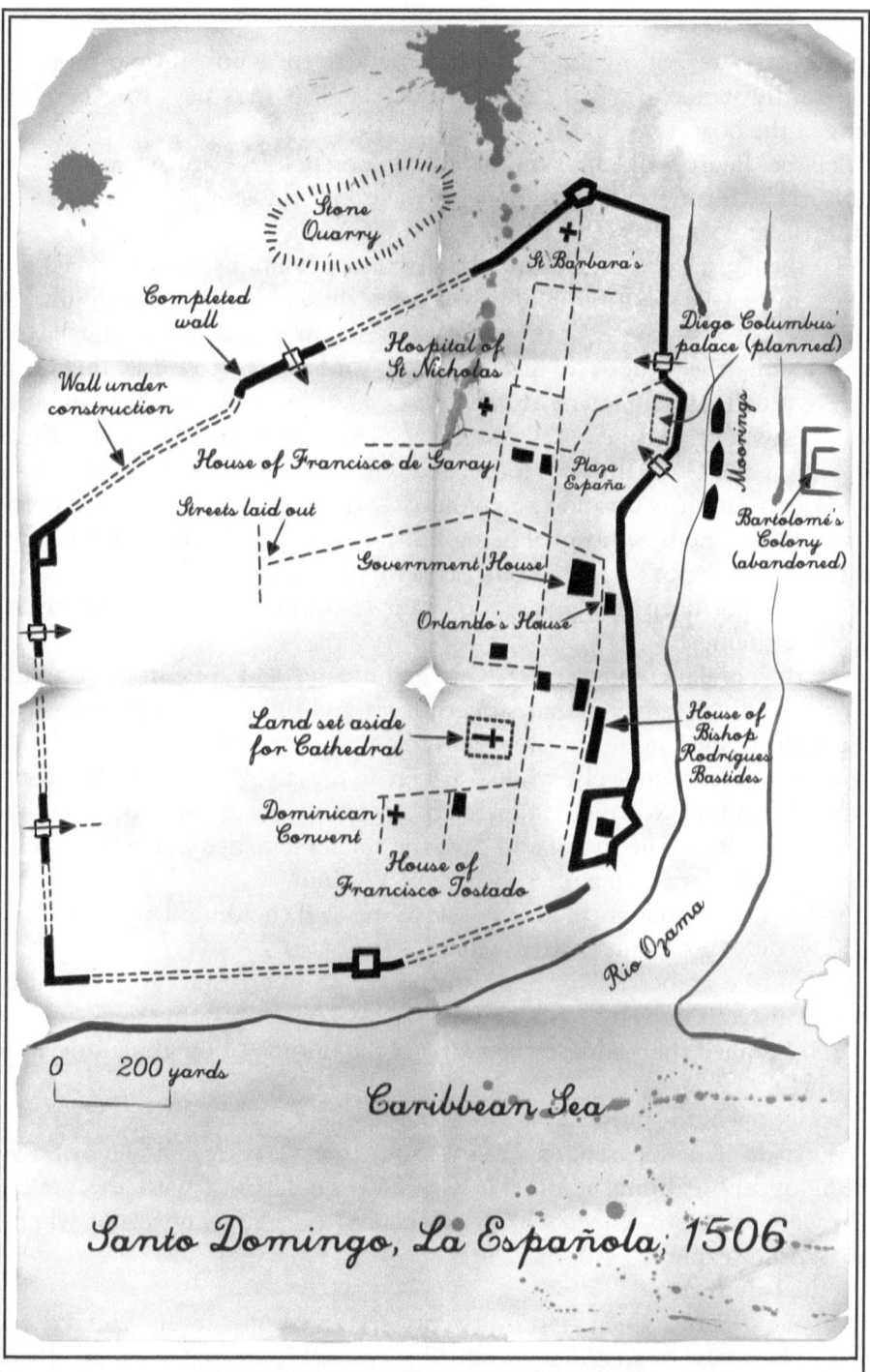

Stone
Quarry

Completed
wall

St Barbara's

Diego Columbus'
palace (planned)

Wall under
construction

Hospital of
St Nicholas

Moorings

House of Francisco de Garay

Plaza
España

E

Bartolomé's
Colony
(abandoned)

Streets laid out

Government House

Orlando's House

Land set aside
for Cathedral

House of
Bishop
Rodriguez
Bastides

Dominican
Convent

House of
Francisco Tostado

Rio Ozama

0   200 yards

Caribbean Sea

Santo Domingo, La Española, 1506

PEDRO'S SKETCH MAP OF SANTO DOMINGO, 1506

'That's where we got off the boat when we arrived,' said Antonio proudly. 'I could hardly stand up when I got onto dry land. It took days to get over the rolling of the boat.'

'Tell me, Pedro,' asked his mother, 'how long does the journey take?'

'Nearly two months overall, Mama, including the stop in Gomera to take on animals and supplies.'

'Has the lawyer you met, Francisco Tostado, got a house there?' asked Eva.

'Yes, in fact he's got two, and they were almost the first ones built. One stands by a grassy space near where the cathedral will eventually be constructed, and the other's a few hundred yards away towards the Ozama Fortress. But there are many other houses now built. A fine building, again made of this lovely white coral stone, is well underway near the Plaza España. This will be the Government House, and will also house the Treasury. Almost directly opposite it is Ovando's new house, with an ornate columned portico. There's also a fine new hospital being built up the road from the main square, and a new prison not far from Francisco's first house.'

'And it's got deep dungeons, too!' said Antonio. 'Señor Tostado took us down into them.'

'Yes, they're dark, and already damp and musty,' added Pedro. 'So, all told,' he concluded, 'already a dozen stone houses and buildings exist along streets made with crushed stone left over from the quarrying.'

'Did you meet anyone else while you were in the city, Pedro?' asked Miriam.

'Yes, Grandma, we did,' interjected Antonio, 'a lady in a beautiful long dress. She took a shine to me and gave me this.' He fished out of his pocket a piece of polished, golden amber the size of a walnut.

'And it's got a dragonfly inside it, too!' he said, holding it up to the light. 'But how did it get inside?' he frowned.

'I think the amber f-f-forms from the sap of trees, Antonio,' replied Mat very seriously. 'It traps insects when the sap s-s-seeps out of the trees.'

'Ugh!' replied the youngster, looking at the outline of the dragonfly against the light.

'But who was the beautiful lady?' asked Raquel.

'María de Toledo,' replied Pedro. 'She's the very elegant wife of Diego Columbus, the Admiral's son. He was away in Jamaica with the governor when we were there. Diego's likely to succeed Nicolás as governor when his term of office expires.'

'Is the lady very old?'

'Oh no, Raquel. Diego's only twenty-six or twenty-seven, and I'd guess María to be a year or so older. In fact, she's probably around your age, Raquel, twenty-nine.'

'I'd like to meet her.'

'I'm sure you will. There are precious few Spanish ladies in La Española and you, Mama, Francesca and Eva will be a source of unlimited attraction among all the settlers when you arrive. You can be sure of that!'

'And Claudia!' added Francesca. 'Don't let's forget Claudia.' By now the seventeen-year-old had blossomed into a beautiful young woman, tall and fair.

'No, of course not,' corrected Pedro. 'All you womenfolk will be a sensation there!'

Miriam blushed. It was a long time since she was a 'sensation'.

'But you didn't stay the whole time in Santo Domingo, did you, Pedro?' she asked, keen to change the subject.

'No, just the two weeks. We then travelled inland by mule to one of the new "villas" which Ovando has established in the central valley called Santiago. It's one of the places where gold is mined.'

'That's where we met Bechy and his family,' said Antonio, winking at the young Taino. 'He's got lots of brothers and sisters. The youngest don't wear any clothes at all!' he added with a boyish giggle.

'We spent most of our time there and at La Vega, another villa not far away,' continued Pedro, describing the country around the other settlements.

'So you located Juana's two concessions?' asked Francesca.

'Yes, but with difficulty. The land is very green and fertile, in sharp contrast to here. I'm sure we'll all be able to make a real go of living there and raising our families. With Behechio's help and that of his family, we'll settle in really well.'

The Taino lad nodded enthusiastically. He had a disarming smile.

'Show them your dried leaves, Bechy,' prompted Antonio.

The Taino boy leaned to one side, extracted from a pocket a small pouch made of turtle skin and took out some dry brown leaves the size of his palm. He held them up. They were veined and flaccid and let off a fragrant aroma. Antonio giggled and Pedro laughed in anticipation; he knew what was coming. Everyone else looked perplexed. The Taino boy placed a leaf on the table and carefully rolled it up into a tube, holding it tightly in his hand. Antonio ran into the house and brought out a lighted spill and handed it to Behechio.

'This is what Behechio's father and uncles do with the leaves,' Antonio said mischievously.

Then Behechio put the leafy tube in his lips and lit the end, blew out the flame and then puffed at the other end, blowing out the smoke from his mouth in a blue-grey cloud. He grinned from ear to ear.

'What is it? What are you doing, Behechio?' asked an appalled Miriam.

'It's what Behechio's father and uncles do of an evening at sunset, Mama,' explained Pedro, 'when they're sitting outside their huts. They say it helps them relax and recover from their daily toils. I saw the Indians smoking these leaves during Columbus's first visit to Cuba. Sometimes they stuff it into the end of a hollowed-out wooden tube before setting fire to it, and at other times they chew it.'[1]

Everyone fell about laughing at such a preposterous activity.

'So what's the plan now?' asked Abel, continuing to nodding his head in disbelief.

'If you're still keen to go, we'll start making our moves. There'll be a lot to arrange. But I did take the opportunity when we returned to Seville of reserving twelve places for us on the autumn fleet next year, and another for Behechio.'

With a comet bright in the night sky, an augury of doom was at hand as Philip and Juana entered Burgos on 7 September 1506. Ten days later, Philip lunched with his courtiers and, in expansive mood, indulged himself in an enormous repast. Afterwards he challenged a young noble to a game of tennis, which was hotly contested. It was a cool September day and the match lasted for well over an hour. Afterwards he drank a large glass of cold water and then stood idly by talking to his companions. Whether it was the drink of cold water or the cold air of the high plateau, within a short time he was being racked by chills and fever. On the following morning, still with a fever, he set forth for a day's hunting in the country. He continued to suffer in silence through the third day until late into the afternoon when, shivering and sweating, he summoned his doctors. By this time, the illness had taken hold, with Philip spitting and coughing blood and complaining of an acute pain in his side. For two days, the physicians in attendance did all they could, bleeding him and purging him, but to little avail. Finally, priests were summoned, and extreme unction was administered. Fearing a coup d'état by the Flemish contingent, Cisneros, ever to the fore, called the Spanish nobles together, who agreed the appointment of a Council of Regents to guide the ship of state until Fernando could be summoned from Italy.

On the afternoon of 25 September 1506, Philip departed this life. Throughout his week-long fever, Juana remained by his bedside, never leaving him once, while seeming oblivious that Philip was close to death. His body lay in state all night under a brocade and ermine-covered dais with a large cross of precious stones placed on his chest. When the sun rose next morning, his body was lowered from the dais to be embalmed by two surgeons summoned to

---

[1] Rodrigo de Jerez brought the habit back from Columbus' first voyage in 1493 and became a confirmed smoker. He so frightened his neighbours that he was imprisoned by the Inquisition for seven years. By the time he was released, smoking was common in Spain.

perform the task. His heart was extracted and placed in a small gold casket to be sent to his homeland to repose beside the remains of his ancestors. After his cranium had been cut open, his brain was removed and then, after opening his abdomen, his entrails. His body was then sewn up, after having been filled with crushed chalk and aromatic herbs. It was then laid in a lead coffin which was itself placed inside a wooden casket. This was taken and secured in a locked sepulchre until Philip's wishes to be buried in Granada beside Queen Isabel could be fulfilled.

Thus the fairest prince in Europe was snatched away at the age of twenty-nine. He left behind a state in utter turmoil. In reality, the life of Philip as king was of brief duration and, like the comet in the night sky, he would pass into celestial oblivion.

On 1 November, the pregnant Juana suddenly decided to go to the Monastery of Miraflores to hear Mass for the repose of the dead. Then, in an act which would dictate the course of history for several decades to come, she ordered that Philip's sepulchre be unlocked. Making her way into the silent tomb, she commanded that the coffins be opened in her presence.

She remained capricious much of the time; distant, unapproachable and uncaring for those around her. At other times, she emerged from her darkness to take the reins of government, revoking all the grants and deeds issued by Philip after the death of her mother, thereby siphoning back into the royal treasury millions of *maravedís* which had found their way into the pockets of Philip's adherents, both Flemish and Spanish. The Royal Council concurred with alacrity. Fortuitously perhaps, Juana's action saved Spain from financial oblivion.

Two months earlier, on 4 September 1506, a few days before Philip's fatal game of tennis, Fernando left Barcelona with his new queen, Germaine, in a squadron of Catalan galleons which met up with Doña Maria Manrique, who was travelling to Naples to join her husband, the Gran Capitán. The King reached Genoa on October and was met by Gonzalo, who climbed on board the King's ship to meet him and embrace his wife, María, whom he had not seen since he left Spain during the Granada rebellion six years before. News then arrived of the death of Philip the Fair. Much jubilation followed – Fernando would rule Castile again as Regent!

With government in Spain in limbo, Fernando wrote from Genoa confirming the succession of six-year-old Charles and naming Cisneros and the Royal Council as governors during his absence. Many of the nobles insisted that Juana should be declared unfit to rule. Others wanted Charles declared king forthwith, while another group wanted the Holy Roman Emperor Maximilian, Philip's father, to be the new ruler, since he was a well-respected and astute figure. King Manuel of Portugal, to whom Juana's younger sister

María was married, was also put forward. Yet others backed three-year-old Fernando, Juana's fourth child, as king. At least, unlike his elder brother Charles, he had lived and had grown up in Spain in Isabel's care, and Castilian was his native language. Henry VII of England, then forty-nine, was even proposed as a future new husband for Juana. Few rulers in Europe escaped the list of candidates being advocated.

Fernando and Gonzalo's joint armada sailed on down the coast of Italy to Naples, disembarking via a long wooden jetty extending out from quayside. There, quite intentionally, Gonzalo presented to the King every officer and humble soldier who had served with him during his long campaign. This brought home forcibly to Fernando the esteem in which Gonzalo was held by his forces and by the people of Naples. The pageantry was unsurpassed. Italian princes, captains and soldiers, cardinals and ambassadors filed past Gonzalo to the sound of eight kettledrummers, twenty-six trumpeters and a bevy of musicians playing sackbuts and pipes. In Naples Cathedral, an anthem was sung which had been composed especially for the day. Both Queen María of Hungary, Juana's younger sister, and the Duchess of Milan were present. The following day, Fernando paid a state visit to Gonzalo in the palace where he resided, showing him every courtesy and honour.

But then the King started to scrutinise Gonzalo's governance of the Kingdom of Naples, and the mean streak in Fernando, held in check during Isabel's life, surfaced to blight the crowning years of the Gran Capitán's triumphs. He forced most of Gonzalo's captains to relinquish the lands and possessions granted to them. Through jealousy and spite, Don Gonzalo himself was forced to relinquish the Duchy of Sant'Angelo which had been bestowed on him by the King of Naples. As a sop to this and his earlier stripping Gonzalo of the viceroyalty of the kingdom, Fernando offered Gonzalo the Grand Mastership of the Order of Santiago. This was the greatest of the three Spanish grand orders, and carried immense prestige and revenues. It was the highest honour in the King's gift and would place Gonzalo second only to the King in power and influence in Spain. But this was an empty promise, and it would turn out to be the meanest act of all against his most loyal subject.

One minute the benefactor and the next the malfeasant, the King instigated a inquiry into the Gran Capitán's expenditure and demanded to see his accounts. Furious that his honesty and honour were being questioned after his near eleven years of campaigning in Italy, Gonzalo presented his own detailed accounts. These showed that the costs he had personally incurred of 600,493 gold pieces far exceeded his incomes of 200,736. At that point, knowing that he had met his match, the King laughed and terminated the audit.

The new Pope, Julius II, three years into his incumbency, offered Gonzalo the command of his papal forces, formerly in the hands of César Borgia. This was the highest honour he could bestow on the Spanish commander. Fernando then knew that he had gone too far in his open criticism of Gonzalo, and again offered him the Grand Mastership of Santiago.

At Christmas that year, Juana insisted that Philip's body be removed from its confines. The priests and her courtiers protested against this sacrilege, but she ranted at them and threatened all of them with dire consequences if they did not accede to her demands. The wooden and lead caskets were opened for everyone to identify the body therein. The corpse was truly horrible to behold, with its face calcified into a solid white mass, and the stench was stomach-churning. Under cover of darkness, the resealed coffins were lifted into a hearse drawn by four horses and a procession formed. With monks intoning dirges, the funeral train wound its way down the road leading from the monastery. Doleful chants floated through the cold December mist, while the flickering flames from the torches of the procession cast eerie shadows along the highway. Behind the bier rode the black-veiled Queen, followed by bishops and priests. Throughout the long night they journeyed, resting during the next day, only to continue after the sun had set, Juana preferring to hide during the daylight hours away from prying eyes. On the third night, they reached the village of Torquemada, thirty-five miles from Burgos and almost halfway to Valladolid. With Philip's body still in tow, Juana declared that she wished to remain there until after the birth of her sixth and last child.

In a temporary palace in Torquemada, a rotating guard was obliged to take turns to stand vigil beside the coffin. Funeral services were held three times a day. Then, on Juana's instructions, the guard of honour was doubled, so that when her husband rose from the dead he would have around him old acquaintances and servants to assist him in arising from his temporary sleep.

XXXV: Triumphant Return

On 14 January 1507, Juana gave birth to her sixth child in Torquemada. The baby was named Catalina in honour of her aunt in England and was baptised in a simple ceremony. But Juana was left in a state of such weakness after the delivery that she shrank more than ever from facing the tasks of a ruler. Open fights were erupting among the nobles as they contrived to advance up the ladder of power, and some strengthened their positions by gathering soldiers around them. The stage was set for a civil war. Simultaneously, a pestilence was reaping a grim harvest upon the plains of Castile, indiscriminately striking down rich and poor alike. Living in constant fear of the mortal disease, the nobles pleaded with the Queen to escape with them from the area of infection, but they received only a vapid stare. Although terrified of catching the contagion, not one among them dared flee from Torquemada lest he be accused of abandoning his queen.

Not until April did Juana stir herself, when she descended on the local church to oversee the movement of Philip's body. Her ministers implored her to move that day to the nearby and larger town of Palencia, but she declared that it was unseemly for a poor widow to be seen moving among the populace. Henceforth, she affirmed, her preoccupation would be to flee from the sunshine and seek the darkness. Her goal, she stated, was to go to Granada, where the body of her mother lay. This would also be the final resting place of her dead husband. That night, Juana led her gloomy procession from the village with no clear idea of her destination. Shunning a nearby nunnery, she had the caskets placed in a nearby field beyond the influence of females, whom she had come to abhor from her early days in Brussels. There, in the field under the stars, with candles set on a temporary altar flickering in a fierce wind, she had the double coffin opened. Once again, the macabre ritual was enacted. She studied the decomposed corpse, servants were called to identify the remains, and the two coffins were resealed. Only then did the cortège proceed on its way, a dark shadow among shadows.[1]

In the darkness, Juana spied a farm which caught her fancy and determined to commandeer it – disregarding the interests of her retinue, who were left to

---

[1] This image of Juana standing in the windswept field at night in front of a temporary altar is famously illustrated by Francisco Pradilla's painting *Juana la Loca*, which resides in the Prado museum in Madrid.

search for lodgings in the miserable hamlet of Hornillos that boasted only twenty-eight hovels. Many of her despairing courtiers sought a haven in nearby Palencia. Juana wanted her father to find everything in Castile just as he had left it. To this end, the next day she summoned her council members from Palencia and dismissed all those who had been Philip's appointees, thereby freeing her government from the influence of the Flemish fortune-hunters. Thereafter Juana was to emerge less and less frequently, seeking to remain in the shadows. The unexpected flashes of reasoning which lit up her mind were short-lived and as few as the beads on her rosary.

Yet some innate spirit of patriotism lingered in the hearts of the people, and this somehow held the crumbling nation together. In spite of foreign meddling and native ambitions, the throne did not collapse beneath the weight of the problems it faced. By an odd quirk, Juana's stubbornness became an obstacle to the rapacious sharks who surrounded her and, by her aloofness, suspicion and avoidance of decisions, the integrity of her kingdom was somehow preserved. Fortunately, the able Cisneros, ever alert, was by her side to seize the torch when she faltered, shrewdly stepping aside when he sensed Juana could grasp the reins. Held in her trembling hands, the flickering flame of nationhood was miraculously nursed along until it could be passed back to Fernando, and eventually to Charles, to cast its glow upon the empire.

Fernando's departure from Italy was precipitated by a rumour that Emperor Maximilian was planning to march on Spain at the head of an army to ensure that Queen Juana would be obeyed, but mainly to secure the succession of his grandson Charles. Fernando had failed to meet the Pope while in Italy, and having settled the affairs of the Kingdom of Naples he departed Ostia on 4 June with sixteen galleons. Don Gonzalo prepared to follow him a few days later, but first he had to settle his debts by selling some property and estates, and also hold a sumptuous outdoor party for all his loyal Neapolitan and Spanish friends. When his ship finally weighed anchor a week after the King, the throng on the quayside made it nigh impossible to move, and many of the ladies openly wept at his departure.

Before leaving Ostia, Don Gonzalo wrote Pedro a short letter.

Ostia, Naples, 8 July 1507

My Dear Pedro,

I have just received your letter of six weeks ago and was keen to pen you a reply before I depart from here in a few days. My first reaction to your news that you are all (and I mean you and your family, Mat, Francesca and the brave Claudia, Abel and his wife) are emigrating to La Española was incredulity. But the more I think about it, the more I can understand your reasoning. Firstly, you have had much family sadness in recent years with the death of Sara at a tender age, of your mother's husband Agustín and, I now learn, your uncle Joshua during the Cardona earthquake. This, incidentally, also badly damaged my family home at Montilla when several sections of the castle wall collapsed. And, of course, there was the dastardly murder of your boyhood friend, Yazíd, who, you'll remember, I managed to save from the galleys all those years ago. So all this makes a change of life and a change of scene understandable.

But equally so is the suffering Spain has recently endured, with years of famine followed by the devastating floods two years ago. Now, I hear, plague is again ravaging Castile and spreading its deathly mantle across the land. I hope you manage to depart before it reaches you.

So what can I say? To remember with affection and gratitude the services which you have rendered me, your comradeship and friendship and, of course, to hold in esteem your charming mother, Miriam, and your beautiful wife, Raquel; and to remember the prodigious strength of Mat and the resourcefulness of Francesca, who together saved you on the brink of death from the crypt at Canevare. So many memories to cherish. With a tear in my eye, I send you all my best wishes for the future.

There is one last thing I can do for you, Pedro. I attach a testimonial which you can use as a means of introducing yourself to Nicolás de Ovando in Santo Domingo. I met him many years ago and he struck me as a sound man.

Yours affectionately,

Gonzalo Fernández

Lately commander, Spanish Forces in Italy

To whom it may concern:

This letter constitutes a letter of introduction and a testimonial for Don Pedro Togeiro de Tedula of Vélez Blanco, Andalucía. I have known Pedro since he was fourteen years of age when I rescued him from the hands of Tomás de Torquemada in Jaén. I have followed his adventures ever since and shared the fortunes, tribulations and disappointments which he and his family have enjoyed or endured over many years. I was honoured one snowy winter's day some years ago to attend Pedro's wedding with his young bride, Raquel, in Vélez Blanco and I will long treasure memories of that day.

Pedro is one of those people who have the knack of being in the right place at the right time, and he was on hand to save Queen Isabel and King Fernando from the fire which nearly took their lives in the months before the fall of Granada in 1492. He was also on hand to find Christopher Columbus's crucial maps of the Ocean Sea, lying in the street in Seville, just a few weeks before his departure from Palos and, fortuitously, he was there to join the crew of the *Pinta* on that historic voyage.

On his return, in recognition of his saving their lives, the monarchs honoured him with a knighthood and appointed him as their ambassador to Morocco, where he represented Spain's interests well in difficult circumstances. Later, I was delighted when he joined me in Italy as my aide-de-camp. Here, he served me with loyalty and distinction, incurring the loss of his hand to Tuscan partisans while en route to Flanders with the Pope's son, Jofré, with a wedding gift for Princess Juana and the Duke of Burgundy. Lastly, since returning to Spain he has been administering the estate of Juan Chacón, the 1st Marquis of Vélez Blanco.

Pedro Togeiro speaks Arabic fluently, as well as good Italian and some French. He is resourceful, totally dependable and reliable, honest and discreet. For all these reasons and many more, I can commend him to you.

Signed,

Gonzalo Fernández of Córdoba

Lately Commander-in-Chief, Spanish forces in Italy

Grand Master (designate) of the Order of Santiago

Count of Montilla and Aguilla

Duke of Terranova

By midsummer, the packing up at Vélez Blanco was well underway. Everyone had a task. Pedro was little help in lugging boxes and crates around, so he sorted out the paperwork, winding up his work for Juan Chacón, arranging the sale of his and Miriam's family house, as well as the house across the small square where Mat, Francesca, Carlos and Claudia were living, and boxing up writing materials he would need in the future. Fortunately, there were ready buyers for the two houses, since so many craftsmen and artisans had arrived in the town to work on the new castle on the hilltop above them which was progressing apace. Miriam, with six-year-old Eva's help, concentrated on the household items such as pots and pans, crockery, cutlery, her wools and dyes, needles, cottons, buttons and all the domestic minutiae which might be in short supply in the new colony. Mat took responsibility for crating and transportation. Luckily, every week wooden crates arrived from Cartagena by wagon bearing construction material for the castle, and many of these he was able to commandeer. Abel took charge of all the iron tools which would be vital for farming and cultivation, such things as spades, hoes, picks, ploughshare tips, buckets and chains... the list was endless. Since every crate had to be manhandled onto the ships at Seville, Abel ensured that they were not overfilled. Smaller carpentry tools, such as hammers, chisels, squares, smoothing planes, saws of all sizes, files, screws and nails, Antonio and Behechio assembled between them and boxed them up under Mat's supervision. A mounted grinding stone was not overlooked. Lastly, Francesca and Claudia sorted out what furniture was feasible to take from the two houses. Altogether it was a huge task, but by August it was nearly done.

En route to Spain, Fernando arrived at the small port of Savona in Liguria to meet his former arch-rival, Louis XII of France, face to face for the first time. Their conversation was relaxed and friendly. In due course, they were joined by Gonzalo, who was fêted like a hero at the banqueting table of the French sovereign against whom he had battled for so many years. Louis declared that Gonzalo was a man of such mental and physical superiority that he was justly accorded the title 'great'. It was with genuine sadness that eventually Fernando set sail for Spain.

Gonzalo left for Spain a few days later. Louis refused to let Gonzalo kiss his hand and, as he departed, the King took from around his neck a massive gold chain of exquisite workmanship and presented it to the Spaniard. In the last days of July, nearly the whole of the Spanish nobility – so disdainfully treated by Fernando since the death of Isabel – went to welcome Gonzalo when he arrived in Valencia. So many gifts had been bestowed on Gonzalo by knights, great lords, ladies and citizens of every class, that there was more than enough to savour for every soldier and sailor who had served with him, down to the very last man. Not one of them entered the city for the banquet on foot, such was the reception for his victorious *tercios*.

A few days later, when all had recovered from the voyage and the celebrations, they marched northwards in fine order to the court in Burgos, with the cities and their citizens on the way opening their gates and their houses to welcome the thousands who followed their commander. Never before or since has Spain seen such an army of splendour, such fine clothes, such burnished armour or such headdresses adorned by such gold emblems. The common people applauded them, chanting the words of a song composed for the occasion: 'Gonzalo the Greatest, not the Great!'

Back in Hornillos, Juana's condition remained the same. In early August, the church caught fire, and only by a miracle was Philip's body saved from the resulting inferno. In a state of agitation, Juana had the coffin placed in her room and would not let it out of her sight. Word then arrived from Valencia of the arrival of Fernando. On 24 August, in the middle of the night, Juana renewed her funeral odyssey. The coffin of Philip was reopened once again for inspection, and four horses hitched to the hearse. The monks began their doleful dirges, the bishops mounted their mules, and with the Queen in her black mourning garb they set off once more in the darkness. When the first glimmer of early dawn lit the eastern sky, they stopped and did not resume until well after sunset. Eventually the group reached Tórtoles de Esgueva, thirty miles on across the plateau. There they awaited the arrival of Fernando.

Finally – *finally* – Juana and Fernando met. After the years in Flanders when Philip prevented Isabel's emissaries seeing her daughter, and then in Spain when he stopped her meeting her father when he was only miles away, at last father and daughter were reunited. Surrounded by many nobles who had sheepishly returned to the fold and by the ever-present Archbishop of Toledo, Fernando's cavalcade came to a halt in a swirl of dust before the village inn where Juana waited impatiently. At the sight of her father, she removed her mourning hood and rushed to him. With tears coursing down his cheeks, he gathered her in his arms. He had not seen her for five years. Hand in hand, they disappeared into the King's lodgings. After much uncertainty as to where to establish their courts, they settled on Santa María del Campo, a small village halfway back towards Burgos. Here a Mass was held for the repose of the soul of Philip. One year had elapsed since his death, and his mortal remains had yet to find peaceful interment.

Fernando had returned from Italy with the coveted gift from Pope Julius II of a Cardinal's hat for Cisneros. The elaborate plans for the ceremony to mark his attainment of this exalted office were thrown into chaos when Juana refused to allow the ceremony to take place in the church where Philip's body lay. In her confused mind, life and death, black and white, darkness and sunshine, should never meet. Instead, the investiture was held in a small, undistinguished village a few miles away. Soon afterwards, with Fernando travelling by day and Juana by night, they reached Burgos. Speedily and efficiently, Fernando took hold of the affairs of state as appointed Governor and Administrator of Castile, patching up and overlooking his differences with the grandees who had earlier deserted him. But one man he singled out with great harshness. The Marqués of Priego, the nephew of the Gran Capitán, who had seized and held prisoner one of the King's officers, was sent against his will to raze the fortress of Montilla, the magnificent castle south of Córdoba which, in its number of its towers and splendour, rivalled Ávila in Castile. Montilla was the family seat of Don Gonzalo himself. This wilful and barely disguised act of malice, aimed at his loyal subject who had given him a life-time's service, would further sully Fernando's crumbling reputation.

In the autumn, Fernando left and went south to Córdoba and Seville, leaving Juana near Burgos. But in no time he received reports from his courtiers there that although the Queen lived quietly she had not once changed her shift nor touched or washed her face. They reported that she slept and ate on the floor in darkness, shunning her many attendants. Evidently sufficiently shocked to believe that it merited comment, they reported that she relieved herself 'very frequently and in a manner never before seen in any other person…' When Fernando saw her next, she appeared before him a walking wraith, and in a shocking state of tatters and filth.

What lay ahead for the deranged Queen was one of the saddest and most wretched episodes of self-imposed solitude witnessed in European history.

For months on his return, Don Gonzalo followed the royal court around, acting as equerry to Fernando's new young queen, Germaine. As the weeks passed, everyone began to take him for granted as just another presence in the royal court. This is precisely what the King wanted, as the Gran Capitán was gradually relegated to the background and excluded from discussions of state and national importance. With his wife, Doña María, and daughters still in Genoa, Fernando offered Gonzalo the Dukedom of Loja, a town near Granada which had been the scene of one of Gonzalo's early triumphs during the Granada wars when he led the assault on the then Muslim fortress. Don Gonzalo felt utterly humiliated and deflated when the King rescinded the promise he made in Naples of making Gonzalo the Grand Commander of the Order of Santiago. Little choice remained to him but to accept the Dukedom of Loja, and he consoled himself in his retirement from active service by being able to escape the suffocating atmosphere in court and return to the place of his birth, his beloved Andalucía.

By early September, Pedro and his family and friends were ready to leave. Mat had already transported several wagonloads of their belongings to Cartagena. All that remained was to say their sad farewells to their many friends and neighbours in Vélez Blanco and be on their way. Their new life beckoned.

XXXVI: A New Land and a New Life

September 1507

The party of thirteen, with their boxes and crates of belongings, arrived in Sanlúcar at the mouth of the Guadalquivir River in the middle of the month, the coastal transport ship from Cartagena having battled against strong westerly winds most of the way. Eighteen ships were already at anchor in the wide shallow estuary. Smaller boats were plying back and forth in the slow and arduous task of provisioning them for the journey. Pedro's coaster from Cartagena anchored among them while he and his party were rowed ashore. Pedro renewed his acquaintance with Juan Quintero, who was commander of the fleet of ships, and he directed Pedro to the port burgomaster's office. Pedro paid him the passage fee for the thirteen of them and for suitable accommodation for the ladies and children.

He learnt that the ship which they would be sailing on was to be the *Santo Cristo*, a 150-ton caravel, a little bigger than the *Pinta* on which he sailed with Martín Pinzón in 1492. The *Santo Cristo* had also been constructed in Palos but had been modified to take some forty fee-paying passengers, plus it had wider hatches for loading larger cargo into the hold. Pedro and Mat returned to the coaster, leaving the rest of the party ashore with the task of finding accommodation until the fleet's departure. In the calm waters of the estuary, the boat manoeuvred alongside the *Santo Cristo* and, with a block and tackle affixed to end of the latter's mainsail's stout yardarm, the dozens of crates and boxes were swung across to the bigger ship and lowered into the hold. With Mat supervising, they were stacked carefully and secured in place. Satisfied that all was ready for their journey, Pedro paid off the captain of the coaster and he and Mat returned ashore. They had a week or two to enjoy what pleasures the busy port might offer.

It was not until 2 October that all was ready for departure. The late afternoon offshore breeze was ideal. With the ship's pilot, Cristóbal García, keeping the ship in the centre of the channel and clear of the other ships which were all in different stages of making headway, he steered a course west-south-west. An hour later, after all three sails – foresail, mainsail and mizzen – were fully raised and they were well clear of land, the *Santo Cristo* turned to the south-west, taking the lead from Juan Quintero in his ship, *La Concepción*.

In four days, the fleet reached Gomera, the customary port of call in the Canaries for voyages to the Indies. There, they refilled their water casks and took on fresh meat, eggs and vegetables. In two more days, they were underway, again heading south-west. Gomera lay at a latitude of 29°N and Santo Domingo, their destination, lay further south at 18°N. For a couple of weeks, they followed the Canaries Current to the south-west until their quadrants showed the height of the midday sun (local time) was also 18°N. Then, by turning due west to join the current[1] which circulated clockwise around the Ocean Sea, they would reach La Española or strike a nearby landfall. This was by now well-practised navigation, and apart from the risk of severe storms it had proved reliable. With these ocean currents flowing at some two nautical miles an hour, propelled by the counter rotation of the Earth, the fleet, aided by the wind in their sails, could expect to make landfall in the Indies in four to six weeks.

With the womenfolk and children accommodated below deck and the menfolk and boys above deck in the low open space below the quarterdeck and the captain's cabin, Pedro and his companions were comfortable enough. For Raquel, it was infinitely better than the nightmarish journey she had had ten years before, when she accompanied Juana to Flanders. In Pedro's case, it was a pleasure not to be an innocent cabin boy suffering the rough edge of the bo'sun's voice or the chiding and bullying of the rest of the crew.

It was towards the end of November that 'Land ahoy!' was shouted by a sailor on lookout at the bows. Everyone rushed onto the deck to see a line of white clouds in the far distance and the faint tops of mountains on the horizon. It was the presence of clouds, birds, floating debris or often a change in sea colour that gave a clue to the proximity of land. As they got closer, the distinctive profile of the mountain of Puerto Rico came into view, with its single 4,500-foot peak rising in the centre of the island. As the fleet approached the seventy-mile-wide Mona Passage between Puerto Rico and La Española, the ships divided, with eight continuing along the northern coast to Puerto Plata and the remainder passing through the straits into the Caribbean and then westwards along the south coast of La Española, reaching Santo Domingo half a day's journey on.

All the passengers crowded the ship's starboard rail, watching with growing excitement as their new homeland slid by ten miles away, with Antonio and Behechio clambering halfway up the rigging to get a better view. As the ships arrived off Santo Domingo in the early evening of their final day on board, five weeks after leaving Gomera, the ten ships lowered their yardarms and furled their mainsails to lose headway. Soon the strong outflow

---

[1] The North Equatorial Current

from the River Ozama abated, and as the tide turned the ships raised their foresails and lateen-rigged mizzen sails and moved slowly into the river, allowing the current to carry them forward to their riverside moorings alongside the burgeoning city.

'Look, Papa!' shouted Antonio as they entered the river. 'There's the Ozama Fortress.' Pointing to his right, he added, 'And there's Señor Tostado's new house!'

The Taino lad, Behechio, was equally excited, and with a huge, toothy grin kept saying the words Antonio had taught him: 'I'm home, I'm home, I'm home.'

Indeed, Antonio was right; it was the lawyer's house. It stood in an open space half a mile from the new city square. Close by, the foundations of a Dominican convent were being set out. Beyond Tostado's fine coral limestone house was a cluster of square timber huts roofed with palm fronds. These fronds were split along the central stalk and laid horizontally one over the other. Such roofs would last fifteen years before needing replacement. These clusters of huts accommodated most of the population of 300 in the city, as well as the immigrants destined for other parts of the island.

With great skill, the ships lost headway in the river. Mooring ropes were thrown ashore by the crews, and the first five ships moored against the wooden staging that formed the quay. A loud cheer went up from crew and passengers that they had arrived safe and sound, and this was answered in the city by those who had congregated in the Plaza España overlooking the quayside as news of the imminent arrival of the ships had spread. The remaining five ships patiently waited their turn and then tied up against the first five – there simply was not enough quayside to accommodate them all. But no matter; passengers and crew could all go ashore, and the outer ships would be unloaded when they could be warped into place against the quay in a few days time. It had all been done before.

Francisco Tostado was there to welcome Pedro and the others ashore. The portly, well-dressed middle-aged lawyer embraced everyone cordially, ruffling Antonio's hair. He had taken a liking to the effervescent youngster earlier in the year. Using some of the Taino language which he had learnt, Antonio introduced Behechio to him. Francisco replied in the same native language. He was one of the few Spaniards who could speak a little of the local language. The seventeen-year-old Behechio was now almost full-grown, and although sturdily built he was no taller than Antonio and barely reached Pedro's chest.

The lawyer led them through the port gateway into the city and then up the zigzag path to the Plaza España, with its view across the river to the decaying remains of Bartolomé Columbus's earlier fort. Most of the city's residents, it seemed, were there. Several four-wheeled wagons drawn by yoked pairs of long-horned oxen stood in the square, ready to collect the ships' cargoes which were already being unloaded onto the quayside. Fifty or more Tainos, barefoot but clothed by orders of the late Queen Isabel, all tiny by comparison with their Spanish overseers, laboured with the boxes and crates up the zigzag path to the square. Antonio and Behechio stayed behind with Mat to see the party's belongings safely ashore.

In the Plaza España stood a very solid-looking covered wagon. Six Spanish soldiers in steel helmets and upper body armour, and bearing pikes and swords, guarded it jealously, eyeing suspiciously anyone who took more than a passing interest in it.

'Why the guards?' asked Pedro.

'It's gold from the Bonao mines,' whispered the lawyer. 'It's this year's output. It's going to be loaded onto the ships for their return to Spain.'

'How much is there?' asked Raquel.

'Shhh, I'll tell you later,' was the guarded reply she received.

Francisco Tostado fitted the ladies into a horse-driven chaise and led the rest of the party on foot out through the square, past Nicolás de Ovando's house on the left, past the partly built Government House opposite, past the fine home of Francisco de Garay, with the Hospital of San Nicolás a short distance beyond up the slope. All the while, the lawyer kept up an endless commentary about the developments in the new city. Within minutes, the party arrived at the lawyer's second house, located a short walk further on, where they would stay for several days. The governor, Nicolás de Ovando, was in another part of the island, but they would make his acquaintance soon.

Although rather cramped in the lawyer's house, they were comfortable enough and immensely grateful for Francisco's generous hospitality. So, for several days, they had a chance to look around the city; to enjoy the balmy tropical warmth, the sea breeze and the towering white clouds of the late afternoon in the deep blue sky; to walk through the grassy fields and among trees decked with huge, plate-sized leaves, with everywhere so green and verdant; to hear the ring of iron striking stone carrying across the city from the quarry beyond its northern boundary; to witness the toil of the friendly Tainos, labouring to transport dressed stone through the streets; to sample the local coconuts, yams, plantains, squashes, breadfruit, maize and mangoes, and the flat-baked cassava bread made from grated yucca root; but, above all, to get caught up in the pure dynamism and vitality of the island. It was no wonder Francisco Tostado spoke with such pride about the new colony.

'Señor Tostado,' said Raquel. 'You were very coy earlier on about telling us about the wagon of gold. Why was that? Is much gold found on the island?'

'Yes, Raquel, more and more. The most important mines are in the central part of the island, which is called Cibao. It's a Taino name. The records are scarce for the earlier years, but in the last three years nearly 50,000 ounces of valley gold have been found.'[2]

'Heavens, that much!' she exclaimed. 'But what's valley gold?' she asked, looking puzzled.

'It's how the gold is found. It's not found in veins, but as grains and nuggets in the soft ground along the floors of the valleys, where over the years it's been washed down from the hills on each side. Men are searching for the source of the gold, but as yet they haven't found it. But they're still looking. One day someone will be very rich! But the working conditions in the open, muddy pits are terrible, and not many of our people stick it for long.'

'What happens to the gold?'

'It's melted down into ingots and sent to Seville in Spain.'

'All of it?'

'Yes, all of it. Well…'

He opened a drawer in his desk and took out a smooth nugget of pure gold the size of a bean.

'That is, all except this!' he chuckled. 'Don't worry, I'm sure you'll find small nuggets of gold on your new land, just like this.'

Francisco Tostado passed to Pedro the deeds of the two concessions which Juana de Torres had bequeathed him and, for good measure, Pedro gave him a copy of Don Gonzalo's testimonial to pass to Nicolás de Ovando. Francisco unrolled a map of part of the island which Bartolomé Columbus had carefully drawn three years before. It was an exquisite piece of work. Tracing his finger over the map, Francisco described the geography of the island.

'As you can see,' he started, 'La Española possesses three main rivers. One river, the Yaque, flows north-westwards past Santiago to the Ocean Sea. A second, the River Ozama, flows out into the Caribbean, here at Santo Domingo. In fact, the island's almost cut in two by these two rivers. Both start in a flat, wide plain around the mining town of La Vega, where the soft clays seem very thick. Even the gold mines twenty or thirty feet deep don't seem to "touch bottom", so to speak. The Indians also obtain amber from these clays, and there's a lot for sale in the city here. You'll see, when you travel across the island, that the central valley has been largely cleared of forest by the Tainos using their traditional "slash and burn" methods, and many hillsides have also been cleared in the same manner for timber.'

What Juana de Torres had told Pedro in Seville before about the locations of the concessions which Christopher Columbus had granted her and her brother Antonio proved to be wrong. The lawyer's plans showed these to be much larger than she had described, and they were conjoined. In effect, there

---

[2] Now known as placer or alluvial gold.

was one farmstead, not two, although Francisco Tostado had drawn up separate legal deeds in case Pedro chose to split them at a later date. This landholding lay on the right bank of the Rio Yaque, two miles downstream of the new villa of Santiago. It lay between two tributary streams two miles apart, so the land enjoyed water on three sides. The farmstead extended back a similar distance from the river through grassy pastures to the wooded slopes of the adjacent hills. A Taino village lay nearby. Overall, the concessions totalled over 2,500 acres. Some accommodation on the farmstead existed, but Francisco was not sure what it comprised. That remained to be discovered. Stone and brick houses were being constructed in Santiago, where most of the Spanish settlers chose to live.

Two weeks after arriving in La Española, Pedro and his party set off. Horses as yet being few in number and expensive, he had bought five mules in the city market as well as several sturdy donkeys, and with four ox wagons and their drovers they set off into the island's interior with much excitement and anticipation. Behechio could barely contain himself, since he would return to his family near La Vega on the way. While in Spanish terms Pedro was the legal owner of this holding, he was sensible enough to realise the land had been in the hands of the Tainos for centuries, and that the deeds which he had been given by Francisco Tostado really conferred on him the stewardship and not ownership of the land. He determined very early on that this would be the basis of his tenure.

Travelling at a leisurely speed dictated by the yoked oxen, they passed through the new villas of Bonao and La Vega, the main centres of gold production, stopping to return Behechio to his family, who insisted on roasting a pig to celebrate his safe return from Spain. Two days later, they reached Santiago, a hundred miles overall from Santo Domingo. They entered the new villa. Like the other new settlements in the central region of Cibao, it had a central plaza with a dozen or so buildings set around it and space left for a church. These single-storey houses had been roughly fashioned using local stone and poorly fired brick. Dozens of wooden huts with palm-frond roofs lay beyond them. All lay within a bank and ditch offering no more than token defence, quite unlike the small fortress at La Vega. Dozens of people were milling in and around the square, the men mostly unshaved and scruffy, the women shabbily dressed and barefoot, and the children filthy and barely clothed. An air of resignation, if not despair, pervaded the small town of 100 or so souls. Santiago had all the appearance of a frontier mining town, and was a world apart from the elegance of Santo Domingo.

Pedro and Mat approached an elderly man sitting on a stool in the shade outside one of the more substantial buildings. The man admitted to being the elder of the community, but knew nothing of Pedro's land tenure and was not able to read the deeds which Pedro's showed him by way of evidence of his entitlement. He waved Pedro and Mat perfunctorily in the direction of the Taino village, which Francisco Tostado said existed on or near Pedro's holding. But he suggested as an afterthought that if they intended to stay in the neighbourhood they could make use of three or four cabins which had recently been abandoned by their occupants – who were returning, destitute, to Spain.

Four empty cabins lay beyond the bank and ditch, and everyone set to, to make them habitable. Francesca liked nothing more than rolling up her sleeves and getting stuck in, and in this she was well aided by Claudia, who was devoted to her. With Mat 'holding the fort', Pedro and Abel rode out to survey their farmstead, calling in at their Taino village of Cutupú. Using the little Taino he had learnt from Behechio, Pedro introduced them, and if their reception was not cordial it was at least civil. Over the next couple of weeks, as the new settlers got acquainted with their surroundings, Miriam, Raquel and Francesca and the children broke the ice with the Taino villagers, who were spellbound by them.

It was a month after their arrival when, unannounced, Friar Nicolás de Ovando arrived to welcome Pedro and his party to La Española. He was accompanied by his secretary and four mounted soldiers. The governor of La Española was sixty. Tall and robust, he had a stern countenance and clearly did not suffer fools gladly. But in the cool of the evening, he and his secretary, Friar José Pradera, sat with the newcomers around their dining table brought from Vélez Blanco, and as Ovando's bottles of imported Rioja were downed the Governor relaxed noticeably.

The next morning, he called Pedro, Mat, Abel and Miriam together. He recognised Miriam as being the matriarch of the family group, and understood that no one, not even Pedro, would go against her wise counsel.

'So,' the Governor said to them, 'what have you learnt? What are your plans? You first, Señor Jiménez. You come from farming stock in Galicia, don't you?'

Abel gathered his thoughts for a moment.

'Yes, Father, I do. I like the look of the land here,' he replied. 'There's lots of good pasture and lots of water. I believe that this farm would be ideal for rearing cattle. What's more, there's no pause in the growing season, so there'll always be ample forage for the animals. Moreover, there are enough trees on these meadows to afford the animals shade in the heat of the day.'

'Astute observations, señor. Your ideas seem very sound,' answered the Dominican friar.

'And apart from the beef,' added Miriam, 'there'll be fresh milk for the children, and we can make butter and cheese…'

'And sell it in the m-m-market,' added Mat.

'And there's the leather from their hides,' offered Pedro.

'Yes, so many benefits. So what would you need, Señor Jiménez?' asked Ovando.

'Obviously we need to start with a small herd, including a fine bull! With twenty, in a few years we'd soon have a good-sized herd.'

'That can be arranged. I'll be returning to Spain in the next few months when Diego takes over from me. I'll see that a herd of fine animals is sent over to you, including a lusty bull!'

'And you, Señor Matute. What are your thoughts?'

Mat was very nervous in front of the Dominican priest and could hardly get his words out.

'I'd like to s-s-see us be self-sufficient in f-f-food, apart from the cattle. We need to learn from our T-T-Taino neighbours and harvest yuca roots from the manioc trees to grate cassava flour for bread, and also from m-m-maize. And we could plant olives on the s-s-slopes of the hills up there and make our own oil.'

'The one thing you haven't mentioned, gentlemen, is sugar cane,' said Ovando. 'The King is very keen to see sugar cane grown on this island, as it is in the Canaries.'

'Well, that's something we can consider, too,' answered Pedro. 'And with the amount of land we have here, thanks to Juana de Torres' generosity, we should be able to accommodate arable farming as well as animal husbandry.'

'Excellent gentlemen... and señoras, please forgive me! But it all sounds first rate. Rest assured, I and Diego will give you all the support and encouragement you need. But now, Don Pedro,' he said, turning to Pedro and adopting a serious tone. 'What will be your role?' He did not give Pedro a chance to respond.

'I have a proposition for you, and this is the real reason I came to visit you here. As you will have seen, the villa of Santiago is in a bad state and virtually lawless. It needs knocking into shape, and quickly. Your testimonial from Don Gonzalo comes like manna from Heaven for me. What with your ambassadorial role in Morocco for the Catholic Monarchs, and then your working alongside the Gran Capitán himself in the Italian campaigns – as well as your management of the Vélez Blanco estate for Juan Chacón – you're exactly what I've been looking for to administer this town. Of course, you'll need a governor's residence for you and your family, plus half a dozen good soldiers to ensure the peace, and they'll need a no-nonsense officer to direct them... and who better than you, Señor Matute...? On second thoughts,' Ovando added, assessing the size of the man sitting across the table from him with a mop of fair hair, 'maybe you won't need the soldiers!'

Taken aback, Mat's response caught in his throat. He simply nodded approvingly.

'And, Don Pedro, you'll need someone to act as your intermediary and translator with the Tainos here. Who better than Antonio's young friend in La Vega, Behechio? I'll speak to his father on my return.'

'But if I and my family are to be resident in Santiago, Father,' said Pedro. 'I'll need someone…'

'…someone to run your farm here?' interrupted Ovando.

He seemed to have thought of everything.

'Well,' he continued, 'Abel can be your man, can't he? Who better?'

Who better, indeed? Abel's eyes lit up.

'So what do you say, Pedro? Will you be the Mayor of Santiago, and govern the new villa in my and Diego's name?'

'Yes, I will, Father,' replied Pedro without hesitation.

'Excellent,' Ovando replied, relaxed and smiling. 'But do please call me Nicolás. You and your family must come and be my guests in Santo Domingo. There's much we need to arrange with Diego. Do come soon.'

Historical Postscript

Whether or not Don Pedro Togeiro of Tudela, mayor designate of Santiago, was aware of it when he settled in La Española, Spain was in a poor shape: exhausted, battered and bruised. Tens of thousands of country folk had perished in the four-year famine which had devastated the land, and hundreds of thousands had perished in the plague which followed in 1507. Thousands more had fled Spanish shores during the expulsion of the Muslims in 1502. All told, the population of Spain had declined by more than a third.

Throughout their dual reign, Isabel and Fernando had held in check the power and independence of the grandees and nobles of Castile. Then Philip of Austria landed in Galicia from Flanders with promises of returning their lost heritage if they supported him in his bid to take over the kingdom. Many did. Juana, being the lawful Queen on the death of Isabel, and in a rare burst of sanity, revoked Philip's changes, bringing the grandees and nobles back to heel. Sanity prevailed. By good fortune, she had saved Spain from virtual dissolution.

But Spain was rudderless. Fernando was consumed by his marriage to eighteen-year-old Germaine, hoping that she would produce for him a male heir for the thrones of Castile and Aragón. As Governor and Administrator of Castile, so designated by Isabel in her will, he chose to keep Juana, the legitimate Queen of Castile, out of harm's way in the palace in Tordesillas. She would remain there for the rest of her life. Often forcibly restrained, sometimes forcibly fed, she occasionally appeared from the life of solitude and darkness in which she chose to live to meet her father or her son, Charles, or to sign state papers. But such glimmers of lucidity lasted just days, and the sad Queen soon reverted to her tragic way of life. As so often had happened in earlier years, Spain turned to Cardinal Jiménez de Cisneros, now approaching eighty years of age, as Regent to steer Castile through these troubled times. This he did with his customary astuteness and incisiveness. Cisneros died in November 1517, not having set eyes on the new king whom he had placed on the throne of Spain.

In November 1515, Don Gonzalo Fernández of Córdoba was taken ill in Loja and carried to Granada, where he died in his home in the Plaza de San

Juan de la Cruz.[1] On his deathbed, he expressed deep remorse over his hasty action thirteen years earlier in despatching King Federico's fourteen-year-old son, the Duke of Calabria, to Spain after capturing Taranto, and bitterness at Fernando's broken promises in not awarding him the Grand Mastership of the Order of Santiago. So passed away Spain's greatest military commander, who had served Spain loyally from the time he was a fourteen-year-old page in the court of Queen Isabel. Within three months, Fernando also died, not having secured a surviving male heir through Germaine. Twice widowed, Germaine went on to marry the Duke of Calabria.

In 1516, Juana's elder son, the precocious Charles, her recognised heir to the thrones of Castile and Aragón, demanded of Cisneros that he be crowned king as Charles I of Spain, four years before his accession decreed in Isabel's will. Cisneros, worn out and with little more than two years to live, concurred. Two years later, Charles was elected to succeed his grandfather Maximilian as Holy Roman Emperor, taking the title Emperor Charles V.

French-speaking Charles visited Spain just a few times in his forty-year reign to see his melancholic mother Juana in Tordesillas. Just once, in 1522, a handful of nobles in Castile, angry and bitter at being governed by an absent and profligate Charles, rose up against their Flemish overlords and implored Juana to emerge from her solitude as the reigning Queen to recover and rule her impoverished kingdom. But it was not to be. Within weeks, Juana's enthusiasm for their cause waned and she returned to the darkness. Racked by malignant sores, the Queen died at the age of seventy-five in 1555. Her emaciated body was laid in the Monastery of Santa Clara, next door to the palace where she had lived the greater part of her life. In 1573, her remains were interred in Granada alongside her husband and parents.

Charles died at the age of forty-eight in the monastery at Yuste in northern Extremadura where, physically worn out, he had retired two years before, after relinquishing the Imperial Crown. He outlived his mother by just three years. In his time, Spain effectively lost its independence to become part of the Austrian Empire. Such was Charles' profligate expenditure on incessant wars against the Turks in the Balkans, the French in Italy and the Muslims in North Africa, that he impoverished Spain's coffers to four times the value of gold and silver by then arriving in abundance from the New World.[2]

---

[1] This house, with a commemorative plaque, is situated alongside the Convento Carmelitas Descalzas. The building is dilapidated and in a sorry state. One hopes that it will be restored by the state as a historic monument.

[2] Nothing illustrates this more than the collection of lavish body armour on display in the Armoury of the Royal Palace in Madrid, including that for his hunting dog.

His son Philip II took on the mantle of King of Spain and strove diligently to manage its vast empire. By then, Cortés had conquered Mexico, Pizarro had marched into Peru and Mendoza had headed south into the vast new continent to found the city of Buenos Aires. In North America, De Soto had explored as far as the Mississippi, and in the Pacific Magellan had discovered the Philippines, named after the King. But the empire had simply grown too large to govern effectively, and from around 1590 – two years after the loss of Philip's grand expeditionary fleet that had set out to conquer England – it was prey to other countries with colonial ambitions, notably Holland and England.

By then, Spain was inextricably linked with Flanders and the Low Countries. As might be said of the Norman invasion of Saxon England in 1066, the House of Austria invigorated Spain with new art, architecture and culture. But on the downside, as European history unfolded in the centuries which followed, this link drew the Spanish Low Countries (Belgium and the Netherlands) into the bitter and bloody rivalry between Catholicism and Protestantism during the Reformation and the Thirty Years War.

So was Isabel and Fernando's pursuit of destiny fulfilled? Sadly, the answer must be 'no'. Although the illustrious monarchs made a number of cardinal errors, such as the expulsion of the Jews in 1492 and of the Muslims ten years later, and foolishly expanding the rights of the sheep drovers to the detriment of the impoverished peasants tied to the land, it was the series of tragic family deaths in just three years which broke Isabel's heart and deprived Spain of its rightful heirs. One or other of Juan, Isabel or Miguel would have united Castile and Aragón, or even the whole of Iberia with Portugal. As it was, following Isabel's death in 1505, Spain hung on grimly through some difficult years, now historically largely overlooked and forgotten, until the accession of Charles, who ruled Spain from afar as part of the German-based Holy Roman Empire. Sadly, the Spain of Isabel and Fernando, proud and independent and on the verge of greatness twenty years before, would be transmuted into a fiefdom of continental Europe.

Appendix A: La Española

La Española is by far the oldest of the Spanish colonies in the Americas, having had Spanish settlements as early as 1494 (cf. Cuba 1511; Mexico 1521; Peru 1531; Ecuador 1534; Argentina 1539). *La Isla Española*, to give it its original Colombian name, comprises the present-day republics of Haiti and the Dominican Republic (DR). It lies between Cuba and Puerto Rico, 500 miles across the Caribbean from Venezuela. To the east, the Leeward and Windward Islands curve around clockwise to nearly reach South America and enclose the Caribbean Sea. Haiti forms the western end of La Española and makes up about one-third of it. Although in Columbus's time La Española referred to the whole island, this note is essentially about the Dominican Republic, which is about 125 miles east–west and 75 miles north–south, just a little smaller than Wales. With a population approaching 9 million, it seems crowded. The capital, Santo Domingo, located on the sheltered southern Caribbean coast, has a population of 2.5 million, and Santiago, the second city in the north of the island, around 1 million. The island encompasses rain forest, mountain ranges reaching 10,400 feet, mangrove swamps and traditional white palm-bordered beaches. Ethnically, the population is essentially Negroid, although some vestiges of the original Tainos population are still evident in people's faces.

Christopher Columbus first landed on La Española in 1492 during the first of his four voyages to the New World. Then, on Christmas Eve, the largest of his three ships, the *Santa María*, foundered on a sandbank and was lost. As his two smaller ships, the *Pinta* and *Niña*, were unable to accommodate the large crew of the *Santa María*, Columbus was forced to leave behind some forty of them with sufficient provisions to sustain themselves and build a fort. He returned there within a year on his second voyage with seventeen ships and 1,500 crew and passengers, but no trace of men or the fort were found, save the *Santa María*'s iron anchor. The Taino chief, Guacanagarí, whom Columbus had befriended on his first voyage, told him that the local Ciguayos, more warlike than the Tainos, had killed the Spaniards a couple of months before for stealing and molesting their women.

In the following year, 1594, as the Spanish settlers moved across the island, there was a pitched battle with the Indians on a hillside (now called Santo Cerro) in the centre of the island, but the Spanish arquebuses and raw steel prevailed over the Stone Age Tainos, who were enslaved. A mile away, the Spanish used their captives to build a stronghold which became the first proper settlement in the New World. This old settlement of La Vega, set around the brick and stone fort with two round stone bastions on opposite corners, has been subject to an archaeological excavation.

The northern Atlantic coast of La Española, like that of Cuba, is fringed by coral reefs. This did not prevent Columbus forming a settlement twenty miles inland at the western end, close to where Martin Pinzón, captain of the *Pinta*, claimed he had found gold on the first voyage. A circle of cabins was built around a central plaza through which a river flowed, and the community of La Isabela was thus established. However, it had a short life. The south coast of the island was more sheltered, and the large tidal reaches of the River Ozama offered a good anchorage. Columbus soon established a settlement there close to the river mouth, and returned to Spain from his second voyage in 1496 with some gold from the hinterland and many slaves.

He returned to La Española on his third voyage in 1498 with just five ships. Although a brilliant sailor and navigator, his administration of the island was disastrous, and Isabel and Fernando had little option but to appoint governors from Spain to administer the growing colonial population. Even these were not that successful, and Rodriguez Fonseca was removed from his post after sending Christopher Columbus and his brothers back to Spain in chains for fomenting discord. This was too much for the monarchs. Francisco de Bobadilla, a highly experienced administrator, followed Fonseca, and during his term of office Bartolomé Columbus, Christopher's younger and faithful brother, founded a colony on the left bank of the river. Nothing remains today of this wooden fort, although its location on a low bluff overlooking the river is outlined in a park. Christopher Columbus continued to believe that the island of La Española was his personal domain, and enjoyed privileges in land and a percentage of the gold found; although by now Isabel and Fernando had opened up the wider exploration of the New World to other explorers without interference from 'the Admiral of the Ocean Sea'. Nevertheless, they gave him the right to assign land to members of his family and to colonists who agreed to stay and cultivate the land for five years.

The Dominican friar Nicolás de Ovando took over the governorship in 1501 and relocated the burgeoning town to the right bank, thereby abandoning Bartolomé's wooden-built colony. Soon afterwards, in 1502, a hurricane devastated the wooden structures springing up in the new city, and Ovando determined that thereafter all the buildings would be made of stone. This same hurricane in 1502 sunk all but two ships of Antonio de Torres' fleet of thirty-three ships off the coast of Samana on the northern Atlantic coast, taking with it a prize nugget of gold destined for Queen Isabel. The remains of one vessel, the *Concepción*, have been recovered from the sea bed and form the bulk of the Museum of the Atarazaras in Santo Domingo. Who knows? It might well be Antonio de Torres' very ship.

Reconstruction of the city after the hurricane soon got underway, with many fine stone buildings dating from then. A city wall was started, enclosing an area around two-thirds of a mile square. The relocation of the city to the right (west) bank placed the city on higher ground, which rose in a step to a low plateau composed of an ancient coral reef. Colonists and Taino forced labour excavated, cut and dressed the stone from a quarry located outside the northern wall of the city, and this white coral limestone makes up the fabric of most of the very many fine buildings in the city which date from this time. Indeed, the sectioned corals exhibited in the blocks of stones of the capital's buildings would be the envy of many geological collections. The Spanish bishop Geraldini commented on his arrival at Santo Domingo in 1525 that the 'buildings are as tall and beautiful as those in Italy, and the streets, wide and straight, are superior to those of Florence'.

Diego Columbus, Christopher's son, became governor after Ovando in 1508 at the age of twenty-nine. He had been living with his celebrated wife, María de Toledo, in the Ozama Fortress near the mouth of the river, but they moved into their fine new fortified palace overlooking the river on the Plaza España in 1510 on its completion. Building continued apace in the city, especially along a street laid out by Ovando, aptly named Calle de Damas, and it was along this thoroughfare that María and her ladies promenaded to matins on a Sunday morning. The main square, the Plaza España, was bordered by the Government house and treasury; Ovando's house lay directly opposite and the Hospital of San Francisco a short distance away. Space was set aside for the cathedral alongside what is now the Parque Colón, and this was started in 1521.

Being on a wide, tidal river, ships could enter the harbour on the incoming tide to moor just below Diego's palace and leave on the ebb tide to catch the trade winds blowing through the Caribbean. It made a perfect anchorage, attracting many mariners, including the piratical Francis Drake, who sacked and burnt the city in 1586, two years before the demise of the Spanish Armada.

But it was not just Santo Domingo that was developed. The island is split in two by a cleft running diagonally across the island with mountains on each side. The Central Highlands to the west comprise smooth-profiled mountains of crystalline rocks, and they rise in steps to a height of over 10,000 feet. Bordering the northern coast is another mountain range where the softer, more recent shales, turbidites and sandstones – folded and distorted by geological movements – provide an attractive, hummocky range of hills reaching over 3,000 feet; and where landslides from tropical downpours have led to sharp, irregular wooded slopes. Between the two sets of mountains lies a central valley opening up south-eastwards to Santo Domingo and the Caribbean coast. This central trough subsided over millions of years as it was filled with sediments eroded from each side to produce a huge thickness of valley alluvium, and it was into these that gold in the form of nuggets or grains settled out from the sluggish rivers traversing this central cleft. These same deposits, once covered by pine forests, accumulated amber formed from resin seeping from the pines, for which the island is renowned.

Gold was the magnet which drew Christopher Columbus to the island, and by the late 1490s various mines (in reality, soggy open pits) in the central valley were producing significant quantities of gold and giving rise to hazardous and dreadful working conditions which cost many lives. Early records are sparse, but between 1503 and 1510 some 10,900 lbs of gold was returned to Seville and some 20,1400 lbs during the next ten years.

'Villas' were established by Nicolás de Ovando around these centres of mining at Santiago, La Vega, Moca and Bonao, and these became the foci of agriculture production, with manioc, maize, cattle rearing, sugar cane and later tobacco.

The small community at Santiago lay on a fertile plain alongside a tributary stream of the Yaque River. This land had been cleared over the years by the Indians. Here, bricks were fired from the river clays and brick and stone buildings erected around a central square along with a governor's house, church and prison. All that remains today of Santiago Viejo (Old Santiago), in a grassy parkland owned by a welcoming octogenarian, Don Pepe, are the walls of a single dwelling and various foundations spread over a couple of acres. La Vega, some fifteen miles to the south and at the apex of a huge flat, fertile plain, was established on lower, sloping ground close to Columbus's hillside battle with the Tainos in 1494, and it took a similar form to the other Ovando villas. The ruins of La Vega Vieja occupy a couple of acres, and constitute the foundations of a rectangular fort with two round bastions with gun ports on opposing corners, and the remains of several other buildings constructed of red brick and black lava. A small museum on the site holds the remains of Colombian and Taino artefacts. Both the original villas of Santiago and La Vega were destroyed in an earthquake in 1562, and modern towns were built a few miles away from the scenes of the devastation. Santiago Viejo lies four miles from the sprawling city and is less easy to find than La Vega Vieja, which is more substantial and well signposted.

The introduction of sugar cane after about 1515 transformed the island, as it did Cuba and the other Caribbean islands. By then, the native populations had been almost eliminated by Spanish conquest, disease and their exportation to Spain as slaves, and were replaced by slaves brought from Africa to work on the sugar plantations.

Appendix B: Chapter Components

I   The End of a Brave Man: April 1494

The graveside of Mohammed Abú Abdalá, El Zagal,
in Tlemcen   p.19

II   Letter from the King

The King invites Pedro and Raquel to attend negotiations
with the Portuguese in Tordesillas   p.24

Arriving home at Vélez Blanco. The family   p.26

III   The Mob: May 1494

Start of journey to Tordesillas   p.33

Capture by the mob at Jódar   p.38

The start of Columbus's second voyage   p.40

Abel returns from Úbeda with a squadron of lancers   p.48

IV   Tordesillas: May–June 1494

Journey across Spain to Toledo   p.51

Treaty of Alcáçovas 1479   p.53

Ávila, Medina del Campo, Tordesillas   p.54

V   The Treaties

Isabel and Ferdinand. Doña Ana of Beamonte   p.60

The negotiations with the Portuguese. Antonio de Torres   p.64

The two treaties   p.67

VI   The Banquet

Meeting the King and Queen at the reception   p.72

The music, the banquet   p.74

Juana shows Pedro and Raquel the palace tapestries   p.78

VII   Yazíd

Pedro and Raquel leave Tordesillas   p.80

Columbus's second voyage: off the coast of Cuba   p.80

	The murder of Yazíd	p.86
	Mat revenges Yazíd's death. The burial	p.89
	Miriam receives a request from Queen Isabel	p.90
VIII	Columbus's Ambitions: January 1495	
	Raquel has baby son, Antonio	p.92
	Letter from Antonio de Torres from the Indies	p.93
	Columbus sends slaves to Spain from La Española	p.94
	Manuel Manzano arrives with message from Don Gonzalo	p.96
IX	Storm Clouds over Italy	
	Charles VIII of France invades Italy	p.99
	Rodrigo Borgia	p.100
	French forces enter Rome	p.103
X	Don Gonzalo Fernández of Córdoba: February 1495	
	Don Gonzalo	p.104
	Pedro and Abel arrive in Granada	p.105
XI	The First Italian Campaign: March 1495	
	Betrothals of Prince Juan and Princess Juana	p.110
	Pedro and Mat reach Málaga and confront a bully	p.110
	They meet Don Gonzalo at his headquarters	p.113
	French forces reach Naples	p.114
	Gonzalo's forces land in Sicily and take Reggio	p.115
	Pedro writes to Raquel	p.116
XII	A Royal Invitation: April 1495	
	Columbus falls out of favour with the monarchs	p.120
	Raquel receives a royal invitation from Ana of Beamonte	p.123
	Gonzalo continues his advance through Italy	p.126
	He takes Laino and then Atella from the French	p.126
XIII	Wedding Bells: August 1496	
	Raquel and Agustín depart overland for Laredo	p.130
	Juana and her party depart by sea for Flanders	p.132
	Juana and her future in Flanders	p.133

XIV   Flanders: October 1496

Columbus returns from his second voyage   p.135

Juana's fleet shelters from storm in England   p.136

Raquel writes to Pedro from Antwerp   p.136

Pedro departs with Jofré for Brussels with wedding gift   p.140

The Pope requests Don Gonzalo's assistance at Ostia   p.140

XV   The Partisans: October 1496

Raquel writes in her diary about the arrival of Philip
    in Brussels   p.141

Juana and Philip are married   p.142

Don Gonzalo enters Rome   p.144

The Spanish take Ostia   p.144

Jofré arrives back in Rome with disturbing news   p.146

Gonzalo's grand triumphant entry into Rome   p.150

XVI   Tuscany: March 1497

Mat prepares to set off to find Pedro   p.151

Letters from Miriam and Antonio de Torres   p.152

Margaret of Austria finally departs Flanders for Spain   p.154

Mat and Francesca learn of Romano Latini in Tuscan village   p.158

XVII   The Cottage in the Clearing

Queen Isabel receives news of her mother's death   p.162

Margaret arrives in Spain and marries Prince Juan   p.162

Juana in Brussels shows Raquel the tapestries of Miriam   p.163

Mat, Francesca and Rosa reach Romano Latini's cottage   p.164

Tina tells them of her ordeal   p.166

Gonzalo in Rome worries about Pedro's fate   p.167

Gonzalo's forces take Rocca Guillermo and he returns
    triumphant to Naples to end the first Italian campaign   p.168

XVIII The Crypt: April 1497

Don Gonzalo's letter to Miriam about Pedro's disappearance   p.170

Mat and Francesca arrive at Canevare and locate Pedro   p.171

Mat, Francesca and Rosa arrive back in Fanano with Pedro   p.175

	Mat writes to Gonzalo that Pedro is safe	p.177
	Pedro has surgery	p.178
XIX	Annus Horribilis: Summer 1497	
	Death of Prince Juan	p.179
	Pedro returns to Sicily and narrates his adventures	p.180
	Raquel assaulted in her room	p.185
XX	The Sorceress	
	Miriam writes to Pedro and Raquel about death of Sara	p.186
	Raquel confides in Ana of Beamonte about her ordeal	p.187
	Raquel leaves Brussels for Rome on coach	p.191
XXI	Scandal and Intrigue in Rome: June 1497	
	Murder on the banks of the Tiber	p.193
	Lucrezia's marriage to Juan Sforza annulled by cardinals	p.193
	César revokes his cardinal's hat	p.195
XXII	Columbus's Third Voyage: Spring 1498	
	Columbus departs from Sanlúcar with five ships	p.196
	He discovers the north coast of a new continent	p.197
	Raquel sets off for Rome with papal delegation	p.198
	During the journey she receives letters from Miriam and Gonzalo	p.199
	She arrives in Florence	p.201
XXIII	The Baron of Montecorvino: June 1488	
	Pedro meets Raquel on the quayside at Messina	p.203
	Over a banquet Raquel learns of Pedro's ordeal at Canevare	p.205
	Gonzalo confers on Pedro the title of Baron of Montecorvino	p.209
	Mat and Francesca to marry	p.210
	Don Gonzalo arrives in Zaragoza. Another royal tragedy	p.211
XXIV	The Granada Revolt: January 1499	
	Ana of Beamonte writes to Raquel about Juana in Flanders	p.213
	Juana gives birth to her first child, Eleanor	p.213
	Mat and Francesca arrive back in Vélez Blanco to a state of unease	p.214

Cisneros precipitates revolt in Granada — p.216

Rebellion breaks out in the Alpujarras — p.216

Agustín joins Pedro Fajardo's forces from Murcia — p.218

Agustín dies at Velefique — p.221

Don Gonzalo's elder brother Alonso killed in battle — p.223

XXV Affairs of State: February 1500

Juana gives birth in Ghent to her second child,
  and first son, Charles — p.224

Prince Miguel dies and Isabel urges Juana to return to Spain — p.225

Don Gonzalo sets off from Málaga for second campaign — p.226

He defeats the Turks at Cephalonia — p.227

Antonio de Torres writes to Pedro about events in La Española — p.228

Juana gives birth in Brussels to a third child, Isabel — p.231

Friar Nicolás de Ovando named new governor of La Española — p.232

XXVI Home at Last: Autumn 1501

Pedro starts to administer the Fajardo estate.
  Mat returns to Italy — p.233

Don Gonzalo starts his campaign at Taranto — p.234

Ana reports on Juana's and Philip's departure from Brussels — p.236

They finally arrive back in northern Spain — p.238

Developments in La Española — p.239

XXVII Nobility and Peasantry

The social and economic situation in Spain — p.241

The importance of sheep — p.243

XXVIII Caribbean Catastrophe: Autumn 1502

The effects of the famine — p.244

Letter from Juana de Torres reporting death of her brother — p.245

Nicolás de Ovando starts reconstruction of Santo Domingo — p.245

Francesca assaulted by French soldiers — p.246

XXIX The Orphan Girl: May 1502

Juana and Philip in Toledo — p.250

	Juana has a fourth child, Fernando, in Madrid, while Philip leaves for France	p.251
	Claudia comes to Francesca's rescue	p.253
	Gonzalo remodels his army into the *tercios* and takes Ruvo	p.256
	Claudia witnesses battle at Cerignola and locates Mat	p.257
	Philip succumbs to fever in Lyon but finally arrives in Brussels	p.259
XXX	**Action on All Fronts: May 1503**	
	Mat and Claudia rescue Francesca at Montecorvino	p.260
	Spanish forces take Castel Nuovo at Naples	p.262
	Columbus starts his fourth voyage to the Caribbean	p.263
	Juana flees from Isabel for Medina de Campo	p.264
	New controls for commerce in the Indies	p.265
	Death of the Pope, Rodrigo Borgia	p.266
	The Spanish and French face each other across the Garigliano River	p.267
XXXI	**Shock Waves across Spain: December 1503**	
	Gonzalo's men rout the French at Garigliano	p.268
	Gonzalo arrests César Borgia	p.269
	Juana departs for Flanders to join Philip	p.270
	Letter from Ana of Beamonte on Juana's conduct	p.270
	Isabel's health continues to worsen	p.271
	Columbus and his brothers arrive back in Spain	p.271
	Isabel dies	p.272
	César Borgia escapes from La Mota but dies in Pyrenees	p.273
XXXII	**Forces Unleashed: 1504**	
	The Carmona earthquake	p.274
	Philip foments unrest among nobles	p.276
	Juana has her fifth child, María	p.277
	Fernando takes a new bride, Germaine	p.277
	Floods across Spain follow the drought	p.278
	Pedro discusses Juana de Torres's offer with family	p.278

XXXIII A Kingdom Pulled Three Ways: October 1505

A rebellion in La Española   p.283

Pedro and Antonio meet Juana de Torres in Seville   p.284

Pedro meets Juan Quintero again, the fleet commander   p.287

Philip and Juana set sail from Middleburg   p.288

Columbus dies in Valladolid, aged fifty-six   p.289

Fernando and Philip confront each other in Castile   p.290

XXXIV Spain in Turmoil: August 1506

Spain in disarray   p.293

Pedro reports back to his family on his trip to La Española   p.293

Philip dies of fever in Burgos   p.298

Fernando leaves with Germaine to meet Gonzalo in Naples   p.299

Juana demands to see Philip's corpse   p.301

XXXV Triumphant Return: January 1507

Juana gives birth to her sixth and last child, Catalina   p.302

Don Gonzalo writes to Pedro with testimonial   p.303

Pedro and family start to pack for departure   p.305

Fernando and Gonzalo meet the French King   p.306

Juana and Fernando meet after five years   p.307

Don Gonzalo humiliated by Fernando   p.308

XXXVI A New Land and a New Life: September 1507

Pedro and his party arrive in Sanlúcar   p.309

They arrive in Santo Domingo   p.310

They settle in Santiago and meet Nicolás de Ovando   p.315

Historical Postscript

A review of later years   p.318

Appendix A: La Española

The geography and history of the island   p.321

Appendix C: Calendar of Historic Events

Year	Month	Isabel and Juana	Gonzalo Fernández	Columbus	Rodrigo Borgia	Elsewhere
1492	Jan					Muslim Granada surrenders to Catholic Monarchs
	May					Jews ordered to leave Spain
	Aug			Sets off on first voyage	Installed as Pope	
1493	Jan	Treaty of Barcelona with France				
	Mar			Returns from Indies		
	May				Bull of 3 May over division of New World	
	Jun				Marriage of Lucrezia and Sforza	

Appendix C: Calendar of Historic Events

Year	Month	Isabel and Juana	Gonzalo Fernández	Columbus	Rodrigo Borgia	Elsewhere
	Aug				Marriage of Jofré and Sancha. Marriage of Juan and M Enrique	
	Sep			Sets off on second voyage		
	Oct					
	Nov			Arrives at Navidad fort		Boabdil leaves Spain El Zagal dies
1494	Jan			Establishes La Isabela on La Española. Twelve ships return to Spain		
	Apr			CC sails on to Cuba		
	May			Arrives in Jamaica	Alfonso crowned King of Naples	
	Jul	Treaties of Tordesillas				
	Aug		Charles VIII invades Italy	CC returns to home at Española	Pope seeks help of Turkish Sultan	

Appendix C: Calendar of Historic Events

Year	Month	Isabel and Juana	Gonzalo Fernández	Columbus	Rodrigo Borgia	Elsewhere
1495	Jan		French ravage Rome. Gonzalo asked to lead Spanish forces			
	Feb		French enter Naples	Antonio de Torres returns with 500 slaves		
	Mar	Double wedding of Juan and Juana with Margaret and Philip agreed		CC explores Española	Treaty of Venice and Holy League formed	
	Apr		Spanish fleet leaves Malaga	Monarchs invite new explorations		
	May		Gonzalo lands in Italy. French abandon Naples. Spanish take Seminara			
	Jun		French enter Rome again	CC receives reprimand from monarchs over slaves		

Year	Month	Isabel and Juana	Gonzalo Fernández	Columbus	Rodrigo Borgia	Elsewhere
	Aug	Cisneros made Archbishop of Toledo				
1496	Feb	Proxy weddings in Brussels of Juana and Margaret	Makes Nicastro his HQ			
	Mar	Proxy weddings in Valladolid	Takes all of Calabria	Sails home from second voyage		
	Jun		Takes Laino	Arrives in Cádiz		
	Jul		Takes Atella. French flee Naples			
	Aug	Juana's fleet sets sail from Laredo. Shelters in England	Ferrante dies. Federico new King of Naples			
	Sep	Fleet arrives in Vissingen in Flanders		Meets monarchs in Burgos		
	Oct	Juana and Philip married in Brussels				
	Dec	Margaret's ships assemble in Ramua				
1497	Jan	Leave Flanders	Gonzalo takes Ostia			

Appendix C: Calendar of Historic Events

Year	Month	Isabel and Juana	Gonzalo Fernández	Columbus	Rodrigo Borgia	Elsewhere
	Mar	Ships reach Spain	Enters Rome in triumph			
	Apr	Wedding of Juan and Margaret	Spanish take Rocca Guillermo			
	May		First Italian campaign ends			
	Jul		Gonzalo sails for Sicily			
	Aug			Bobadilla made new governor of the Indies		
	Oct	Death of Juan in Salamanca				
	Dec			CC and brothers arrive in chains in Cádiz		
1498	Apr		Charles VIII of France dies			
	May			CC starts third voyage		

Appendix C: Calendar of Historic Events

Year	Month	Isabel and Juana	Gonzalo Fernández	Columbus	Rodrigo Borgia	Elsewhere
	Jun				César Borgia made Duke of Benevento. Juan Borgia murdered. Lucrezia enters convent	
	Jul		Gonzalo and army sail home			
	Aug	Queen Isabel's daughter, Isabel, dies in Zaragoza	Arrive in Zaragoza to a royal welcome		César relinquishes purple for military role	
	Oct				César leaves for French court	
	Nov	Juana bears first child, Eleanor				
1499	Mar	Five-month-old Miguel, Isabel's son, sworn in as heir in Aragón				
	May				César marries Carlota, Princess of Navarra	
	Dec					Cisneros arrives in Granada for mass baptisms

Appendix C: Calendar of Historic Events

Year	Month	Isabel and Juana	Gonzalo Fernández	Columbus	Rodrigo Borgia	Elsewhere
1500	Jan					Muslim rebellion breaks out
	Feb	Juana bears second child, Charles				
	Mar					Fernando sacks Lanjarón
	Apr	23-month-old Miguel dies				
	Jun		Spanish forces sail from Málaga for Italy			
	Sep					Revolt spreads to Níjar
	Oct	Relations between Juana and Philip worsen further				
	Dec		Gonzalo takes Cephalonia from Turks			
1501	Jan					Muslims finally surrender Velefique

Appendix C: Calendar of Historic Events

Year	Month	Isabel and Juana	Gonzalo Fernández	Columbus	Rodrigo Borgia	Elsewhere
	?		Spain and France sign Treaty of Granada			
	Jul	Juana bears third child, Isabel				
	Sep			Ovando named governor of La Española		
	Nov	Philip and Juana leave for Spain via France				
1502	Feb			Ovando leaves Sanlúcar with huge fleet		
	Apr			CC sets off on fourth voyage		

Appendix C: Calendar of Historic Events

Year	Month	Isabel and Juana	Gonzalo Fernández	Columbus	Rodrigo Borgia	Elsewhere
	May	Philip and Juana arrive in Toledo. Cisneros establishes University of Alcala. Prince Arthur dies in England. Isabel very sick. Aragón Cortes declare Juana as heir.				
	Jun			Hurricane destroys La Española and fleet		
	Aug		French attack Gonzalo at Barletta			
	Dec	Philip flees Madrid				
1503	Feb	Juana placed in Cisneros' care				
	Mar	Juana bears fourth child, Fernando. Philip arrives in Lyon. Philip and Louis sign Treaty of Lyon				

Year	Month	Isabel and Juana	Gonzalo Fernández	Columbus	Rodrigo Borgia	Elsewhere
	Apr		Spanish march out of Barletta			
	May		Battle of Cerignola. Start of the *tercios*			
	Jun		Gonzalo marches north to Gaeta	CC sails along Cuba and reaches Honduras		
	Jul		New French army crosses the Alps			
	Aug			Casa de Contratación established to control Indies gold	Rodrigo Borgia dies. Julius II new Pope. César arrested	
	Oct	Juana shows real signs of madness				
	Nov	Philip arrives in Flanders		First Casa de Contratación fleet sets sail		
	Dec		Battle on the Garigliano River			
1504	Feb	Famine continues in Spain	Gonzalo enters Naples, but is sick			

Appendix C: Calendar of Historic Events

Year	Month	Isabel and Juana	Gonzalo Fernández	Columbus	Rodrigo Borgia	Elsewhere
	May	Juana leaves Spain for Flanders	César Borgia arrested by Gonzalo on Fernando's orders			
	Aug	Juana scandalises Flemish court	César sent to Spain			
	Sep			CC and brothers arrive in Sanlúcar from fourth voyage		
	Nov	Queen Isabel dies in Medina	News reaches Naples		César escapes from La Mota fortress	Major earthquake at Carmona. Tremors felt in Medina
1505	Jan	Cortes oath of allegiance to Juana, rightful heiress				
	May		Philip canvasses Gonzalo's support in Naples			
	Sep	Juana's bears fifth child, Maria				
	Oct	Fernando's marriage with Germaine approved. Spain deluged by storms	Peace treaty with France	Rebellion by Ciguayos Indians		

Appendix C: Calendar of Historic Events

Year	Month	Isabel and Juana	Gonzalo Fernández	Columbus	Rodrigo Borgia	Elsewhere
	Nov	Power sharing between Philip and Fernando ratified by Cortes				
1506	Jan	Juana and Philip depart Middleburg				
	Mar	Fernando marries Germaine				
	Apr	Juana and Philip arrive in La Coruña				
	Jun	Fernando and Philip meet				
	Jul	Final meeting between Philip and Fernando. Cortes declare Juana their queen				
	Sep	Juana and Philip reach Burgos. Philip dies of fever after playing tennis	Fernando and Germaine sail for Naples to meet Gonzalo			
	Nov	Juana refuses to sign state papers	Fernando's fleet arrives in Naples			

Appendix C: Calendar of Historic Events

Year	Month	Isabel and Juana	Gonzalo Fernández	Columbus	Rodrigo Borgia	Elsewhere
	Dec	Fernando recognises Charles as rightful heir and makes Cisneros his governor in his absence. Juana opens Philip's coffin			Julius II offers Gonzalo command of papal forces	
1507	Jan	Juana bears sixth child, Catalina				
	Mar				César killed in Pyrenees	
	Apr	Juana 'seeks the darkness'				
	Jun		Fernando sails home from Naples. Gonzalo follows			
	Jul		Gonzalo arrives in Valencia to a rapturous reception			
	Aug	Juana and Fernando meet after five years. Cisneros made cardinal				

Appendix C: Calendar of Historic Events

Year	Month	Isabel and Juana	Gonzalo Fernández	Columbus	Rodrigo Borgia	Elsewhere
	Oct		Humiliated by Fernando and retires to estate in Loja, near Granada			

Appendix D: Bibliography – Alphabetical

Anon, *The Letter of Columbus*, Lenox Library Reprint, New York, 1892

Bennassar, Bartolomé, *Inquisición Española: Poder Político y Control Social*, Editorial Critica, Barcelona, 1981

De Gaury, Gerald, *The Grand Captain: Gonzalo de Córdoba*, Longmans, Green and Co., London, 1955

Dennis, Amarie, *Seek the Darkness: The Story of Juana la Loca*, printed in Madrid by the Successors of Rivadeneyra Press Inc., Madrid, 1961

Dunn, Oliver and Kelley Jr, James E, *The Diario of Christopher Columbus's First Voyage to America, 1492–1493*, University of Oklahoma Press: Norman and London, 1991

Fernández Álvarez, Manuel, *Juana la Loca*, Editorial Espasa Calpe, SA, Madrid, 2000

—, *Isabel la Católica*, Editorial Espasa Calpe, SA, Madrid, 2003

Fuson, R H, *The Log of Christopher Columbus*, International Marine Publishing Company, Camden, Maine, USA, 1987

Gala, Antonio, *El Manuscrito Carmesí*, Editorial Planeta, Barcelona, 1990

Galán, Lola, and Deusgala, J C, *La Papa Borja*, Santillana Ediciones Generales, SL, Madid, 2004

García-Frías Checa, Carmen, *The Royal Convent of Santa Clara de Tordesillas, Valladolid*, Patrimonio Nacional, Palacio Real de Madrid, 2003

—, *Guide to the Royal Convent of Santa Clara de Tordesillas*, ALDEASA, 2003

Garrido Atienza, Miguel, *Las Capitulaciones para la Entrega de Granada. Estudio preliminar por José Enrique López de Coca Castañer*, Granada, 1910

Gibbons, W, and Moreno, T [ed.], *The Geology of Spain*, published by the Geological Society of London, 2002

Harvey, Sean, *The Rough Guide to the Dominican Republic*, Rough Guides, New York, London, Delhi, 2006

Headworth, Howard, *The Al-Andalus Chronicle*, Athena Press, London, 2004

—, 'Early Arab Water Technology in Southern Spain', *Jour.Inst.Water and Env.Mangmt*, Vol. 18, No. 3, 161–165, 2004

—, *Los Molinos Hidráulicos de Huebro Revisitados: sus Características Técnicas. Revista de Humanidades y Ciencias del Instituto de Estudios Almerienses. Diputación de Almería*, Vol. 19 (2003–2004), 331–248, 2004

Instituto Tecnológico Geominero de España, *Mapa de Peninsula Ibérica, Baleares y Canarias*, scale 1 to 1 million, Madrid, 1994

Kamen, Henry, *La Inquisición Española: Una Revisión Histórica*, Biblioteca Historia de España, 1997

—, *Spain's Road to Empire: The Making of a World Power, 1492–1763*, Allen Lane, an imprint of Penguin Books, 2002

Kelly, Ian, *Cooking for Kings: The life of Antonin Carême, the first celebrity chef*, Short Books, 2003

Larousse, *Historia Universal Larousse: Renacimiento, Humanismo y la Era de los Descubrimientos, 1492–1581*, Editiones Larousse, pp.17–19, 2005

Mezcua, J, Socías, I, and Rueda, J J, 'Seismicity and Magnetic Structures in South Spain', *Fisica de la Tierra*, No. 4, 135–149, Editorial Complutense, Madrid, 1992

Munrow, David, *Music for Ferdinand and Isabella: Instruments of the Middle Ages and Renaissance*, EMI Recordings, compact disc SBT 1251, 1996

Norris, Herbert, *Tudor Costume and Dress*, Dover Publications, Inc., Mineola, New York, 1997

—, *Medieval Costume and Dress*, Dover Publications, Inc., Mineola, New York, 1999

Parker, Geoffrey [ed.], *The Times Illustrated World History*, Harper-Collins, 1992

Posadas Chinchilla, AM, and Vidal Sánchez, F [ed.], *El Estudio de los Terremotos en Almería, Instituto de Estudios Almerienses, Diputación de Almería*, 1994

Purcell, Mary, *The Great Captain: Gonzalo Fernández de Córdoba*, Alvin Redman, London, 1963

Quintana Lacaci, Guillermo, *Armería del Palacio Real de Madrid*, Editorial Patrimonio Nacional, Madrid, 1987

Ruiz García, Alfonso, *El Castillo de Vélez Blanco (Almeria), Revista Velezana*, 2nd Edition. Ayuntamiento de Vélez Rubio (Almería), 2002

Sach, Jan, *Enciclopedia Ilustrada de las Armas Blancas*, Susaeta Ediciones SA, Madrid, 1999

Tapia Garrido, José Angel, *Historia de la Baja Alpujarra, Instituto de Estudios de Sur de España*, pp.109–130, 1964

—, *Breve Historia de Almería, Editado por el Monte de Pieded y Caja de Ahorras de Almería*, pp.132–135, 1972

—, *Almería Musulmana, 1172/1492: Historia General de Almería y Provincia*, pp.432–523, 1986

Thomas, Hugh, *El Imperio Español de Colón a Magallanes*, Editorial Planeta, Barcelona, 2003

Times Books, *The Times Concise Atlas of World History*, revised edition, Times Books Ltd, London, 1982

Verdegay Flores, Francisco, *Historias de Almería: Experiencias Realizados por los Alumnos de El Ejido*, pp.45–115, 1983

Vincent, Bernard, *1992: El Año Admirable*, Editorial Crítica, Barcelona, 1992

Wade-Matthews, M, and Thompson, W, *Music: An Illustrated Encyclopedia of Musical Instruments and the Great Composers*, Annes Publishing Ltd, 2002

Wert, Juan Pablo, *El Reino Nazarí de Granada*, Ediciones AKAL SA, Madrid, 1994

Williams, Mark, *The Story of Spain: The Dramatic History of Europe's most Fascinating Country*, Ediciones Santana SL, Fuengirola (Málaga), Spain, 2000

Yanko, Aroní, *Los Silencios de Juana la Loca*, Belacqva de Ediciones y Publicaciones SL, 2003

Appendix E   Bibliography – by Subject

General Subjects

García-Frías Checa, Carmen, *The Royal Convent of Santa Clara de Tordesillas*, Valladolid, Patrimonio Nacional, Palacio Real de Madrid, 2003

—, *Guide to the Royal Convent of Santa Clara de Tordesillas*, ALDEASA, 2003

Harvey, Sean, *The Rough Guide to the Dominican Republic*, Rough Guides, New York, London, Delhi, 2006

Kelly, Ian, *Cooking for Kings: The life of Antonin Carême, the first celebrity chef*, Short Books, 2003

Munrow, David, *Music for Ferdinand and Isabella: Instruments of the Middle Ages and Renaissance*, EMI Recordings, compact disc SBT 1251, 1996

Norris, Herbert, *Tudor Costume and Dress*, Dover Publications, Inc., Mineola, New York, 1997

—, *Medieval Costume and Dress*, Dover Publications, Inc., Mineola, New York, 1999

Quintana Lacaci, Guillermo, *Armería del Palacio Real de Madrid*, Editorial Patrimonio Nacional, Madrid, 1987

Sach, Jan, *Enciclopedia Ilustrada de las Armas Blancas*, Susaeta Ediciones SA, Madrid, 1999

Wade-Matthews, M, and Thompson, W, *Music: An Illustrated Encyclopedia of Musical Instruments and the Great Composers*, Annes Publishing Ltd, 2002

General History

Kamen, Henry, *Spain's Road to Empire: The Making of a World Power, 1492–1763*, Allen Lane, an imprint of Penguin Books, 2002

Larousse, *Historia Universal Larousse: Renacimiento, Humanismo y la Era de los Descubrimientos, 1492–1581*, Editiones Larousse, pp.17–19, 2005

Parker, Geoffrey [ed.], *The Times Illustrated World History*, Harper-Collins, 1992

Times Books, *The Times Concise Atlas of World History*, revised edition, Times Books Ltd, London, 1982

Williams, Mark, *The Story of Spain: The Dramatic History of Europe's most Fascinating Country*, Ediciones Santana SL, Fuengirola (Málaga), Spain, 2000

Almería and Granada

Gala, Antonio, *El Manuscrito Carmesí*, Editorial Planeta, Barcelona, 1990

Garrido Atienza, Miguel, *Las Capitulaciones para la Entrega de Granada. Estudio preliminar por José Enrique López de Coca Castañer*, Granada, 1910

Headworth, Howard, *The Al-Andalus Chronicle*, Athena Press, London, 2004

Ruiz García, Alfonso, *El Castillo de Vélez Blanco (Almeria), Revista Velezana*, 2nd Edition. Ayuntamiento de Vélez Rubio (Almería), 2002

Tapia Garrido, José Angel, *Historia de la Baja Alpujarra, Instituto de Estudios de Sur de España*, pp.109–130, 1964

—, *Breve Historia de Almería, Editado por el Monte de Pieded y Caja de Ahorras de Almería*, pp.132–135, 1972

—, *Almería Musulmana, 1172/1492: Historia General de Almería y Provincia*, pp.432–523, 1986

Verdegay Flores, Francisco, *Historias de Almería: Experiencias Realizados por los Alumnos de El Ejido*, pp.45–115, 1983

Vincent, Bernard, 1992: *El Año Admirable*, Editorial Crítica, Barcelona, 1992

Wert, Juan Pablo, *El Reino Nazarí de Granada*, Ediciones AKAL SA, Madrid, 1994

Christopher Columbus

Anon, *The Letter of Columbus*, Lenox Library Reprint, New York, 1892

Dunn, Oliver and Kelley Jr, James E, *The Diario of Christopher Columbus's First Voyage to America, 1492–1493*, University of Oklahoma Press: Norman and London, 1991

Fuson, R H, *The Log of Christopher Columbus*, International Marine Publishing Company, Camden, Maine, USA, 1987

Thomas, Hugh, *El Imperio Español de Colón a Magallanes*, Editorial Planeta, Barcelona, 2003

Gonzalo Fernández of Córdoba

De Gaury, Gerald, *The Grand Captain: Gonzalo de Córdoba*, Longmans, Green and Co., London, 1955

Purcell, Mary, *The Great Captain: Gonzalo Fernández de Córdoba*, Alvin Redman, London, 1963

Princess Juana

Dennis, Amarie, *Seek the Darkness: The Story of Juana la Loca*, printed in Madrid by the Successors of Rivadeneyra Press Inc., Madrid, 1961

Fernández Álvarez, Manuel, *Juana la Loca*, Editorial Espasa Calpe, SA, Madrid, 2000

—, *Isabel la Católica*, Editorial Espasa Calpe, SA, Madrid, 2003

Yanko, Aroní, *Los Silencios de Juana la Loca*, Belacqva de Ediciones y Publicaciones SL, 2003

Rodrigo Borja, Pope Alexander VI

Galán, Lola, and Deusgala, J C, *La Papa Borja*, Santillana Ediciones Generales, SL, Madid, 2004

Spanish Inquisition

Bennassar, Bartolomé, *Inquisición Española: Poder Político y Control Social*, Editorial Critica, Barcelona, 1981

Kamen, Henry, *La Inquisición Española: Una Revisión Histórica*, Biblioteca Historia de España, 1997

Technical

Gibbons, W, and Moreno, T [ed.], *The Geology of Spain*, published by the Geological Society of London, 2002

Headworth, Howard, 'Early Arab Water Technology in Southern Spain', *Jour.Inst.Water and Env.Mangmt*, Vol. 18, No. 3, 161–165, 2004

—, *Los Molinos Hidráulicos de Huebro Revisitados: sus Características Técnicas. Revista de Humanidades y Ciencias del Instituto de Estudios Almerienses. Diputación de Almería*, Vol. 19 (2003–2004), 331–248, 2004

Instituto Tecnológico Geominero de España, *Mapa de Peninsula Ibérica, Baleares y Canarias*, scale 1 to 1 million, Madrid, 1994

Mezcua, J, Socías, I, and Rueda, J J, 'Seismicity and Magnetic Structures in South Spain', *Fisica de la Tierra*, No. 4, 135–149, Editorial Complutense, Madrid, 1992

Posadas Chinchilla, A M, and Vidal Sánchez, F [ed.], *El Estudio de los Terremotos en Almería, Instituto de Estudios Almerienses*, Diputación de Almería, 1994

www.ingramcontent.com/pod-product-compliance
Lightning Source LLC
Chambersburg PA
CBHW030400030726
47497CB00002B/417